HERO AD HOC

888-555-HERO #2

SUZAN HARDEN

To John and Kay, a classy couple
who bends over backward for their legal clients

This is a work of fiction. All characters, organizations and events in this novel are products of the author's imagination and are not to be construed as real. Any resemblance to persons, living or dead, is entirely coincidental.

HERO AD HOC (888-555-HERO #2)

ISBN-13 - 978-1-938745-45-4

Published by Angry Sheep Publishing
Findlay, Ohio

Interior Design by QA Productions
Cover Design by For the Muse Designs

More books by Suzan Harden
(Each series is in suggested reading order)

Bloodlines
Blood Magick
Zombie Love
Zombie Confidential
Zombie Wedding
Amish, Vamps & Thieves
Blood Sacrifice
Love, War & a Bulldog
Zombie Goddess
Ravaged
Sacrificed
Reality Bites (Coming Soon)
Ghouls in the Grocery (Coming Soon)
Resurrected (Coming Soon)

Seasons of Magick
Spring
Summer
Autumn
Winter

Justice
Sword and Sorceress 28 ("Justice")
Sword and Sorceress 30 ("Diplomacy in the Dark")
Justice: The Beginning
A Question of Balance
A Modicum of Truth
A Matter of Death (Coming Soon)
A Touch of Mother (Coming Soon)

888-555-HERO
Hero De Facto
Hero Ad Hoc
Hero De Novo

Miscellaneous
Sword and Sorceress 31 ("Pig-Headed")
Sword and Sorceress 32 ("Unexpected")

For more information or to join her mailing list, visit Suzan's website at
www.suzanharden.com

Legal definition from the *Merriam-Webster Dictionary*:

ad hoc – for the particular end or case at hand without consideration of wider application

CHAPTER 1

Aisha Franklin stared at her brand-new office carpet nearly a yard beneath her favorite Christian Louboutin stilettos. And the carpet was drifting farther away by the second.

"How the hell do I get down!"

Her best friend and legal partner Harri Winters stared up at her. "Honey, I don't even know how you're flying to begin with."

"I'm not flying!" Aisha yelled. In her panic, she bounced up another foot. "I'm floating, and I can't get down!"

Harri waved her hands. "Keep your voice down. We don't need to freak out the neighborhood."

Aisha glared at Harri. "I'm pregnant, I'm floating in mid-air, and we exclusively represent superheroes. Not to mention, our IT guy is a former supervillain. I doubt if this is the weirdest thing they've ever seen or heard."

But Harri was right. Aisha glanced at her windows. She'd opened her office blinds when she came downstairs. Thankfully, their building was on the downtrodden Canyon Block, and no one was on the sidewalk this early in the morning.

"It is when you're not a super." Harri crossed her arms. "I can't leave you like this, but I can't reach you. Do you want me to call Rey?"

"No!" Aisha winced as her head bumped against the plaster medallion on her office ceiling, but it gave her an idea. She reached up and pushed hard against the ornamentation.

The floor rushed toward her, and she stumbled slightly on her leopard print stilettos when she landed. She straightened. So far, her feet remained in contact with the carpet.

Harri sagged. "Do I need to get a rope and tie you to your desk? Because I can't stay here and babysit."

When the weird light-headed feeling rushed through her again, Aisha grabbed the edge of her desk. Just in case. "What are you talking about? We've got a meeting with a new client this morning."

"You can handle Screaming Orgasm. Rebranding her will be totally in your court anyway." Harri dropped her arms to her sides. "I came in to let you know Patty's in labor. I need to get to the hospital."

"Why are you in here yakking with me?" Aisha made shooing motions. "You need to get her there before her water breaks. You're her birthing coach."

"It already broke, and Arthur already took her."

At Harri's grimace, Aisha realized the real problem. "He spent the night with her, and she didn't tell you before they left for the hospital."

"Keep your phone in your pocket." Harri looked around the office, ignoring her own feelings as usual. "If you get into trouble again, call Tim. He's downstairs tinkering." She finally met Aisha's gaze again. "We'll talk about your situation as soon as I get back. I promise."

"I know." She gave Harri a wry smile. "Sorry, I freaked out on you."

Harri chuckled. "It can't be any worse than what Rey did."

Aisha nibbled her lower lip.

Harri's face fell. "You did tell him, didn't you? Oh, God, please tell me he's the father."

"Of course, he's the father," Aisha snapped. "Why do think I was freaking out? He doesn't need this shit when he's just getting his career off the ground!"

"Given the circumstances, I totally get why you're upset, but I really need to go. I'll call you once Patty has delivered." Harri waggled the fingers of her right hand before she marched out of the office.

Aisha held her breath until she heard the side door shut, followed by the distinctive thud of the deadbolt and the beep of the security system. Was Harri that irritated about Aisha's pregnancy she was abusing the building?

Aisha released her breath and her hold on the edge of her desk. No, Harri was probably freaking out about being Patty's birthing coach, and half-afraid she would ask the same. Which she wouldn't do because Rey would be there.

Wouldn't he?

The panic from the six pregnancy tests reared its ugly head again.

And she immediately started floating upward again.

She dug her fingertips around the wooden lip of the desk and pulled herself down. She couldn't lose it. Not today. Not with a new client coming in this morning.

Ah, who the hell was she kidding. She'd already lost it.

How the hell was she going to explain this to Rey? She'd told him she couldn't get pregnant. That's what all those damned expensive fertility experts had said after she'd already lost one ovary to an ectopic pregnancy. Calvin had left her because of what those doctors had said. The kicker had been last month when her doctor said she'd started perimenopause.

Her fingers twitched. God, she needed a cigarette. But she didn't dare. Not now.

She rubbed her still flat belly. There was someone else she needed to worry about for the next eight months. And she knew exactly what she was going to tell Rey.

Because Captain Justice sure as hell couldn't be seen with a family, no matter how she felt about the man behind the mask.

CHAPTER 2

Harri pulled into the parking garage for Canyon Pointe General Hospital and immediately started cursing. Even at this early hour, the first nine floors were packed. No one wanted to park on the roof between the ninety-degree temps and the likelihood of a super or debris falling on their vehicle.

Well, she was supposed to go car shopping with Aisha after work since the bad guys from Corvus, the not-quite-legal arm of the National Superhero Bureau, had trashed her partner's beloved BMW while trying to kill her and capture Rey a month ago. Harri pulled into a spot partially covered by the hospital roof's overhang. If Captain Mojave landed on her ancient Accord, maybe they could get a two-for-one deal. God knew Aisha would have to cut back on her designer fashions and BMWs with a kid on the way.

Harri squelched that thought. Just because she lacked anything resembling a maternal instinct, it didn't give her the right to judge Aisha.

Her best friend had wanted kids of her own forever. Calvin the Asshole had dumped her because she couldn't provide him with the biological heir he desperately desired. But Rey was still a kid himself. Okay, so he was twenty-one, but still . . .

Any super sperm jokes would have to wait until Aisha calmed down. Maybe after the baby headed off to college.

Harri climbed out of her car, slammed the door shut, and headed for the elevator. Rey being the father didn't explain Aisha's levitation trick in her office this morning. The kid was human, not an alien. Tim and Arthur had tested the hell out of him. Or they tried to. The guys still hadn't devised a way to get a blood sample.

But the mixing of bodily fluids shouldn't have affected Aisha's DNA—

Aw, crap. If Aisha had developed HRSP from the pregnancy, she needed a specialist, which meant the government would know, and she could lose her license for sleeping with a client. The state supreme court didn't take ethical breaches of that magnitude lightly

Harri frowned as she jabbed the call button. On the other hand, Rey didn't know who his biological father was, much less how he got his powers. Maybe Tim and Arthur could run more tests.

The elevator doors parted, and she stepped aboard.

"Hold the 'vator!"

At the shout, she automatically hit the button to keep the doors open. A man plunged through, out of breath, and Harri released the button. The elevator doors slid shut, and the machine hummed to life.

"Thanks," he said between panting breaths. The stranger was tall with sparkling blue eyes, but what really stood out was the huge bouquet of yellow daisies.

Patty's favorite flower. "Crap," Harri muttered.

"You're mad because you held the elevator for me?" He shot her a charming smile.

She grimaced. "No, I'm mad because I forgot to pick up flowers for my friend who's having a baby."

"You, too?" He grinned, the ridiculous grin of someone in love. It reminded her of her reflection this morning, though she wasn't ready to admit her feelings to Tim. Maybe things were getting better for her and her little . . .

Crew? Gang? Family?

Part of her veered away from the F-word. Too many bad connections with her crazy parents.

But if their worst problem was Aisha's unplanned pregnancy on top of Patty's—

"Is this your first one?" she asked to distract herself.

He hesitated. "Yeah. Sort of."

"Sort of?"

The garage elevator doors parted, and they stepped into the hospital's main lobby.

"We broke up before I knew she was pregnant." He scowled as they crossed to the elevator bank for the hospital itself. "I didn't find out about it until I got back to town."

The nagging familiarity of his voice was superseded by her own feelings in regards to deadbeat parents. "You left town?"

His scowl deepened. "I travel a lot for work. When I stopped by her apartment to try to work things out this morning, one of her neighbors said she'd left for the hospital. I want to do the right thing—"

"Glad to hear someone does," Harri grumbled. The elevator dinged, and she followed the crowd onto the car.

"Excuse me?" Blue-Eyes stood next to her as the elevator started climbing.

"Sorry, it's not you." She shook her head. "My friend's ex took off right after she learned she was knocked up. I've seen too many irresponsible parents." *Mine top the list.*

A rueful expression twisted the man's features. "I hate to side with a scumbag, but, and this is speaking from experience, are you sure he knows?"

Harri opened her mouth, then stopped. No, she wasn't sure. Patty had said so little about her ex and their circumstances. How many conclusions had she jumped to because of her own childhood issues?

"You're right." She matched his slight, sad smile. "I don't know. I hope things work out better for you and your baby's mother."

"So do I," he murmured.

The bell dinged, and the doors parted. Harri rushed out, but she whirled around and gave her walking companion a thumbs-up gesture while he was still trying to squeeze past the other passengers.

She jogged down the hallway to the room number Arthur had texted her.

"GET IT OUT OF ME!"

Harri winced at Patty's volume as she entered the delivery room. Despite the screaming, Arthur held Patty's hand, stroked her forehead with a damp washcloth, and murmured encouraging words to her. He may not be this baby's father, but he was doing pretty damn good in Harri's book.

The nurse looked at her. "You Harri Winters?"

Harri nodded.

The nurse grinned. "I think you lost your spot as birthing coach, but let's get you gowned up anyway." She took Harri's bag and chucked it into a closet before she opened a second one and pulled out a bunch of blue material.

"Oh, thank god." Patty groaned.

Disappointment flashed across Arthur's face, but when he tried to rise, Patty yanked him back down into his chair.

Patty started bawling, real tears for once. "I need you both here!" she wailed.

"We're here," Harri crooned as the nurse shook out the plastic-coated disposable gown and held it for Harri to shove her arms in the appropriate spots.

"Yeah, sweetie, we're both here," Arthur said. "Everything's going to be fine."

The nurse spun Harri around to tie up the back, and she got a glimpse of Blue Eyes with Yellow Daisies outside in the corridor. Poor guy looked totally stricken. Things must not have gone well with his ex. Once he realized she saw him, he pivoted away and took off down the hall.

Damn, if she didn't have her hands full, she'd go after him. Try to help. But today, there were responsibilities in her personal life she couldn't shirk. Not when the two women she was closest to needed her. Funny how they both dealt with her personal kryptonite—babies.

Aisha pushed one more time, but once again, she only went down a couple of feet before she bobbed right back up to the third-floor overhang. She'd managed to distract herself with contracts for other clients and the proposal for Screaming Orgasm. Long enough, she wanted, no, needed a mocha.

She was halfway to the espresso machine when a part of her realized caffeine wasn't good for the baby. That thought sent her floating through the air until she grabbed the second-floor balcony railing. She had worked her way hand-over-hand to the overhang, but the trick she'd used earlier in her office wasn't working.

Irritation fluttered through her. She couldn't stay here. God only knew how long Harri would be at the hospital. And she definitely couldn't let Rey see this before she figured out how to tell him she was pregnant. Not to mention Screaming Orgasm would arrive for her meeting soon.

Damn it! She definitely needed help this time.

Aisha handwalked along the overhang ceiling until she reached one of the antique light fixtures. Clinging to the chain with her legs, she pulled her phone out of the front pocket of her slacks. She stared at the device for a full minute before she thumbed Tim's number.

"Hello?"

"Can you come up to the law office, please?"

"What's wrong? Can you talk?"

Aisha rolled her eyes. Of course, he went right into superhero mode. "I'm okay. I just need a little help reaching the espresso machine." She hesitated for a second before she added, "And can you bring a pole?"

"O-o-o-kay. I'll be right up." The signal went dead. Of course, he'd be checking the security cameras first, wondering what the hell was going on. But the micro devices were all pointed toward doors and windows, normal entry points, not at the art deco light fixtures hanging from the atrium ceiling.

The basement door to his lab and quarters opened, and Tim's red hair poked through. "Aisha?"

"Up here."

He entered the law office proper, dragging a pole with a loop of rope attached, and stared up at her. "Should I even ask?"

"No," she growled.

Tim glanced around the reception area. "Where is everybody?"

"Rey got called in before our alarm went off. Professor Triassic unleashed a herd of dinosaurs on downtown Hermanville, and the governor issued a state of emergency. Arthur took Patty to the hospital since she's in labor, and Harri followed them."

"Patty's having her baby, and you led with the dinosaur story?"

"Forget about both of them, and get me down!"

Tim tried to reach her from his spot on the floor, but the pole wasn't long enough. He climbed up on Patty's desk. Aisha prayed the used furniture would hold under his weight. Most their money had gone into security measures for the Lechuza Building instead of furniture once they'd learned a top-secret black ops division of superheroes had made problems for both Rey and Tim in the past.

And then tried to kill her and Harri over the last month, though they backed off after one of their operatives, Seismic Shift, was busted by the FBI, thanks to their law firm.

Aisha held her breath until Tim managed to lasso her right ankle on his third try. He carefully climbed down from Patty's desk as she worked her way down the light fixture's chain until she clung to the wide glass and steel bowl that shielded the actual bulbs.

"You need to let go so I can get you the rest of the way down," Tim said gently.

Aisha glanced up. She couldn't stay here forever. But if he couldn't hold her down, they could both float up to the third-floor ceiling. And it was an awfully long way to the first floor if this floating ability of the baby's, and she was pretty damn sure it was the baby, cut out. Tim could be seriously injured. Or die.

And Harri would never forgive her.

"Aisha?"

She let go of the light fixture. He slid the pole backwards, hand over hand, until she could grab his shirt. He let the pole drop, but his firm grip on her waist helped her settle on the antique tile floor. She blew out a deep breath.

"You okay?"

She nodded.

He peered into her eyes. "You gonna tell me what's going on?"

Aisha couldn't meet his earnest gaze. "I can't. Not until . . ."

"You tell Rey."

She lifted her head and stared at him.

He ran a hand through his unruly red hair. "I guess the office nursery has just been bumped to the top of the priority list."

"Wha—NO!"

Tim glanced down for a split second before his eyes met hers again. "Then why have you been rubbing your abdomen?" A wry smile tilted his mouth before he added, "My wife used to do the same thing before our son started moving. Like she couldn't believe it was really happening."

The light-headed feeling returned with a fury, and Aisha flailed as she started to rise. Tim grabbed her hand and pulled her back down.

She clung to him. "Please, please, give me a chance to tell Rey myself—"

"Tell me what?" said a familiar male voice from above them.

She looked up to see Rey peering over the balcony with an odd expression. At least, he was wearing civilian clothes since her new client would be here any minute. With a start, she realized she was still clinging to Tim. She abruptly let go, only to shoot toward the ceiling.

Rey launched himself from the balcony and caught her. Before Aisha could say a word, knocking on the glass partition made them both look down.

A woman with wild purple, green, and blue hair stood behind the bulletproof glass at the main entry. She was bent over so she could look up at them, showing off ample cleavage in the process. The woman reached up and jabbed the intercom button. "Excuse me. I've got a ten o'clock appointment." She grinned. "I didn't realize when y'all said you were superhero attorneys, you meant it literally."

Aisha's face heated. Of course, Screaming Orgasm would arrive in time to see this fiasco. This whole situation was rapidly turning into a TV sitcom, and that definitely wasn't the image she or Harri wanted to portray.

"Tim, would you be kind enough to buzz in Ms. Orgasm?" Aisha called down. She turned to Rey and lowered her voice. "Honey, we need to talk, but I've got to deal with our client first. Patty went into labor, and Harri's at the hospital with her."

"All right." His brilliant smile lit his entire face. "But I expect full disclosure over lunch because I don't think Harri would be happy seeing you hugging Tim either."

No, she definitely wouldn't. Tim and Harri each had a ton of personal baggage to fight through before either one would openly admit they had feelings for the other.

Aisha smiled back, even though her stomach was a mass of knots. "I promise, honey. Full disclosure. After Screaming Orgasm leaves, which may be later this afternoon. Right now, I need to be on the first floor."

He carefully flew them both to where Tim waited with Screaming Orgasm.

After he released her, she kept a firm grip on his arm with her left hand while she held out her right one. "Hello, I'm Aisha Franklin."

The superheroine shook her hand. "Pleasure to meet you." Her gaze flicked between Tim and Rey. "Do you have an all-male staff, Ms. Franklin?"

Not sure if the emotion in Screaming Orgasm's eyes was speculation or concern, Aisha shrugged. "We're evenly split, but the firm's other partner is at Canyon Pointe General—"

Orgasm's eyes widened.

"—because our paralegal went into labor this morning. I haven't had a chance to call the temp agency yet."

"Yeah, the floating around thing would put a crimp in your day." Orgasm's eyes twinkled. Aisha could have sworn the superheroine's irises were made of glitter.

Aisha gestured at the two men. "Tim handles security for Winters & Franklin. I assure you any information you give us will remain private within the bounds of the law. Rey—" She faltered for a moment before she could come up with a good excuse. "—works for our contractor. We're renovating the upper floors for expansion."

"Hi." Orgasm batted her eyelashes and shook the men's hands.

"Would you like some coffee before we get started?" Aisha said.

"Rey, why don't you help Ms. Franklin to her office?" Tim interjected. He turned to Orgasm. "What's your drink? We have a full-service espresso machine. Ms. Franklin's usual is a large no-fat, no-whip mocha with sugar-free peppermint."

"That sounds delicious!" Orgasm gave him a coy look. "But I don't suppose I could have mine with raspberry syrup instead?"

"No problem." Tim waved toward Aisha's office. "I'll bring them in for you ladies."

Aisha bit her tongue to keep from objecting. Maybe a little caffeine wouldn't hurt the baby if it calmed her down enough to do her job.

Aisha led the way to her office. Sort of. Rey had to act as her guide dog so she wouldn't float up to the ceiling again. Once inside, she said, "Office chair."

Normally, she and Harri conducted initial client interviews on the couches that took up a good chunk of her office. The mood felt homier and relaxed the client.

However, Harri wasn't here. And Aisha could hook her toes under the wheel braces of her desk chair so she wouldn't float away. As soon as she and Orgasm were settled, Rey left the room, closing the door behind him.

"Wow!" The superheroine giggled. "My sister was not joking about how good-looking Captain Justice is in person."

"Excuse me?" Aisha paused in reaching for a pen and raised an eyebrow.

"It's the eyes, Ms. Franklin. Those gold-brown eyes of his are a dead giveaway." Orgasm fanned herself. "But the TV does not do him justice if you'll pardon the pun."

Enough was enough. Aisha could be honest enough to admit there was a wee bit of jealousy over the superheroine ogling her boyfriend, but the rest of her trepidation was pure lawyer. They didn't need a plant by Corvus. She folded her hands over the legal pad in front of her. "Why are you really here, Screaming Orgasm?"

She blinked her glittery eyes. "Like I said on the phone, I need help rebranding my image. Cobblestone said you were awesome, not to mention I saw you on TV—"

"What's your relationship with Seismic Shift?" Aisha asked coolly.

Screaming Orgasm's glittery eyes hardened. "I don't care what Seismic Shit told you or anyone else, I didn't sleep with him. I mean, come on! He's old!"

Aisha bit her tongue to keep from smiling at Orgasm's use of Harri's favorite nickname for the disgraced and jailed superhero. It would be a lot funnier if he hadn't come so damn close to killing Harri.

More than once.

"Did Byron Trubble ever mention us?" Aisha asked.

"Who?" A perplexed expression appeared on the superheroine's face.

"A friend of Shit, er, Shift's." So much for professional demeanor.

"Doesn't ring a bell." Orgasm shook her head and spread her fingers wide. "Look, I know Shit threatened the nurse Cobblestone has a crush on. If you think I'd go along with that stuff, you're wrong. The reason I'm here is because Cobblestone said you weren't sleazy assholes looking to make a buck. I was also under the impression he had already talked to you about me—"

"He did." Aisha gave her best client-reassuring smile. "But he's a very sweet guy with the proverbial heart of gold. I had to make sure you weren't taking advantage of him. I look out for my clients." She leaned forward. "All my clients."

An impish grin replaced the girl's disturbed expression. "Understood. I'll keep my hands off Captain Justice."

Aisha leaned back. The superheroine wasn't as dumb as the image she liked to project. And unless Screaming Orgasm was one hell of an actress, she hadn't been sucked into Corvus's orbit.

"So, Ms. Orgasm, what exactly would you like Winters & Franklin to help you with?" Aisha picked up her pen.

The superheroine took a deep breath. "I want the public to take me seriously as a hero. Everyone takes my sister Sourpuss seriously. Hell, we come from a line of heroes. Our grandmother was Rue Liberty for crying out loud. But the only endorsements I can get are for the legal brothels in Nevada!"

Aisha bit her tongue to keep from pointing out the obvious. "About your powers—can you use your sonic blast when you're not, um, in the throes of, um . . ."

A confused expression appeared on Orgasm's face. "Of course I can, but where's the fun in that?"

Thankfully, Tim brought in their mochas. It was going to be a very long day.

Chapter 3

Arthur gazed lovingly through the nursery window. "Isn't she absolutely adorable, Harri?"

Grace Harriet Ames looked like every other capped, red-faced, squalling infant in the hospital to Harri, but she nodded and said, "Absolutely," anyway.

The nurse had shooed them out of Patty's room in order to take care of the clean-up. When Harri had objected to the baby's name, the same nurse also threatened to stab Harri with a scalpel for upsetting the new mother. She just wished Patty had warned her of the plan to give the baby the worst middle name ever.

"I could get the birth certificate changed," Harri muttered. "The judge will understand Patty was on drugs when she filled out the form."

"Quit acting like a baby yourself," Arthur murmured. "Patty planned to name her after you and her aunt all along. You two have been the biggest influences in her life."

Harri looked at the former-supervillain-wannabe turned tech-guy and doting daddy-wannabe. "Jeremy's makeover has gone to your head."

"No." Arthur returned her gaze with a steady one of his own, something she wouldn't have thought possible even a month ago. "Do you know why I targeted you last year? You were the heir to the Winters empire and one of the most prominent lawyers in the city. I thought you had the perfect life. One with power and prestige. The one I was cheated out of. When Corvus tried to set me up for the destruction of City Hall, I knew you would be the only one strong enough to find the real culprit. And you did.

"But on top of that, I got to know all of you, and I realized all of your lives were just as screwed up as mine. When none of you had a family to rely on, you made your own."

He turned back to watch Grace with an even more lovestruck expression on his face. "The best I can do is take everything you guys have given me and give it to Gracie. Give her the family all of us wanted, but none of us had."

Harri swallowed hard to get the lump out of her throat. Who would've thought the former Professor Venom was a sentimental sap? "You're right, Arthur. That's the best present we can all give Grace."

She sniffed to get the snot out of her sinuses. Otherwise, she'd start bawling, and the babies didn't need to be frightened by her ugly-cry face. "I need to let Aisha and the guys know how Patty and Grace are doing."

"Okay," he murmured, but Harri was pretty sure he hadn't heard a thing she said.

She headed out to the cell phone patio. Thankfully, she was the only one there. She pulled out her phone and dialed the office number.

"Winters & Franklin, attorneys at law. How may I direct your call?"

Harri laughed. "Why, Ms. Franklin, you almost sounded like a professional receptionist."

Aisha answered with a creative epithet for a female cat. "Gimme the stats."

"Grace Harriet Ames. Born at four-fifty-eight p.m. Seven pounds, two ounces. Eighteen inches. All the fingers and toes, and healthy as a horse. On the other hand, Patty may be here an extra day."

"What happened? Is she okay?" Panic edged Aisha's voice

Harri winced. That had been careless of her. Aisha was already hyper over her own situation.

"Patty's blood pressure was a little high, and she had more bleeding than the OB was comfortable with. She wants to make sure everything is under control before she sends Patty and Grace home."

"Room number?"

"No. No flowers." Harri gestured emphatically even though Aisha couldn't see her. "That's one more thing we'll have to haul home. Have 'em delivered to the apartment when she's released from the hospital. If you want to help, decorate Patty's place. It's not like you need a ladder."

A groan vibrated through the receiver. "Can we not talk about this right now?"

"Fine." A zillion issues dammed up behind the idea of her best friend being pregnant. By one of their clients, no less. "How'd the meeting with our indecent proposal go?"

"I think I have her convinced that changing her atrocious hero moniker would go a long way toward improving her image."

"Uh-oh. That implies there are other issues."

"She claims she gets the biggest power boost by, um, you know."

Harri sat down on one of the decorative benches. "You're kidding me, right? I always thought her Meg Ryan imitation was part of her shtick."

"Nope, not an imitation. That may be a bigger hurdle than the name change."

"Keep her or drop her?"

"She didn't even blink at our rates, and Cobblestone did recommend her. He's been our best referral for new clients."

Harri rolled her eyes. Maybe it was a good thing they couldn't see each other. She still thought Aisha should have pressed assault charges even though Corvus had extorted Cobblestone to deliver their warning to her. However, the condo association bought out Aisha's upside down mortgage at the full amount just to get her out of the building after the destruction Cobblestone and Rey had wrought in their battle. The insurance settlement had been a nice bonus, even though they immediately dropped her policy due to the excessive payout.

"That didn't answer my question," Harri muttered.

"She wrote the check for the retainer on the spot."

Harri snorted. "What happened to discussing a client together before we agree to represent them?"

Aisha chuckled. "When I told her that, she wrote the check for three times our requested amount. I said you still had final say in the matter no matter how many zeros she wrote."

Time to address the pink elephant in the room. "Did you make it through the day without any more floating?"

"No."

Harri could have sworn she heard Aisha's teeth grinding. "You're not on the ceiling right now, are you?"

"No, I am not. Can we please talk about this later?"

"You're going to need to tell Rey—"

"I know that!"

"Hey! I'm just trying to—"

"Fix it. Just like you do with everyone's problems. But this isn't your thing to fix, Harri." After three Mississippi's, Aisha added, "I love you. You know I do, girl, but this is between me and Rey." She groaned. "And he's knocking on my office door right now because I said I'd discuss my floating problem after five since I had to cover the phones as well."

"Didn't you call the temp agency? I had one already lined up!"

"No yet." A burst of static was followed by a muffled "Come in!" Aisha muttered, "I've got to go. Talk to you later." The signal died.

Harri stared at her phone. Maybe Aisha was right. Maybe this wasn't her business. Hell, she couldn't get her own shit together with Tim.

No, this literally was her business. If Aisha would be out on maternity leave in eight months, they needed to get their ducks lined up now. Harri scrolled through her contacts list for potential replacements.

———•———

Rey peered around the door. "You still busy?" he mouthed.

Aisha resisted the urge to slam down the receiver and replaced it gently in its cradle. Harri was simply the way she was. She gestured to Rey. "No, come on in."

Tim followed Rey into the office and closed the door behind him.

The light-headed feeling struck, but after Screaming Orgasm had left, she'd managed to fashion a rubber band chain that kept her tied to her office chair.

She tried to imitate Harri's patented look-of-death glare. "Did you need something, Tim?"

"Information," he said.

Both men plopped down on the visitor chairs across from her desk.

"Why didn't you tell me you were a super, too?" Rey frowned.

"I'm not, honey." She turned to Tim. "Can I have a private conversation with Rey first?"

"No," they replied in unison.

"If something's wrong, it affects us all," Rey said sternly.

"Oh, god." Aisha buried her face in her hands. "This wasn't how I wanted to tell you."

"Tell me what?" Rey's large warm hands drew hers away from her face.

She looked up at him, or the blurry vision of him. Damn, she thought she'd gotten the waterworks out of the way this morning. "I'm pregnant."

"B-b-but you said—"

Aisha tamped down the urge to scream the words. "I know what I said. I don't know how this happened."

"Really? You don't know how this happened? Do I need to have 'the talk' with you two?"

She and Rey glared at Tim.

Tim's smile faltered. "It is Rey's, right?"

"Why do white men always assume anyone with their lack of pigment can't control their urges and screw everything in sight?" In her righteous indignation, Aisha started to stand and was quickly reminded of her rubber band belt.

"It's called ruling out other possibilities," Tim said dryly. "If you're carrying a super baby, it would explain your floating." He pulled out his phone. "Have there been any other side effects, and when did they start?"

"She needs a doctor," Rey said. "And you're not one."

"True, but she can't go to her regular doctor." Tim eyed her as if wanting to know whether her ob/gyn could be trusted.

Aisha shook her head. "Given my medical history, there'd be too many questions. And I don't want to put Rey's identity at risk."

"Your health and the baby's are more important than my secret identity." Rey crossed his arms, a stubborn look on his beautiful face.

"She's right," Tim said softly. "If you care about her, we need to keep this quiet. For everyone's sake." He regarded her once again. "Any other symptoms?"

She wanted to sag in her chair, but she couldn't. From the rocking of the wheels, she was barely on terra firma as it was. "Just the floating. And it started this morning after the last pregnancy test."

"Time?" Tim asked at the same moment Rey blurted, "Last pregnancy test?"

"Around seven." She met Rey's incredulous stare. "After the governor called you in, I couldn't sleep. Normally, when I have insomnia, I'd go out on my balcony and smoke." Rey's mouth opened, and she held up her hands. "I know I promised to quit, honey. That's when I realized I hadn't touched a cigarette in a couple of weeks. And my period was late," she finished in a tiny voice.

Aisha sucked in a deep breath. Neither Rey or Tim said anything, waiting for her to finish. Harri hadn't let her get this far during their morning discussion. "So I walked down to the bodega and bought a test kit. They were both positive."

"Both?" Tim looked at her askance. "You said you bought one."

"Celia carries the two-packs because they are cheaper," Rey offered.

Tim cocked an eyebrow. "How would you know?"

Rey's face turned a deep scarlet. "I overheard Marta talking to her daughters when I was washing dishes at the restaurant."

Aisha cleared her throat. "Anyway, I went back and bought two more two-packs. They were all positive as well."

"Does anybody else know?" Tim asked.

Aisha shook her head. "Just Harri."

"You told Harri before you told me?" Hurt filled Rey's gold eyes.

"Honey, you were off fighting dinosaurs, and well—" Guilt overrode Aisha's anxiety. The last thing she wanted was to hurt Rey. "She walked in here when I was freaking out about the whole thing and started floating the first time."

"It'll be okay." He smiled that glorious smile of his. "I promise." He turned to Tim. "Serena?"

Tim nodded firmly. "Serena."

Suspicion tingled along Aisha's nerves. She shot each man a look. "What's a Serena?"

CHAPTER 4

Aisha bobbed in the air above her new couch, which was where Tim tethered her with her bathrobe belt while he fiddled with stuff in his equipment bag. Thankfully, the rest of her furniture arrived three days before everything hit the fan. Nothing else in the loft was heavy enough to hold her down other than their mattress. After the hugging incident in the atrium this morning, she didn't want Rey to get the wrong idea about her and Tim by being alone with him in the bedroom.

The loft door rolled open. Rey entered with a woman she presumed was the mysterious Serena.

She turned out to be a green-haired young woman with a variety of features that said mixed-race and skin a shade darker than Aisha's. Serena's hand covered her mouth when she spotted Aisha. From the glint in her gorgeous, and equally green, eyes, Serena was trying not to laugh.

Aisha crossed her arms and glared at the younger woman. "If you can't help, then get out of my home."

The younger woman immediately sobered. "I apologize, Ms. Franklin. I know the sudden appearance of powers can be frightening."

"I'm not frightened. I'm pissed," Aisha snapped. And it was true. Any fear from this morning had disappeared when she had to grab the freaking toilet seat and hold on for dear life in order to do her business. "It's bad enough I'll look like a Macy's balloon in eight months, but I'm already floating like one!"

Serena tossed her large bag on the couch. "First, we need to figure out if it's the baby who has the powers or if it's you."

Aisha threw her hands up in the air. "Why the hell would I have powers now when I've never had them before?"

"You might have HRSP. Pregnancy hormones can do some strange things to a woman's body." Serena grinned. "My mom was also non-powered when she wasn't pregnant, but she had a different ability with me and each of my four siblings. In my case, she was constantly setting stuff on fire."

Aisha swallowed a groan. Hormone related super powers, AKA HRSP, wasn't the worst thing that could happen in a pregnancy, but it would be damn inconvenient if she started to float in front of cameras during a press conference for one of their clients.

"I guess I should be thankful I don't have some destructive ability," she said.

"Yep, my aunt started developing pure calcium deposits on her skin," Serena tugged on the terrycloth tied to Aisha's ankle, pulling her down toward the couch. "Couldn't take a shower without blowing up the bathroom. Can you imagine not bathing for nine months? Rey, you wanna hang on to your girlfriend and keep her within my reach?" She turned to Tim. "You got my payment?"

The inventor grinned and held out a blue plastic rectangle the size of a shoebox with a wand attached. "One portable ultrasound device, madam."

Rey flew up a couple of feet and wrapped Aisha in his arms before settling them both on the couch. Aisha wouldn't have minded sitting on his lap if they didn't have company, but it was aggravating as hell that it was the only way she could stay in place.

As she untied the belt from her ankle, she eyed the green-haired woman suspiciously. "Do you have a medical degree of some kind?"

"Does school count?" Serena pulled a stethoscope out of her bag.

"Not really," Aisha said sourly.

"I'm working on my degree to become a physician's assistant." Serena looked at her, all joking gone. "You can go to your regular doctor, but do you know what's going to happen if you do?"

Aisha knew all too well. Part of the Superhero Act of 1945 allowed the federal government to "rescue" babies with powers if they could justify to a judge the parents' inability to handle things. With the recent attacks by Corvus, the Attorney General could easily claim hers and Rey's lifestyle put any baby in eminent danger, which was why she hadn't called her own doctor. In theory, the reason for a government guardianship was to give the kids a safe place to learn control of their abilities, but a lot of childcare experts questioned what the government nannies did to the kids. "Obviously, Rey didn't tell you what I do for a living."

If possible, Serena became even more somber. "Ms. Franklin, everybody in the neighborhood knows who and what you and Ms. Winters are. Rey isn't the only super living around here. And the only reason I'm making a house call is because Rey and Jatz'om Kuh vouched for you."

Two realizations struck as hard as one of Sparx's electric bolts. The first being Serena knew Tim's secret identity. The other made her heart break. "Your parents hid you and your brothers and sisters."

"Not on purpose at first. Actually, my dad's gift is the ability to hide a super's freaky EEG readings, including his own." Serena's smile was gentle. "Now, shush while I check your heart."

Biting her tongue, Aisha remained silent while the younger woman checked her heartbeat, her breathing, and her blood pressure. But when Serena took Tim's invention from him, Aisha couldn't keep quiet any longer.

"Don't you need gel for an ultrasound?"

Tim shook his head. "Nope. Serena wanted something a little more powerful than standard equipment so she's not limited in what she can do with it. This can resolve internal pictures closer to the level of an MRI machine than a standard ultrasound." He grinned. "It's one of the patents I want you to file."

Serena reached for the top of the blue box, and his grin disappeared. "Wait! Don't turn it on yet!" He headed back to the island that separated the kitchen from the living area and reached into his equipment bag. He produced a set of headphones. "For Rey's ears."

Once Rey was wearing the noise canceling headphones, Serena lifted the lid on top of the blue box, which had a screen, and pulled out a wand connected to the box by a long cord. She flipped on the power

A high-pitched noise pierced Aisha's eardrums. She cried out and slapped her palms over her ears.

Serena instantly punched the power button. "What is it? What's wrong?" Alarm showed on Tim's face as well.

"What's wrong, *azúcar*?" Rey murmured.

Aisha lowered her hands. "It was like that thing rammed an icepick through my brain."

"You could hear the subsonics?" Tim's expression was a cross between puzzlement and expectation.

"Yeah, I guess." Aisha peered over her shoulder. Rey had taken off the headphones. "Does it hurt you when you don't have protective gear on?"

Rey nodded, looking a little embarrassed. "That's what really happened with the kitchen counter in Patty's apartment. Tim tested the unit when Miguel and I were installing the granite."

Aisha cupped his cheek. "Oh, honey, why didn't you guys just say so?"

Tim laughed. "You have met Harriet Winters, haven't you?"

Harri had gone ballistic over the crushed stone countertop. She had wanted to have Patty ensconced in the Lechuza Building before she gave birth, regardless of what her poor, pregnant assistant wanted. And Harri's interference in Patty's life probably had more to do with Patty and Arthur's budding romance. Harri still didn't trust the former supervillain, even though he hadn't been much of a supervillain to begin with by her own admission.

Aisha rolled her eyes. "You can't let her bulldoze you. Follow mine and Patty's example."

The two men exchanged glances that implied she and Patty were just as much under Harri's thumb as they were.

Tim turned back to his bag of tricks and pulled out another set of ear protection.

Aisha eyed him suspiciously. "Do you bring spares for every contingency?"

"No, but I thought we might need them." Tim's face quirked in the weird way she'd come to recognize the genius was working out some theory in his big brain. He stayed by the island. "Rey let go of her."

"But I'll just float to the freaking ceiling," she snapped.

"Aisha, I need you to concentrate on wanting these headphones." Tim held up the set. "You want them as bad as you want a cigarette."

"But I don't want a cigarette," she protested.

"Hey, I used to smoke, too." He grinned at her. "Haven't touched 'em in twenty-five years, but I still remember the desire. Focus on wanting the headphones as much as that morning cigarette."

Rey released her waist, and she immediately started to rise into the air.

She pushed down the threatening panic. It wasn't like he couldn't fly up and pull her off the damn ceiling. But she sure didn't want to feel that icepick-through-the-brain thing again either. If the headphones covered her ears—

She moved, not upwards, but across the room toward Tim. In that realization, she lost her focus and started drifting upward again.

This is no different than taking the bar. Concentrate on one thing at a time.

Aisha narrowed her eyes and stared at the headphones. She shot across the space and stopped right in front of Tim.

Now, feet on the floor.

The sudden contact of her stilettos with the floor made her stumble, but Tim saved her from falling on her face. Behind her, applause erupted.

"Good job." Tim grinned and released her.

"How'd you know I could control this?" Suspicion ran through her.

"Because I told him how my abilities manifested." Rey swept her into a huge hug. "I knew you could do it." His lips claimed hers, and she fell into the emotions swirling through her.

Someone cleared their throat, and she reluctantly pulled away.

"Now you know why she's pregnant," Tim said dryly to Selena.

"Shut up," Aisha muttered.

"Can I check the baby now that we know you might actually be a teachable super?" Sarcasm ran thick in Serena's voice.

"Fine," Aisha muttered.

Serena gestured back toward the couch.

Aisha had to concentrate fiercely in order to reach the couch on her feet. It was like gravity was no longer her default setting. She sat gingerly on the edge. Rey perched on the couch beside her. They both donned their ear protection.

Serena plopped down on Aisha's other side. She checked them both before she flipped the power switch on Tim's device again.

A bit of a hum penetrated the noise-cancelling headphones, but it was nothing like the brain-piercing pain of the first time. Serena slowly drew the wand across Aisha's abdomen. A picture developed on the screen.

Aisha just stared at the little white blob about the size and shape of a peanut. Her baby. The one she'd wanted for so damn long.

Rey tapped her shoulder, and she jumped. He wasn't wearing his earphones, and he gestured for Aisha to remove hers.

"Is it in the right place?" she asked once she could hear.

Serena raised an eyebrow. "It's not an ectopic pregnancy if that's what you're worried about. He's definitely in your uterus."

"Oh, god!" Tears blurred Aisha's vision. "This is really happening."

"When was your last period?" Serena pulled out a notepad.

Aisha swallowed hard at the standard question. Too many doctors asked the same damn thing at too many appointments. "Six weeks ago, but with the loss of one of my ovaries, I've started perimenopause, and I've never been regular before that."

The younger woman chewed her bottom lip for a few seconds before she said, "I'd like to use my powers to check both you and the baby."

"You said your mom started fires when she was carrying you. How do I know you won't set me on fire?"

Serena's grin was a little rueful. "If the issue is HRSP, the mom and the baby don't necessarily have the same abilities. Like I said, once Mom delivered me, no more powers."

Aisha leaned away from her. "Won't x-ray vision hurt the fetus?"

"I can sense bodily functions." Serena hesitated for a moment before she added, "And I can affect them."

"Affect them how?"

"She's a healer," Ray murmured.

"Or she can make you sicker than a dog if you try to pimp little girls on River Street." Tim chuckled.

Well, they needed to know what was going on. Aisha sucked in a deep breath and nodded.

Serena leaned forward and rested both her hands on Aisha's abdomen.

Nothing really seemed to happen. Aisha half-expected the girl's hands to glow or to feel something other than the touch.

Serena straightened and smiled. "You're about four weeks along, and he's a perfectly healthy baby."

"He? You keep saying he?"

"Oops." Serena winced. "Are you one of those moms who wants to be surprised?"

"No, I just, I . . ." Aisha's voice faltered. This time, her waterworks weren't from panic or pain. She swiped at the tears and cleared her throat. "I never thought I'd hear those words."

Serena closed up the equipment Tim had given her. "My place is above Celia's bodega. I'll get you started on prenatal vitamins." She hesitated. "If it's okay, I'll contact a friend who has a medical license. She'll keep quiet. I swear. But we'll want an ally just in case."

"In case something goes wrong," Aisha murmured.

Serena nodded, even as Rey hugged her and growled, "Nothing's going to happen to you or the baby."

Aisha couldn't help rubbing her stomach. She'd wanted a baby for so long. This should have been the best thing to ever happen to her.

So why did she feel like something awful would occur in return for getting her wish?

CHAPTER 5

The next morning, Harri filled her coffee mug and headed to her office. She had no doubt Tim showing up on her loft's doorstep with dinner last night had been his way to keep her from walking across the hall to Aisha and Rey's loft. He hadn't said a word about them though, and she didn't ask.

She jabbed the power button on her computer.

As much as she hated to admit it, Arthur was right. She went overboard helping other people because she couldn't save her own family. Not Mom from the skiing accident. Not Dad from his various addictions. Not even Grandma Harri from lung cancer.

But when she saw both Aisha and Patty doing stupid things with their lives—

Aisha burst into Harri's office. "Have you seen the news?"

Harri held up her super-sized mug of black coffee with a splash of cream. "First one, so no, I haven't."

Aisha scooped up the remote and flipped on the large screen monitor/TV that hung on Harri's office wall. She thumbed through channels to reach Action 12 News! Harri grimaced as the blow-dried, orange-skinned buffoon the station called an anchor popped up larger than life. If it wouldn't ruin Rey's reputation, she'd pay the kid to place Ted Meadowfield's Corvette on top of the Canyon Building five seconds before the city demolished the eyesore.

Meadowfield stood in front of a building Harri was too familiar with, microphone in hand.

". . . acting district attorney Calvin Johnson had no comment on the suspicious death. If you are just tuning in, Darryl Bloch, AKA disgraced superhero Seismic Shift, was found dead in his cell at Lake County jail this morning. Cause still unknown. This is Ted Meadowfield. Action 12 News!"

The camera lingered on Ted after his sign-off. He looked at someone off-camera. "I wouldn't put it past that Winters bitch to use one of her supers to sneak into the jail and murder the sonovabitch out of revenge."

The feed immediately cut off to be replaced by Essie Morales in the studio.

Harri had no doubt the co-anchor's tight smile was held in place through sheer willpower. "Thank you for that informative report, Ted. We'll be bringing you further updates regarding Seismic Shift's untimely death as they become available. In other headlines today, reconstruction of City Hall has been delayed. The building suffered extensive damage after the devastating fire Seismic Shift is accused of allegedly setting—"

Aisha thumbed the mute button. "Corvus?"

Harri frowned and stared at Essie's lips moving onscreen. "For failing to kill me, losing both Sparx and Captain Justice, and getting caught? Yep, I'd definitely say General Trubble wasn't happy with Bloch."

"Why kill him though?" Aisha dropped into one of the visitor chairs. "That will only bring more attention down on them. All they had to do was get his case transferred to Federal court. Once it was out of Cal's hands, they could quietly hush everything up."

Harri tilted her head. "Based on what?"

"The Supervillainy Act of '47." Aisha shrugged. "Fed trumps state if they decide to get involved. And if a high-profile super goes bad like Shift, the U.S. attorney general jumps all over it. Corvus has to have someone inside the Justice Department."

"Normally, I'd agree with you." Harri shook her head. She wished she could shake away her bad feeling as easily. "Something else is going on. Something other than Bloch going off the reservation and exposing Corvus to us. Trubble wanted Rey too bad to give up, much less kill one of his assets out of spite."

"What the hell could Bloch have done to get whacked?" Aisha shook her head. "All of our real evidence concerned his illegal property transactions and his attempts on your life. That's normal, run-of-the-mill criminal acts. Like I said, Trubble sending in one of his pet supers to kill Bloch would only attract attention Corvus wouldn't want."

A chill ran through Harri not even her hot mug could dissipate. "Not if Trubble sent Black Death."

"Who?" Aisha cocked her head.

"According to Tim, he's the assassin of last resort for Corvus." Harri sipped her coffee. "Not even Jatz'om Kuh has been able to discover his secret identity. Supposedly, he can kill with a touch. Tim's description of Black Death's ability sounds an awful lot like Patty's mysterious baby daddy who was supposed to make my death inside that very same jail look like Mother Nature."

"That's not a comforting thought." Aisha shook her head. "Someone like that under the thumb of General Bat Crap Crazy?"

"Yeah," Harri muttered. "If Trubble decides we're more trouble than we're worth, I don't think even Rey is going to be able to take down Black Death." Except the man in her cell had pleaded with her to keep Patty and the baby safe when Harri had been illegally held at the county lockup. He didn't assassinate Harri as ordered, which made her pretty sure the command came from Shift, not Trubble. Would Black Death actually kill Patty if Trubble ordered him to?

Guilt assaulted Harri when Aisha rubbed her belly. Dammit. She could have worded things a bit differently.

Harri cleared her throat. "You ready to talk about your situation?"

Aisha sighed and dropped her hand to her lap. "I told him after I got off the phone with you last night. I couldn't really hide it either when he saw me floating two stories above Patty's desk yesterday morning."

"How did Rey take it?" Harri took another sip of her coffee.

"He's . . . ecstatic." Aisha covered her face with her palms for a moment. When she lowered her hands, she stared bleakly at Harri. "Why aren't I just as ecstatic? This is what I wanted. Or I thought it was. But I turn forty-one in a couple of months. And Rey? Dammit, he's just getting his career off the ground."

"Not to mention he's young enough to be—"

"Stop," Aisha snapped. "Just stop." Her hand slashed through the air. "I don't need the I-told-you-so, and if that's all you can offer—"

Harri set down her mug and raised both palms. "I'm sorry. You're right." She exhaled and leaned her elbows on her desk. "I just wasn't planning to open a daycare in the office despite what Tim suggested."

"Wow." Aisha shook her head. "I never thought I'd hear Ms. Women's Rights acting like my previous employer. When the hell did you become an old white man?" She jabbed an index finger in the general direction of the basement door. "Tim has been more supportive in the last twenty-four hours than you have."

"I said I was sorry. I just wish one of these children were planned."

"Really?" Aisha stood. "Look, I get how your screwed-up childhood affected you, but if all you're going to do is throw your resentment at your parents and stepmonster in my face, this law firm, hell, our friendship won't survive."

"Maybe it's because I know what happens to the kids when the parents can't get their shit together!" Harri rose as well. Aisha using her superior height got under her last nerve.

Aisha threw her hands up. "I can't talk to you when you get like this. Come see me when you're ready to apologize for acting as bat crap crazy as Trubble." She flew out of the office.

Literally. Flew.

Harri's jaw dropped. All of her arguments with Aisha had been dealt with by the end of the day, usually through a phone call as they lay in their respective beds. But this time—

How the hell could she possibly win a fight with her best friend if Aisha was getting Rey's powers?

Maybe Aisha had been right. Maybe both of them living in the same building was putting too much of a strain on their friendship.

Or maybe the real problem was Aisha taking that step into motherhood Harri had avoided like the plague.

Patty was one thing. As much as Harri adored her assistant, she didn't have the history with her that she had with Aisha. And now Aisha was leaving her behind just like her parents had.

That realization made her want to hit something.

Harri charged out of her office and straight for the basement door.

———— • ◆ • ————

After changing, Harri stomped into the gym Tim had put together only to find Rey already in there, laying on a reinforced bench and holding a ton of weight over his head. Literally, a ton.

Her anger deflated faster than a Macy's parade balloon. "Sorry," she muttered. "I didn't think anybody would be in here."

Rey set the weight down, sat up, and eyed her. "Are you going to lecture me about not using protection the way you did Aisha?" He grabbed his towel, and wiped at the non-existent sweat on his forehead. "Because if you are, Miguel beat you to it."

"No." She sat on the other bench and clasped her fingers together. "And I didn't lecture her."

His dark eyebrow arched over his golden eye on the right side of his face. "Really?"

Harri glared at him. "I don't want you to tell Aisha you want this child and back out when you realized it's not all cuteness and giggles twenty-four-seven. You're barely old enough to drink—"

"I'm not your father, Harri." His stern expression and quiet voice shook her to her core.

"I know that," she snapped.

"Do you really?" Rey said. "With what little Aisha hinted at about your own past, I can guess the rest. You think I don't see what happens in this neighborhood? Drugs don't care if you're rich or poor, Harri. I'm sorry you're still hurting because your father abandoned you to get high, but I won't let you pit Aisha and me against each other because of your hang-ups. This baby is a blessing, and we will raise it together."

He stood abruptly and stalked out of the exercise room.

"Well, I'd say you handled that with aplomb."

Harri turned to see Tim, dressed in a tattered t-shirt and knit shorts, leaning against the doorframe that led to his apartment. A brace still covered the knee the Corvus assassination team had messed up, but Tim had been stalling on getting the necessary surgery out of worry Trubble would send his goons at their little team again.

Which only made her angrier. "Shut up, Canyon."

"Take it from someone who has tried and failed miserably, Winters. You can't fix everyone's problems the way you think they should be fixed."

"Says the man who's too much of a wimp to get the surgery he needs," she snapped.

Tim exhaled loudly. "So now you're trying to fix me?"

"I'm not trying—" She closed her mouth. She wasn't trying to fix anything, and she sure as hell didn't need his advice.

"Uh-huh. Keep telling yourself that." He grinned, the cocky one that made her think about things she shouldn't. "You gonna stay and watch me work my rock-hard abs?"

"You wish." She jumped to her feet and practically ran from the gym. The problem was she did wish. But then, she'd wished a lot of things in her life that hadn't come true. Why should this whole superhero boutique law firm thing working out be any different?

CHAPTER 6

"What the hell is she thinking?" Harri's margarita sloshed over the edge of her glass at her sharp wave. La Churro's had been her and Aisha's hangout when they'd been in law school. Cheap food and the drinks weren't watered down. Jeremy had insisted on meeting here though he could afford better these days.

"Woman, that is a waste of perfectly good tequila." He mopped the spill on the table while Harri set down her drink and wiped off her hand.

"Sorry, it's just that-that—"

"You're pissed off that for once, everyone else is right, and you're wrong?" Jeremy topped off both of their glasses from the pitcher they'd ordered.

"You're supposed to be on my side!"

Jeremy set down the pitcher. "Has it even occurred to you they're right? I'm not going to pretend I understand Aisha's obsession with having a rugrat. But that's her decision, not yours." He tilted his head and regarded her. "Unless you were having fantasies of the two of you living happily ever after?"

"Be a queen on Lady Jaye's time, not mine. Besides that fantasy included you, and we'd be like the Golden Girls." Harri fiddled with the stirrer. "It's just that Rey's too young for her—"

Jeremy held up his hand. "And that attitude right there is why I don't bring any of my boytoys around to meet you."

Harri snorted. "You're not a boytoy person any more than I am."

"You're right." He picked a chip from the basket and pointed a sharp corner at her. "Neither is Aisha."

"What's that supposed to mean?" Harri glared at him over the salted rim of her glass and took a huge gulp.

Jeremy dipped his chip in the creamy cilantro sauce he preferred to salsa. "Unlike us, she had fairly good relationship role models in Betty and Marvin. She doesn't have your hangups about commitment, and that bugs the hell out of you." Jeremy popped the chip in his mouth.

"Not as good of role models as you think," Harri muttered. Maybe Aisha's parents hadn't kicked her out of their home for being gay like Jeremy's had or driven their Porsche off a cliff like her dad and stepmother, but they weren't perfect either.

He shook his head. "Betty's snit fit when she was here last month had more to do with her than Marvin. No queen likes facing old age in the mirror. Speaking of which, when are you going to let Leonardo do your gray? It's driving me insane."

Harri ran a hand over her ponytail. "What's your obsession with youth?"

"I'm not the one pissed over Aisha's twenty-something thang." Jeremy lifted an eyebrow and sipped his drink.

The discussion had come full circle, and Harri didn't like the new view. She groaned and covered her face with her hands. "I really am wrong this time, aren't I?"

"You said it. I didn't," Jeremy said primly as he selected another chip. "Why haven't you focused on the other luscious tidbit living in close proximity to you? Or is he too old, Miss Picky?"

"Crap." She had been rather brutal to Tim this morning when her pissy mood took over. They claimed they were taking things slow. They both had a ton of personal baggage. But neither of them were taking the emotional chances Aisha and Rey were.

To be honest, she wasn't taking an emotional chance at all.

Harri leaned back in her chair and examined the other patrons. Maybe this was more about Aisha finding someone, than about who that someone was. People laughed around her and Jeremy. Lots of groups flirting. Lots of folks on dates. All ages, colors, and orientations. Everyone was with someone.

All except the one guy in the back. Their eyes met for a split second before he rose, threw some bills on the table, and strode out of the restaurant.

She squinted through tequila vision at his backside. Those intensely blue eyes of the stranger's were familiar.

Jeremy followed her line of sight and twisted on his stool. He turned back to her and grinned. "Not bad, but you were a little too slow."

"No, I think I know him." She slapped her forehead. "Oh, crap. He was the guy in the garage elevator with me yesterday morning at the hospital."

"Any hanky-panky?" Jeremy waggled his eyebrows and leered.

"No." She shot a dirty look at him. "I was on my way to Delivery after Patty went into labor. That guy's girlfriend was pregnant, and he'd just found out."

Jeremy cocked his head. "That she was pregnant or that she'd had the baby?"

"Both from what he implied on the elevator." Harri shook her head and reached for another chip. "From his expression the last time I saw him, I don't think things went too well with her." She dunked her chip in salsa. "He did make me question about whether Patty actually told her baby daddy."

"Harri—"

She popped the chip in her mouth and held up her hands in surrender. When she chewed and swallowed, she said, "Not fixing, just speculating."

Besides, the super sent to kill Harri had definitely known Patty was pregnant. But it didn't mean her assistant had told him. He could have learned through Corvus's surveillance of their little cadre.

"So when's the new mommy and kid coming home?" Jeremy asked.

"Day after tomorrow."

Jeremy frowned. "Isn't that a long stay for mom and baby?"

"Patty's blood pressure was a little high and she had more bleeding than usual after delivery, but I chalk that up to all the stress we've been living with the last few weeks." Harri shook her head. "Anyway, her doctor's not taking any chances."

"Want me to decorate the new apartment while you pick up Patty and Grace?" Jeremy's anticipation over a party, any party, was legendary.

"No welcome home party tomorrow."

Jeremy's face fell.

Harri smiled to take edge off her veto. "We're doing it next week when Grace goes in for her well-baby checkup so it's not too much for the mom or the baby."

Jeremy managed to dance on his stool without falling off.

"Aisha's already ordered the cake . . ." Double crap. Harri buried her face in her hands. She was supposed to go car shopping with Aisha tonight. But she'd been so freaking mad about their fight, and then Rey and Tim piling on, she'd left the office early and met Jeremy at his salon.

He gently pulled her hands away from her face. "She'll forgive you for being a butthead. You two always make up. Now, let's talk theme . . ."

By the time she and Jeremy were done discussing Patty and Grace's welcome home party, they both needed rides home. The taxi driver wasn't keen about taking them to the northeast side either at this time of night.

Jeremy laughed. "Don't you pay attention to the news? Captain Justice and Sparx patrol the Canyon Block these days."

The driver snorted as he pulled away from the curb. His statue of Ganesh hanging from the rearview mirror danced at the sudden acceleration. "That bullshit with Seismic Shift? It's all for show."

"Hey, R—" Harriet quickly corrected herself. Maybe that third pitcher of margaritas wasn't such a good idea. "Captain Justice is the real deal!"

"Yeah, sure," their driver replied derisively. "They're all wonderful until it's time to pay their cab fare. Then it's 'my supersuit doesn't have pockets'. Crisp high five, my ass! In the meantime, they're making a ton in residuals for their commercials, toys, comics, and shit. Do you have any idea how much of that super crap my kids beg me for? I moved from New York to get away from that circus."

"Then believe this—" Jeremy squinted and leaned closer to read the driver's ID. "—Dopinder. Captain Justice isn't going to let anything happen to his attorneys or their cab drivers."

"None of those bigshot lawyers live on that side of River Street." The driver glanced at them in the mirror, a frown on his face.

"You've got one in the backseat who does." Harri leaned her head back and closed her eyes. "One who definitely drank too much tequila tonight."

"You'd better not puke in my cab, Ms. Hot Shot Lawyer," Dopinder growled. After a few seconds, he added, "I don't suppose you could get me his autograph."

Harri couldn't help chuckling. "Not tonight. I'd have better luck getting you Jabba, er, Jutta, Jadda—"

"Jatz'om Kuh," both Jeremy and Dopinder said at the same time.

She groaned. Yep, that third pitcher was definitely a mistake. "The Ghost Owl's."

"You represent a famous vigilante, too?" Wonder filled the man's voice.

Oops. No more tequila. Ever. "No. Just had a couple of run-ins."

Thank goodness, Jeremy didn't call her on her little white lie. Technically she didn't represent the Ghost Owl, only his alter ego Tim Canyon.

Well, even more technically, Aisha represented Tim because she was the IP whiz. Which was even more of a reason to make up to her partner. While she could get their supers out of paying for damages to the city, or at least minimize the amount, Dopinder was right. The real money was in subsidiary licensing, and Aisha was the one who knew how to milk that cash cow.

Jeremy nudged her shoulder, and she blearily opened her eyes and raised her head. The cab pulled to a halt in front of the Lechuza Building.

Dopinder twisted in his seat to look at them directly. "So why can't you get me Captain Justice's autograph?"

"Because she stuck her foot in her mouth with him," Jeremy muttered. "Which was why I tried to lubricate an apology out of her before she loses her biggest client. Thanks, amigo. I just need you to wait a couple of minutes."

Harri shook a finger at their driver. "Here's my tip: Don't ever let your kids grow up to be superheroes."

Jeremy hauled Harri out of the back seat. With an arm around her waist, he guided her to the side entrance.

"Maybe I should sleep in my office tonight," she muttered.

"Why is that?" Jeremy sounded like he was trying really hard not to laugh at her.

"I don't think I can make it up four flights of stairs," she said as the side door swung open.

The streetlamp highlighted the silver in Tim's red hair. "Well then, it's a good thing the elevator was repaired today."

"You take advantage of our girl, and I'll have Eddie beat the shit out of you," Jeremy warned as he passed her to Tim.

"Not Rey?" Harri peered blearily up at him.

"Harri, sweetie, these days I could take Tim with a baseball bat." Jeremy rolled his eyes. "That wasn't the point I was trying to make."

"Dude," Tim drawled. "You know me better than that."

"You're right. I do." Jeremy grinned and turned to her. "Harri, you take advantage of my boy, and I'll have Aisha beat the shit out of you."

Harri flipped him off as Tim guided her inside. He paused once he got her past the doorjamb. Jeremy climbed back into the cab, and Dopinder merged with the light traffic.

Tim pulled his phone from his pocket.

"What are you doing?" She leaned closer to see what he was texting and nearly fell over.

"Something I forgot to tell Jeremy when he was here." Tim let the door swing shut, and a series of beeps followed.

"How'd you know I was out there?" She peered up at him while they walked. "Are you spying on me?"

"There's a far simpler explanation, Harriet. Jeremy texted me from the cab." Tim paused in front of the antique elevator gate.

"Don't call me Harriet," she muttered.

"When are you going to stop taking out your anger on me?" Indigo blue eyes bore into hers.

She sighed. "I'm sorry about this morning."

"Have you thought about counseling?" He pulled the gate open.

"For what?"

"Your daddy issues." He led her onto the car.

"I've been to enough fucking shrinks in my life, thank you." She glared up at him. "And my life is none of your business, so keep your nose out of it."

"You have no problem poking yours into everyone else's business."

The car started its upward climb. A wave of nausea threatened the cheese burritos she'd eaten when Jeremy insisted she needed something in her stomach besides chips, salsa, and margaritas.

"I know," she muttered.

"Was that an admission of guilt?" Humor flowed in his voice.

"At least, I don't deal with my issues by running around in public clad in only my underwear."

The arm holding her up stiffened. "I don't wear my underwear in public. And this is exactly what I'm talking about. The more you care about someone, the nastier you are to them. Your dad seriously screwed up your wiring because that's not how it works."

"And you think you can fix everything with your Swiss army knife, MacGyver," she growled.

He sighed. "If I hadn't promised Jeremy, and you weren't drunk, I'd show what I can do with the rest of my toolbox."

She blinked, trying to make sense of his words. "Are you making a pass at me?"

"I've been making passes at you." He grinned down at her. "But the subtle ones obviously aren't working."

A shiver went through her that had nothing to do with the tequila. She liked Tim. She really did. Her sight blurred even more with the hot liquid in her eyes.

"It wouldn't work," she said.

"Why?"

"Because I am so fucked up, and not from the alcohol." She swiped at the one tear that had escaped. "Everything I touch turns to crap."

The elevator ground to a halt, and he guided her off and towards her loft. At her door, he turned her to face him.

"Harri, when you're sober in the morning, take a good look around you. You already have the family you want and need."

"They're all mad at me," she wailed.

He entered her security code. Something in the back of her mind said he shouldn't know her loft code.

"Yeah, they are right now, but you need to apologize to them like you did me." He guided her to her couch, the cute aqua blue one she'd bought after her divorce from Eddie. The one that now seemed overwhelmed by the huge space of a downtown loft.

"But what if they don't forgive me?" She sounded like a little girl. Dammit, she hated that voice. She lay down on the couch and stared up at Tim.

"They'll forgive you." Tim pulled the throw from the back and spread it over her. Eddie had done the same thing for her when she would fall asleep on the ratty old couch in their first cockroach-infested apartment. Damn, she really had taken her ex-husband for granted.

"I fucked up," Harri murmured. "I really fucked up."

"You can fix it in the morning." Tim kissed her forehead. "Good night."

She watched his backside as he crossed the living area and pulled the door shut behind him.

Yep, she'd definitely screwed up. But was she ready for a relationship with the quirky inventor-turned-vigilante if she couldn't keep things straight with her best friend?

And if she was, could she deal with Aisha dishing back the same crap about not sleeping with clients Harri had given out?

CHAPTER 7

The alarm blared. Aisha slapped the snooze button, but it wouldn't stop ringing. A warm, strong arm wrapped around her and an equally warm chuckle tickled her ear.

"That's mine. Not yours." The alarm finally stopped.

"Another emergency so soon on top of Professor Triassic?" she murmured sleepily. "The supervillains have stepped up their game."

"Yeah, but a man's gotta buy the bacon for his woman and their baby." Rey kissed her soundly before jumping out of bed.

Aisha rolled on her back and propped herself on her elbows in order to admire his luscious backside as he stalked over to his wardrobe. It made her want to hunt down whatever supervillain caused this alarm and shoot him.

Cognizant thought about earning money for bacon intruded. "Don't forget you and Sparx have a *People* photo shoot this afternoon at two."

"I won't." Rey turned and smiled at her. His little jade pendant at his throat gleamed in the ambient glow thrown off by the streetlights. He quickly dressed in his Captain Justice uniform and flew back to the bed and hovered over her.

"Show off," she muttered. He'd made her practice for a solid two hours last night. Just in case she started floating when someone wasn't around to pull her back down to the ground.

"Go back to sleep, baby. I love you." He kissed her again before he zoomed out of sight.

"I love you, too," she said to his afterimage. She snuggled back under the covers and did as he suggested.

Later that afternoon, Aisha paced in front of the condemned Canyon Building. Heat shimmered off the sidewalk in waves. Why the hell the *People* magazine team wanted to shoot these photos outside in the hottest summer on record was beyond her.

Well, she knew why they wanted this place. It was the site of the Winter & Franklin team's confrontation with Seismic Shift. The one that led to their national exposure and his arrest. She didn't have to like it though.

Thank god, she wore her cream-colored linen suit. Otherwise she'd be sweating through her dress shields. How the hell did Sparx deal with the heat in her superhero outfit? It was mainly black with a few white lightning bolts thrown in for contrast.

Aisha glanced at her watch. Two-fifteen. She'd worked with some supers carrying diva attitudes in her time, but she never expected this from Rey. Not this soon anyway.

Sparx leaned against Aisha's rental car and yawned. A reminder that Harri hadn't gone with Aisha last night to shop for a new car, even though she planned to bow out anyway. She didn't trust her ability to control her new power despite Rey practicing with her. But Harri hadn't called last night to make up from their morning fight.

A twinge of guilt hit her. She hadn't called Harri either because she was still pissed over the lecture Harri had launched. She and Rey were adults, dammit!

She looked at her watch again. Two-eighteen.

Okay, one of them was an adult.

Another twinge of guilt. Treating Rey like an irresponsible twenty-something wasn't fair. She hadn't heard from him since this morning's emergency alarm.

There hadn't been anything on any of her news feeds this morning about accidents, natural disasters, or supervillain shenanigans either. Was Rey in trouble? Had some new creep been more than he could handle?

Or had Trubble taken another shot at him despite the stalemate between Corvus and Winters & Franklin?

The photographer, photographer's assistant, and the makeup artist all fidgeted with their equipment. The interviewer pointedly looked at her.

Aisha plastered her fake, ingratiating smile on her face no matter how much doing so galled her. "Why don't you start with some individual shots of Sparx while we wait for Captain Justice?"

The interviewer crossed her arms. "I can't sell her without him."

"I can hear you, you know." Sparx glared at the interviewer.

"Sorry, hun." The interviewer shrugged. "It's the business."

Sparx shot a look at Aisha that said, "Fix this."

"I'm sure Captain Justice will be here soon." Aisha waved airily. "You know how the new superheroes have to keep up appearances to protect their secret identities. If he got stuck at his day job—"

The light-headed feeling struck her, and she clawed at the chainlink fence behind her. The last thing she needed was to start floating. Outdoors. In front of someone with a camera.

Sparx pushed off from the hood of the rental. "You okay, Ms. Franklin?"

"Yeah." Aisha clung to the fence and concentrated on how much she wanted-ed to stay on the concrete. "I missed lunch."

"Just making sure." Sparx didn't relax, but she didn't question the lie in front of the magazine crew either. But from the set of her mouth, Aisha would defi-nitely be questioned later since the two of them had wraps from Marta's shop while they went over an endorsement campaign from a battery manufacturer.

"Look, I'll give him until two-thirty, but we've got a schedule—"

A high-pitched whistle from overhead interrupted the reporter. The entire group waiting on the sidewalk, including the spectators on the opposite side of the street, looked up.

A red and white blur flashed overhead. Rey circled back around and sim-ply dropped into the three-point hero landing. The one that made a splashy entrance.

The one that had driven Harri crazy during her time as city attorney when other supers did it. Despite the audience loving the spectacle, the stunt left huge, crumbly divots in concrete and asphalt. Divots that cost Canyon Pointe millions to repair annually.

Aisha glanced across the street. *Please, God, don't let Harri have seen that.*

Besides, Rey abhorred the flashy bullshit of the other supers as much as Harri did. Why the hell had he pulled that particular stunt?

Apparently, he got the response he wanted. Bystanders enthusiastically ap-plauded, including the *People* magazine crew, who Aisha was sure had seen it all before.

However, Sparx was looking at him like he'd lost his damn mind.

Aisha wanted to breathe a sigh of relief she wasn't the only one who thought so. Instead, she put on her game face and approached Rey.

He rose to his full height and flashed his panty-melting smile. "Sorry I'm late."

That wouldn't work. Not today, especially since she reminded him of the shoot before he left this morning. "They're ready for you, Captain Justice." Her tone was barely above freezing. This was business, not personal. If he couldn't separate the two, their relationship was already on ice.

"You're mad at me," he whispered.

"We'll talk about this later." The light-headed feeling struck, and she managed to loop her arm around his elbow before her heels left the ground. Damn, she hoped that looked like she stumbled on the cracked concrete.

The weird sensation disappeared by the time they reached the *People* crew. Aisha quickly made introductions, and the photographer lined up shots. When the reporter asked questions during lens and lighting changes, both Captain Justice and Sparx stuck to their rehearsed scripts. Other than Rey's stupid landing stunt, no one went off the reservation.

Until Sparx jumped right as the photographer pressed the camera button on a shot with Rey standing behind her. Her mouth opened, and she looked at Aisha with a shocked expression.

"You okay there?" the photographer called out.

"Yes." Sparx glanced over her shoulder at Rey. Her face carried a mix of perplexion and embarrassment while Captain Justice maintained an innocent air.

Old rage rose inside Aisha and mixed with disbelief. Had Rey just grabbed Qiang's ass? From the superheroine's rapid shift from embarrassment to anger, he certainly had. Slimeball Stuart Cheatham, the so-called development manager at Aisha's previous employer, had tried that same stunt once with Aisha.

Only once.

"You sure?" Aisha asked, trying to give the other woman an out.

"Yes," Sparx bit out. "Let's get this done."

After another five minutes, the *People* crew had everything they needed for the upcoming issue. Captain Justice thanked them and shook their hands, but he held on just a little too long with the ladies. He launched himself into the sky without a word to Aisha.

Sparx sidled close to Aisha as the magazine folks packed their gear. "Did you see—"

"Yeah, I did." Aisha shook her head. "I'm so sorry."

"Wanna tell me what that was all about?" Sparx's frown underneath her mask promised someone would get his balls electrocuted if he didn't make amends.

Aisha stared in the direction Rey had flown. "I have no freakin' clue."

"I thought you two were an item," Sparx whispered.

"Maybe not much longer," Aisha growled. How dare he put her in this position!

She faced Sparx. "Again, I'm sorry for his unprofessionalism. I'll make him apologize."

"I didn't think he was the type. Just tell him if he pulls something like that again, I'll fry his balls off for you."

As Aisha suspected, but Sparx's tone was far milder than her words. From what she could see of Sparx's face, the superheroine appeared more concerned than angry now that the initial shock had worn off.

"You sure you're okay?" Sparx asked. "You looked like you had some trouble staying upright."

"Dizzy spell from overheating." Aisha hated lying to the other woman, but news of her pregnancy getting out would be problematic at best. "I've been in the sun too long thanks to you-know-who."

Sparx didn't look convinced, but thankfully, she didn't question it. "Anything else we need to discuss before I take off for the day job?"

Aisha shook her head again. "I'll let you know what they say about our requested contract revisions for the endorsement offer."

Sparx nodded. Using the magnetic side of her abilities, she also flew away.

None of Rey's behavior for the last hour made any sense. And running, er, flying away because she was mad wasn't like him either. Was he having second thoughts about the baby? She rubbed her abdomen as she crossed the street.

Little Francisco Esperanza raced up to her at the entrance to the Lechuza Building. Down by the corner bodega, his brother watched with what seemed to be vague interest. But thirteen-year-old Javier and his middle school cronies kept pretty tight tabs on the neighborhood now that the two oldest Esperanza brothers were helping their father with the build-out on the upper floors of the Lechuza Building for the summer.

"Where's he going?" the seven-year-old said breathlessly. "He didn't stop to say hi."

At the kid's stricken expression, Aisha placed a hand on his shoulder. "I'm sorry. Captain Justice had some things he had to do."

"But what about my book report on *The Hobbit*?" Wide, brown eyes stared up at her.

The Hobbit? She blinked. That was way beyond the reading level of most second graders. What else had Rey been pushing the kid to read?

She smiled. "Ask your dad if you can stop by after supper and give your book report to him then."

The boy brightened at the invitation. "Thanks, Ms. Aisha." He raced back toward his brother.

Despite hers and Harri's protestations that the Esperanza boys use their first names, Miguel still insisted his children address them respectfully. Their contractor and maintenance man reminded her too much of her own parents.

Which only reminded her she needed to give them a call as she nodded at the temp receptionist and entered her office.

Mom should be back from visiting LaShun in Seattle by now. Hopefully, Dad had taken Aisha's advice and called a marriage counselor. Her parents' major blow-up when they'd been visiting her two months ago worried her more than she wanted to admit. She couldn't imagine throwing away a nearly fifty-year marriage on some petty shit.

She was digging her cell phone out of her purse when a knock on her door grabbed her attention. Harri peeked around the edge.

"Can we talk?"

"That depends," Aisha said cautiously. She dropped the cell back in her purse, closed the drawer, and straightened.

Harri looked away for an instant before her attention returned to Aisha. "Was the three-point your idea?"

Damn. She had seen Rey's stupid stunt.

"No," Aisha replied coolly. "And I'll speak to him about it."

Harri's cheeks pinked. "Don't yell at him. It may be my fault."

"How so?" Though Rey had told Aisha what had happened between him and Harri yesterday morning, she waited for her partner's confession.

"Yesterday, I said some things I shouldn't have. To both of you." She entered Aisha's office, and she wrapped her arms around herself. A good sign that she knew she'd stepped way across the line. "He may have done it to piss me off. He's still at that age—"

"Excuse me?" Aisha's tone was as icy as it had been with Rey earlier. She didn't need both of them throwing bullshit at her. Not when her plate was overflowing. "Are you seriously trying to make the lecture you gave me yesterday Rey's fault?"

Harri inhaled deeply, dropped her arms, and eyed Aisha squarely. "No. You're right. This is on me. I'm sorry for what I said to you yesterday. It's not my business."

"And?" She cocked her head.

"I'm sorry for blowing you off when we had plans to go car shopping."

Aisha leaned back in her chair. "Actually, I'm more pissed you and Jeremy went to La Churro's without me."

Harri frowned. "Tim blabbed?"

"Actually, Jeremy called me this morning to warn me my partner might be crabby and hungover. He now owes me a free straightening."

"What? Why?" Harri appeared totally confused as she sat on one of the visitor chairs.

"He said you'd apologize before noon."

"You were with clients," Harri protested.

"We live in the same building now." Maybe her diatribe was a little too much at her best friend's expense, but Aisha couldn't help it. "Not to mention you could have drunk dialed me from the restaurant or the cab. But no, you let a client escort you up to your loft. Alone."

"Nothing happened!" Harri glared at her. "And even if it did . . ." Her face crumpled, and she sighed. "Okay, point made."

"Good." Aisha smiled. "Then you are forgiven. But speaking of Captain Justice . . ." She hesitated for a moment and prayed she was making more out of this than it was.

Thankfully, Harri kept her mouth shut and waited.

"Have you heard anything about any superhero incident with him this morning?"

Harri slowly shook her head before she grimaced, rose, and closed Aisha's office door. "The girl the temp agency sent over is great for phones and filing, but I'm going to be ecstatic when Patty's back from maternity leave." She plopped back down in the same visitor chair. "Arthur swore he and Patty set up alerts for us. They should have been in your e-mail for the last three mornings."

"The alerts were. It's just . . ." The light-headed feeling hit with a rush, and she hook her stilettos under her chair's wheel braces to keep from floating to the ceiling again. "Rey's government pager went off this morning. I didn't see him again until his stupid landing stunt in front of the *People* crew. But there's been absolutely nothing on the news."

"It could have been something the feds hushed up." Harri's expression turned sympathetic. "A nuclear meltdown or something they don't want to freak the public about. You know how some of that crap goes."

"Yeah, and you also know that stuff doesn't stay quiet for long."

"Do you want me to make some inquiries? I still have some contacts in the government." She raised her hands, finger spread. "I can't guarantee anything."

The light-headed feeling grew worse. "I'm being silly, aren't I?"

"No, you're rightly concerned about the man you love."

Tears blurred her vision. Deep down, it wasn't a disaster she feared. At least, not the epic superhero type.

"I am being stupid. Damn Cal and his cheating—" She banged the top of her desk with her fist.

Crack!

She and Harri scrambled back as the splintered wood paused as if thinking about staying together before it collapsed on itself, taking her laptop, office phone and everything else with it.

They stared at each other, then at the remains of the desk again.

The door swung in and crashed into the wall. Tim stood in the entry, his weight on the balls of his feet. The temp peered over his shoulder, her eyes so wide Aisha could see white all around the girl's irises.

Tim relaxed a fraction. "You two okay?"

She and Harri nodded, but it was the temp who worried Aisha.

She cleared her throat. "Harri, I told you not to buy the IKEA knock-offs for the office."

CHAPTER 8

Harri sent the temp home early with the promise of a full day's pay. She walked back to Aisha's office with the vacuum and a box of trash bags.

The first trash can was already full. Aisha and Tim had started a pile of files and office supplies on one of the couches while they sorted through the damage. He climbed laboriously to his feet and accepted the trash bags. His initial adrenaline rush must have worn off if his arthritis and cartilage damage was bothering him bad enough to show.

"I'll call Miguel and the boys to come down and help," Harri said.

"If you're trying salve my manhood, don't bother." He waved at Aisha. "The person with super strength can handle the big pieces. I'm just thankful we have an extra dumpster behind the building due to the renovations."

"Hey!" Aisha scowled at them. "I'm pregnant. I'm not supposed to be exerting myself in the first trimester. Especially since—" A wave of horror crossed her face.

Harri waggled an index finger at her partner. "Uh-uh, girl. If you're going to blame me for my furniture selection, I'm going to side with Tim on this one. Not to mention, you're not going to lose this baby, not with his super genes."

"If I'm getting Rey's powers . . ." Aisha picked up her bronze letter opener from the debris, the one Grandma Harri had given her for middle school graduation. Harri's matching one sat in her own top drawer in her office desk. But it was Aisha's thoughtful expression that triggered alarm bells in Harri's head.

"Aisha, no!"

Her partner jammed the opener into her opposing palm.

Or tried to.

The bronze crumpled like paper against her skin.

Harri marched over and grabbed the letter opener away from Aisha. Or Aisha was in the process of dropping it. There was no way Harri could have wrestled the bit of metal away from her best friend. Not if she now had super strength and invulnerability on top of the floating issue.

Aisha's face crumpled as well. "Oh, god, what's happening to me?" Sobs racked her frame.

Harri toss the lump of metal into the trash bag Tim held open and pulled Aisha into her arms. Tim, bless him, grabbed the full trash bag and quietly exited the office.

She guided Aisha over to the unoccupied couch and grabbed a handful of tissues from the decorative box Patty insisted they purchase. This wasn't like Aisha to bawl like this. Maybe the hormones were doing weirder things to her than they all realized. She stroked Aisha's hair and held her while her best friend released all her fear and frustration. The sobbing finally died to the occasional hiccup.

"What am I going to do, Harri?" Aisha whispered.

"Well, the first thing I would suggest is collect on your bet with Jeremy. These roots desperately need some attention."

"Bitch." But it was said with a bit of a chuckle.

Harri sucked in a deep breath and released it. "Talk to him. He's not Calvin the Asshole."

"What if he doesn't want this baby?" Aisha said softly.

"Trust me. He wants this baby." Harri took another breath and let it go as she saw through her own bullshit yesterday morning and actually heard Rey's words. "He wants the family he lost. You want this baby as much if not more than he does. And you'll be a great mom. You're the only one out of all of us who had anything close to a normal childhood. You don't get how fucked up the rest of us are."

"The rest of us?" Aisha hiccupped again.

"Me, Jeremy, Patty, Rey, Tim, Miguel. Crap's happened to all of us."

"You think I don't have problems?"

"No, it's not that." Harri leaned away as Aisha sat up to snatch some more tissues. "It's Betty and Marvin sticking together for forty-five years, through thick and thin. You had a good example of a healthy relationship. And despite Calvin the Asshole's bullshit, you know what you want in a man."

"Even if he's twenty years younger?"

"Uh-uh." Harri waggled her index finger. "You're not sucking me into another argument after I already apologized. You only get one apology a day."

A soft knock on the door drew their attention. Tim poked his head around the edge. "Serena's here to check your vitals, Aisha."

——— •◆• ———

An hour later, Serena stopped by Aisha's office to let Harri and Tim know the attorney was resting.

"You sure nothing's wrong with her?" Harri said.

"Nothing that doesn't happen to any other pregnant woman." Serena's smile was meant to be reassuring, but it only sent another frisson of worry through Harri.

"And how many pregnancies have you handled where the mom develops flight, super strength and invulnerability?" she shot back.

Rey appeared in the doorway. "Aisha's developed powers?"

"No thanks to you." Harri set aside her armful of files and marched up to the super. "What the hell was with the stupid landing stunt this afternoon?" She poked his chest to emphasize her irritation. "You know what that does to concrete. Aisha's stressed out enough as it is without you doing stupid shit. That kind of stress isn't good for the baby. Do you have any idea of how many babies that poor woman has already lost?"

"I-I—" Rey looked flabbergasted, but she wasn't having any of it.

"Not to mention pinching Qiang's ass!"

"What?"

She wasn't buying his innocent act. "If you don't want to be Captain Justice and are going out of the way to sabotage your career, that's your choice. But so help me, you are not acting like a dick and treating my best friend like crap. Otherwise, I will find something in Tim's lab and kick your ass with it! Now, get upstairs and dote over the mother of your child!"

"Yes, ma'am," he said meekly. He didn't bother with the stairs and flew straight up through the atrium.

"Maybe I need to leave Rey some burn ointment." Serena grinned.

Harri glared at the woman. "Are you sure there's nothing wrong with Aisha?"

"Honestly, she just needs some rest." Serena crossed her heart.

"What do we owe you?"

"De nada. This one's on the house." Serena flicked her fingers. "However, I do want to set up a legal appointment with you. A friend of mine wants to apply for a federal grant to open a low-cost clinic on this side of the city."

"Sure!" Harri rocked on her heels. A clinic in this neighborhood would go a long way toward stabilizing the area. She pulled a business card out of her pocket. "Have your friend call me."

"Is this friend of yours a super?" Tim asked.

"Does that make a difference?" Suspicion danced in Serena's eyes.

"Only if it means you'll have a job at this clinic," Harri quickly added. "I'd like to have someone I can refer my other clients to when extraordinary situations happen like in Aisha's case."

Tension flowed out of Serena's shoulders. "Yes, it would mean a steady job for me. I told her about you deliberately moving your practice here, but having Captain Justice as one of your clients sealed her interest. I'll have her call you."

Tim escorted her out of the building. More beeps from Patty's desk said he'd engaged the building's security system.

"I thought we were going to finish cleaning up this mess," Harri said when he returned. "It's a little hard to do when you lock the doors."

"Since this is partly Rey's fault, he can finish in the morning while you pick up Patty and the baby from the hospital." Tim folded his arms over his chest. "Qiang's ass?" he asked with a raised eyebrow.

There was no way to explain what happened without sounding like a jerk herself, but if anyone could get through to Rey concerning his behavior, it would be Tim. Harri flopped back on Aisha's couch.

"I was watching the photo shoot across the street." She told him about Rey's tardiness, his three-point stunt, and his grope of Sparx in front of the *People* team.

"So you were spying on Aisha and Rey because you were too guilty to apologize?" Tim flopped on the couch beside Harri.

She turned her head to look at him. "Out of my entire story, that's all you came away with?"

"The rest doesn't sound like Rey," he admitted.

"Did you hear anything about a supers incident this morning involving him?" she asked.

Tim shook his head. "Isn't the news alerts system Arthur and Patty set up working?"

"It is, but there wasn't anything listed today regarding Captain Justice." She related Aisha's story about Rey's government pager going off early this morning. "It's not like him to disappear for that long."

"Well, Aisha did have a pretty full schedule here until the photo shoot." Tim shrugged. "Maybe he found something to keep him busy." Except he didn't sound any more sure than Harri felt.

"Aren't you supposed to be telling me it's none of my business at this point?"

"Like that's going to stop you?" He grinned.

"Nope," she said and grinned in return. "How does Marta's sound for dinner?"

"Are you asking me out, Ms. Winters?"

"Well, I owe you for taking care of me last night. And the dinner offer lasts as long as you can deal with a poor heiress and her penny pinching." She pushed herself to her feet and held out her hand. He surprised her by taking it. She braced her body as he pulled himself up.

"Sorry. I'm afraid I can't afford something as fancy as Nolan's right now." She waved a hand at the demolished wood. "Especially since my partner's going to need a new desk."

"You know I was only trying to show off that night, right?"

"With which part? The expensive restaurant, beating up the bad guys, or nearly ending up in the hospital?"

"I'll make you a deal—no bad guys, no flashing cash wads, no severe injuries on either of our parts." He gestured for her to go out the office door first. "Just good eats and good company."

"That I can handle."

— ·•· —

For all of Harri's insecurities about relationships in general, Tim kept it light while Anna, Marta's youngest daughter, served them at the taqueria. Harri almost felt sorry for the girl when she discovered her crush wasn't meeting Harri and Tim for dinner.

"I wonder if she'd change her opinion if she saw Rey's performance today," Harri whispered after Anna delivered their plates.

"He had a bad day," Tim murmured. "We've all had them."

"So why do I feel like there's something more to this?"

"Because you are neither a glass is half-empty or half-full type of person," Tim said as he precisely sliced his chicken burritos. "You're a—" He waved his knife and fork dramatically in the air. "Oh, my god! The glass is empty! We're-all-gonna-die-of-thirst type person."

Harri rolled her eyes, but she couldn't help laughing with him as well. "If I wanted drama queen psychoanalysis, I would have called Jeremy."

"So you're telling me none of the superheroes you've dealt with haven't let the attention go to their heads?"

"Those are the only type I ever dealt with when I was a city attorney." She placed a dramatic hand to her head and lowered her voice an octave. "It couldn't possibly be my fault the senior center collapsed. I was just saving Canyon Pointe from Doctor Dumbshit!" She lowered her hand and glared at Tim. "Well, if you hadn't thrown Doctor Dumbshit's Dumbmobile at the senior center, it would still be standing, wouldn't it?"

Tim roared with laughter. "That's the best Ultramegaperson imitation I've heard," he finally said.

"He-she should rename herself to Ultramegatwat."

"Are you sure that's not what's really bothering you?"

"What do you mean?" She dipped a chicken taquito in guacamole.

"That Rey's not going to live up to the pedestal you've put him on." Tim forked a bite into his mouth.

"I haven't done any such thing!"

Tim chewed as he watched at her.

Harri stared at the pupusas on her own plate. Is that what she'd done? Create an impossible standard for Rey to live up to?

"He's a good kid," she mumbled.

"Not arguing that," Tim said. "But even good kids screw up once in a while. Anywhere from not putting away their toys when it's bedtime to joyriding in a golf cart around Whitechapel Country Club before dunking it in the Number Six water hazard."

Harri's head jerked up. "What?"

He pointed his knife at her. "Don't try the innocent act with me, Harriet Mathilda Winters. You know exactly what I'm talking about."

"How'd you know about that?"

Tim chuckled. "And here I thought Granddad blamed it on you just to get a rise out of your grandmother."

Her face grew hot at the realization she fallen for one of the oldest tricks in a lawyer's playbook and admitted her culpability. "Well, I got blamed for nicking the door on Old Lady Harrison's Rolls Royce when Reginald Samuels did it."

"Yeah, funny how Reggie's class ring was found under some paperwork in the equipment office." Tim grinned at her.

Her eyes widened. "You didn't."

He shrugged.

Harri's heart caught in her throat. She'd been a stupid kid. Angry at her mom for dying. Angry at her dad for loving drugs more than he loved her. "Why did you cover for me? You were in college at the time."

"Guess I started the vigilante act earlier than you thought." He sipped his soft drink.

She cleared her throat. "Are you trying to impress me again?"

"A little bit." Damn, if his eyes didn't twinkle.

"Why didn't you say anything then?"

He laughed out loud. "Because a twenty-one-year-old man interested in a fourteen-year-old girl is illegal."

With the thoughts running through her head, her face heated again. "And what about a totally adult genius inventor and a totally adult attorney?"

"I'd say there's a reason Jeremy warned you to behave yourself last night." The look Tim gave her was pure lust.

"I'm not drunk tonight."

"Neither am I."

Harri reached into her bag and laid bills on the table, including a healthy tip for Anna. She climbed out of the booth, grabbed Tim's hand, and headed for the door. The wave of outside air felt cool against her overheated skin.

Maybe this was a totally stupid idea. Maybe this was nothing more than hero worship. Maybe this was a really huge mistake after the lecture she'd given Aisha.

"Stop it," Tim whispered in her ear

"Stop what?" She looked up at him.

"You're thinking too much."

She gulped. "It's, um, been a while."

"And?"

"Well, it's just that . . ." Geez, she hadn't been this nervous in the back seat of Jimmy Novak's ancient Buick on prom night.

"Would it help if I said it's been a while for me, too? Well, unless you count my shower."

Harri couldn't help it. She giggled like she was Anna's age. "I guess that means we need to go to my loft. I wouldn't want your shower to get jealous."

She halted as another thought occurred to her. "We need to make a stop at the bodega."

"If it's for what I think it is, we're covered." Tim tugged her hand and they continued down the sidewalk.

"You're packing?"

"Yep."

Part of her was a little offended at his presumption. Another part was ec-static about not wasting time. "Since when?"

He remained silent, and she glanced up at him. His face was an even bright-er red than his hair.

"Tim?"

"Since the day Miguel called me up from the basement to meet you."

"Oh." The idea sent warm fuzzies through her until her damn lawyer train-ing kicked. "But you told me a couple of nights later you wanted my help in exposing Corvus and faking your death."

"Maybe part of me wanted you to talk me out of that damn fool plan." He squeezed her hand. "I think I knew then that things just weren't going to work out with my shower."

"But it's been twenty . . ." The last thing Harri wanted to do was bring up Tim's murdered wife. She swallowed hard. "Surely, you've met other women over the years."

A sharp, bitter laugh knifed its way out of him. "How when I'm the rich as-shat who got away with murder? Yeah, the ladies were beating down my door."

Under his tone lay a bit of regret. And like a terrier with a rat, she leapt and shook that hint.

"What was her name?"

"Who?"

Fewer and fewer cars glided by them as they walked, and even fewer pedestrians passed. Harri let the silence speak for her.

"All right." Tim sighed. "But can I preface my admission by saying I'm not proud of this?"

"I kind of figured that due to your reluctance to mention her."

"Miss Purrception."

Not sure if this was the funniest thing she ever heard or the most wrong, Harri settled on incredulous disbelief. "Your only fling in the last twenty years was with a supervillain?"

"I wouldn't exactly call it a fling," he said sourly.

"What was it then? Sweaty sex on a rooftop with your masks on?"

The setting sun couldn't compete with Tim's flaming red cheeks and ears.

"Oh. My. God." She covered her mouth with her hand in a desperate attempt to hide her grin.

He glanced at her, then stared straight ahead. His grimace said it all.

Once she was sure her humor was under control, she lowered her hand and cleared her throat. "Well, that beats my prom story. Did you two even reveal your secret identities to each other?"

"No," he ground out.

"Speaking as your attorney, that's a good thing." She paused for a moment. "We wouldn't want any sex tapes leaking out to the press."

"Har-de-har-har."

"So why'd you two quit having rooftop sex?"

"I was in a bad place at the time." The agonized expression was back, the one that he got whenever he thought about his wife and son's murders. "She claimed to have information on Trubble and Corvus. She was just using me to cover her own tracks with them."

"How deep was she in with Trubble?"

Tim ran his hand through his hair. "She stole a microchip encoded with some pretty damning information. She gave me a fake and sold the real one to a foreign power."

"Wow. And she didn't offer to split the proceeds?"

"She did."

Harri looked up at him. Nope, Tim wasn't joking about this.

"She wanted me to run away with her. Live off her take. Travel the world."

After a whole block of silence, Harri asked, "Why didn't you take her up on her offer? It sounds exactly like what you wanted when you first approached me about the tell-all."

"Because I couldn't let go of what Corvus, what Shift had done to Rebecca and Shane." His voice lowered even further. "Because I realized I was using Miss Purrception as much as she was using me, and I really didn't like myself for it." He looked down at her. "Because I realized I wanted something more even if I might never have it again."

Harri swallowed hard. She could fall into those indigo eyes, and if she did, she might lose everything she fought so hard for in her life.

Including her soul.

"I don't know how to compete with that," she whispered.

"Harri, my dear, there is no comparison." He tilted his head and leaned toward her. His kiss felt new and old, soft and claiming, all at once.

It went on forever and wasn't long enough.

Only when they parted did she realize they stood next to the service entrance of the Lechuza Building. Tim's throat bobbed. Good to know he was as off-kilter as she felt. He turned and held his palm to the lock pad.

The door burst open before the light turned green. Little Francisco Esperanza wailed and launched himself into Harri's arms.

CHAPTER 9

Harri looked over Francisco's head at Tim, but even he looked dumbstruck. Francisco continued to sob, so Harri stroked his hair.

Tim knelt beside the boy. "Where's your papa, *mi amigo*?"

"At-at home."

Harri knelt as well now that Francisco sobs had shifted to sniffles. "What are you doing here by yourself, sweetie?"

"Miss—" He swiped at his nose with his arm. "Miss Aisha said I could bring my book report over after dinner for Rey to look at." His little face crumpled. "He-he said—"

More wailing filled the air. He flung his skinny arms and a crumpled sheet of notebook paper around Harri's shoulders, nearly knocking her off balance. "He said it was awful!"

Her gaze met Tim's. Anger sparked in his eyes. Anger that burned through her as well. Francisco was only seven for crying out loud.

"Tim, why don't you take Francisco down to the bodega for some ice cream? Then walk him home, please. I've got this."

"Sure." Tim smiled at the little boy. "While we're eating our ice cream, you can read me your report." He rested a palm on Francisco's shoulder. "What book did you read?"

"*The Hobbit*." Francisco sniffed and wiped at his tears with his free hand.

"Really? That's one of my favorites!"

Harri slapped her hand on the lock pad while the guys headed down the street, discussing the book. The light shifted to green, and she charged through the door. For a moment, she considered running off her fury on the stairs, but chewing someone a new asshole while huffing and puffing after four flights wouldn't be as effective. The toe of her right shoe jiggled an impatient rhythm as the antique elevator took its sweet time coming back down to the first floor.

She yanked the two gates open, walked inside, and more carefully closed the gates. No sense adding more expenses to their fledgling enterprise by wrecking the recently restored elevator. Her right shoe picked up where it left off on the slow crawl up to the top floor.

Once again, she yanked the gates open and marched up to Aisha's door. Raised voices penetrated the thick walls, and she wanted in on this action. If a crying kid came out of a building with her name on the deed, she would dish out her share of pain. She banged on the sliding barn door Miguel had salvaged and restored.

The loft door rolled open. Aisha's expression shared the fury roiling through Harri.

"We're in the middle of something. Can this wait?" Aisha's voice was relatively calm despite the same spark of anger in her eyes that had been in Tim's.

"No, it can't." Harri marched past her. "And you shouldn't be getting upset right now."

"I'm pregnant," Aisha snapped. "Not an invalid."

"This isn't about you anyway." Harri turned and glared at Rey. Her glower was totally wasted from the way he nonchalantly flipped channels from his seat on the couch. She marched over and snatched the remote from his hand.

"Hey!" He stood. "Give that back!"

"Not until you and I talk."

He crossed his arms. "You mean after you lecture me about how I'm living my life."

Harri took a deep breath and released it. "You know something, kid. I was out of line yesterday, and I was coming up here to apologize to you. Then I ran into a heartbroken seven-year-old boy.

"You can be as mad at me as you want. Hell, I'll set up some demolitions through the city for you if you need to take your super-pissy attitude out on something." On her tiptoes, she waved an index finger under his nose. "But don't you dare take your crap out on Francisco again. You got me?"

"And I don't need the two of you nagging me!" Rey moved so fast he was nothing but a blur through the room and out the doorway. A second later, a sonic boom rocked the building.

Harri turned to Aisha and noticed three melting bowls of ice cream on the counter. "What the hell happened up here? Francisco said you invited him over after dinner."

"I did." Aisha sighed and walked over to the refrigerator. "That was the other thing I wanted to mention to you earlier. Before I ruined my desk."

"That you invited Francisco over?" Harri cocked her head. "I'm not his mom. Why would I care?"

"Not Francisco." Aisha gingerly opened the refrigerator door and produced a bottle of chocolate syrup. "Want some? No sense letting Häagen-Dazs go to waste."

Harri nodded and crossed to the counter. She divided the third bowl's contents into the other two while Aisha squirted an unhealthy amount of chocolate over the vanilla ice cream.

"So what's the other thing?" Harri prompted after they both had a bite.

"You know how Rey always talks to the kids who hang outside the bodega, no matter which guise he's in?"

"Yeah, fistbumps and high-fives all around." Harri swirled her spoon around the goopy mess in her bowl. "I noticed he simply took off after the photos were done."

Aisha nodded. "The older kids were playing it cool, but Francisco was pretty upset. So, I told him to stop by tonight." She shook her head and played with her melting dessert. "Never in my life would I have imagined Rey acting as shitty as he did with Francisco." She met Harri's gaze. "Your dad was a giant dick, but nothing like this."

Harri released her spoon and held up both her hands. "Sorry for intruding on your smack down. I just got so pissed when Francisco told Tim and me what had happened."

"You and Tim, hmmm?" Aisha's sly smile could have given the Cheshire Cat a run for his money.

"I bought him dinner for helping me clean up *your* office."

"I'd believe you if you didn't look so damn guilty." Aisha chuckled. "I'm sorry we ruined your date."

"It wasn't a date."

"Sexcapade, then."

"It wasn't—" Harri stared at the brown and cream mess in her bowl. Aisha was right. Tim's confession about Miss Purrception left her feeling a little guilty. Not about the fact that it happened, but that she'd be using him to scratch an itch just like the supervillainess had. He'd made his feelings and intentions about Harri perfectly clear.

"I almost wish it was just a sexcapade," she murmured. "I like him, but I think he likes me too much more."

Aisha's smiled faded. "Did he say that?"

"It wasn't an undying declaration or anything." Harri gulped. "He just mentioned he was looking for something a little more . . . long term."

"Wow." Aisha shoved her bowl aside and leaned her elbows on the counter. "What did you say?"

"I didn't have a chance to say anything before Francisco ran out of the building, crying his little heart out."

"Where is he right now?"

"Walking Francisco home."

"Okay, then. Do you need condoms for tonight?" Aisha straightened and reached for her designer purse.

"Aren't you a little late for those?" Harri rolled her eyes.

"Unless you want to have a joint baby shower with me, you need them." Aisha waggled her finger. "And I was going to give you the cash to run down to the bodega. Trust me. He will be back up here. Tonight." She grinned. "Or were you two planning to get kinky in the Owl's Nest?"

"Tim's bed is too small."

The return of Aisha's Cheshire Cat grin made Harri realize how her words sounded.

"We haven't done anything in anyone's bed yet," she muttered.

"Hey!" Aisha raised both hands. "At least with Tim, you don't have to worry about smashing furniture in your enthusiasm."

"Hell, you can do that without the enthusiasm." Harri took another bite of chocolate and vanilla mush. "Are things okay with you two? I mean, really okay. It's only been a couple of days since you realized you're pregnant."

Aisha sagged. "I wish I knew. He was fine when he left the loft this morning, but he wouldn't tell me about the reason for the a.m. alarm when he got home this evening. If this were a comic book, I'd suspect Rey was replaced by his evil twin."

"Well, as far as we know Maria didn't have any other kids. So, robot or clone?"

Well, if he's a robot, he's a damn good imitation." Aisha wiped her hands down her face. "I think the initial excitement has worn off, and the reality of being a father has sunk in."

"Want me to stay here?" Harri waved her spoon. "Just until he comes back. Or do you want to go to a hotel?"

"Oh, sweetie." Aisha circled the island and hugged Harri from behind. "He's not going to hurt me."

"You don't know that," she grumbled. She set the spoon back in the bowl and patted Aisha's hands.

"We've all been under a ton of pressure the last month. My very unexpected pregnancy was simply the proverbial straw." Aisha released Harri. "We had a fight. You were the one saying Rey was too good to be true. Guess what? He proved he is just as human as the rest of us."

"If you're sure . . ."

"I'm sure." Aisha smiled. "I've always got the panic button. Besides—" She lifted her arms in a bodybuilder's pose. "I've got super powers, too." With that statement, she started floating toward the ceiling.

Harri couldn't help laughing. "Need some help?"

"Nah." Aisha's face scrunched, and she floated back to the floor. "I'm starting to get the hang of this."

"All right." Harri shook her head, still chuckling. "I'll see you in the morning."

———•———

Tim wasn't waiting in her loft, so Harri headed for the basement. This time, she took the stairs. When the biometric scanner let her through the door to the Owl's Nest, she realized all the other security measures had been turned off.

He was expecting her.

The good manners Grandma Harri had drilled into her made her pause and knock on the entrance to his main lab. No answer.

She pressed her palm against the black rectangle on the wall, and the door slid open.

In the furthest niche on her right, an exoskeleton stood on a platform. Tim worked on the thing's left leg. Between the ear protection and the high-pitched whine of his grinder, no wonder he didn't hear her knock.

She crossed the workshop to where he could see her and waved. He hit the power switch on the grinder, flipped up the protective mask, and yanked out his ear plugs.

Concern filled his eyes. "Is Aisha okay? We heard the sonic boom at Celia's."

Harri shook her head. "I'm used to Rey's maturity. Maybe too much. When he does something a normal twenty-one-year-old guy would do, it throws me off."

"But Aisha's okay, right?"

"Yeah." Harri smiled. "She's dealing with his temper tantrum better than I am." But her best friend's offhand comment sat in the back of her head. "I know this is going to sound weird, but has Corvus been doing anything in robotics or cloning?"

Tim's eyes widened, and he sat down the grinder. "Are you actually trying to suggest that was Rey's evil twin being a shit?"

"No." She gave a half-hearted laugh. "Definitely not. That's a totally ridiculous notion. How's Francisco though?"

"Calmer." Tim removed his safety gloves and head gear. His hair stuck up in all directions. The look was actually sexy. When he pulled off his flame resistant jacket, the snug, sweat-stained t-shirt underneath was even more appealing for some reason.

"If it had been one of his older brothers acting like a jerk, it wouldn't have fazed the kid." He shook his head. "What would it take to set up a private trust for Francisco from the proceeds of some of my patents?"

"Just drawing up the paperwork and taking it to a bank to set up the account." Harri frowned. "Why just Francisco?"

"He needs a better education than we can give him here. I spoke with Miguel about sending the kid to a private school."

"Private school?" She threw her arms up. "Why on earth—"

"Because Francisco's a genius." A wry smile tilted his mouth.

"So are you—"

"He's way beyond me, Harri." Tim crossed to the dorm-sized refrigerator and pulled out two bottles of water. He returned and handed one to her before he pointed to a nearby white board. "Francisco was down here yesterday while Miguel was helping me with the assembly of George."

"George?"

He waved at the exoskeleton. "I took your suggestion to heart. An armored exoskeleton will cut down on the Ghost Owl's speed and flexibility." A wry smile tilted Tim's mouth. "But he's losing that already. However, it will definitely extend his durability."

"But Francisco . . ." she prompted.

Tim pointed at the board. "He corrected one of my equations."

"You mean you forgot to carry a one on a multiplication problem?"

"No." Tim strode over to the white board and pointed out a line of what looked like gibberish to Harri. "I mean the differential equation regarding power consumption for the exoskeleton."

She blinked. "The kid just learned how to read."

"Yeah, and his understanding of the themes in *The Hobbit* goes beyond most masters' theses." Tim sat on one of his work stools. "He's coming by in the morning to borrow my copies of *The Lord of the Rings*."

Harri unscrewed the cap and took a drink of her water as she eyed the exoskeleton. She turned back to Tim. "He's too young to be sent away yet. What if you take him on as an apprentice?"

Tim chuckled. "That's what Miguel said."

Harri shrugged. "Francisco can keep Rey's secret. He can keep yours, too."

"No." A sharp shake of Tim's followed his negation. "Being Tim Canyon's apprentice is one thing. Francisco's not going to be related in any way to the Ghost Owl."

"Your decision, but I still think he'd learn more from you than any other teacher." She raised her water in the direction of the exoskeleton. "What did you tell him that was? Surely, he asked."

"I said it was a new idea for astronauts' spacewalks."

Harri shook her head. "That's not going to work for long if he's as smart as you think he is."

"I know." He set his now-empty bottle on a work bench and crossed to her. "Didn't we have other plans before real life intruded?"

"Yeah." She took his hands in hers.

He winced. "Maybe I should shower first."

"After," she murmured. "I like the way you smell." She tugged him toward the door.

"You can't be serious." He laughed.

"Canyon, if you want to get laid, shut up."

Chapter 10

Aisha sprawled on the couch with a patent application she was reviewing when the loft door slid open. Rey came in with a sheepish expression on his face.

"Hey," he muttered and closed the door.

"Hi."

He swung his arms, the gesture reminiscent of a guilty little boy. "I, um, suppose I need to apologize."

"To Francisco, yes." She glanced at the clock on the microwave. "But in the morning. He's in bed, and Miguel will not be happy if you wake his kid."

"Are you mad at me?"

She set aside the patent application she hadn't been able to concentrate on anyway. "No. As your attorney, I am disappointed in your behavior today. Are you having second thoughts about the superhero gig?"

"No."

"Then why did you pinch Sparx's ass in front of everyone today?"

He shrugged and shoved his hands in his jeans' pockets. "I was just kidding around."

Aisha closed her eyes and pinched the bridge of her nose. This was the real reason attorneys weren't supposed to sleep with clients. If she and Rey weren't living together, weren't expecting a baby, she'd be chewing him a new asshole about propriety and public relations.

She opened her eyes and lowered her hand. "Listen to me, Rey. Fair or not, the kids in our neighborhood look up to you. When they see you act like a shit to women—"

He opened his mouth, and she held up a hand.

"Let me finish. When they see you act inappropriately to Sparx and the ladies from *People*, they emulate that behavior because you're their hero." She looked down at her abdomen and rubbed it. "And our son will do the same. That's not how I want to raise my child."

Aisha rose from the couch and walked over to him. "Honey, you need to understand something. I've seen the effects of bad fathers. Harri's was a drug addict, and she ruined her relationship with Eddie because of her fears. Jeremy's dad beat him, which is why he's terrified of adopting, though Leonardo is begging him to once they're married. And from what your mother told Miguel and Beatrice, she took you and ran away from your father for probably some damn good reasons.

"But, Rey, you've got to be better than that. You don't have a choice. We don't have a choice. Especially since Serena says our baby is a super, too."

"Okay." He nodded, but his expression still appeared embarrassed. "Do you really think I can?"

She smiled and took his hand. "I know you can, baby. It's late. Why don't we go to bed? You apologize to Francisco in the morning, and things will be a whole lot better."

As they readied for sleep, light caught his amulet. Something was off. She stepped in front of him as he headed toward the bathroom and laid her hand on his chest.

This stone wasn't the same one. The markings were different. Nor did it have the vein of blue running through the middle.

"Baby, where'd you get that amulet?"

Rey blinked, then frowned. "I told you the story the first day we met. I've always had it."

"Has it ever changed color before?"

"What are you talking about?"

Aisha ran her finger over the surface of the amulet. It felt cold to her touch. The stone had always been warm from Rey's body heat. "I could have sworn there was a little blue streak in the middle."

His frown deepened. "No, it's always been red."

Despite the thread of unease worming its way through her brain, she laughed. "Damn pregnancy. I didn't need my reading glasses when I was reviewing paperwork tonight." She tried to shrug as nonchalantly as she could. "I guess the hormones are messing with my color perception, too."

Rey merely shook his head, the same expression on his face she'd seen on her brother-in-law Eric's every time LaShun had been pregnant. He kissed her forehead, went into the bathroom, and closed the door.

Aisha swallowed hard. It wasn't the same amulet. But the bigger question was why had Rey just lied to her?

CHAPTER 11

Aisha's first glance in the bathroom mirror the next morning said Harri was right. She paused, lifted her strands, and examined the roots. Curly with a touch of gray. She let the locks drop and stared.

It couldn't be.

She peered closer and smoothed the framing edges of her style along her jaw. Nope, it definitely wasn't her eyesight. Her hair had grown nearly an inch overnight.

Well, the book about what to expect during a pregnancy she'd downloaded yesterday said hormones changed the growth pattern and texture of the mom-to-be's hair and nails. But damn!

A phone call to Jeremy was definitely in order, even though she'd been to his salon only three weeks ago for straightening and color.

Oh, god! Had the hair treatments hurt the baby? She'd avoided them when she and Cal had been trying to conceive.

No, Serena stated the baby was healthy. Surely, she would have said something. Aisha sighed at her old paranoia raising its ugly head and shoved it away while she finished applying her makeup and dressed.

Rey was still sprawled facedown across their mattress when she returned to their bedroom. Aisha frowned. That man was always up at sunrise. It was his only trait she could bitch about until yesterday, but at least, he made coffee for her every morning even though he didn't drink it himself.

Or he did until today.

"Baby?" She bent over and shook his shoulder.

Nothing.

"Baby?" She shook his shoulder again.

Nothing.

"Rey!"

He jerked upright, and only her new reflexes kept them from knocking heads. "What!"

Aisha concentrated on landing back on the floor. "Weren't you going to help Miguel bring up the appliances for his apartment this morning?"

"Not until eight." He flopped back down on the bed.

"Baby, it's five after eight."

Rey jumped up, muttering to himself. She definitely caught the word "nag" as he stomped into the bathroom. So, they were back to that, hmmm?

Nope. She was not dealing with it. Not right now. She needed coffee first.

Aisha stuffed the files she'd been reviewing into her bag and headed downstairs to her office.

———•———

Luckily, the morning was busy enough Aisha didn't have time to brood about her own life issues. Even better, two endorsement checks arrived with the morning mail. Harri danced around the office, but Aisha suspected her partner's good mood had more to do with her company last night than the money.

However, Harri's practical side quickly reasserted itself. She left early to deposit the checks on her way to pick up Patty and Grace from the hospital.

A knock on her door interrupted Aisha's doodling on a legal pad.

Tim poked his head around her door. "You going to be okay if I run an errand? I'll be gone for a couple of hours."

"Does it have anything to do with the knee brace you're trying to hide?" She leaned back in her chair.

Tim glanced at her office door, which he was mostly hiding behind, before he looked at her askance. "X-ray vision?"

"Super hearing, remember?"

His face turned even redder than his hair. "Ummm, I guess we should have stayed down in my apartment."

"Oh, honey." She laughed. "You think that's the first time I've heard Harri? We used to live together. It could have been worse. It could be Jeremy living upstairs beside me. He puts you and Harri together to shame. I just can't figure out how Rey slept through it."

"Not what I wanted to know about the guy who measures me for Kevlar." Tim chuckled. "And Rey's had longer to learn how to tune out background noise. To answer your original question, I've got an appointment with my orthopedic specialist at eleven." His amused expression turned serious. "I don't want to leave you here alone with everyone else out."

She gave him a reassuring smile. Even though it had been twenty years, the loss of Tim's son made him exceptionally paranoid when it came to kids. Even unborn ones.

"Miguel, Rey, and the boys are unloading appliances for the fourth-floor apartments, I'm taking Screaming Orgasm out to Jeremy's for a makeover, and Harri will be back once she and Arthur get Patty settled. I think I'll be okay for a half hour or so alone." Aisha shrugged. "Besides, I've been practicing my landings."

Tim shook his head and laughed. "All right. I'll see you later." He closed the door quietly behind him.

Aisha turned back to the list of potential new monikers for Orgasm she had been composing. Nothing felt quite right. Too cutesy. Too stupid. Too used.

"Too bad Soundgarden's been taken," she muttered to herself.

A girl screamed. It was followed by the shattering of ceramic. A lot of ceramic.

Anna at the restaurant.

Aisha jumped up and raced for the main doors. She slapped her hand on the security pad. It didn't seem to want to recognize her print. All this security felt like a prison.

She ran back to her office, opened a window, and climbed out. The handful of people on the sidewalks merely stared in the direction of the sounds. She sprinted past the idiots standing around instead of doing something.

Aisha reached Marta's restaurant and yanked on the door. Glass and steel went flying into the street.

Shit. Something else she'd have to pay for.

A man with the proverbial ski mask aimed a gun at Marta. His other arm was wrapped around the neck of Christina, her middle daughter. Jagged pieces of smashed plates lay in the middle of the floor. Standing by the debris, Anna had opened her mouth for another scream.

Aisha grabbed the man's arm and yanked him away from Christina. A deafening clap dropped her to her knees. She slapped her hands over her ears, but it didn't block the wall of sound.

"Ms. Franklin?" Golden eyes peered into her hers.

She blinked. Wearing his Captain Justice outfit, Rey crouched next to her.

"Are you all right?" From the tension in his voice, he'd asked the question more than once.

"I'll take her back to her office, Captain." Miguel's voice. "The police are on the way."

The two men helped her upright. A groan from behind her drew her attention. The ski-masked gunman was partially embedded in the drywall. In fact, his head had punched through a stud.

She opened her mouth, but Rey hissed, "Don't say anything to anyone." He turned to Miguel, and in a little deeper voice, he said, "Thank you for your assistance, citizen."

Miguel wrapped an arm around her shoulders and guided her out of the restaurant.

Part of her knew it was the smart thing to do. She wasn't registered, but she didn't like the idea of Rey taking the blame for what happened. What *had* happened though?

Miguel's handprint worked just fine on the security system. He set her on a couch in her office.

"You relax while I'll get you a mocha, Aisha."

"Wait."

He paused at the door.

"What exactly did happen back there, Miguel?"

"That's what we'd like to know." He folded his arms over his chest. "You beat Rey to the restaurant. Marta and Anna were doing lunch prep when the man used Christina to force his way inside the door. None of them saw you until Christina's assailant went through the wall and you were on the floor. Marta said his gun went off point blank at your head, but there's not a mark on you. Let me get your coffee."

Oh, crap. She laid her face in her hands. Why hadn't she call the police? Hell, why hadn't she called Rey upstairs? Reacting instead of following a carefully considered plan? Charging into an unknown situation like the proverbial bull was Harri's style, not hers.

"What the hell do you think you were doing!" Rey roared.

She jerked her head up. He stood in front of her makeshift desk in his skivvies.

"This is a law firm! Put some clothes on!"

"Don't do it on my account." Screaming Orgasm leaned against the doorframe of Aisha's office. She tilted her head to examine Rey's backside. "Do you have any openings, Ms. Franklin? This place would be a blast to work at. You definitely don't have a dull moment here."

CHAPTER 12

Harri could feel Patty's eyes bore a hole in her skull as she flipped her turn signal for the upcoming exit.

"You're not planning a party for when I get home, are you?" Suspicion ran thick in her assistant's voice.

"Have you known me to be a party person?"

An asshole in a bright red pocket rocket swerved and cut Harri off. She swore and laid on her horn.

"Harri!"

She glanced at Patty. "Sorry."

"You should be." Patty peered over her shoulder at Grace. "I'm the mother. I get to teach her all the good curse words."

Harri chuckled. "If you teach her the good English ones and Aisha the good Spanish ones, what does that leave me with?"

"You get to show her how to flip the bird at reporters while you're in deathly peril."

Harri's chuckle turned to outright laughter. "It's a deal. I swear there's no party today. Arthur wanted to make sure everything was perfect when you got home."

"What do you think of him?"

Sensing a trap ahead, Harri hesitated. "What do you mean?"

Patty played with the hem of the maternity t-shirt she wore. "Do you think he's really given up being a supervillain?"

"He was never that good of a regular villain, much less a supervillain." They traveled another two blocks before she added, "I think Arthur is just like all the rest of us. He wants someone to love who loves him back."

"Grace's father—" Patty sounded on the verge of tears. "He was so charming with the most mesmerizing blue eyes, but he was so secretive. Arthur is such a better man than him. So open, so sweet. But I don't want to make the same mistake. It's not only me I have to think about now. I want a—I want—"

"You want something better for your daughter than what you had," Harri murmured.

"Yeah." Patty reached for the tissues Harri kept in the console and blew her nose. "I never told you what happened with my parents."

"No." Remembering the guys' lectures, Harri quickly added, "And it's none of my business if you don't want to tell me."

Patty emitted a sharp bark of laughter. "Since when did you stop poking your nose in everyone's business?"

"Since both Captain Justice and the Ghost Owl pointed out I'm a busybody," Harri replied dryly.

"If I'd known it took a superhero or two . . ." Patty blew her nose again. "My parents were junkies, too. In their case, heroin. I was almost five, but the memory is still so clear."

Harri glanced at her assistant again.

Patty's smile was almost wistful. "They always told me not to touch their special medicine or their needles. That last day, they'd picked up their supply from their dealer. Daddy pulled over on a little dirt township road. He and Mommy took their medicine and they went to sleep.

"When they didn't wake up, I knew something was wrong. I thought about getting out of the car and finding another grown-up, but I didn't want them to be scared if they woke up, and I was gone."

Patty plucked another couple of tissues and swiped at her face. "The sheriff's deputy found us the next morning. I was sent to live with my grandmother. She wasn't the nicest person. I could almost understand why my mother would shoot heroin. But the last thing my mother said to me before she died was that she loved me more than anything. But she lied."

Harri didn't say anything. What was there to say? She and Jeremy had been damn lucky they had Betty and Marvin. Poor Patty didn't even have that.

"Luckily, my grandmother decided she couldn't deal with me and sent me to live with my aunt Grace." Patty blew her nose again. "She's the reason I didn't end up in the system. So now you know."

"What happened to her?" Harri asked.

"Ironically, she overdosed, too, a couple of years ago. It was an accident. Prescription painkillers for a slipped disk in her back."

"Shit." Harri glanced at the woman next to her, but Patty stared out the windshield, lost in her memories. "I'm sorry things weren't different for both of us."

"Except none of us might have met if our childhoods were different," Patty said.

Arthur's comments from the night Grace was born ran through Harri's mind. "The other day, someone pointed out to me we made our own family to make up for our crappy childhoods."

"He's a smart cookie." Patty sniffed. "You know, Arthur's parents weren't as crappy as ours. They didn't hurt him. They didn't take drugs. They just didn't care what he did, good or bad."

Silence reigned for a long time in the Honda. Harri pulled up in front of Patty's building, but neither she or Patty moved.

Harri took a deep breath and turned to her assistant. "Can I repeat something Tim said to me the other night?"

Patty nodded.

"Take a good look around you. You already have the family you need and want."

Patty wiped her eyes again. "He's a sweetheart. How was he in bed?"

"What?" Harri stared at her assistant who giggled.

"I thought so. I've never seen you in such a good mood." Patty pulled the door release and waggled her eyebrows. "You need to get laid more often."

Harri still sat in her seat staring at the vehicle in front of her. A Honda just like hers only tan. Or she thought it was under the layers of dust. So much dust, it obscured the license plate.

Yeah, thinking about dust on a car was much safer than thinking about Tim. Or what he did when he . . .

"Harri!"

She jumped.

"Are you coming?" Patty deliberately drawled the last word and watched Harri with an amused expression through the passenger window. She already had the infant carrier.

"Yeah." Harri punched the trunk release and yanked on the door lever.

Patty still wore that damn amused smile when Harri climbed out of the car and strode back to the trunk.

"Stop it," she ordered.

Patty smiled down at Grace. "There's your grumpy godmother."

Grace yawned and stretched, but otherwise didn't comment.

"Can you get the rest of our stuff?" Patty asked.

"Yeah." Harri lifted the lid. "I think I can manage all of two bags."

"Don't forget the infant seat base."

Harri slung the diaper bag over one shoulder. "Yes, Ms. Ames."

Unfortunately, Patty's building didn't have an elevator. By the time she reached the third floor, Harri's shirt was damp despite her extra-strength antiperspirant.

She really needed to send a complaint e-mail to the manufacturer.

When Harri nudged the apartment door open with her knee, Patty was already enthroned on her rocking chair, her feet propped up by the matching ottoman and a glass of ice tea in her hand. Arthur held Grace.

He looked up from the baby and his mouth dropped open before he turned an accusing glare at Patty. "You said she didn't need any help." He turned back. "I'm sorry, Harri. I should have come down when Patty arrived."

"I'll be the new mommy's beast of burden." Harri shot a nasty look at her all-too-smug assistant. "But I'm not changing any dirty diapers."

Grace took Harri's statement as her cue. She let out a horrendous wail.

Arthur felt the baby's bottom. "Yep, definitely wet."

Patty started to rise, but he waved her down.

"I've got this one." He and Grace headed into the only bedroom.

Harri followed them and plunked the bags on the bed. She looked around the room. Yep, it was as immaculate as the living room and kitchenette had been.

"Did you get a cleaning service?"

"What? No." Arthur dropped the dirty diaper into the special sealed disposal contraption that supposedly reduced odors. Harri had rather thought it was a good investment when she bought it for Patty.

"I just wanted to make things as clean and pleasant as possible before the girls came home." Arthur expertly unfolded a new diaper with a flick of his wrist and slid it into place.

Harri frowned as she watched the former Professor Venom apply lotion to the baby's bottom. "This isn't your first babysitting gig, is it?"

Arthur blushed while he fastened the diaper. "No. I-I was a nanny for four kids to pay my way through school."

"Wow. I'm impressed." And she really was. The more she got to know the former supervillain, the more facets he showed. No wonder Patty was falling for the guy.

He shrugged as he snapped Grace's onesie. "It was just a job."

"Arthur, anyone who can handle one baby, much less a herd of them, has my respect. Does Patty know?"

He nodded and carefully lifted Grace to his shoulder, cradling her fragile head and neck the whole time. "I think she's relieved she has someone here who knows what to do."

From Patty's confession on the ride from the hospital, Harri had no doubt on that issue. It sounded like her assistant had even fewer maternal examples growing up than Harri did.

"Thanks for giving me the time off to help here," Arthur added. "How are things at the office?"

The last thing she wanted was to burden either of their miniscule staff with the soap opera drama the Lechuza Building had become. Maybe that's why she wanted Patty to move there. Everyone would behave around her and the baby.

Maybe Harri was fooling herself about that, too.

"Fine," she said as she tailed Arthur back to the living room. "In fact, do the three of you need anything before I take off? I promised Aisha I'd help her look for a car later this afternoon."

Both Arthur and Patty shook their heads.

"Did you see how many boxes of diapers he bought?" Patty laughed. "I think we're set until Grace starts having babies."

"You don't realize how many one kid can go through in a day. You'll thank me."

Grace burbled which she followed by smacking her lips.

"She's hungry," he announced.

Patty smiled as she accepted Grace from Arthur. And that was Harri's cue.

"See you tomorrow, Arthur! Call me if you need anything, Patti." She sped out of the apartment to her assistant's laughter.

Heat shimmered from the sidewalk when Harri jogged through the building's entrance. The same Honda was parked in front of hers. The driver wore huge aviator glasses, and she would have sworn on a stack of Bibles he stared at her. There was something terribly familiar about him. Then he faced forward, his engine revved, and he pulled into traffic. She took a few steps toward the street and concentrated on the plate. The first alphanumeric could have been an "N", but he switched lanes in front of a city bus before she was certain.

It was nothing. She really wanted to believe her internal voice, but the last time she listened to the damn thing had been when she'd been mugged three months ago. Her first encounter with Corvus though she'd been blithely ignorant at the time. If only Seismic Shift hadn't screwed up when he tried to kill her the first time, he might still be alive himself.

Harri pulled her phone out of her pocket as she ran to her car, all too aware of how exposed she was on the sidewalk. She got in and locked the doors, but hesitated before she turned the key. She activated the app Tim had installed on all their phones, a little something none of the tech companies had. After a few seconds, the app flashed green.

The phone itself rang. Of course. The app had notified Tim she'd activated it.

She thumbed the answer icon. "I'm fine."

"But you're not paranoid, so what happened?" he answered.

Maybe that's why she liked him so much. He didn't feel the need to beat his chest when it came to her.

Harri told him about the tan Honda in front of Patty's building.

"You've seen it before?"

"No, it was the driver . . ." Okay, she had been pretty damn drunk the other night. "Maybe I did see the car, but through tequila glasses. I think it may have been parked down by the bodega when Jeremy brought me home the other night. His face was familiar." Tim's behavior registered from that blurry night. "You noticed something out of place that night, too."

A long pause stretched out before he said, "Yes, but it's not wise discussing it even over a secured phone."

"You don't think our mutual friend is messing with us again, do you?"

"I haven't heard any chatter, but that doesn't mean he or someone else isn't up to something." He paused. She could hear a female voice paging a doctor. "You feel safe enough to make it back to the office?" he asked.

She chuckled. "Yeah, your little app already did its job."

"Don't take my toys for granted, Harri," he said. "They can be circumvented. Trust your gut. If you don't feel safe, go to a public place—"

And he had to go and ruin everything by switching into overprotective mode.

"I'm fine. Get your ass home so we can go through the security footage from the other night. And you can tell me how your appointment went."

He laughed. "Yes, ma'am."

She ended the call and placed her phone in the cup holder she kept clean for the device. And she kept an eye on her mirrors the whole way across town because her gut said that wasn't the last they'd seen of the guy in the Honda.

———— •❦• ————

Aisha was hanging up from her call to the shop that sold refurbished office furniture when Harri knocked on her door. "A new desk will be delivered next Monday, and it's coming out of my share of our funds. As is the door for Marta's restaurant."

"Damn straight it is." Harri crossed the room and flopped into a guest chair. "Wait. What happened with Marta's door?"

Aisha gave her the short version of the attempted robbery. "And to top it off, Screaming Orgasm arrived early for her consultation with Jeremy while mostly-naked Rey was bitching me out. We've rescheduled for later this week."

"Crap," Harri muttered. "I really hope she doesn't spread any gossip about us."

"Don't worry. Rey sweet-talked her." Aisha forced a smile. If she didn't change the subject, she'd do something to their new client they'd all regret. "Things go smoothly with Patty and Grace's discharge?"

"New mom and baby are home. Arthur will be doing half-days for the next week." She frowned and leaned forward. "Did you get extensions or something?"

"No." Aisha frowned as well and sat on her hands to keep from scratching her scalp. She could practically feel her hair growing with her pregnancy-augmented senses.

"You need to schedule some salon time." Harri shook her head. "Your roots are seriously showing, girl."

Aisha rolled her eyes. "I can't take you seriously since it's coming from the woman who refuses to do anything with that salt-and-pepper mess on her head."

Tim knocked on her door, a laptop in his hand. "Sorry to interrupt, but I've got the security footage, Harri." He faced Aisha. "What happened down at Marta's? There's plywood on her door and a 'Closed for remodeling' sign."

"Don't bullshit me," she said sourly. "I know damn well you already hacked the police report."

"All right." Tim eyed her warily. "Rey's been short-tempered the last few days, but I also know he's not going to destroy Marta's livelihood to stop a robbery."

"He didn't." She stared down at the table top. "I did."

"I thought you said you accidentally ripped the door off its hinges," Harri said.

"I also accidentally threw it into traffic." Aisha winced.

"You responded to the robbery, and Rey covered for you?" Harri asked.

Aisha nodded.

"Where is he now?" Harri bit out.

"He went with Miguel, Dom and Emilio to pick up the new door, wood, drywall and paint."

"Do I even want to know?"

Aisha forced herself to face Harri. "Captain Justice is probably going to get sued for excessive force. I—sort of—um—threw the robber through a wall stud."

Harri jumped to her feet and, as she paced, let off a stream of invectives that could have peeled the rest of the paint off the walls in Marta's restaurant. She stopped, propped her fists on her hips, and glared at Aisha. "Anything else?"

Tim eyed her as well. "People outside of the restaurant heard a single gunshot. Police found the bullet embedded in the ceiling. Captain Justice claimed it bounced off him, but according to witnesses the gunshot happened before he arrived at the scene."

Harri's eyes widened, and she threw her hands in the air. "Dammit, Aisha! You're lucky you didn't get yourself killed! What if that bullet had hit the baby?"

"Did you forget the letter opener?" she said dryly.

"This isn't funny!" Harri shrieked.

"I know it isn't," she answered quietly. "The robber shot me point blank in the head. Rey already read me the riot act about bullets bouncing off my invulnerable skin. I could have accidentally killed Marta or the girls. And I've been sitting here thinking it could be even worse. These powers may result in our baby's death."

Harri dropped back into the chair she'd vacated. "What are you talking about?"

The fear bubbling through Aisha turned into a full boil. She hooked her toes under her chair to keep from floating toward the ceiling.

"What happens if something goes wrong during the delivery?" She swallowed the bile at the back of her throat. "How can the doctor do a C-section if there's no way to operate on me?"

"You can't think that way," Harri said at the same time Tim asked, "What did Serena say?"

Aisha scowled at him. "She tried to mollify me with babble about how we have eight months to find a solution."

"Then I need to have a little conversation with her." Harri started to rise again.

"No!" Aisha and Tim said at the same time.

"Let's deal with the more immediate problem." Aisha jabbed a finger at Tim's laptop. "Why are you two so concerned about the security footage? Is Corvus up to something again?"

Harri and Tim exchanged concerned looks before they turned back to her.

"It's probably nothing," Tim said.

"Just me being paranoid," Harri added.

"Uh-huh." Aisha carefully laid her palms on her makeshift desk before she hit something. "I'm pregnant. Not a fucking moron. Try again before I put the two of you through a wall." She narrowed her eyes. "Because you know I can."

Harri sucked in a deep breath and blew it out before she held up her hands. "All right. No need to resort to threats. We've both seen a Honda recently, same model and year as mine, but tan instead of white."

"That's all?" Aisha shook her head. "Do you know how many people drive Accords in Lake County alone?"

"10,746 are registered," Tim answered. "That doesn't include out-of-town visitors and folks with cars registered in the surrounding counties."

"So what's the story?" Aisha's gaze swung back and forth. "You think Corvus is actually trying to be inconspicuous instead of intimidating?"

Harri and Tim looked at each other again.

"We're not sure, which is why I wanted to see the security footage from the other night," Harri admitted.

"Well, let me see, too." Aisha rolled around the desk on her chair. Everyone's overprotectiveness was getting on her nerves. Now, she understood Patty's peevishness the last month of her pregnancy.

Except Corvus was actually trying to kill the entire staff and client base of Winters & Franklin at the time.

Tim set his laptop on the table and clicked a couple of buttons before he sat in the chair between Harri and Aisha. The footage started playing in clear sepia-toned glory. It came from the camera on the northeast corner of the Lechuza Building. The view encompassed most of the abandoned Canyon building and hotel across the street, the street itself, and a couple of the storefronts between their office and Celia's bodega on the corner.

Traffic zipped up and down the street and the timer counter off minutes as fast as seconds until Tim tapped another key. The images slowed, and a tan Honda Accord pulled into a parking space between the bodega and the nail salon.

"I can't make out his face from this distance," Harri complained. "Can't you zoom in?"

"Not on a recording," Tim said, his irritation clear. "Those stupid procedurals on TV make it look like all it takes is the press of a button to catch the bad guys."

A cab whipped past the bodega and pulled to a halt at the edge of the Lechuza Building. Jeremy jumped out of the backseat before he turned to help an obviously drunk Harri out of the cab.

"Wow," Aisha muttered. "Jeremy wasn't joking about how wasted you were the other night."

Harri leaned over to glare directly at her. "Am I all you two talk about when I'm not around?"

Jeremy and Harri disappeared beneath the bottom edge of the screen. Right about where the side door to the building was.

"It's the only time we can complain about your straight white tendencies," Aisha shot back.

Tim's aborted laugh turned into a cough. "Here we go."

On screen, Jeremy walked back to the cab and slid into the backseat. The Honda pulled away from the curb the same time as the cab. Tim hit a key to halt the playback. Harri's face scrunched as she tried to see the driver's face.

"Do you want to borrow my reading glasses?" Aisha asked.

Harri exhaled gustily. "If I didn't need them so bad, I would flip you off for calling me old."

Aisha grabbed the purple pair that matched her Saint Laurent pumps and handed them to Harri. She slid them on and peered at the screen again.

"The asshole has aviator sunglasses on just like he did this morning at Patty's apartment," Harri said. She pointed at the front of the car. "See? The in-state license plate is obscured with mud here just like on the rear plate. Only an 'N' shows."

"How's he able to see while driving with those glasses on at night?" Aisha asked.

"Because I doubt if they're sunglasses," Tim said. "See the faint static pattern?"

Both Aisha and Harri nodded.

"Those are modified night vision glasses," Tim explained. "Something halfway between regular vision and military grade goggles."

"Another one of your inventions those asshats at Corvus stole?" Aisha's hands shook, and she clenched them in her lap. She'd never felt this level of anger on any client's behalf. Keeping her cool when everyone else was losing their shit had always been her trademark.

Another side effect of her pregnancy? Emotional ups and downs were to be expected according to her book.

"No, I can't claim this one." An impish grin appeared on Tim's face, one that made him appear twenty years younger. She could see why Harri liked him so much. That poor girl had lost her funny bone the day her mom died, and despite his own tragedies, Tim was pretty damn mellow as a civilian.

"But that didn't stop me from borrowing their tech, just like they borrowed mine," he added. "I found a couple of other instances where this guy's shown up on our surveillance." He pushed the mouse to another tab and clicked on it.

This video was taken early in the morning. No one was on the street except for a few guys entering the bodega. Celia's egg burritos were a fixture on the street, which was why Aisha worked on engineering a partnership between the shopkeeper and Marta's son Rueben to open a breakfast café in the empty store between the Lechuza Building and the check cashing place. Rey had even offered to front the money, but right now, their neighbors' pride was the biggest obstacle.

The tan Honda was parked in front of the nail salon again, but other movement caught Aisha's attention. At the bottom left side of the screen, she could see leopard print heels flailing in the air through her office window.

"Oh, my god! That's the morning I found out I was pregnant!"

Harri leaned closer. "Yep, that's definitely your long legs." She turned to Aisha. "Told you no one was on the street to see you."

"Let me jump to the more interesting part," Tim murmured. He fast-forwarded the video, then tapped a key. "Here we go."

Onscreen, Harri's white Accord turned left from the garage and zipped up the street. The other Honda pulled out of its parking space before the driver made an illegal U-turn. The rising sun highlighted his unobscured features.

"Holy shit!" Harri stared at the screen, her skin whiter than Aisha could ever remember. "That's the guy from the hospital!"

CHAPTER 13

"What guy from the hospital?" Aisha watched Harri. From her partner's expression of shock, maybe she should run upstairs and grab the bottle of bourbon she kept on hand for her dad. Lord knew she wasn't going to touch the stuff over the next eight months.

"After I parked, I got into the hospital garage elevator." Harri's throat bobbed. "He yelled for me to hold the door, and he went up to the maternity ward with me. He may be Grace's father."

A chill ran through Aisha. "Wait a minute. You said the super who was supposed to kill you that night in jail was Patty's baby daddy."

"I didn't see his face. He had on the same mask the Corvus guys wear with their tactical gear," Harri murmured.

"But if he was supposed to give you an aneurysm—" Aisha started.

"Are you're saying Black Death spared you because you're his ex-girlfriend's boss?" Tim stared at Harri.

She shrugged. "I guess so."

"It would explain Seismic Shock's death while in custody." Aisha pointed at the screen. "If Bloch's been screwing up more than we know, and—" She shuddered at how close this assassin was to her home. "If Black Death managed to blame his failure to kill Harri on Bloch, Trubble would want to cut his losses. Did he see Patty at the hospital?"

Harri nodded. "I'm sure he did, but he didn't come into the delivery room. He stood in the hallway and looked shocked, but he took off when he realized I noticed him. Then Jeremy and I saw him the next night at La Churro's. Again, once he realized I spotted him, he left."

Aisha looked at Tim. "Have you identified him? I mean his real name."

"No. I've been trying to for years, but this is the first time I've gotten a clear look at his face," he said. "Arthur's facial recognition program is still working on an ID."

"I know you've checked the FBI database, but run this guy past Eddie, too." Harri scowled. "Somebody here in Canyon Pointe must have seen him before."

"You sure you want me talking to your ex-husband?" Tim said with a lift of his eyebrow.

"Actually, I would prefer if it were the Ghost Owl who contacted him," Harri replied, her voice deceptively mild.

"And why is that?"

"Your mask will cover that smug I-banged-your-ex-last-night expression you have," Aisha supplied.

Tim and Harri both stared at her. "I do not!" he said at the same time she yelled, "That's not what I meant!"

"It's what I see," Aisha said. "And if it's that obvious to me, then it's going to be super obvious to Eddie. So yeah, do what my partner said and have the Ghost Owl visit Agent Lewis of the FBI because that bum knee of yours isn't going to last one round with the ex-husband. We need to warn Arthur and—"

Kids' shrieks in the lobby brought the three of them to their feet. The cries resolved into "Ms. Harri!" and "Ms. Aisha!" right before Javier and Francisco tore into Aisha's office.

Once again, Francisco threw himself into Aisha's arms. "It's not true! It can't be!"

"You need to see this!" Javier snatched the remote off the table currently doubling as her desk, whirled, and pressed the power button. The Action 12 News! city emergency logo flared to life on the wall screen.

An all-too-familiar voice blared through the speakers. "—at the Omega Avenue Builder's Loft. Police have closed down streets in a three-block radius, and emergency services are evacuating the area. Acting Mayor Alfred Benevides recommends that commuters avoid the area and citizens shelter in place unless directed to evacuate by emergency personnel. This is Ted Meadowfield. Action 12 News!"

The camera switched to Essie Morales, Ted's co-anchor, in the studio, the city emergency emblem behind her. She wore her concerned journalist expression on her beautiful features.

"Thank you, Ted, for that on-the-scene update. For folks just tuning in, an unknown supervillain attacked civilians at the Omega Avenue Builder's Loft location and set the store on fire this afternoon before fleeing the scene. Local superheroes Cobblestone, Sparx, Sourpuss, and Captain Mojave are assisting police in their search and rescue efforts. So far, our newest superhero, Captain Justice, has not made an appearance—"

Javier pressed the mute button and turned back to the adults. "That's where Dad and the guys were headed, and if Rey was there, why didn't he do something?"

"Rey didn't do anything wrong," Francisco shrieked at his brother before he buried his head against Aisha's shoulder again.

"Then why isn't he or Dad answering their phones!" Javier yelled back.

Aisha briefly closed her eyes. Leave it to the kids to verbalize her fear.

Tim thrust his laptop into Harri's hands. "I'll call once I know something."

"I'm coming with you," Aisha said as she tried to disengage Francisco from her waist.

"No," Tim and Harri said.

"But Sparx and—" Aisha started. Can't panic or lose it in front of the kids.

"They have superpowers," Harri enunciated slowly and clearly.

Irritation swelled at her overprotectiveness. As much as Aisha hated admitting Harri was right, she couldn't go off half-cocked again. Not when she had a second life to think about.

"We good here?" Tim's query only added to her anger.

"Yes," she muttered.

Tim turned to Harri. "Talk to you soon." He pecked her lips before he charged out the door, which prompted Javier to roll his eyes.

The teen's reaction only turned Harri's cheeks even more pink than the kiss had.

Aisha stroked Francisco's back. "I'm sure your dad and brothers are fine. They probably got caught in the mess of people evacuating."

The boy looked up at her with big watery eyes. "Rey wouldn't do anything wrong."

"No, sweetie, he wouldn't." She exchanged a look with Harri before she turned her attention back to the heartbroken child. "But he'd put your dad and brothers in danger if he took on a bad guy in public without his superhero outfit. Tim will find all of them and make sure they're okay."

"In the meantime," Harri interjected. "Why don't you two come upstairs, and I'll make you some dinner?"

"It's not dinner time," Javier growled. "And we can take care of ourselves. Besides, you can't cook."

Aisha couldn't help grinning at the teen's attitude when she looked at Harri. "He's got you on the last one."

"Then we'll go down to Marta's, and you're buying," Harri snapped.

"Then you're driving," Aisha replied. "I'm not walking all the way to the restaurant in this heat."

"Aw, crap." Harri smacked her head in an exaggerated motion, which sent Francisco into a giggle fit. "We were supposed to go car shopping tonight."

"Not a good idea," Javier said with a gravity beyond his thirteen years. "Traffic's gonna be a bitch with a supervillain attack."

"Javier!" Harri stared at him. "Language!"

"I'm not a little kid." He crossed his arms with a sullen expression.

"Use *puta*. It sounds classier to *gringas'* ears." Aisha winked at Javier.

He relaxed slightly, but her joke didn't ease the little line of worry on his forehead. Javier was too young to have worry lines.

She looked at Harri again. "Why don't we call in an order to Marta's for everyone? The guys will be starved when they get home. While we wait for them to get back or an appropriate dinner time, whichever comes first, you can work on your Foxstar score."

"My Foxstar score is just fine," Harri grumbled.

"You suck at that game," Javier said with a cheeky grin. Thankfully, he was going along with the need to keep his baby brother occupied.

Harri propped her hands on her waist. "That's because you cheat."

"It's not my fault your reflexes deteriorate with age."

"Ooo, Ms. Harri needs burn ointment!" Francisco chortled.

The teasing continued on their ride down to Marta's.

— •◦• —

Harri breathed a sigh of relief when Marta didn't mention what Aisha had done to her store or ask why Miguel hadn't come back. Luckily the take-out window hadn't been destroyed in her partner's rescue attempt. The proprietress cheerfully reminded everyone the restaurant seating section would be open in a couple of days.

Hours after dinner, video games, and snacks, Francisco had passed out on her couch. Javier sprawled on the old futon that formerly graced her office in her old townhome, snoring slightly.

Harri waved for Aisha to join her in the kitchen. She pulled out a bottle of zinfandel from the pantry and set it on the island before she searched for her wine glasses. The new cupboard arrangement still threw her off once in a while, like when she'd had a damn long day.

She withdrew the goblets and turned to find Aisha staring forlornly at the bottle of wine on the counter. And immediately felt like a total shit.

"I'm sorry. I wasn't thinking."

"It's okay." Aisha waved airily. "No reason you can't have a glass for both of us."

"I've got some sparkling water." She reached into the refrigerator and grabbed a bottle. "I swear it's the only thing Tim will drink besides regular water and the occasional whiskey."

Aisha chuckled as she accepted the bottle. "That's okay. I need to get used to it for the next few months."

Harri had barely poured the wine when both hers and Aisha's phones buzzed. Harri pulled hers out of her pocket and scanned the text. "Tim found Miguel, Dom, and Emilio, but their pickup is trapped behind the police line, and they need a ride."

Aisha looked up from her phone where she thumbed an answer. "Where are they?"

"About a mile from the Builder's Loft. Why?"

Aisha's forehead crinkled. "Rey says he's at Westerville Park."

Harri cocked her head. "That's on the other side of Lake Del Oro."

"Yeah, thirty miles away in Washington County."

"What the hell happened? Why can't he just fly back here?"

The device buzzed again, and Aisha shook her head. "All he says is that someone's after him, and he's laying low at the park."

Worry threaded through Harri. "Corvus?"

"I don't know." Aisha looked over her shoulder at the sleeping boys. "If Trubble's up to something again, we can't leave them here unprotected."

"Jeremy?"

Aisha frowned. "With the detours around the barricaded area, it'll take him an hour to get here." She bit her lower lip before she said, "I'll call Serena."

Harri clenched her jaw muscles. Things were changing too much. She'd only met this woman once, but Aisha was ready to trust her with Miguel's kids? Dammit, she was the one who'd almost died keeping Shift's attention on her while the Ghost Owl was saving Francisco!

Except she didn't have any better idea on what to do. The Ghost Owl couldn't bring three grown men back on his Owl Cycle, much less help Rey.

"Do it," she muttered, but Aisha had already hit speed dial.

———— • ————

Harri guided Miguel's minivan behind the closed department store off of Mercy Drive. Thankfully, Aisha had remembered she still had his spare keys from when she and Jeremy helped Harri move. Until that point, Harri wasn't sure how she was going to fit four grown men into her Honda either.

But Javier and Aisha had been dead on about how bad the traffic would be after a supervillain attack. It took Harri nearly an hour to get to Tim's rendez-vous spot.

A shadow stepped from behind the dumpster. Her headlights illuminated the grays of the Ghost Owl's outfit. However, she waited until Tim flipped up his matte face shield before she released the air caught in her lungs.

He strode over to her window, and she hit the switch to roll it down.

"Open the rear hatch for me."

She punched the button for the hatch on the console and the one for the sliding side door. Dom and Emilio quickly climbed in and folded down the last two seats before they claimed the two middle seats. Miguel gingerly sat in the front passenger seat, his expression one of pain and exhaustion.

"You okay?"

"I'm getting too old for this *guano*," he muttered.

Tim hoisted himself into the back. "Harri close the hatch and douse the interior lights."

"Dad, cold pack for your ankle." Dom handed the blue gel-filled bag to his father from where he and his brother perched in the middle seats.

"You are fucking awesome, Ms. Harri!" From Emilio's excitement, he'd found the burritos and drinks under the gel packs.

"Language!" Miguel barked.

"Sorry, Ms. Harri," Emilio muttered from around a mouthful of burrito.

"I figured someone else might need the ice." She glared at Tim's reflection in the rearview mirror. "What the hell happened at the hardware store?"

"Something weird happened with Rey," Emilio said as he dug in the cooler for another burrito. "He was with me, ordering paint while Dad and Dom were taking care of the door and drywall. All of the sudden, he drops to his knees and slaps his hands over his ears right in front of the paint counter."

"Was the paint mixer on?" Tim asked. He peeled off his special-blend tactical jacket and turned it inside out.

"No." Emilio shook his head and talked around a mouthful of burrito. "He dropped, then this thing that looked like a giant crocodile made out of lava waltzed right through the front doors. And I mean through the doors. The glass and metal started to melt, the prefab concrete simply crumbled, and everything else caught on fire."

He swallowed his bite. "I tried to get Rey up on his feet. The lava crocodile said something I didn't understand before it walloped Rey through the roof."

"A caiman," Miguel said quietly. "It was a caiman."

"What's a caiman?" Harri stared at the contractor who hadn't opened the foil-wrapped burrito Emilio had handed to him.

"It's a relative of alligators and crocodiles, native to Central and South America," Tim answered when Miguel remained silent.

Rey's story of what had killed his mother ran through Harri's head. "Did Rey know what it was saying?"

Emilio stopped chewing and nodded. He swallowed his mouthful before he said, "Yeah, I think so because he answered in kind."

Harri sucked in a deep breath and turned to Miguel. "I know you want to protect your kids, but you need to be straight with me. Was this monster like the things that attacked Maria all those years ago?"

Fear shone in Miguel's eyes under the faint glow of the dashboard lights. "I don't think this was like the creatures that killed her. There were no burns on her body. The thing in Builder's Loft was exactly how my abuelito described Zipacna, the Mayan demon of volcanoes."

"A . . . demon?" Harri twisted in her seat to look directly at Tim.

He shrugged. "Is that possibility any crazier than a bunch of humans with superpowers?"

"Damn," Harri muttered. "It means his mom's amulet isn't protecting him anymore." She unlocked her seatbelt and dug in her jeans pocket for her phone. Aisha's phone rang four times before it rolled over to voicemail. Harri tried twice more with the same result before she looked at Tim, trying to ignore the fear churning in her stomach.

"She's not picking up."

"The bluffs along the east side of the lake can interfere with reception," he said in his reassuring superhero mode. "Let's get everyone home. If we still can't reach her, we'll make a plan."

Harri wasn't sure which was more upsetting—the fear that something could have happened to Aisha and Rey, or that Tim's idea of a plan would be to go out to Westerville Park by himself.

CHAPTER 14

Aisha tapped her Bluetooth as she drove east on the freeway, heading for the causeway over the lake.

Surprisingly, Arthur picked up on the first ring. "Ames residence."

"Sorry for calling so late. Is everything okay with Patty and Grace?"

"Patty's asleep," he said softly. "I'm taking the midnight and two a.m. feedings so she can get an uninterrupted six hours. But yeah, everything's fine. Aren't you, little cutie-patootie?"

If someone had told her she'd be listening to a former supervillain baby talk an infant over the phone once she had her own law firm, Aisha would have laughed her ass off. Now?

It was the only relatively normal thing in her life.

"Arthur, don't come into the office tomorrow."

"What? Why? Does it have something to do with the attack and fire at the Omega Avenue Builder's Loft?"

"No, this is a separate matter." Aisha sucked in a deep breath, praying Arthur would keep his cool. "Has Patty told you who Grace's father is?"

"No," he drawled out. "At least, not anything more than she's told Harri. Why?"

"There's a guy following Harri around."

"That's sounds more like Corvus's style," Arthur said.

The whine of the engine forced Aisha to check her speedometer. Twenty-five miles over the speed limit. She eased off the accelerator. If most of CPPD weren't dealing with the mess on the south side, she'd be looking at one hell of a fine.

"We think the guy who knocked up Patty is a Corvus assassin codenamed Black Death." Only static crackled across the line. Had she lost the signal? "Arthur? You still there?"

"Yeah." Another pause. "This isn't good. I heard of this guy even before Tim asked me about him. You sure he's after Harri?"

Aisha hit her right turn signal for the causeway exit. How much did she tell

Arthur? The last thing she wanted was to panic the poor guy. Part of the truth would have to do.

"So far, he's only been spotted following Harri. He's driving the same model and year as her Honda, but it's tan, not white. The last thing we want—"

"Is for him to hold Patty and Grace hostage like Seismic Shift did with Francisco." A new strength carried through Arthur's voice. "You think he's behind Shift's death."

It was a statement, not a question. "It's a possibility."

"When Patty wakes up, I'll move her into my apartment at the Lechuza Building."

Aisha laughed. "Man, she is going to fight you tooth and nail on that one."

"When it's Harri bullying her, yeah, but if it's Grace's safety . . ." A tiny baby burp came through the receiver. "We'll be there after Grace's four a.m. feeding."

"I'll let Serena know in case Harri and I aren't back from picking up the guys."

"Who's Serena?" Arthur sounded genuinely perplexed.

Crap. So much had happened since Patty had gone into labor Aisha totally forgot he hadn't been around the office the last few days.

"She's a future physician's assistant who lives in one of the apartments above the bodega." Aisha couldn't help a small laugh. "Going back to the Builder's Loft fire, Miguel, Rey, and the two older boys had run over there to pick some paint and supplies when the crap hit the fan. They got separated in the mayhem, and none of them could get to Miguel's pickup." That was assuming the vehicle was intact from some of the video they saw on the news, but she didn't want to freak out Arthur. "Harri's headed to get one group, and I'm picking up the other."

"Oh, dear," Arthur breathed. "That explains why Captain Justice didn't make an appearance. It had to have killed Rey to get caught without his supersuit in the middle of a supervillain attack."

A chill hit her as she passed the spot where her beloved BMW had flipped over the causeway retaining wall. If Rey hadn't been with her, Corvus would have made sure she sunk into the lake with her car. Part of her still wanted to give Byron Trubble, the head of Corvus, a good swift kick in the balls for the loss of her baby. But that night had been before Rey had a supersuit. He hadn't thought twice about using his powers to save her life.

"Arthur, I need to call Serena before it gets too much later," she said. "If you run into trouble—"

"I'll text Tim or Qiang," he said. "Don't worry. I've got this end of things. Talk to you in the morning."

The call ended, and Aisha smiled to herself in relief. Arthur had come a long way in the last couple of months. She tapped the speed dial for Serena's phone. The woman insisted on it in case anything else weird happened during this pregnancy.

"Yeah." The med student sounded groggy. She must have fallen asleep on the couch Aisha had carried over to Harri's from her own loft.

"Serena, I'm calling to let you know that Arthur and Patty will be on their way to the building when Patty wakes up at four. I didn't want you to be surprised."

"Okay." Serena yawned. "Thanks for letting me know. How are you feeling?"

"I'm fine." Aisha didn't quite snap. Rey was acting weird, and everyone else seemed to be overcompensating for his . . . whatever the hell was going through his head the last two days. The extra solicitousness was getting tiresome.

"Drink the smoothie I made for you. Lots of vitamins." Another yawn. "Anything else?"

"How are the boys?"

Serena laughed, a very feminine one. Something Aisha had never managed.

"Cisco and Javi are still out cold. Miguel may be pissed, but I'll keep 'em here tomorrow. They've had a rough day."

"Thanks again for watching them, Serena."

"*De nada.* See you when you get back."

Aisha tapped her Bluetooth and set it on the console slot with her phone. She glanced at the sippy bottle of green sludge Serena had given her when Harri let the woman into the Lechuza Building.

Tim wouldn't let his friend poison me, would he?

She took a sip. Strawberries. Banana. But she couldn't identify the slight vegetable flavor. *With my luck, it's kale.*

All the eastbound traffic continued on as she exited from the causeway on the opposite shore. Her little rental was the only vehicle headed north on the scenic lake drive.

———— •●• ————

Forty-five minutes later, Aisha reached the entrance to Westerville Park. Under the headlights of her car, the padlock on the gate was obvious. She tapped her fingers on the steering wheel. The smart thing would be to text Rey and let him know she was here. But what if something like the monsters that had slaughtered his mother when he was little and later attacked him at the White Chapel Country Club were looking for him?

The text tone could alert whatever was hunting for Rey. Or he could have his phone turned off as a safety precaution.

Well, I'm already paying for the damage I did to Marta's restaurant.

Aisha climbed out of her rental and strode over to the gate. With a quick yank, the padlock snapped, and she tossed it aside. Nothing appeared on the other side of the gate. If Rey didn't hear it, he must be hurt worse than she thought.

Hinges squealed as she pulled the gate open wide enough for her car to enter. She paused and listen once again. After a few seconds of silence, the park animals resumed their normal nocturnal activities.

But still no Rey.

She strode back to the car and climbed in. No sense acting like anything but a lowly mortal. Besides, she didn't trust her flying abilities out in the open.

The rental slowly rolled through the park, but she didn't see a sign of anything out of place. A worry niggled through her. What if this was a set up? What if whoever had attacked the hardware store had managed to snatch Rey's phone? Or worse, they'd taken Rey captive somehow?

What if this was all a bunch of Corvus bullshit to break the fragile truce and kill her?

Glowing green eyes shown out of the scrub thicket ahead. Aisha tapped the brake in case it decided to run out in front of her. The last thing she needed was to hit an animal with her rental car in the middle of the closed park.

Except the creature that stepped out onto the concrete wasn't a white tail deer or a coyote.

It had the brilliant plumage of a parrot, but it was roughly the size of her brother's Rottweiler. Instead of wings, it had four scaly legs that were much too long for a dog, much less a parrot, but they ended in wicked talons.

It opened its misproportioned beak, revealing short, sharp teeth. Its cry sounded like something from a CGI dinosaur.

More of these things stepped out of ditches and from behind bushes. A quick glance in the rearview mirror said she was surrounded.

Those legs looked as fragile as a flamingo's. Aisha gritted her teeth and jammed the accelerator to the floor. The engine whined before the car leapt forward.

Whatever these creatures expected, a full-on charge wasn't it. She struck the parrot-Rottweiler. Its legs broke with sickening snaps, and its body bounced off the hood before it flew to the left.

The rest of the flock screeched at the mistreatment of their partner. Aisha risked a glance in the side mirrors as she raced for the entrance. There was enough starlight to see six figures running after her rental.

She didn't want to abandon Rey. However, the logical part of her mind kept pointing out how stupid it was to come up here by herself. Sparx may have been engaged in search and rescue duty with the authorities, but Aisha could have waited for Tim to get back or called Jeremy or Eddie to come with her. Hell, even Screaming Orgasm would be more useful right now than she was. The open entrance to the park came into sight.

And next to it was a familiar figure, waving. Rey's expression grew alarmed as the posse chasing her registered.

Aisha weighed her options. She didn't have any weapons—

Her mouth stretched into what Harri, Jeremy, and her siblings called her scary smile at her idea. The gate itself was on her side of the car. And she had been pretty damn good at tossing a discus back in high school.

She slammed on the brakes. Tires screeched and the acrid smell of burning rubber filled the air. Rey yanked the passenger door open as she bailed out the driver side.

"Aisha!"

She didn't look back at his yell. "Get in the damn car!"

Her fingers locked around the top cross bar and yanked. The hinges shrieked and snapped.

She pivoted once. Twice. On the third spin, she released the gate. The parrot-Rottweilers tried to scatter, but the gate sliced through them like the proverbial knife through butter.

Rey stood at the open car door and stared at her.

"Get the fuck inside!" She dived into the car as one of the creatures screamed its peculiar cry.

Both car doors slammed shut. Aisha threw the shifter into "Drive" and pressed the accelerator. The car shimmied before she regained control.

"Why the hell didn't you fly home?" Her heart threatened to pound its way out of her chest. This kind of stress couldn't possibly be good for the baby.

"I couldn't," Rey growled. "Something happened to me at Builder's Loft. It's like I didn't have my powers. The only reason I survived when the damn thing hit me is because I landed in the lake."

That explained his fishy smell. She glanced at him. "I'm sorry, baby." She checked her mirrors and blew out a deep breath. No sign of pursuit.

"I'm sorry," she repeated. "What happened inside the store?"

"I don't know." He stared out at the inky black of Lake Del Oro beside them. "It felt like someone shoved a knife into my skull. Emilio was yelling at me and tugging on my arm. Then something was in front of me. It looked like an alligator on fire except it walked on its hind legs."

A self-deprecating chuckle rumbled out of his chest, and he finally looked at her. "That sounds crazy, doesn't it?"

"After some of the shit you've been through?" She shook her head. "That barely cracks the top five." She tapped her index finger against the steering wheel. "Did it say anything to you? Most supervillains like making proclamations of why they're about to trounce the superhero."

"Yeah, it did, but I couldn't understand it."

"Did you recognize the language?"

"No. All I can tell you is it wasn't speaking English or Spanish."

"You didn't lose your amulet, did you?"

"No." He reached beneath his t-shirt and pulled it out. "It's still here. I never take it off."

Aisha glanced at it. The ugly red streak on the jade seemed to glow in the dim interior of her rental. She refrained from saying anything more. He'd already lied about the amulet once. If he'd lost the original that had protected him his entire life, why replace it with a fake? He had to know the things that had hunted him and his mom would find him without the original.

She reached for Rey's hand and squeezed it. "It's okay, baby. We'll figure out what's going on."

Her reassurance sounded lame to her own ears. She'd revealed her hand to the parrot-lizard things, and at least one had survived. They weren't going to get as lucky on the next round with whatever these creatures were.

CHAPTER 15

Harri jerked awake when the side door security alarm beeped. Not wanting to wake Serena or the boys, she'd crashed on her office couch when she returned with the older Esperanzas. Even Miguel agreed the younger boys were better off getting some sleep at Harri's place, and he settled for leaving a note under the loft door.

A quick check of her phone said it was four-thirty a.m. Hopefully, it was Aisha and Rey.

Please be Aisha and Rey.

Harri pushed herself upright and slipped on her shoes. Voices echoed from the reception area's high art deco ceiling. The antique elevator ground to life.

She strode out of her office, but it was Arthur and Patty standing by the gate, fully loaded with infant carrier and assorted baby accoutrements. "What are you two doing here at four in the morning?"

Arthur faced her with a frown. "It was Aisha's idea. She called around midnight."

"And why didn't you call me to let me know my ex was stalking us?" Patty gave Harri a full-out evil glare.

"I just had a slight suspicion."

If anything, Patty's scowl deepened.

"All right. I didn't say anything because I didn't put it all together until yesterday afternoon."

A slim blond eyebrow climbed Patty's forehead.

Damn. Harri rubbed the spot between her own eyebrows. Grace would never get away with anything.

"All right," Harri said. "I didn't want to scare you."

"I'm assuming Tim has the security video," Patty said tightly as the elevator groaned to a halt.

"Yes."

"I'll check it and confirm it's the asshat who dumped me." Patty strode onto the elevator car with Grace. She whirled to face Harri again. "But I will do it at a decent hour."

Arthur simply looked at Harri and shrugged as he boarded the elevator.

On one hand, she was pleased the two were taking Aisha's warning seriously. On the other, it was a little embarrassing she hadn't been the one to call them. She'd been too worried about Tim zipping around town with an unknown threat on the loose.

The side door security alarm beeped again, and Harri automatically searched for a weapon. Aisha charged into the building with a bedraggled Rey in tow. She reset the alarm before she noticed Harri staring at her.

"What are you still doing up?"

"Waiting for you to get back." A wave of day-old fish hit Harri's nose. "What the hell were you two doing?"

"The monster knocked Rey into the lake." Aisha turned to Arthur. "Thanks for making sure he had the waterproof phone."

"No problem." Arthur waved Rey toward the elevator. "Come on. It smells like you need a shower more than I do."

Rey shot Aisha a curious glance. "Aren't you coming?"

"I'll be up in a few minutes. Harri and I need to talk spin control about Captain Justice's non-appearance."

"And keep the noise down on our floor," Harri added. "Francisco and Javier are asleep in my living room."

Rey entered the elevator and closed the gates. Patty made a face when his smell hit her. Arthur punched the button, and the car began its upward climb.

Harri eyed Aisha who watched the elevator as it disappeared from sight above the third floor. "Want some coffee?"

"What I want is a pitcher of margaritas." She seemed to shake herself out of whatever world she was lost in. "But coffee will do. And don't give me any of the decaf shit either."

Harri sauntered into the break room and opened the cupboard to find two boxes, each with a single pre-packed filter, plus the full box of decaffeinated coffee for the drip machine. No espresso beans to be seen. Crap, how had they gone through that much espresso in so short of time?

She pulled out the last two filters and held them up. "Cinnamon or hazelnut?"

"No mocha or espresso?" Aisha's big brown eyes shimmered under the overheads as she filled the clear glass pot.

"You've gone through all of it, sweetie."

Aisha turned off the tap and filled the reservoir. "It's not just me," she muttered. A little louder, she said, "Cinnamon."

Harri slapped the pack into the basket, slid it into place, and pressed the button to start the brewer.

"Any problems picking up your set?" Aisha asked.

Harri shook her head. "Nothing a couple of checkpoints and everybody having their ID on them couldn't handle."

"Tim had his ID with him while dressed as the Ghost Owl?" Aisha stared at her in horror.

Harri chuckled. "I swear Tim's secret identity has more outfits than Jeremy's. He had on a reversible jacket and an extra, more conventional helmet in the sidesaddle of his motorcycle."

"He was riding his bike with that bum knee?"

"Vitamin I does wonders," Harri admitted.

"Vitamin I?"

"Ibuprofen."

"Okay. I guess that's better than opioids if he's riding on the streets." Aisha reached into the cupboard by the sink for a couple of mugs. Harri recognized the delay tactic.

The coffee maker trickled, condensation sizzled, and the aroma of cinnamon filled the break room. Aisha played with the handles until Harri rested her hands on her partner's.

"What happened when you went to get Rey at the park?"

Aisha sucked in a deep breath before she met Harri's gaze. "You know how weird Rey's been acting since that mission a couple of mornings ago no one has said boo about?"

Harri nodded.

"I don't think the person who came home is Rey."

CHAPTER 16

"What are you talking about?" A frisson of fear ran up Harri's back. Aisha wasn't prone to drama. If she suspected something was off, she was usually dead on the money.

Harri released Aisha's hands, and her own fingers curled around the edge of the counter as Aisha laid out Rey's version of the events at Builder's Loft and the creatures they'd encountered at the park.

"What makes you think the man in your shower right now isn't Rey?"

"Only his spare Captain Justice outfit is in the secret compartment of our closet."

Harri cocked her head. "Maybe he gave the other one to Jeremy for cleaning after the dinosaur wrangling he had to do the other day."

"Describe his amulet to me."

What an odd question. Harri frowned. "It's green jade with a streak of Olmec blue through the middle on a leather thong. You sketched out the symbols on it, and e-mailed a copy to your dad. He translated the symbols and said it was a combination of the Mayan words for love and protection."

"That was the stone he was wearing when his alarm went off Thursday morning. The one he's been wearing since we got ready for bed that night is green jade with a red streak through it, and the stone has a totally different symbol. When I asked him where he got it, he claimed it was the same amulet he's always worn."

Harri swore under her breath. Rey didn't lie. He just didn't have it in him. Thank goodness, she didn't have superstrength. If she did, the granite counter would have been nothing but pebbles.

"Surely you'd know just by kissing him . . ." her voice trailed off as Aisha's expression hardened. "You haven't kissed him in the last forty-eight hours?"

"Not since he left on the mysterious call." She sagged under the weight of her revelations. "He gave me a patronizing kiss on the forehead when I questioned him about the amulet before he went into the bathroom."

"Oh, god." Harri swallowed hard. This was bad. So, so bad. "Could it be

Rey and he's been brainwashed? Or the new amulet is exerting some kind of influence on him?"

Aisha shook her head. "I can't put my finger on the difference other than that damn amulet and his taste in music."

"Taste in music?"

"He was humming along with a Mozart concerto on NPR during the ride home."

"And?"

"If it ain't Beyoncé, it's Bon Jovi for him."

"Maybe you've had more of an influence on Rey than you think."

Aisha gave her the "Are you kidding me?" glare. Their long moment of silence was interrupted by the little hiccup the coffee maker made when the reservoir emptied.

"So what the hell is going on?" Harri stared at the stupid poster Patty had put up in the break room. A cat hung from a tree limb with the words "Hang in there!" along the bottom. "Why send in a spy if Black Death is following me around the city?"

"I don't know," Aisha whispered. "I'm worried about Rey. Corvus has been after him for years, and we still don't know why. They could be doing god-knows what to him right now."

"Do we tell everybody else what we suspect about your imposter?" Harri finally asked.

"Not . . . yet." Aisha wore her analytical face, the one that didn't bode well for any opposing attorney. Or for whoever had kidnapped her lover.

And for the first time, Harri realized how wrong she'd been about Rey and Aisha's nascent relationship. She couldn't picture Aisha having that kind of "I'll rip someone a new one" reaction if Calvin the Asshole had been abducted back when they were in college.

"So what's our play?" Harri pried her fingers from the edge of the counter and poured their coffee.

"Let's see if we can find out who he really is. And where Corvus is holding Rey."

— ◆ —

Harri headed down to the basement after she and Aisha went through the pot of cinnamon coffee while they put together a tentative plan to out their imposter. At the bottom of the stairs, she punched in the second security code for the hermetically sealed door. When it swung open, she frowned. Most of the security was deactivated. Metallic banging echoed through the hallways.

She followed the sounds to the larger of Tim's two labs. Inside, the exoskeleton he'd been working on all week had taken on the appearance of modern armor mixed with the gray and brown insignia of the Ghost Owl. The only thing missing was the chest plate.

Which Tim was pounding into shape on one of his machines. He paused when he caught sight of her. He laid aside his mallet, pulled out his earplugs, and pushed up his safety goggles.

"What's the word?"

"Aisha got Rey home." Harri shook her head and crossed her arms. "She also called Arthur and told him about my stalker. He convinced Patty to bring Grace here."

Tim stripped off his gloves and reached for his ever present water bottle. "You look upset about that."

"It's my ego in the way again," she said as he took a swig. "Aisha has more influence over Arthur than I do."

Tim swiped his forearm across his forehead. "She wasn't involved in his sentencing or community service either."

"There's also the fact that my assistant listens to a former supervillain more than she does to me."

Tim chuckled. "Well, by your own analysis, Arthur sucked at being a supervillain, but he's been one hell of an IT and baby-wrangling asset."

"And now one of my clients has been up all night."

He shrugged and set aside the bottle. "I couldn't sleep. Not until I knew everyone was home."

Harri rolled her eyes. "So you've been keeping an eye on the security cameras, and you already knew everyone arrived safely before I came down here."

"Well, I was waiting for a visit from my favorite attorney." He pulled her into his arms and kissed her.

Tim holding her felt so good after the day they'd had. She didn't want the kiss to stop. A whimper escaped her when he gently pulled away.

"Come with me. I want to show you something," he whispered in her ear.

"I've already seen it."

He laughed. "That's not what I meant. I took your advice to heart about teaching Francisco." He took her hand and led her out of his large lab to the smaller one.

Inside, a smaller replica of the exoskeleton stood on a frame.

She turned to Tim. "You made him a toy version of your suit?"

"Not exactly." He released her hand and shoved both of his in the back pockets of his jeans. "I had a few small scale models to work out my concepts. He took those pieces and ran with his own ideas."

"You let him use an acetylene torch?" Harri glared at him.

"Not without me or Miguel supervising and helping."

She shook her head and stared at the smaller suit. It didn't have the Ghost Owl's colors, but otherwise looked the same until she peered closer. She circled the platform, taking in the detail.

"Is that a rocket pack on its back?"

"Yep." Tim chuckled. "The military's been trying to develop one for decades. The kid figured it out in an afternoon. This is what I mean. Francisco's way ahead of me."

Harri knelt and examined the framework more closely. Unlike Tim's suit, the longer steel pieces were thinner, doubled, and designed to slide from the way other pieces were connected. "This looks like a locking mechanism on the bigger support rods. Why is it adjustable?"

"So Francisco could adjust the size as he grows."

She looked up at Tim. "Seems to me if you're serious about creating an EVA suit for astronauts, an adjustable size would be very useful on the International Space Station."

"You almost look like you want to try it on, Ms. Winters?"

"Oh, no, no, no." Harri stood. "I'm not running around in my underwear."

He stepped closer to her. "Then let's go to bed."

She shoved playfully at his chest. "Your bed's too small."

"Still coming up with excuses, Winters?" He eyed her.

Not an excuse. She was scared shitless of leaving Aisha upstairs with a total stranger, but as her partner pointed out, she had super strength, invulnerability, and flight abilities now. There was a chance the imposter didn't have all of

Rey's powers, and the ones he'd displayed so far could have been faked somehow. Harri prayed Aisha was right as she turned and eyed the suit once again.

"What's wrong, Harri?" Tim murmured in her ear.

And the fact Timothy Mitchell Canyon, acquitted murderer and vigilante superhero, could read her moods better than any other man didn't help.

She swallowed her fear for her best friend. "You're right." She looked up at him again and sighed. "I'm letting old stuff get in the way. But that doesn't change your bed size."

"Well," he drawled. "It's either my apartment or take a chance of waking the kids up. Do you want to get yelled at by Miguel for setting a bad example in front of his children?"

"Not really," she admitted.

"Besides, I did mean sleep." Tim grinned. "We've both been up nearly twenty-four hours."

She glanced at the clock. It was already past six a.m. "All right," she grumbled. "We'll use your bed."

Tim limped beside her as they headed into the apartment section of the basement.

"By the way, what did the specialist say this morning?" Harri asked.

"You mean yesterday morning?" He grinned down at her.

"Don't make me beat up on a crippled guy." She scowled up at him.

"You're so insensitive and politically incorrect," he mocked. "The proper term is differently abled."

"Quit mansplaining, and just tell me what the doctor said."

He dipped his head for the retinal scanner, and when the lock clicked, he yanked the door open. "Partial tear of the LCL. Given the state of the joint, she's suggesting a total knee replacement, which is nothing new, but . . ." He shrugged and waved for Harri to proceed him.

"The Ghost Owl needs to stop patrolling," she said softly as she entered his living room.

"I had a plan." He closed the door to his living quarters and reset the basement security alarms. "Until a couple of attorneys took my prospective protégé and turned him into part of the underwear brigade."

Fear grabbed a hold of her throat. If Rey was hurt or dead, it would be all her fault. She's the one who pushed him into getting registered and becoming a legitimate superhero. All that did was put a bullseye on the kid's chest.

"Hey, what's wrong?" Tim cupped her face. "You weren't this squirrely when Seismic Shift was trying to kill you."

"I'm worried Black Death may try to hurt Patty." She shook her head at her not-quite-outright lie, but telling Tim her second worst fear seemed a more prudent move. If she told him the truth about the stranger upstairs, he'd charge up to Aisha's loft. Nothing good would come from a confrontation now. Harri swallowed hard. "From what he said to me in the elevator, Patty didn't tell him she was pregnant."

"Black Death probably already knows who's living here through Corvus, which is why he hasn't done anything stupid."

"Yet. Give him a chance." She wanted to believe Tim, but her gut said things were definitely going to get worse.

◆

Harri woke to the intercom beeping. Low lighting illuminated Tim's bedroom. Like the rest of his underground apartment, it was neat and functional. However, she was alone.

Voices came from somewhere else in the apartment. She blinked, and it seemed as if the bedroom was a little brighter. Time to face the day, like it or not. Harri flipped back the covers and shuffled out of the bedroom and into the main living area.

"I'll be upstairs once I get my shower and some breakfast," Tim said.

"You either give me access to that video right now," Patty snarled over the intercom speaker. "Or so help me, I'll ram Grace's stroller into your bad knee."

"What happened to you would talk to him at a reasonable hour?" Harri said.

Tim smiled at her and shook his head.

"It's eleven a.m., boss." Patty's tone turned saccharine sweet. "You didn't put your morning absence on the calendar."

"Really? That's how you want to play this right now?" Harri leaned against the wall on the other side of the speaker.

"You should have told me about Cade following you, not Aisha through Arthur." Patty's bad attitude was back. But she slipped for the first time and mentioned her ex's name, their first clue to Black Death's real identity. Something she'd never done before.

"You're right," Harri said. "I should have. I'm sorry."

Her apology silenced her assistant.

Harri cleared her throat. "Patty, I have to ask you something. Did you know Cade was a super?"

"What?" The sound came through the speaker as more of a squeak than an actual word.

"Sweetie, this is important," Harri said softly. "I need to know."

"No! N-no, he couldn't be." Patty's voice faltered. "I thought he might be, but I figured his mystery act was due to me being his side chick. Not to mention, my pregnancy was totally normal."

"Not every super conceives a super baby," Tim added. "Not every mom gets powers carrying a super baby. And sometimes, a super may lose her powers or develop new ones while she's pregnant. The researchers haven't quite figured out how or why certain hormones affect a super's abilities."

"Sweetie, if Grace was a super, you'd know," Harri said. "The hospital was legally required to test newborns for the super gene, just like they have to test for phenylalanine. And we both know she tested negative."

"B-b-but how do you know Cade . . ."

Harri eyed Tim. "Can you skip the shower for a bit? We need to deal with this now."

He held up his hands in surrender. "You ladies are the ones who have to deal with my body odor."

"Patty, we'll be up in five." Harri thumbed the intercom button. "And for the record, I already told you I like the way you smell." She whipped off Tim's t-shirt she'd worn as pajamas last night as she headed back to the bedroom.

He groaned. "Couldn't you have made it ten minutes?"

She looked over her shoulder and laughed. "That's not a time limit a woman wants to hear."

Aisha opened one eye when her phone buzzed. So much for getting a little extra sleep on a Saturday after not getting to bed until nearly six this morning. She reached for the phone and checked the text and the time.

Damn. Harri wouldn't be calling in the cavalry unless Patty was having a serious meltdown over Grace's biological father.

She glanced at the man lying beside her, snoring softly. He was going through most of the right moves as Rey, but it was the little things he was slipping on.

Like not hearing her phone signaling a text.

Or like being already asleep by the time she got up to the loft this morning. Rey insisted on cuddling. Every freaking night. There were times she would have felt like a child's blankie if she didn't need the touch as much as he did.

This guy's whole act, and it was definitely an act, was based on observing Rey in public settings. In a way, she was relieved to know Corvus couldn't have possibly planted any bugs or cameras in her loft.

She texted back to Harri she'd be down as soon as she dressed. The stranger in her bed didn't move as she donned slacks and a blouse. She picked up one of her Valentino Garavani T-straps and seriously thought about shoving the stiletto heel through the imposter's sensitive parts until he told her where Rey was.

The blood wouldn't be obvious on the scarlet leather without a black light.

In the end, she slipped on a pair of Ferragamo flats. The guy pretending to be Rey didn't stop snoring as she walked out of her bedroom and out of her loft.

Once on the main level, she followed the voices to Harri's office. Her partner looked up at Aisha, and she schooled her expression to the appropriate concern.

Patty's face, on the other hand, gave new meaning to white. Tim sat on one side of their assistant with his laptop on Harri's desk. On the screen was the paused spot on the security recording where the Harri's stalker could be clearly seen in the morning light. Arthur sat on the other side of Patty, and she gripped the poor guy's hands so tight his fingertips were turning purple.

"Th-that's definitely Cade," Patty said as Aisha crossed the office and perched a hip on a corner of Harri's desk.

"We need a last name, Patty," Aisha said softly.

The girl seemed to collapse in on herself. "The name he gave me was Cade Wilson. I doubt if it's his real name. He said he worked for Netware Technologies."

"If we start running a search on his name, it'll flag Corvus." Arthur appeared worried, which was normal, but it was the first time Aisha heard an edge of anger in his voice.

"He's right," Tim added.

"You all think he's Corvus?" White ringed Patty's brilliant blue irises.

Aisha glanced down at Harri. "You need to tell her everything."

Her partner grimaced before she faced Patty. "I'm sorry for not bringing this up sooner, but I know you didn't want to talk about your ex, and . . ." Harri leaned her elbows on her desk.

"The night I spent in jail, a man came to my cell. He said he was sent to kill me, but he asked me to make sure you and Grace were kept safe. After he left my cell, he called Aisha and told her to get her ass down there before his accomplices discovered he hadn't done the job he was sent to do."

Harri cleared her throat. "Tim and I have been comparing notes. There's a super called Black Death. He's the guy Corvus calls in to make an assassination look like natural causes. He can kill with a touch."

Patty pulled her hands from Arthur's and shivered as she examined each of their faces. "And you suspect Cade is Black Death? You suspect that's what happened to Seismic Shift, don't you? Trubble had this Black Death kill Bloch before he talked?"

Arthur, Tim, and Harri all looked terribly guilt-ridden and wouldn't meet Patty's gaze.

"Yeah, sweetie," Aisha said. "That's exactly what we think. He was also at the hospital the day you gave birth. He accidentally—" She made air quotes. "—ran into Harri. He claimed you didn't tell him you were pregnant. And it sounds like he's not too happy about that."

"I-I didn't tell him." Patty's fingers folded and unfolded in her lap. "The day I found out, the day I planned to tell him, was the same day he broke up with me. He said he was going overseas for a few months." A couple of tears trickled down her pale cheeks, and she swiped at them. "He said it wasn't fair to keep me hanging. I was so mad. He was just another asshole. I didn't want that for Grace."

Tim blew out a deep breath. "Ironically, he was probably telling you the truth about having to leave the country for a few months. There were at least two assassinations in Asia and one in the Middle East over the last year I can link to Black Death."

"You really think it helps telling me Grace's father is a murderer?" Patty snapped. Her attention shot back to Harri. "Wait a minute If he's pissed at me for not telling him I was pregnant, why's he after Harri?"

"It's a loyalty test," Tim stated grimly. "Even though Shift didn't have authorization to kill Harri initially, Black Death disobeyed one of Trubble's lieutenants. Trubble will want to make sure Black Death is under his thumb."

"Or it could be far simpler," Arthur said. "He may be jealous Harri and I were there for the birth of his daughter, and he wasn't."

The man had a point, but conjecturing about Black Death's motives didn't mean a damn thing.

"The real question is what do we do about him." Aisha eyed each of her officemates. "We can't lock Harri, Patty, and Grace in here forever."

"So far, he's not paying too much attention to the kids on the street," Tim mused.

"Javier would be ecstatic if he had a real live Ghost Owl phone." Aisha smirked.

"You can't put Javier and his friends in danger." Patty waved her hands, a sheen of anger on her face.

"Are you saying Javier is irresponsible? Where is he right now?" Aisha asked. The question was more for her colleagues' benefit. With her super hearing, she'd already heard the thirteen-year-old teaching Francisco how to change Grace's diapers in Arthur's office, though their IT guy might want to double-check his desk for contaminates.

"All right." Patty's anger faded, and she sighed. "Point taken."

Aisha stood. "If this staff meeting is finished, I need to get to Jeremy's."

"Finally, the roots will be done!" Harri cheered.

"Actually, the chemicals used on a black woman's hair can cause birth defects," Arthur said.

Everyone turned to stare at him.

He shrugged. "Ms. Johnson went for the natural look and used henna to color while she was pregnant. You might want to suggest something similar to Jeremy."

Tim's expression was almost comical. "Gaia Johnson? The tennis pro?"

However, Patty gave the blushing IT guy an admiring look. "You didn't tell me you were the nanny for her kids." She turned back to Harri. "I have Gaia Johnson's nanny!"

Harri sat back in her chair. "Well, that explains her character reference and plea for leniency at your sentencing hearing. And here, I thought you refinished her furniture."

Aisha back-handed Harri's shoulder. "Be nice. We need him more than he needs us. I'm out of here. I've got to turn a wild child into a real hero."

CHAPTER 17

An hour later, Aisha watched as Jeremy examined Screaming Orgasm's roots.

He whistled. "Totally natural colors. I love it." He eyed the super in the mirror. "Normally, I'd work with this, but I'd listen to your lawyer if I were you."

"But blond is sooo boring," Orgasm whined.

"I can certainly refund your money." Aisha smiled at her client. "Minus the fees Mr. Harkness and I have earned so far, of course."

"I know you're right." Orgasm pouted at the mirror. "But I was hoping for a beauty product contract."

"First, we need to establish your new hero brand," Aisha said. "Once we show you're a serious power to the marketing departments of sponsors, then we can add some of your natural flash back into the mix."

"Do you have to cut off my curls, too?" Orgasm looked on the verge of tears.

Or it could have been her glittery irises.

"Not all of them, sugar pop," Jeremy crooned. "But I do want to take several inches off. You need to look badass, not sex-kittenish. You want the bad guys to fear you, not lust after you."

"You really think I can be as good as my sister?" The super swiped at her eyes.

"Of course, we do." Aisha smiled at the younger woman's reflection. "We wouldn't have taken you as a client if we didn't."

"But I had to bribe you—"

"Molly, listen to me." Aisha swiveled the beautician chair around to face the super directly. "It's called a partnership for a reason, and it's no different than the relationship you registered heroes have with each other. I trust Harri Winters to have my back, and I have hers. I meant what I said about taking you on had to be a joint decision. I would have returned your check, regardless of the amount, if Harri said no. And I meant what I said about our hourly rate. It's going to be the same no matter how much you give me for a retainer fee, but it's up to you to spend that retainer wisely. I can advise you, but the decisions, and the consequences, are ultimately yours."

Orgasm nodded. "Okay." She sucked in a deep breath and looked up at Jeremy. "Do it."

—•—

"You have way better people skills than Harri," Jeremy shook out a new plastic cape and draped it over Aisha's shoulders as she sat on the seat Molly Reinhold had vacated. "Or me. I would have killed that kid by now."

Aisha had been close to killing Molly a few times herself, but professionalism meant she couldn't say it. Not even to Jeremy.

Screaming Orgasm, now dubbed Nix, had practically skipped out of his warehouse/superhero factory with her new hairdo and the costume she'd selected out of the designs he'd put together. The question was whether the superhero could keep her shit together during Monday's press conference.

"Don't ever say my skills are better to Harri's face." Aisha laughed. "Or not anywhere she can hear you." She smoothed out the cape. "Besides, it wasn't like she had many good examples growing up."

"Are you saying Grandma Harri wasn't a good example?" Jeremy waved his pick dramatically.

"Of course not. She was a perfect example of how to boss people around."

They both laughed, but Jeremy turned serious.

"Harri still giving you shit about the baby?"

"No." Aisha frowned. "Something else has distracted her." She described the car Black Death was driving. "Have you seen a vehicle like that?"

"Of course, silly." Jeremy grabbed the sides of her head and tilted her forward. "Who do you think texted Timmy about the suspicious car the night Harri got wasted?"

Aisha breathed a little sigh of relief. "That explains the taxi. You were afraid her Honda had been tampered with."

"Yeah. Let me guess. Hot brunette with a tight ass and intensely blue eyes?"

"You saw him at La Churro's, didn't you?" She couldn't help chuckling at Jeremy's analysis of such a dangerous super.

"Honey, just because things are getting permanently serious with Leonardo doesn't mean I can't look at the other desserts." He poked through her hair. "But yes, I spotted him keeping too close of an eye on Harri at La Churro's. And he had the same ugly look that some of the bullies in school had."

New concern rippled through her at his admission, and she lifted her head. "You didn't go straight home that night, did you?"

Jeremy's reflection glared at her. "Aisha, honey, do I look that stupid?" His expression deflated, and he exhaled loudly. "Though if he's Corvus, all my evasive efforts were for nothing."

Aisha shuddered. Corvus knew too much about all of them. They'd trashed Jeremy's salon two months ago in their efforts to isolate her and Harri from all their relationships within the city. So far, they hadn't targeted this warehouse. While she'd been very careful not to reveal Jeremy's identity to her former employers at Dewey & Cheatham, she was under no illusions this place was totally safe anymore.

"You need a new hideout," she said as he tilted her head again.

"Looking into it already."

She lifted her head and glared at him. "I'm serious. They've already tried to kill Harri numerous times."

"I am aware, girlfriend," Jeremy said primly. His eyes narrowed in the mirror, a warning to drop the subject, before his expression switched back to gossipy queen. "Now let's talk about more important things," he added airily. "Like what the hell kind of prenatal vitamins are you taking, girl? I swear your hair has grown more than an inch since the last time you were in the salon."

"I know." She sagged in the beautician's chair. "It's part of my new package of superpowers. I don't know what to do. I can't afford to come to you more often—" She held up her index finger when his reflection opened its mouth. Her nail looked pristine despite the fact she'd bitten it down to the quick the morning of all the pregnancy tests.

"Nor am I accepting charity from you," she finished.

"You've definitely been living with Harri too long," he grumbled. "I know you went for the quasi-white girl look because of the idiots at Dewey & Cheatham, but I think we need to skip the straightening until after you deliver your little bundle and any breastfeeding you might choose to do."

"Can't I use my blow dryer or flat iron?"

"You can, but are you going to feel up to?" He set aside his pick and ran his fingers through her hair.

Aisha glared at him. "Sweetie, I can bench press a ton right now."

Jeremy rested his hands on her shoulders. "And you're underestimating how much this baby is going to change your life. Every mother I've known, super or civilian, has gotten progressively more tired as they haul around an extra person growing inside of them. And that's not even accounting for the lack of sleep once the baby gets here."

"You want to chop my hair off." She stared bleakly at his reflection.

"I'm looking out for your image as a high-power legal badass. Your hair is going to look shitty with it half straightened and half not. I also suggest using henna to color it. I don't want to take the chance Baby Franklin mutates into something you and Rey can't handle."

"Have you been talking to Arthur?"

"No." Jeremy frowned. "Why?"

"He made the same suggestion." Jeremy's image blurred, and she blinked to clear the threatening tears. What would happen if she couldn't find Rey before Corvus did something terrible to him?

She cleared her throat. "That's a little more change than I was planning."

Jeremy swung her chair around to face him. "What did you tell our Nix not three hours ago?"

"Seriously? You're throwing my own words back in my face?"

He laughed and shook his head. "You've definitely been living with Harriet Mathilda Winters too long." He took Aisha's hands. "You've got your dream with that baby, doll. Now listen to your stylist. Short and red. You'll be the hippest mommy in the Canyon Pointe General maternity ward. But like you told Molly, the choice is ultimately yours."

Aisha sucked in a deep breath and blew it out. "All right. Do it."

Her new look might be exactly the trigger she and Harri needed to expose the imposter living in her loft.

— • —

When Aisha returned to the Lechuza Building, the door to Harri's office was closed. From the conversation her new super hearing allowed her to eavesdrop on, Harri was discussing the finer points of civic restitution with someone.

No rest for the wicked. Or for lawyers.

Not wanting to risk any flying mishaps, Aisha took the elevator up to the fifth floor. The fake Rey was nowhere to be found in her loft. Maybe he was so immersed in his role, he was actually helping Miguel with the construction as the real Rey promised.

She took the stairs back down to the fourth floor where Miguel had been working on the large apartment for him and his sons. Even though, Patty refused to move into the one they'd completed for her, Aisha had been able to talk the contractor into moving into the smaller apartment temporarily.

Well, guilted the poor man actually. She'd pointed out that squatting in the abandoned hotel across the street didn't make sense anymore. Not with the two younger boys.

However, voices came from Arthur's apartment, not from the other two. Aisha knocked.

Patty opened the door and smiled. "Welcome to Casa de Kid." Her smile shifted to a brilliant grin. "Love the new 'do!"

"Sounds more like the old Toys 'R' Us in here." Aisha stepped into the apartment. Familiar game music played through high-quality speakers.

"Die, suckah!" Francisco's jeer was followed by an explosion on Arthur's large screen monitor/TV.

"You got me!" But Arthur laughed along with the boy.

"I called winner."

Aisha frowned at Javier's muted voice until she spotted the teenager on Patty's rocking chair. He carefully held Grace.

"Baby swap!" Arthur climbed to his feet and nodded to Aisha. Then did a comical double-take. "You took my advice." He blinked, and a pleased expression crossed his face.

She couldn't help grinning. "You took mine."

Jeremy had done an incredible job with finding a haircut that drew attention to Arthur's soulful eyes and away from his oversized nose. The product her friend suggested had done wonders for clearing up Arthur's acne as well.

"But I came down here looking for Rey." She gestured in the direction of the unfinished apartment. "Where is everyone?"

"Dad and Dom took the minivan to get the stuff they needed for the mess you made at Marta's at the Builder's Loft down on the south side." Javier carefully handed Grace over to Arthur before he sauntered over to the couch, picked up the game controller, and flopped down next to his brother. "Mr. Tim drove Emilio over to get Dad's pickup."

Patty shrugged. "Rey hasn't been down here at all. Have you checked at Marta's?"

Aisha forced a self-deprecating laugh. "I've been trying to forget what I did to her restaurant. Thanks."

Not wanting to interrupt Patty and Arthur's efforts to keep the boys occupied, Aisha headed down to her office. She took the stairs a little more slowly this time. Last night, well, this morning had been hard enough. She didn't know if she could continue sleeping in the same bed with a man who could be responsible for Rey's—

No! she told herself sternly. *You cannot think that way. Rey isn't dead.*

But the internal lecture did nothing to melt the icy ball in her gut. As she entered the reception area, Harri charged out of her office. Her face brightened momentarily.

"Love the new look!" She immediately sobered. "How did things go at Jeremy's?"

"Screaming Orgasm is now Nix, blonde, and wearing a stretchy blue pleather/Kevlar number that doesn't attract hungry infants or pervs."

"Nix?" Harri cocked her head.

"The name of mythological water spirits. The Germanic equivalent of the Greeks' sirens." Aisha shrugged. "And she's supposed to be practicing on her power control over the weekend without doing the other thing which sets off the conservative parent groups. I'm going to do some testing with her over in the delivery docks across the street next week since they're rubble. Do you think Sparx would be willing to mentor her a little?"

"Maybe." Harri rolled her eyes. "Or you could be mixing orange juice and milk."

Aisha shrugged. "Nix needs a little more discipline, and Sparx could loosen up."

"Hey, you want to get a bite?" Harri's mood noticeably darkened.

"Marta's?"

"I'm a little Latin cuisined out." Harri hesitated. "What about White Chapel?"

Aisha frowned. Her best friend was up to something she didn't want to talk about here. Harri hated the country club, even though she had a lifetime membership. "Sure."

Minutes later, they were in Harri's Honda. She detoured past Marta's taqueria. Sure enough, both Miguel's pickup and minivan plus Tim's classic Mercedes were parked in the lot. The front door had already been replaced. Relief spread through Aisha and eased the gigantic knot of fear and worry she'd bottled up around Nix and Jeremy this afternoon. Harri gunned the engine and sped through the miniscule downtown traffic. Her attention kept darting to each of her mirrors.

"Black Death wasn't parked on the street when I got back from Jeremy's," Aisha volunteered.

"We can't take chances," Harri growled. "All he needs to do is get a hand on you or Rey..."

Aisha swallowed the bile at the back of her throat. From the way Harri's voice faltered, she had the same idea that flicked through Aisha's mind—that Black Death already got to Rey.

"Trubble needs Rey alive," she said, trying to convince herself as much as she was Harri. "He's the only leverage Trubble has over us."

"Speaking of which, our friend took off soon after you left this morning." Harri grimaced. "He was in the Captain Justice spare suit. Wouldn't tell me where he was going. Pissed Miguel off to no end. He wanted Rey's help with fixing Marta's place. I wish I could have told him—"

"You can't," Aisha bit out. "Not until we get Rey back."

"I know, sweetie," Harri murmured. "I know. I just don't like letting him trash Rey's reputation in the process."

"Rey's rep isn't Trubble's main goal," Aisha snapped. "Trashing ours is."

"But are our clients going to trust us when this is over?"

Aisha resisted the urge to nibble on a fingernail. Harri was right. By the time this game Corvus played was over, she might not have the means to raise her little boy. And that scared her as much as the idea that Rey was already dead.

CHAPTER 18

Harri strode through the entrance of the White Chapel Country Club's dining room. The same maître d who reported Aisha and Rey to the dining room manager in order to get them kicked out a couple of months ago was at the podium. Good. She had someone to take her pissy mood out on.

"Two for dinner."

"I-I-I'm terribly sorry, Ms. Winters. Th-the dining room is currently full, and I have reservations for the next two hours."

Well, he was smart enough to remember her name.

Harri stomped past him to check. He wasn't lying. Every single table was full.

She whirled and glared at him. "Is there going to be a problem if my law partner and I order dinner from the club bar?"

Whites surrounded his hazel irises, and perspiration beaded on his forehead. "Not at all, Ms. Winters." He grabbed two menus. "This way please."

They followed him into the adjoining section. In Grandma Harri's day, a woman sitting at the clubhouse bar without a man was unthinkable. Several couples and groups took all the small tables, but all the stools at the counter were free.

All except one.

Quentin Samuels, former mayor of Canyon Pointe and all-around snake, eyed Harri over the rim of his highball glass. If he was a super with heat vision, she'd be nothing but sizzling bits of meat.

Silence fell over the club members as they waited to see what drama would unfold. Samuels slammed his glass down on the polished wooden counter before he stormed out of the bar. The maître d laid down the menus in front of Harri and Aisha before he retreated as well. With no explosion, conversation among the diners waiting for their tables resumed.

"Why is he not in jail?" Aisha whispered.

"Out on bail for the state charges," Harri answered as she hoisted herself onto a stool. No getting drunk tonight. It was a long way to the floor, even if her best friend now had super strength and would catch her. She couldn't out Aisha that way. "According to Jim Duncan at the federal prosecutor's office, the grand jury is still deciding on the RICO charges."

"And yet, he can sit here and drink without the snobs throwing a fit." Aisha scowled in the direction of Samuels' retreating back.

"Wait until we have gobs of money." Harri flipped through the menu. "We'll buy out the memberships and change the by-laws."

Aisha snorted in amusement and took her seat. "Is there a reason you picked this place? I know you weren't sparing me the embarrassment of going to Marta's."

"Actually, yes." She signaled the bartender. "Diet cola and lobster salad."

"I'm sorry, ma'am, but we're out of lobster salad." He gave her an ingratiating smile.

Harri smiled back, but hers was hardly ingratiating. "I know damn well the lobster salad for tomorrow's lunch has already been prepped. If you want to retain your job, you will fill my order and without the extra spit, please."

His smile faded, and he did a slow blink.

Harri glanced at Aisha, but her partner looked both pleased at the dressing down since the lobster salad was her favorite and appalled Harri chewed out a poor staff member, who at best was paid minimum wage. She jabbed a thumb in Aisha's direction.

"She'll have a lemonade with her lobster salad."

The bartender took the menus and trotted away.

Harri turned to face Aisha. "Don't give me the 'you've been a bad rich white jerk'. I promise I'll give him a good tip."

"No," Aisha drawled. "This is the 'just because I'm black doesn't mean I can't order my own damn dinner' look."

"Please, spare me. You were going to order the lobster salad and you know it." Time to get to business. "What did you think about Susan Kennedy when she was at Dewey and Cheatham?"

"Why?" Aisha's eyes narrowed.

Harri waited until the bartender deposited their drinks and retreated to the other end of the bar. "Because your vacation time will be here sooner than you think. I've put some feelers out."

"You really want someone who used to be with Dewey and Cheatham?"

Harri took a sip of her cola and shrugged. "Considering Matthew Cheatham has been attempting to blackball her with any potential employer here at the club, I thought you'd have some insight."

Aisha played with her straw. "She's a decent attorney. Knows her stuff from what I saw. According to the rumor mill, she quit because of Stuart's wandering hands, but that's nothing new when it comes to him. She may not want anything to do with us though." She shook her head. "If she says no, what about Lisa Ashcraft? She's one of the few people in Canyon Pointe who doesn't hate your guts."

Harri shook her head. Her divorce attorney had been one of the first people she'd thought of. "I already called her. She's sticking with family law unless one of our supers needs help with a divorce or a custody battle. By the way, Lisa was a little peeved you didn't go to her when you and Cal split."

Aisha's gaze dropped to her lemonade. "I should have. If I'd known I'd have to worry about my kid later, I would have fought harder."

"You mean actually fought at all," Harri murmured.

"That's not fair." Aisha lifted her head and glared at Harri. "You were trying to punish Eddie for not being what you wanted him to be." She waved a hand. "I was just embarrassed, and I wanted it over."

"But Lisa wouldn't have let Cal take advantage of you—" Old anger boiled inside of Harri.

"Stop." Aisha held up her hand. "I don't want to fight. We've been getting enough of that at home lately. All we're doing right now is rehashing old shit. Do you want me to contact Susan?"

"I think she'd have a rapport with you since you also quit." Harri shrugged. "Not to mention, Becky Roth, the gal who was Dewey and Cheatham's receptionist and filed the sexually harassment claim, called today to say she got a new job through Susan—"

Both of their phones started ringing.

"Shit," Harri muttered. "This cannot be good." She pulled out her device. "It's Patty."

"I've got Sparx," Aisha whispered. She rose as she thumbed the controls on her phone and walked over to an isolated corner of the bar.

Harri tapped the answer icon on her own device. "What's up, Patty?"

"Have you seen tonight's news?" Her assistant's breathless voice managed to convey real worry.

"I'm at dinner with Aisha, so no."

"Check the Channel 12 twenty-four-hour newsfeed. One of our clients made the headlines."

Oh, shit! What had fake Rey done?

Harri waved over the bartender. "There's an extra twenty in your tip if you tune the TV to digital channel twelve-point-two and turn up the sound."

The bribe perked up the bartender's demeanor immensely. He pulled out the remote and switched the channel from the insipid sitcom airing on the station's main transmission to its sister newscast. The first image was Cobblestone's massive dark hand coming straight at the camera with his gravelly voice in the background.

"Get that outta my face. Yer scarin' the kids."

The camera shot switched to the exterior of Canyon Pointe General Hospital. Twilight shot fingers of pink and lavender light across the few clouds in the sky. A perky, young reporter stood near the main entrance. He practically shivered with excitement at covering a superhero story.

"At this point, hospital security rushed in and cleared the area." When the hospital's outdoor lights flickered on, the reporter poked at his glasses. "Captain Justice is represented by the Law Firm of Winters & Franklin. Our attempts at contacting them for comment have not been answered at this time."

Harri's heart pounded so hard she half-expected the organ to break through her ribs and escape. What had happened? Even more important, did anyone catch Fake Rey on camera?

Oh, shit. Of course, someone had. It may not have been the Channel 12 cameraman, but if they were in the pediatric wing of the hospital, a given by Cobblestone's words, someone was always filming.

The on-site reporter threw the broadcast back to the station. It was the primetime evening newscast, so it was no surprise when Ted Meadowfield's smirking face appeared onscreen.

"Thank you for that report, Greg." Ted turned to another camera. "To repeat tonight's top story, Canyon Point's newest superhero Captain Justice showed his true colors, and they're not red, white and blue. This additional footage was contributed by a parent at today's health fair."

Harri groaned. Kids. It had to be an event with kids. Why else would Cobblestone be at CPGH?

Ted's face disappeared, and shaky video of Captain Justice surrounded by young admirers replaced the news anchor. A little girl held a pen and what looked like a pink journal up to the superhero.

Fake Rey could be clearly heard on the video. "I don't sign *bleep* pink *bleep*!" Despite Channel 12's efforts to censor the audio, any viewer could read his lips. Parents gasped. Even the children looked shocked at their hero's profanity. The little girl with the journal started crying.

Those words and actions definitely confirmed Aisha's suspicions. That couldn't possibly be Rey. The kid wouldn't even swear in Spanish.

And he definitely wouldn't make a little girl cry.

But he made Francisco cry a couple of nights ago . . .

No, it was the fake who'd upset Francisco if Aisha was right. Harri swallowed hard. No wonder Ted was gloating. If Captain Justice crashed and burned, he might take their fledgling firm with him.

And the news anchor would thorough enjoy watching Harri be publicly humiliated.

Her phone's second line started ringing. She glanced at the caller ID. Cobblestone.

"Patty, let me call you back in a few minutes." Harri thumbed the controls to switch to the superhero. "Is this about the health fair?"

"You saw?" Cobblestone's deep voice rumbled through the receiver.

"It's all over Action 12 News! right now, so I'm assuming it's on every other station in town."

"I swear I tried to pull him aside and talk some sense into him, Ms. Winters." The superhero's voice was contrite. "He took off, and Sparx went after him. I ain't seen either of them since then."

"Thanks for trying. How'd the rest of the health fair go?" Pain throbbed in the middle of Harri's forehead.

"I promised that little girl a personal visit this weekend by a new lady superhero if that's all right," Cobblestone said. "Our mutual friend said she loves Ms. Franklin's makeover. I know the official announcement isn't until Monday, but if it's alright with you and Ms. Franklin?"

A little relief seeped through Harri along with a little guilt. She hadn't given the superhero enough credit for thinking on his feet, which made her just as guilty as the supervillians who underestimated him.

"Not a problem," she said. "I'll let Aisha know. And thanks for trying to clean up this mess." When he didn't say anything more, she asked, "Is there another problem?"

"Just a minute." The sounds in the background changed from muted voices to car traffic. "I know y'all are in tight with the Ghost Owl. Have you had him check out Tighty Whitey the last couple of days to make sure . . . he's the real deal?"

"You think someone's impersonating Captain Justice?"

"I wouldn't put anything past those Corvus assholes, Ms. Winters," Cobblestone stated.

A couple of clone and robot jokes aside, having Cobblestone repeat Aisha's assertion sent a chill through Harri.

"I'll have him check," she finally said.

Cobblestone exhaled gustily. "If you need any help . . . taking care of things, Ms. Winters, you know you can depend on me."

"I know," she replied fervently. "I promise I'll call you, even if it's to let you know this is nothing."

The bartender placed the salads in front of Harri as she signed off on the call. He glanced over his shoulder at the television screen before he looked at Harri and shook his head.

"I swear the attention always goes to these superheroes' heads. Do you need anything else, Ms. Winters?"

She smiled despite the urge to deliver a primal scream. "Just a refill on my diet cola, thanks."

While he trotted to the other side of the bar for her drink, Aisha stomped back to her seat. Or she tried to. Harri couldn't help noticing her partner grabbed anything remotely solid in order to stay on the ground. Aisha's conversation with Sparx must have went as well as hers with Cobblestone. Aisha glared at the TV screen as she resumed her seat.

"How do we spin this?" Harri murmured.

"I don't know yet." Aisha poked at her lobster salad. "He managed to lose Sparx around the warehouse district by throwing a semi trailer at her. So much for playing him in order to find out what his game is."

"We may already know." Harri waved at the TV. "Bad press can destroy a superhero faster than any weapon devised by a supervillain."

Aisha stared at the screen. "We need to find a way to secure this asshole before we question him. Maybe Tim and Arthur will have some ideas." She looked at Harri. "Are you going to throw a hissy fit if I call Eddie for suggestions?"

For once, the mention of her ex-husband didn't irritate Harri.

"Not if it gets us Rey back." Her phone buzzed, and she checked the caller ID. Patty again. Damn, she'd totally forgotten to call back her assistant. She thumbed the answer icon.

"Sorry, Patty. I—"

"Harri, we don't know what to do! Tim's gone after Rey!"

Chapter 19

Aisha forced a bite of the salad into her mouth. The situation with the imposter had killed her appetite, but she was eating for two now. However, Patty's warning buried her appetite and capped it with a headstone.

"Shit," Harri muttered as she pocketed her phone. She waved for the bartender, who nodded at her motions for boxes and the check. "We need to get our dinners to go. Things just went from bad to worse. Tim went after him."

In the midst of the PR disaster, Harri had forgotten about Aisha's blossoming powers. The lobster salad turned to sawdust in her mouth at another awful realization. Once she could finally swallow, she whispered, "We should have told them what was going on."

"We didn't have proof, and we have no idea where Rey is," Harri murmured. She glanced around the room, but most of the patrons had been called to their tables. "We didn't want to spook our imposter."

"But Tim has no idea what kind of mess he's getting into," Aisha hissed under her breath.

From the shift in Harri's expression, the danger to her boyfriend finally sank through her bravado.

The bartender brought over to-go containers and started to box up their dinners. Aisha snagged the crackers from her plate while Harri pulled out a wad of cash from her wallet.

At her overly generous tip, he grinned. "Can I get you ladies drinks to go as well?"

"Please," Harri said. As he headed back to the soft drink dispensers, she turned back to Aisha. "Give Sparx another call."

"And tell her what?" Aisha growled back. "'Please let a fake superhero beat you up instead of my partner's non-super boyfriend'?"

"You ladies have a good evening." The bartender set their to-go cups on the counter.

"Thank you." Harri smiled until he sauntered to the other end of the bar.

She glared at Aisha. "That's not what I meant, and you know it." Harri seized their bag of food and her cola before she stalked out of the bar.

Aisha resisted the urge to roll her eyes. Typical Harri. Run away from an argument because it hit too close to her emotions. Damn, she'd fallen harder for Canyon than either Aisha or Jeremy had suspected. She grabbed her drink and followed Harri to the exit.

The valet brought Harri's Honda to a stop in front of them. Harri handed the kid a tip, and both women slid into their seats.

"Call her!" Harri practically shouted as she floored the accelerator. The little Honda whined in agreement. Or maybe the car was begging for its life.

Aisha pulled out her phone and tapped the icon for Qiang's cell number.

"Reilly residence." Damn, that meant she was at home and her family was in the room.

"This is about the account we discussed earlier."

"One moment, please." Rustling came over the receiver followed by Sparx saying, "I need to take this." A child's voice murmured in the background. "Finish your vegetables, Connor, and then you can have some cake." The background noise faded.

"I'm not your personal errand girl, Franklin," Qiang snapped.

"I know." Aisha blew out a deep breath. "I wouldn't have called if the Ghost Owl hadn't gone after Captain Justice a few minutes ago."

"The Ghost Owl . . ."

Aisha could have sworn she heard Qiang's brain cells firing.

"You know who Jatz'om Kuh is," she breathed.

"I also know he's in deep shit." Aisha swallowed hard. "He looks at Captain Justice as a protégé, and he doesn't realize—" Her vision blurred. This whole mess was getting worse.

"He doesn't realize some idiot villain is mind-controlling CJ." Qiang's sigh came through the receiver.

Part of Aisha hoped the superhero was right, that someone had replaced Rey's amulet and were using it to control him. But deep down, she knew something worse was happening.

"That's what we suspect."

Qiang clicked her tongue. "I know you didn't want to debut Molly's new look until Monday morning, but I'd feel better if I have some back-up."

"Why her?"

"Because her sonic powers will have some effect on your boyfriend and his sensitive ears." Qiang chuckled. "And we might leave some of the city intact. I don't suppose one of your staff geniuses have a way to track the Ghost Owl."

"They're working on it. Meet us on the roof of the Lechuza Building."

Qiang was silent for a long moment before she made a disgusted sound in the back of her throat. "I am such a dumbass. Look, I'm not going to ask the obvious question right now, but I don't know if I trust a lawyer who's a vigilante on the side."

"What?" Aisha stared at her phone for a second before she returned it to her ear. "Neither Harri or I is the Ghost Owl!"

"Uh-huh," Qiang drawled. "And which one of you has superpowers?"

"Shit," Aisha muttered. "Molly blabbed, didn't she?" When Qiang didn't answer, Aisha continued in a rush, "I've only had my powers for a week, and they are caused by a change in my medical condition. The Ghost Owl's been around a lot longer than that."

Qiang was quiet for a long time. Aisha half-expected her to hang up on the call. Finally, the superheroine said, "If you're going to make me run your personal errands, my babysitter's fees are coming out of your share of my endorsements."

Aisha breathed a sigh of relief. "Deal. We'll see you in a few minutes."

Harri waited until Aisha disconnected the call before she said, "What deal did you make without consulting me?"

"Chill. It's Qiang's babysitting fees for tonight."

"Her parents—"

"—are getting to old to handle a preteen on the spectrum," Aisha bit out. "Her next-door neighbor is the Northside High School's wrestling coach, and his son has an excellent rapport with Connor. The kid deserves to get paid if we're using Sparx as our personal fixer."

A quiver of unease about her own situation ran through Aisha. If something has happened to Rey, and Serena was right about her powers being temporary, how the hell could she handle single parenthood with a super baby?

— ● —

Harri tapped the phone button on her steering wheel.

Arthur answered a moment later with no preface or pleasantries. "The Owl's headed for Veterans Park. CJ's GPS shows him in the center at the memorial statue."

"Are you sure you're not telepathic, Mr. Drallhickey?" She chuckled.

"No, but are you going to tell me what's really going on?"

"We're not quite sure." Harri glanced at Aisha, but her partner stared at traffic.

"What do you want me to tell Agent Lewis when he arrives?"

Harri's heart jumped to her throat. "Why is Eddie on his way to the office?"

"Because he called here, and I couldn't give him a satisfactory answer regarding the events at the hospital this afternoon," Arthur snapped. "When a superhero does something stupid, and the local constabulary doesn't take point, it becomes federal jurisdiction. Not to mention, Agent Lewis is far too involved in firm business based on his prior relationship with you."

Arthur never snapped. Hell, between his shyness and mild stammer, the man never raised his voice unless he was panicking.

"I'm sorry, Arthur," Harri said. "We don't know what's going on with CJ. Aisha and I were debating that over dinner ourselves."

Arthur's voice softened. "Ms. Franklin, whatever is happening, this isn't about you and the baby. He loves you."

"I-I know," Aisha choked out.

"Arthur," Harri interjected. "Sparx and the hero formerly known as Screaming Orgasm are meeting us on the roof. Do you have anything to give them they can use to track our boys?"

"Yes, ma'am," Arthur assured. "They'll be ready when you arrive."

— •— —

Despite working out in Tim's gym for the last month, Harri was out of breath by the time she and Aisha reached the door to the roof.

"Why didn't they put in an elevator that went all the way up when they built this building?" she wheezed.

"People were more fit a century ago," Aisha remarked. "Not to mention, this is supposed to be the fire escape, not a regular staircase.

Of course, the bitch wasn't out of breath. Damn superpowers.

Harri yanked the door open and tried to suck in enough air before she walked onto the roof. Arthur stood with Sparx and the renamed Nix, already in their superhero duds. Harri grimaced at the fourth figure. Somehow, her ex-husband beat them to the office building.

At the creak of hinges, all four of them turned to look at the two attorneys.

"What's the word, Arthur?" Harri asked, deliberately ignoring Eddie.

"I'm tracking both men by the GPS on their phones." He waved at the bulkier device Sparx held. "I designed an insulated tracker I'm hoping will be sufficiently resistant to her electromagnetic abilities." He crossed his fingers on his free hand.

"Can we track the ladies as well?" Aisha asked.

Arthur nodded. "If Corvus is behind this, we should know pretty damn quick."

"Shit. Them again?" Eddie muttered.

Harri blinked. She was long used to her ex's potty mouth, but Arthur swearing made the last two days even weirder than usual.

"All right." She clapped her hands together. "The mission is to get the Ghost Owl to back off Captain Justice."

"You sure this is . . ."

Harri shot an ugly look at Eddie.

Thank god, he got her silent message. "Captain Justice? This behavior is not like him."

She glanced at Aisha. "Actually, we don't know if someone is mind-controlling Captain Justice, or if someone is pretending to be him."

"One of us knows," Aisha hissed.

"Whoa!" Sparx held up her gloved palms. "You're telling us that's not Rey?"

Leave it to another super to out his real identity. Oh, hell, what was she thinking? Everyone on the roof knew Rey Garcia and Captain Justice were the same person.

Again, Harri glanced at her partner, but Aisha's mouth was set in a grim, tight line.

"No, whoever he is, he's not our Rey," Harri said. "We had a plan to get him to out himself, but before we could warn our staff or anyone else, the Ghost Owl decided to take matters into his own hands."

"So my powers may not have an effect on this imposter?" Nix nibbled her bottom lip.

"If he's a fake, you'll both be able to hurt him." Harri shook her head. "I'm hoping you two catch up with the Owl before any of you take on the guy wearing CJ's tighty-whities."

Eddie chuckled at her using Cobblestone's slur for Rey. The other super still hadn't quite forgiven Rey for beating him unconscious. Though in all fairness, Corvus had extorted Cobblestone into killing Aisha.

"The Ghost Owl isn't a super, is he?" Sparx crossed her arms.

"No, he isn't," Harri replied. "And between you ladies, CJ, and Cobblestone covering the east side of Canyon Pointe these days, he planned to retire. I want him off the streets, too, but I don't want to see him get hurt or killed to do it."

"We need to get moving." Nix watched the screen on the little device Arthur had given her. "It looks like the Ghost Owl will intercept the fake CJ in the middle of Veterans' Memorial Park."

Sparx jabbed a finger in Harri's direction. "We are not finished with this conversation, ladies." The superhero rose into the air. Air shimmered, but the wavering wasn't caused by the heat emanating from the roof. Nix leapt and crouched on top of the magnetic disc Sparx created and pulled along with her. The dark hulk of the Canyon Building soon hid the women from view.

Eddie crossed his arms. "Why didn't you two call me when this started?"

Harri jammed her fists on her hips and matched his wide-legged stance. "The same reason I didn't tell Tim. Because you both would have gone on some half-cocked crusade—"

"You mean like the one Tim's on right now?" Eddie shot back.

"Get your dick out of the equation!" Harri waved her index finger under her nose.

"Do you have any idea how many calls my office had to field this evening after Tighty Whitey treated that little girl like shit?"

"Stop it, you two!"

Harri and Eddie both looked at Aisha, who appeared to be on the verge of tears.

"I'm sorry, sweetie," Harri said. "You're right."

Eddie exhaled loudly. "I'm sorry, too. I tried to reach Tim on my way here. He's ignoring my calls."

"He's ignoring my calls, too," Arthur said. "I think he's turned off notifications. I don't dare turn them back on remotely. It may put him in more danger from this imposter."

Their IT guy had been so quiet Harri had forgotten he was on the roof with them.

"I hope Sparx and Nix stop Tim before he does something stupid," Aisha murmured. "I don't envy their task."

"We have the suckiest part of the job." Harri scowled in the direction the two superheroes had taken. "We wait."

She just prayed Tim would listen to them because he sure as hell wasn't answering any of her calls either.

— • —

Sitting on her own couch, Harri jumped when her phone buzzed twenty minutes later. It had taken her five of those minutes to convince Eddie to go home to his pregnant wife and their oldest child. Eddie didn't need to be swallowed up in Harri's problems, but he insisted she keep him updated.

Which meant he was seriously worried about Tim doing something stupid, too.

She checked the caller ID. Sparx.

Harri glanced at Aisha, who set aside her mug of herbal tea and nodded.

Trepidation shivered across her skin. Sparx had never really forgiven Harri for getting the better of the super when Seismic Shift had sent her to kill Harri. She couldn't blame Sparx. Shift had threatened to murder her family if she didn't comply. However, Sparx always called Aisha regarding any interaction since she had become a client.

Harri thumbed the answer icon. "Hello?"

"Meet me at Canyon Pointe General Hospital." In the background, a siren wailed, but it didn't cover the crackle of anger in Sparx's voice. "Tim was mugged. He's in pretty bad shape."

She couldn't speak freely if she was using such an obvious story. Or worse, Tim had been exposed as the Ghost Owl.

Harri's stomach clenched at the possible revelation. Everything they'd worked for over the past couple of months may have been destroyed. "Did-did you catch the person who did it?"

"No." Someone else spoke to Sparx in the background. "Harri?" Her voice shifted to concern. "Does any of Tim's family live close by? The paramedic says Tim is going to need surgery."

"N-no, he doesn't have any family left," she managed to choke out before the phone slipped from her grasp. It was happening all over again. She should never have slept with him. She cursed everyone she cared about.

Aisha caught the phone before it hit the floor. "Sparx?"

Harri buried her face in her hands. This couldn't be happening.

"Miguel Esperanza is Tim's medical power of attorney." Aisha's voice penetrated the fog of fear that enveloped Harri. "We're on our way." Another pause. "Thanks. I'll let Arthur know to expect her." The electronic beep sounded terribly loud in the cavernous expanse of Harri's loft.

Aisha's familiar touch stroked the back of Harri's neck. "Why don't you stay here? I'll go with Miguel."

Harri dropped her hands. Anger replaced the comfort her best friend offered. Anger was an even older companion than fear, as cozy as her favorite bathrobe.

"No." She looked at Aisha and shook her head. "I need to be there." She held out her hand for her phone. "I'll call Jeremy. He can put up Patty and the kids in case the imposter comes back here."

"No." Aisha's expression carried the same resolve it always did when she faced a crisis. "If you don't want me to go to the hospital with you, I won't, but Nix is on her way back here with the Ghost Owl costume. Between the two of us and Arthur, we can protect Patty and the kids if he comes back here."

"But—" Horrible visions danced in Harri's mind.

"I'm not getting chased out of my own home anymore," Aisha said sternly. "Cal and Corvus messing up my life were bad enough. I'm not letting some two-bit imposter hurt the people I love."

"But—"

"We'll be fine." Aisha handed the phone back to her. "Go take care of your boyfriend."

Boyfriend. Shit. Harri didn't have the brain space to make a snarky reply. The rage and fear inside her were too thick.

She rose from the couch. "I'll call you once I know something."

Sure, Aisha said they'd be fine, but Harri's gut said the game had seriously changed.

And not in their fledgling firm's favor.

CHAPTER 20

Harri increased her pace to keep up with Miguel as they headed for Canyon Pointe General Hospital's ER entrance. They had barely spoken a word since she knocked on his door and told him of Tim's situation.

The glass doors whooshed open, and she spotted Sparx pacing the waiting area as far as she could get from the reception desk. The other patients and family gave the superhero a wide berth.

When Harri got closer to Sparx, she understood why. The fine hairs all over her body stood at attention from the static the superhero was throwing off. On the other hand, Miguel headed straight to the nurse behind the reception desk with his wad of paperwork in his fist.

"What happened?" Harri murmured.

"Let's go outside before I accidentally blow the ER's wiring and equipment," Sparx muttered back.

Miguel looked up from his conversation with the admissions nurse as they passed him. Harri gestured at Sparx and mimed talking with her hand. He nodded and turned his attention back to the nurse.

Despite full night, the concrete walkway still gave off waves of heat. Harri followed Sparx to a bench.

"We didn't reach Tim in time," the superhero said without preamble. "I don't know if that bastard spotted him from the air or what, but he changed course and kicked up his speed." Her dark eyes sparked under the halogen security lamps. "You should have told us."

"It wasn't my secret to share." Harri didn't flinch from Sparx's glare.

"Shit, Winters!" Sparx threw her hands in the air. Static crackled and danced along her gloves and the sleeves of her hero togs. "I'm trying to clean up my act. Then I find out the firm I signed with has a former supervillain working for said firm. I thought okay, fine, I can deal with a little white savior attitude. But then I find out you're also harboring a vigilante!"

Harri sighed and leaned back. "Has it occurred to you that you aren't the only one trying to fly straight? Or the only one looking for a second chance?"

Sparx's gaze dropped. Good. Maybe she'd gotten through her head she'd be awaiting trial right now if Harri had pressed charges for attempted murder.

"You said surgery when you called from the ambulance?" she prompted.

Sparx leaned her back against the wooden slats, too. "At least three broken ribs, a concussion, and internal bleeding. When we arrived, the asshole pretending to be Rey stomped on Tim's left femur before he flew off. I called for the ambulance, and Nix and I stripped off anything identifying Tim as Jatz'om Kuh before the paramedics arrived."

Like everyone living on the northeast side of Canyon Pointe, she referred to the Ghost Owl's Mayan name.

Sparx shook her head. "Like I told Franklin, I sent Nix back to your office with his stuff." Despite their predicament, Sparx chuckled. "Thank Buddha, your boy had on shorts and a t-shirt under his tactical gear."

"Thank you," Harri whispered.

"It gets worse." Sparx shook her head. "The imposter must have figured out we were using Rey's phone to track him. Right before the ambulance arrived at the park, his signal disappeared from the screens of Arthur's doohickeys."

Harri stared up at the night sky. With the city's light pollution, she could only make out a few stars. "Well, that's just . . . great," she finished lamely.

"Ms. Winters!" Miguel stood outside the sliding glass doors to the ER. He waved both hands over his head.

Harri jumped to her feet. "Thanks for your help tonight, Sparx. Go home and be with your family."

"Winters?"

Harri paused at the touch on her arm.

Sparx stood beside her and dropped her gloved hand to her side. "Keep me updated on Tim's condition. And if you need help finding this bastard . . ."

Not trusting herself to speak, Harri nodded. The superhero rose into the air until her uniform blended with the night sky. Harri turned and strode towards the ever-patient Miguel.

She felt sick about Rey's disappearance and what the imposter had done to Tim. She couldn't imagine how Aisha was feeling right now.

After Arthur brought Nix upstairs, Aisha let her into Harri's loft and showed her the amenities. She tried to keep her composure, but the younger woman's account of the imposter attacking Tim left an ugly feeling within her. Nothing like her grief over her failed marriage. Now, she understood Harri's uncontrollable rages in their teen years.

"You sure Ms. Winters won't mind?" Molly cocked her head, concern on her pretty, unmasked features.

"You are doing us a favor by staying here tonight." Aisha crossed her arms. "I'm not sure Arthur and I can handle the man impersonating Captain Justice by ourselves."

"You mean you'd have a hard time clocking the man who looks just like your baby's daddy?" Despite her ditz act, Molly was pretty damn sharp.

"You got me." Aisha held up her hands in surrender. "You want some tea?"

"After tonight, you wouldn't happen to have anything stronger, would you?"

Aisha laughed and headed toward the kitchen. "I'm afraid all either of us has are wine and scotch."

"I'll take the scotch."

After Aisha poured the superhero a tumbler of the amber alcohol and made herself a cup of chamomile, she sat on the stool next to Molly.

"Do you have a plan for raising the baby if we can't get the real Captain Justice back?" Molly asked softly as she stared at the liquid in her glass.

Aisha frowned as she regarded the younger woman. "What's that supposed to mean?"

"Without him here, the government's going to make a case the kid is too much for you to handle." Molly waved her hand. "Especially with the chaos you've had in your life the last few months."

There was something more to the superhero's words than the usual mistrust of the feds. "You're talking as if you have experience in this area."

"Yeah, I do." Molly took a sip of her scotch before she turned and faced Aisha. "The government took me and my sister from our mom, who is a super, too. She could totally handle us, but they claimed she couldn't because she wasn't married and she was a bad influence."

"I thought your grandmother raised the two of you." Aisha sipped her tea.

"When Grandmama found out Mom lost custody, she pulled a few favors to get herself assigned as our guardian." From the look in Molly's eyes, she was reliving the past pain. "Mom never forgave Grandmama for not helping her get us back. That's when she turned to supervilliany."

"Wait a minute." Aisha stared at the superhero. "Your mother was a supervillain? You told me your parents died when someone attacked your grandmother."

Molly's new blond hair emphasized the red flush of her cheeks. "Yeah. I'm . . . I still repeat the story Grandmama insisted we tell people. I'm sorry."

"I won't repeat it. Attorney-client privilege applies." Aisha smiled. "What about your dad?"

"We have no idea who he is." Molly shrugged, but the lack of knowledge obviously bothered her a lot. "Grandmama always claimed he was the reason Mom turned to villainy, so she forbade us from asking about him because she didn't want the same to happen to us."

"But you don't think that's the case?"

The younger woman shook her head. "I think Grandmama just didn't like him. And Mom was pretty young when she got pregnant with me and Kerry, not to mention unmarried. Grandmama believed supers have an obligation to exhibit a moral standard to the public."

Dammit. Aisha had to force her fingers to relax before she broke her teacup. Not even Grandma Harri had taken her granddaughter away from her own son, even if it would have been in Harri's best interests. But not to know where you came from?

"Would you like to find your father?"

A glimmer of hope flickered in Molly's glittery eyes. "Is that even possible?"

"Possible, yes." Aisha waved her hand side to side. "Successful, I can't guarantee. Let's get through the current crisis, and I'll see what I can find out for you."

"Thank you!" Molly threw her arms around Aisha.

Aisha carefully returned the hug. Harri was right. She really didn't know how good the Franklin clan had it until she saw the shit other people put their kids through.

Harri listened to Miguel with the same numb horror she'd felt when first her mother had been killed, then her grandmother was diagnosed with cancer, and finally her father, higher on coke than she thought was possible and still be functional, had driven his Porsche over the cliff.

"With the internal injuries and bleeding, they couldn't wait for us to get here." Miguel led her down a hallway in the hospital. One she'd never been down before. "While his injuries are severe, they see no reason why he won't completely recover, barring any complications. The surgeon has been told that family has arrived. I told them you are his fiancée."

"You can't do that," Harri protested. "HIPPA regulations prohibit—"

"I'm the medical power of attorney since Tim is in no position to argue." A rueful smile twisted Miguel's thick moustache into a comical position. "I also told the lady from legal his attorney had drafted a new POA naming you as primary, but he didn't have a chance to sign it before he was attacked. Therefore, in my power, I had you made my backup until such time Mr. Canyon rescinded yours or my powers. So for now, if anyone asks, you are Tim's fiancée, and he's too poor to buy you a ring so he gave you part ownership of the Lechuza Building as a wedding present."

Harri couldn't help herself. She started laughing at Miguel's audacity.

A sign said "Surgical Waiting". They turned into the room. Luckily, no one else was there because they certainly would have questioned her sanity. But at this time of night, the surgical area of the hospital was as silent as a tomb. Someone had even turned off the sound on the TV mounted on the far wall.

However, the screen showed the late-night edition of Action 12 News! Instead of Essie Morales's friendly face, the new kid, Kent something or other, reviewed the day's local headlines. The top of which was the fake Captain Justice at the children's health fair held in this very hospital.

Harri dropped onto one of the empty couches. Miguel crossed to the coffee pot and poured them each a cup of what smelled like stale black java. He returned and handed her one cup before he gingerly lowered himself beside her.

"You want to tell me what's really going on, Harri?"

Miguel rarely called her by her first name, much less her nickname. It showed just how bad things had gotten.

Softly, she laid out the details. Rey's increasingly bizarre behavior. Aisha's suspicions. Their plan to get him to expose himself as a fraud.

"Before we could put anything into motion, this happened." Harri waved her cup at the TV screen.

"You didn't even consult Tim?" Miguel stared at her, aghast.

"We were going to tell him once we had proof and the location of the real Rey—"

"And how exactly were you planning to subdue the imposter?"

"Aisha said Tim has a medical scanner that produces sonics that would stun him like Screaming Orgasm, um, Nix's powers."

"*Mi Dios!*" Miguel gave her the same horrified look she'd given the jury during Doctor Malevolent's trial. "I know you hate kids, Harri, but you'd put your best friend's unborn child in the middle of a possible battle with someone who's likely a supervillain?"

"That's not—" She started, but Miguel slammed his cup on the end table, sloshing the awful coffee over the side. He jumped to his feet and began pacing, muttering in Spanish. She didn't catch much of it, but "puta" stood out loud and clear, and it was pretty obvious who the word was aimed out.

"What the hell were you thinking?" Miguel asked, finally switching back to English. "My sons and Patty's daughter are living in that building, and you didn't think we could handle the truth?"

He was right. God help her, he was totally right. Just like Tim was. In her need to create the perfect family, she put everyone in danger.

"You're right," she said softly.

Miguel stopped his pacing and stared at her. "What?"

"You're right." She met his gaze. "I'm so used to being on my own and fixing my own problems I didn't consider how this would affect the rest of you. I'm sorry."

He grunted. "As long as we got that straight." He exhaled loudly and raked his calloused fingers through his shaggy salt-and-pepper locks. "Your plan wasn't a bad one, but we'll never get close enough to him now to implement it. He'll run or kill any super who gets near him after his encounter with Jatz'om Kuh."

Harri frowned. The idea running through her mind was insane, but it just might work. "What about the new exoskeleton?"

Miguel shook his head. "It's going to take Tim weeks, if not months, to recover from his injuries—"

"What if someone else uses it?"

Shock chased the confusion from Miguel's face as he realized her intent. "Getting yourself killed isn't the way to make things right, Harri!"

"I don't plan on getting myself killed." She reached into her purse for the notebook and pen for the notes too sensitive to commit to an electronic device. "If Francisco can do the math, Arthur, you, and I can finish the suit. Plus, Tim has some of that non-reflective stuff in his lab that absorbs electromagnetic waves. Our fake Captain Justice will never see me coming." She grinned. "Not until it's too late."

Miguel crossed his arms. His bushy eyebrows twitched as he considered her plan. "If he has Rey's abilities, the sonics will not keep him down for long. How do you plan to contain him?"

"We drug him until we get him someplace where Cobblestone can chain him."

"Needles cannot penetrate Rey's skin," Miguel reminded her.

"We can use knock-out gas . . ." Her face dropped into her hands momentarily before she looked back up at Miguel. "That's how his cronies captured Rey the other morning. They gassed him."

Miguel's expression looked as bleak as she felt. "Then let us hope he is still alive, or all of this will be for nothing."

CHAPTER 21

Harri sat beside Tim's hospital bed and held his hand, waiting desperately for him to wake up. Dawn sent streamers of gold through the window. The light glinted off the tubes and lines running from his body to various machines and devices. The déjà vu was what was killing her. Grandma Harri had been in the same straits, but she never opened her eyes again.

She'd sent Miguel home after they'd spoken to the surgeon. The doctor's post-op prognosis was guarded but fairly optimistic. She found herself grasping that little sliver of hope, expecting it to cut her to shreds any minute. But the EKG kept its steady rhythm as the hours had worn on through the rest of the night.

At the knock on the door, Harri half-expected the duty nurse with another offer of a blanket and pillow, but it was Serena's green-haired head that poked around the corner.

"How did you know we were here?" Harri croaked. Her throat was pretty damn sore with the sobs she refused to release.

"Aisha told me. And no, the asshole who did this didn't come back to Lechuza last night." Serena slid the rest of the way into the room and regarded the man in the bed. Glass-sharp irritation radiated from her. "I told him this was how things would end."

"He's not dead," Harri snapped.

"Yeah, because you sent Sparx and Nix after him." Serena shook her head as she stared at Tim's still form. "God help me, where do I even start?"

Relief sparked in Harri's chest. "You can fix his injuries?"

The younger woman frowned. "Not all of them. Not without killing myself in the process, which I will not do." She shot a glare at Harri. "So don't ask."

"What about transferring my life force to him?"

Serena's jaw dropped and hung open a few seconds before she closed it with an audible click of her teeth. After a long pause, she said, "So you're not the big, bad attorney you pretend to be."

"That's not it." Harri stroked the fingers of Tim's hand, the one she'd been holding for the last several hours. "I think I love him."

"I see." Serena sighed and shook her head. "I've never transferred energy from one person to another like that, and I'm not about to try in a very public hospital. I can do little bits here and there to help him without rousing suspicion." She played with the strap of her shoulder bag. "We will help you guard him."

We. In other words, not just Harri's little family, which was already strained to its limits, but the super community. One of their own was down, even if he was an unregistered vigilante.

"I can stay with him until Nix gets here this afternoon," Serena continued. "Cobblestone said he'd take the night shift. So, go home, get some sleep, figure out how to get Rey back, and take down the bastard who did this."

"Thank you." Harri swiped at the one tear that managed to escape. They were doing this for Rey and Tim, not her. It didn't make her any less grateful.

The tension keeping her awake all night drained from her body. "I need to call a ride," she tried to say around a yawn she couldn't stifle.

"I brought your car, assuming you can drive?" Serena's right eyebrow rose. The bitch was probably reading Harri's biorhythms or something from the skeptical expression on the super's face.

"I think I can manage," Harri said dryly as she stood.

Serena hesitated for just a moment, but held out the fob to Harri's Honda anyway. "It's in the third twenty-minute slot on the first floor of the parking garage. Good luck on whatever you and Miguel are planning."

Harri jerked at the accusation, but managed to hold her tongue. The fewer people who knew about their plot to take down the man impersonating Rey, the better.

After a quick kiss on Tim's forehead, Harri marched for the parking garage. When they nailed the fake to the wall and rescued Rey, she was going to have a little one-on-one talk with the head of Corvus about messing with any of her clients.

And she'd be using one of Corvus's cattle prods when she did.

Camera lights flashed in Aisha's eyes while she stood in front of the Lechuza Building at ten a.m. She'd considered cancelling Nix's rebranding press conference, but Molly had insisted on moving it up. Bless her, the superhero pointed out the public needed to see the rest of the Winters & Franklin clientele had faith in the firm, and that the firm had faith in them.

And damn if the superhero didn't have most of the press eating out of her hand. Nix was positive and flirty, but not overtly sexual, as they had practiced.

"Ms. Franklin?" Essie Morales waved her hand for attention. Bob the cameraman stood next to her, a slight frown on the half of his face Aisha could see. Neither seemed particularly happy, which gave her enough warning.

She couldn't fault either of them for doing their jobs. And they couldn't ignore yesterday's incident at the children's health fair without accusations of favoritism. Nella Lopez, the news producer at Action 12 News!, had too much integrity despite their friendly professional relationship.

Aisha nodded.

"Does Winters & Franklin have any comment on Captain Justice's actions at the children's health fair?" Essie breathlessly asked.

Tension crackled amid the silence as the entire press corps of Canyon Pointe waited for Aisha's answer.

"Captain Justice's behavior yesterday does not reflect the tenets our firm. We are currently re-evaluating our relationship with him," she replied coolly. "Beyond that, we have no comment."

"Have you or your partner spoken with Captain Justice since yesterday's incident?" Bill Hallas's question rose above the rest of the chatter. The *Canyon Pointe Tribune* columnist was someone she could normally count on to provide impartial and factual analysis on the super community, but his recent pieces after the Seismic Shift arrest had started to lean towards an anti-hero bias.

Still, she'd never outright lied to the press, and she couldn't start now. Not if she and Harri hoped their firm would survive this mess.

"Bill, you know I can't comment on that. Attorney-client privilege applies to any form of client communications." She prayed her face didn't show her trepidation when she smiled. "Does anyone have another question for Nix?"

"Attorney-client privilege doesn't apply to criminal acts, Ms. Franklin!" Hallas shouted. So much for trying to change the subject.

"Last time I checked, it wasn't illegal to be rude," Aisha replied calmly. "If it were, everyone present would be in the city jail, including you and me."

Most of the journalists chuckled at her rejoinder, but a few had scowls. The incident between the fake Captain Justice and the little girl had hit deeper than she realized.

"Now, does anyone have an actual question for Nix?" When no one immediately jumped, she broadened her smile. "Thank you for coming."

Nix didn't need any additional guidance. She smiled and nodded at the crowd of journalists before she headed into the office building, holding the door open for Aisha. She followed the superhero inside, part of her expecting a tomato in the back.

Or a bullet.

Okay, maybe not a bullet. She didn't need to be outed today. Not so soon after the children's health fair incident.

Patty buzzed them through the second set of bullet-proof glass security doors. Aisha glanced over her shoulder. The reporters were packing up and returning to their vehicles.

All except Bill Hallas, who stared daggers at her. Now what had crawled up his shorts? From his expression, it almost seemed like his feelings were personal.

"That went a little better than I expected," Nix remarked.

"I'm sorry." Aisha shook her head. "You shouldn't be in the middle of this trouble with another super."

"I've been in the middle of trouble with supers since I could walk." Nix gave her a rueful smile. "Thanks for the remake and for letting me park my cycle in here."

Aisha held out her hand. "Thanks again for bringing Tim's gear back here. And for keeping an eye on him this evening."

"*De nada.*" Nix grabbed Aisha's offered palm and shook it. She winced when Aisha applied a little too much force.

Damn. She quickly released the super's hand. If she wasn't more careful, she could seriously injure someone.

Nix pivoted with a final smile and sauntered toward the corridor leading to the side door. Patty followed her in order to turn off the security panel and let Nix out, then reset the alarms.

Aisha glanced in Harri's office, but it was still empty. Last she knew, Serena planned to go to the hospital and send Harri home, but Aisha hadn't seen or heard her partner this morning. It wasn't like her partner to hide from any problems.

Unless she had collapsed from sheer exhaustion.

After the tense press conference, Aisha didn't have the energy to hunt down anyone at the moment either. Fatigue plucked at her as she strode into her own office, closed the door, and flopped full-length on her longer couch. Her new desk should arrive tomorrow, and she could ditch the folding table.

She closed her eyes against the worry threatening to overwhelm her tiredness. A new desk was a relatively minor expense. Tim's medical bills though . . .

He had no insurance. If he ended up in bankruptcy over the medical costs, the court's trustee could and would seize all his assets, including the Lechuza Building. There was no way she and Harri could buy his half out right now. Had their silence regarding the fake Captain Justice condemned their friends living in the newly renovated apartments to homelessness?

Oh, hell, she didn't have health insurance anymore either. The only reason Patty did was due to her wrongful termination lawsuit against the city. After Samuels was arrested, Acting Mayor Benevides had done his best to clean up his predecessor's mess. Patty's settlement had included health coverage for her and Grace for an additional year.

Aisha and Harri had started shopping for a policy for the firm and its employees, but they hadn't gotten far. Aisha rubbed her abdomen. Now, she would be classified as having a pre-existing condition. She and her son were screwed. The government would take her baby because she couldn't provide insurance.

The creak of her office door preceded the scent of cinnamon. Aisha opened her eyes. Patty crossed the room and set one steaming mug on the coffee table. The other she kept in hand and sat on the matching stuffed chair.

"Is it decaf?" Aisha swung her legs to the floor and sat upright.

"Decaf cinnamon tea for both of us." Patty sipped from her own cup.

"Would you please call the temp agency back?"

"Nope." Patty slurped more tea. After last night's crap with the imposter, she'd canceled the temp contract. Aisha hadn't known what their assistant had done until Nix arrived for her press conference, and Patty was sitting at her desk in the reception area.

Good grief, the woman had a baby less than a week ago.

"You're supposed to be on maternity leave, Patty." Aisha couldn't keep the weariness out of her voice. She'd been awake most of the night, expecting the fake Rey to fly into their loft at any moment. The snatches of sleep she'd managed were plagued by nightmares of him killing everyone who lived in the Lechuza Building's apartments.

"I know."

The nightmare version of Patty had shown the same surety before fake Rey had torn her in half. He'd turned to Aisha in her dream and handed her the crushed form of baby Grace.

The light-headedness hit Aisha hard. She grabbed for the couch cushions and missed. Not that they were heavy enough to keep her grounded. She floated into the air, doing a slow somersault as she rose toward the ceiling. Damn. She couldn't even summon the strength to concentrate on landing.

Patty set her mug on the coffee table and stood. With a jump, she grabbed Aisha as she floated by doing a second somersault and pulled her back down to the couch.

Aisha grabbed the closest upholstered arm and forced her tired brain to focus on gravity. Her rear end settled back on the cushion where she started.

"I don't know how you can do the weightless thing without puking," Patty said as she resumed her own seat. "I was worshipping the porcelain god every morning of my first trimester without floating all over creation."

"No offense, but I'm keeping my fingers crossed I don't get morning sick because I won't be able to limit any vomit to the toilet." Aisha picked up her mug and took a sip. "Is Harri up in her loft? I need to let her know the turn public opinion has taken on Captain Justice. We need a PR plan."

"You mean fake Rey, and no, she's not upstairs, but please let her sleep," Patty begged. "A few more hours aren't going hurt us."

"Where the hell is she sleeping?"

Patty sighed. "She went down to the basement when she got back from the hospital. I think she's sleeping in Tim's bed." She frowned as she picked up her mug. "She finally meets a guy she likes, and this happens."

"Harri and Tim have both been through worse." Aisha tried to project a smile over the rim of her cup. "I can't think of anyone better to get him through the physical therapy he'll need."

Yeah, Harri and Tim would be okay when this was all over. Aisha had no doubt about that, but would she?

———— •—•—• ————

Harri blinked the sweat out of her eyes. The two-hour catnap hadn't been enough, but it would have to do until they finished the exoskeleton prototype. She reached for the next bolt only to have a small brown hand press it to her fingers.

"Thanks, Francisco." She placed a rubber gasket over it and pushed the bolt into the pre-drilled hole.

Francisco handed her the necessary nut. She spun the little piece of metal until she was sure it wouldn't fall off the bolt. Miguel's youngest handed her the ratchet, and she tightened the nut.

She wiped the sweat from her forehead, leaned back, and stretched before she smiled at Francisco. "Did you get the math done?"

"Yes, ma'am." He nodded, his brown eyes far more serious than a seven-year-old's should be. "Mr. Tim had enough deuterium batteries to fuel the suit for an hour for him. You'll have enough for one hour and thirty-six minutes."

"Wait a minute," she protested. "I'm like half his size. Shouldn't I have twice as much time?"

Francisco shook his head. "You have to take into account the suit's own weight in the calculations." He glanced over his shoulder at Miguel who was welding a circuit board before he turned back to Harri. "Also, Papa can't get the electronics quite right to keep the power stable. He won't let me help. Says I'm too young to weld."

"If it's any consolation, he probably wouldn't let Grace do it either," she joked.

Francisco snorted. "That's because she's a baby." But her humor did draw a smile out of the boy. "Actually, he probably wouldn't let Dom help either," he whispered conspiratorially.

Miguel cut the gas to the micro welder and pushed up his mask. "What are you two plotting over there?"

"Like any supervillains, the best way to raid Tim's kitchen," Harri called back.

Miguel checked his watch and laughed. "I didn't realize we'd missed lunchtime. You're slipping, 'Cisco!"

Their teasing sent a pang through Harri. They reminded her of her own father, how good things had been before Mom's death when Harri had been Francisco's age. Why couldn't Dad have been more like Miguel?

If she were honest with herself, Dad hadn't used anything stronger than an occasional joint before Mom died. In Harri's own grief and anger, she never acknowledged what he was going through by losing Mom. Maybe if he had someone, another widower, like Tim and Miguel had each other, he wouldn't have turned to the stronger, nastier shit.

Like coke.

Harri pushed back the old memories and new insight, and she climbed to her feet. All of their work today wouldn't mean a damn thing if they couldn't find the fake Captain Justice, capture him, and rescue Rey.

Too many people in this building had lost a parent. She'd be damned if she let Aisha's baby grow up without his father.

CHAPTER 22

Before eating a quick lunch with the Esperanzas, Harri texted Arthur. It was the safest way to check on his progress while he took care of Grace and tried to come up with a way to find the fake Rey.

After lunch, Miguel and Francisco walked down to Marta's to check on the rest of the Esperanza clan's progress fixing the damage Aisha had caused. Moments after they left, Harri's phoned beeped as she contemplated taking another nap.

Nervous anticipation ran along her nerves while she rode the elevator straight up to the fourth floor. The loft door to Arthur's place stood open.

She eased closer and peered inside. He sat at his desk, typing on his computer keyboard with his right hand and holding Baby Grace with the other.

"Is this how you did your homework in college?" Harri asked.

He looked up at her and grinned. "Actually, yes. I don't suppose you can take Grace for a moment. Don't worry. She's had her bottle and a diaper change."

"You make me sound like a total wuss," Harri protested as she crossed his living area. She carefully took the infant from him.

Huge blue eyes stared up at Harri, but Grace didn't complain about the change in adults. She wiggled a bit to get comfortable and yawned. Her tiny mittened fist rubbed at her face.

For the briefest of instances, a pang of regret rattled Harri. Had she made a huge mistake not having a baby with Eddie? Even if Tim were willing, she was too damn old to have one of these adorable things now.

"No, you're not," Arthur said, his gaze still intent on the computer monitor. "Lots of women are having babies in their forties these days."

With a jerk of horror, Harri realized she'd said her last thought aloud. "If you tell anyone what I said, no one will ever find your body."

Arthur looked up at her, and a little of his old insecurity shone in his eyes. "I swear I would never tell." After a second, a small smile lifted his mouth. "No one would believe me anyway."

"What have you got on finding our imposter?"

"The reason Sparx and Nix lost the signal is because he turned off his GPS." He tapped a key, and a grid map of the region around Founder's Park popped up on his monitor. "I turned it back on, but our imposter dumped Rey's phone in a trash can at Riverway Mall."

"How do you know he dumped it?"

"Special Agent Lewis retrieved the phone when I gave him the location."

Harri rolled her eyes. "What is my partner and staff's obsession with my ex-husband?"

"We trust him more than our region's National Superhero Bureau office or the local constabulary?" Arthur gave her a totally innocent look that she didn't buy for a minute.

"Crap," she muttered. "How are we going to track Fake Rey then?"

"A lot of supers can be tracked by their power signature." He turned back to the keyboard. "Our problem is Rey doesn't give off anything specific, at least nothing Tim or I knew how to measure."

And Tim was in no condition to help now, assuming he was awake and coherent. The tightness in her chest returned with a vengeance despite the peace of Grace sleeping in her arms. "Which means we're not going to be able to find Rey directly."

Arthur shook his head while he poked at some more keys. "I was hoping the ladies would get close enough the tracking devices might pick up something from the imposter."

"Like what?"

Arthur shrugged, still without looking at her. "If he's not Rey, he has to be faking Rey's powers somehow." He tapped another key. "Like the subsonics Seismic Shift used to amplify his natural abilities."

"So did they get any readings?"

Arthur shook his head again. "But your friend Jeremy has a proverbial ace up his sleeve."

"Jeremy?" Her voice was a little louder than she intended. Grace squirmed in her sleep and made a burble sound.

"Go put her in her crib before we continue this conversation," Arthur ordered.

"Excuse me?" Harri glared at him.

Arthur finally looked up at her. "If you wake Grace up, you can deal with a cranky baby this afternoon while the rest of us clean up the mess you and Ms. Franklin made by not telling us what was going on."

The wussy nerd who wanted to be a supervillain, the one who didn't have the guts to threaten her to her face, the one who didn't get the attention he craved while growing up, was gone. In his place was a responsible, loyal man. One who cared as deeply about the baby in her arms as his missing friend. Maybe Aisha was right about encouraging a relationship between him and Patty.

"Yes, Mr. Drallhickey," she whispered.

"And make sure you place her on her back," he said softly.

"Yes, Mr. Drallhickey." Harri grinned, and headed toward Arthur's spare bedroom.

A crib just like the one at Patty's sat in the corner next to the made bed. Harri frowned. Both Arthur's car and Patty's were too small to lug the crib from Patty's apartment to here. Especially not in the middle of the night.

Harri carefully laid Grace on her mattress. The baby fidgeted a bit before she settled back down into the sleep only innocents and dogs could find. Harri shook her head as she watched Grace. If she'd missed her time to be a mother, that was fine. She could spoil Grace and Aisha's son rotten, making up for their missing fathers.

Her heart lurched. No, she couldn't give up on Rey. Not yet.

Hell, she wouldn't still be alive if it weren't for him. And it wasn't like he'd left Aisha. At least, not willingly.

Harri carefully closed the door to the spare bedroom behind her and headed back to Arthur's living space. She grabbed a chair from his little butcher block breakfast table, carried it over to his desk and sat.

"Now, what were you saying about Jeremy?"

"He puts an RFID tag in his client's outfits. There have been issues in the past with clients not paying their bills."

"RFID tag? Like a shoplifting tag?"

"Sort of." Arthur smiled. "Instead of triggering an alarm or ruining the superhero outfit, it merely keeps track of the supersuit using a specific radio frequency. Once the total bill's paid, Jeremy removes the tag. If the bill for the outfit isn't paid according to the terms agreed to, Jeremy can send a collector to the super's location."

"Please tell me this collector doesn't approach the super in public or at home."

"Okay, I won't."

Sometimes, Arthur was a bit too literal.

"So what you're saying, or Jeremy is saying, Rey hasn't paid for his suit and it has one of these tags?"

Arthur flicked a glance in her direction before returning his attention to the screen. "Rey's already paid for the first one, which is why I can't find him directly, but he hasn't paid for the spare suit in full yet. Jeremy has him on a payment plan so Rey can pay his share of the grocery bill."

"And our imposter took Rey's spare suit." Excitement thrummed through Harri's blood. The same feeling of an impending win she used to get when she uncovered a supervillain's hidden assets.

Another grid map popped up on Arthur's screen. It showed the obvious outline of the eastern shore of Lake Del Oro. She leaned closer over his shoulder. A red dot blinked in the middle of Westerville Park.

"Why would our fake go back to the park?"

A very grim Arthur turned to her. "Because I think the monsters a few nights ago were a trap for Ms. Franklin."

CHAPTER 23

"Aisha?" Harri stared at Arthur while her mind tried to catch up with the conclusion he'd already found. "Shit. They wanted to use her as leverage against Rey."

"He's practically invulnerable." Arthur shrugged. "Torture isn't going to work on him, and anyone watching us could tell how he and Aisha feel about each other. So whatever they want from him, they would need that leverage. They didn't count on her intelligence, much less her hormone-related powers." He pointed at the red dot. "Whatever is going on, the imposter's lair is in the middle of the park."

Harri's fingernails dug into the back of Arthur's ergonomically enhanced chair. Had she gotten Black Death's motives wrong? What if he didn't give a shit about Patty and Grace? What if he was really surveilling Rey and Aisha all this time, and following her was a way to throw off suspicion?

Corvus. Everything pointed back to Corvus. Byron Trubble had been trying to capture Rey since he was a little kid. The previous attempts on her own life were to keep her from discovering Seismic Shift's connection to assassinations ordered by Trubble. Circumstantial evidence pointed to Black Death killing Seismic Shift at the Lake County jail to keep him from spilling Corvus's secrets.

If Trubble had broken the fragile truce between the Winters & Franklin supers and Corvus to stay out of each other's way, there would be hell to pay. And Harri would be damn sure that Trubble paid it.

Late Sunday afternoon, Aisha lounged on the couch in her office and tried to focus on the battery company's final version of Sparx's endorsement contract. Despite the bad publicity with the Captain Justice imposter, the manufacturer hadn't balked at any of her requested changes. The news reports of Sparx saving a mugged jogger who had been beaten and left for dead had helped immensely in that regard.

Luckily, the hospital took its privacy policy seriously, and they hadn't released Tim's name as the victim. As for the police, a lot of people on the force still thought Tim had gotten away with murder. They believed Tim had gotten what he deserved. Those cops weren't about to paint Tim as an innocent, and so they kept quiet as to his identity.

On the domestic end, Aisha hadn't been able to get Patty to leave her desk despite it being a Sunday afternoon, but a call from Arthur did the trick. Patty couldn't say no to Miguel needing Arthur's help running and testing some wiring.

Aisha jumped when her cell phone rang. After checking the caller ID and catching her breath, she tapped the Answer icon. "Hey, Serena." Sudden alarm ran through Aisha at the possible reason for the PA student to contact her. "What is it? Has Tim—"

"Calm down. He's fine." Serena chuckled. "He's awake and asking for Harri. I told him I sent her home to get some rest. By the way, how's she doing? She looked like hell when I got here."

"Asleep most of the day." Aisha laughed as well. "Us old ladies don't have the stamina of you twenty-somethings."

"That's not true, and we both know it. Molly's arrived, so I'm headed home. Did you get the wrist blood pressure cuff I recommended?"

Aisha sighed. She didn't need another lecture. Not today. "I didn't have a chance to run out yet. I promise I will go down to the drugstore after dinner."

"Um, how about you stay home tonight? I'll pick one up on the way home and bring it over in the morning. You can pay me back."

Needles danced along Aisha's newly shorn scalp. "What's going on, Serena?"

"It may be nothing, but Molly said she's seen a Caucasian guy with intense blue eyes in a tan Accord on your street a lot lately. I've seen the same guy. And Celia mentioned overhearing Javier telling his posse to keep an eye out for that particular color and model."

Shit. Knowing Celia, everybody in the neighborhood now had their eyes out for Black Death. One of their friends or neighbors could end up dead if they decided to run interference for the Lechuza tenants.

"Serena, listen to me carefully. Spread the word. No one, and I mean *no one*, is to approach this man. Do you understand me?"

"Look, not all of us are helpless, you know," the younger woman protested.

"We think he's the guy who murdered Seismic Shift while he was in custody, Serena. He's dangerous. You don't take any chances. No one does. You got me."

"Whoa, there, sister! Calm down."

Aisha sucked in a harsh breath. The super was right. She was on the edge of panic, and that wasn't like her at all. She took a second breath before she said, "I'm not joking. All he has to do to kill you is touch you."

The phone signal was silent, except a PA system requesting a doctor in the background.

Finally, Serena whispered, "You think Black Death is watching you?"

Aisha's blood turned to ice. "What do you know about Black Death?"

"H-he's the super equivalent of the boogeyman." Serena's breath hitched. "The only time I've heard anyone talk about him as if he were real was my parents. I accidentally overheard them one night when I was little. I woke up and wanted a drink, and . . ."

The younger woman sounded as scared as Aisha felt. "Serena, would you do me a favor?"

"Sure."

"After I deal with the Tim and Rey situation, I need you to introduce me to your parents. It sounds like they know more about this guy than we do."

"But Tim—"

"Has gone as far as he can in trying to find out this guy's identity." Tension ran along Aisha's nerves. The power of Serena's dad to hide a super might be reversed. If Serena's dad were willing to assist in finding and apprehending Black Death, putting the assassin behind bars would go a long way into improving the law firm's public relations issue. And tweaking Trubble and Corvus's nose in the process would go a long way to improving her mood since she was pretty damn sure they were behind the fake Captain Justice. "Would your parents be willing to help?"

"I-I don't know. I'd have to ask."

"That's all I can request. Thanks." She reached deep down for her bitch mode. "But whatever you do—"

"Stay away from the white guy in the Honda. Understood." Serena's old confidence was back. "I'll spread the word. See you in the morning."

Aisha breathed a little sigh of relief as she laid her phone on the coffee table. Maybe if she took care of the Black Death problem, Harri wouldn't run off and do something half-cocked in the misguided intention of protecting her friends.

CHAPTER 24

"What's our imposter's location?" Harri held still while Miguel tightened the chest plate to the rest of her armor for an airtight seal. The exoskeleton was surprisingly lightweight and comfortable.

Arthur's attention flicked to his laptop before his gaze returned to Tim's main desktop. Several screens showed various displays where he performed system checks of the suit.

"He's left Westerville Park. Local radar confirms he's crossing the lake. Harri—" Sweat beaded on Arthur's forehead as he looked at her. "His current trajectory will take him straight to the Alpha Cola Stadium."

Oh, god. She licked her suddenly dry lips. "Please tell me nothing's scheduled for tonight."

"The Cannons are playing San Antonio tonight," Francisco piped up from somewhere behind her. "The guys ordered pizza, and they're watching upstairs. Should be almost half-time."

"Well, then, I guess I can't let the guy pretending to be Rey near the stadium," she said, trying to keep her voice light. "Arthur, plot me an intercept course, please."

Miguel met her gaze and scowled. He didn't need to say a thing. His emotions about involving his youngest in this cockamamie plan of hers were written all over his features.

Except she couldn't pull off apprehending the fake Captain Justice without the boy's help.

"Okay, your phone is patched into the suit's comm system, Ms. Harri," Francisco said.

As if on cue, the X-File theme, the ringtone for her ex-husband, filtered through both her headset and Francisco's laptop.

"Answer," she commanded. The receiver beeped in response to her vocal command. "'Bout time you returned my—" She stopped herself from uttering an obscenity in front of the seven-year-old. "—calls."

"That's because I was sure it was a prank," Eddie shot back. "You never call me. I figured you'd make Aisha or Patty give me updates. How's Tim doing?"

"Alive. Conscious. This isn't about him." She tensed, knowing there was about to be a lot of shouting. "Jatz'om Kuh will turn over the imposter pretending to be Captain Justice at—" She looked over at Arthur.

"Intercept course plotted. Dock 25," he answered. "In twelve minutes."

"Dock 25—" she started.

"—in twelve minutes." Eddie growled. "I heard Arthur. What the hell are you doing, Harri?"

"Language!" Miguel snapped.

"Yeah, keep it clean, Edward." Harri had to bite her lower lip to keep from laughing. "Arthur and Tim's protégé is underage and present."

"Harri," Eddie drawled out her name. "I'm in the middle of watching the Cannons game, and we both know Jatz'om Kuh is not available. Which super is apprehending our identity thief?"

"Don't ask questions you don't want the answers to, Eddie. End call." The comm system beeped, cutting off her ex's tirade.

"You should have told him, Harri," Miguel said softly.

"He can't lie to his superiors if he doesn't know." She tried to ignore the caterpillars of guilt crawling around her butterflies of anticipation. All the old anger was still mixed into her feelings about Eddie Lewis, but she'd never lied to him in all their years together. Not like this.

Miguel settled the helmet over her head and locked the seals. He tapped the button on the side of the helmet, and his voice filtered through the receiver. "Powering up the main batteries."

One thing Tim did right was keep the communications on a separate power supply than the main deuterium batteries. If she couldn't take down the fake before she lost main power, she could still call for a ride.

The metal, plastic, and cloth hummed around her in response to the batteries. Air brushed her face as the oxygen generator kicked on. The sensation wasn't as claustrophobic as she expected during their tests. In fact, her body hummed in tune with the power, ready for action.

Miguel slid the secondary visor over the main face plate. The polarized polycarbonate actually made everything sharper.

"Tactical," she murmured. Displays popped up in the corners of the visor, including the intercept course Arthur plotted.

"Pre-flight checks completed," Miguel said in her ear, or seemed to. "Main computer operational and responding to your voice commands. Detaching the secondary computers."

Miguel and Francisco unplugged her from everything they used to check the worthiness of the suit's systems.

"Still green," Arthur reported.

The visor displays shone steady. "Green here," she replied.

"Remember, you're down to one hour and fifteen minutes of power after your practice runs."

"Confirmed." Harri chuckled. "And quit being a mother hen, Arthur."

"If you get yourself killed tonight, I'll be the first one accused of murdering you," he grumbled.

"Don't forget to reset the security systems once I'm clear," she said.

"Quit stalling," Miguel muttered.

"Initiate flight plan," Harri said.

The suit did exactly what it was supposed to do. One second she was in the lab. The next she was flying at breakneck speed through the corridors of the old fall-out shelter in the basement of the Lechuza Building. Her suit zipped around corners slicker than Tim's antique Mercedes on a racetrack.

Harri shrieked in delight. This was way better than Rey carrying her.

But the suit's speed in the basement was nothing. When she reached the old subway tunnel that once connected the Canyon Block with the rest of the city, the suit surged. The pillars that supported the ceiling passed in blurs. When she reached a large ventilation shaft, the suit barely slowed enough for the turn upward.

Harri shot past the empty street and emptier buildings toward the stars. Her flight path shifted in a long arc. The lights of Canyon Pointe spread out beneath her. Not even the whistle of air penetrated her helmet. Ahead and to her right, a section of the shoreline glowed brighter than the rest of the city. The stadium had opened the roof for tonight's game.

"Intercept in fifteen seconds," Arthur said in her ear.

"Keep quiet, Drallhickey," she said. "I don't need you ruining my concentration."

"Yes, ma'am."

The digital display in the top left corner of the visor ticked down the time. At ten, the targeting display moved to the middle of her facemask. It outlined the figure ahead in red and white.

Her breath hitched a moment before the suit fired the first gas pellet at nearly pointblank range. Tim's system worked beautifully. The pellet hit the Captain Justice imposter in the cheek and exploded in a little cloud of yellow around his face.

He faltered and slowed, but he didn't plummet toward the lake. Instead he turned toward her as she crashed into him. They tumbled through the air together, Harri simply trying to keep him from ripping off her Ghost Owl suit.

Harri raised her fist and aimed it at his nose. "Manual! Fire!"

The imposter whacked her arm up, and the pellet disappeared into the night sky. He managed to wrench his foot between them and kicked. If it weren't for the armor, Harri was certain his boot would have gone through her spine.

She lost her grip on him and somersaulted backwards a few times. It took a second for the gyros to stabilize her.

The imposter stared at her before the disbelief turned to a snarl. "You're dead! I killed you!"

Well, that definitely settled his intentions toward Tim last night.

She tapped the external mic. "Oh, my dear fake, don't you know what a ghost is?"

The vocal scrambler in the system made her sound like Tim's alter ego. As she hoped, the imposter charged her. She darted left. When he spun around to face her again, she fired another pellet of knock-out gas.

Once again, the imposter breathed in the vapor and faltered. This time though, he dipped a moment before he regained his altitude.

Damn! Tim had sworn these things were strong enough to take down Cobblestone and Captain Mojave, but he obviously hadn't bothered to try them out on Rey. Oh, hell, they still weren't sure exactly what Rey's duplicate was. Maybe he really was a robot, or some shit like that, and was merely trying to fake her out.

She aimed her left fist at him. "Tasers!"

The prongs shot from their housing and lodged in his chest. Electricity sparked, but he didn't seem affected. Golden eyes glared at her, and he yanked the wires out of her left sleeve.

The display on her visor fluctuated.

"Harri, the suite's power is dropping too fast." In his panic, Arthur used her first name. "And I just lost the RFID signal."

The battery gauge on the heads up display shifted from green to yellow. He wasn't just panicking. She was in trouble.

"You can't pierce my skin, fool," the fake Captain Justice growled.

Double crap. The prongs had merely snagged his suit and shorted out the damn tag Jeremy had inserted.

The impostor charged her. With the power drain, she couldn't move fast enough. He grabbed her right foot and flung her toward a stack of shipping containers.

Well, she got his focus off the stadium. But she couldn't let him use her to trash the docks and put a bunch of longshoremen out of work for weeks. She managed to roll so she was stomach down.

"Right turn!" The computer was sluggish, but it responded to her vocal command. The tips of her boots scraped the side of the topmost container with a screech that penetrated her exoskeleton.

Maybe she couldn't penetrate his skin, and drugs had no effect, but he still needed to breathe. She had to keep him on this side of causeway, closer to the deeper water of the lake.

A little too close to his original target for her comfort.

But the imposter was a little too intent on doing bad things to her. Despite her zigzagging over and under the docks, he gained on her. The one saving grace was he hadn't thrown any of the boulders protecting the shoreline from erosion at her.

Harri tapped the helmet to make her conversation private. "Arthur? Miguel? How waterproof is Tim's suit?"

"Not very," Miguel responded. "We didn't think you'd be swimming in it." In the background she could hear Francisco and Arthur, but it didn't sound like they were talking to each other. "Cisco says twenty feet at best. You need to tranquilize him."

"I tried." Harri swung left to avoid a crane. "Twice. It had about as much effect as chamomile tea!"

"Tase him then!" Miguel yelled.

"Really? You think I haven't already tried?" She dove under the next dock. "Computer, ninety-degree turn up."

The display on her visor shifted from yellow to orange. She was in deep, deep shit.

More talking in the background that she couldn't make out. "Guys! I need a plan that doesn't involve me dying. Otherwise, I'm taking him into the lake."

"Eddie says lead him back to the dock," Arthur said. "He's got some heavy-duty gas grenades."

The visor display turned red. A soft beeping filled her helmet. She was officially out of time. A quick glance below her showed the imposter reaching for her right foot.

A wild idea hit her, but desperation was a crazy bitch.

"Computer, cut power to flight."

Gravity took over. Somehow, she managed to snag the fake Captain Justice's cape as she fell. She wrapped her legs around his waist and shoved her right fist under his nostrils.

"Manual. Fire."

He shuddered under her grip, then relaxed. They started to fall toward the inky blackness below.

Oh, god, how'd we get this high? Harri couldn't maintain her hold on the imposter, and he slipped from her grip.

"Computer, reactivate flight." The thrusters in the back of the suit hummed. Below her, the red and white suited figure plummeted into the lake. "Descend."

The warning beeps started again. The power reading blinked. She headed for the docks. Eddie would help her scrounge a boat to retrieve the imposter and secure the bastard.

The hum of the thrusters stopped and the displays went blank. Harri had enough time to mutter a choice obscenity before she hit the surface of the water.

CHAPTER 25

Something cracked in Harri's right leg when she slammed into the lake. She tumbled a few times, not knowing which way was up. But the leg didn't hurt. Not like it should if she broke it.

And the liquid trickling down it would feel warmer if it were blood. One of the joins must have broken. It meant water leaked into her suit, and from the sensation on her calf, it was more than a seepage.

"Arthur? Miguel?"

Static crackled through her comm. Bubbles floated past her visor.

"Guys? Can you read me?"

Nothing.

She looked around wildly. Everything was black. So was everything above her. But at her feet . . . a rapidly receding irregular row of lights. That had to be the shoreline.

Harri flipped around and struck out for the surface. But all the years of swimming lessons and laps in Grandma Harri's pool meant nothing when she was wearing superhero armor that weighed half as much as she did.

Cold water filled her right boot and seeped past her knee. The leak must be worse than she thought. And the lake was rapidly filling the suit. Without the battery pack, there was no oxygen generator. And the little air left in the suit wouldn't last long. Panic spurred longer, faster strokes.

The lights drew further away.

"Guys?" Her voice wheezed. "Arthur? Miguel? I'm in trouble." Nothing.

She didn't even have the comfort of static. The comm was on a separate circuit. It shouldn't be affected by the loss of the main batteries. But she'd hit the water pretty hard. The force must have damaged the comm system.

Her shorts grew damp. She didn't have much time. As much as she hated losing all of Tim's initial work, it could be replicated. She wrenched the oversized right boot. The seal broke, and she pulled it off.

Cold water tickled her belly. She wasn't going to get the suit off in time. The little air left in the suit was turning stale. Dizziness swept over her.

Yep. This time she really was going to die.

And it was her own damn fault.

———•◦•———

Fury raged through Aisha as she landed next to Eddie on Dock 25.

Except she wasn't sure who she was more angry at. Her only consolation was Patty being equally pissed at Harri and the idiots in the basement. Thank goodness, Patty had gone downstairs to grab Arthur when she couldn't get Grace to settle down for the night, and he didn't answer his phone.

Eddie's mouth dropped open. "When did you—"

"Later." Aisha swept her hand in a cutting motion. "The guys lost contact with her. Where'd she go down?"

He pointed to the right of a signal buoy floating a few yards from the end of the dock. "There. About three-quarters of a mile out."

She leapt into the air and zoomed in the direction Eddie indicated. Of all the stupid, bull-headed ideas Harri had ever come up with, taking on a su-pervillain of unknown skills and strengths by herself topped the friggin' list. Dammit, she'd better still be alive so Aisha could yell at her.

Sucking in a huge breath, Aisha dove into the lake. The water was fairly warm for the first few feet, but rapidly cooled the deeper she went. This part of Del Oro had been a canyon thousands of years ago until the sides collapsed in on themselves to block enough of the river to form the lake. It meant the depth was easily four hundred feet in this section.

She paused and listened. Sounds echoed weirdly through the water, but . . .

Yep, definitely something thrashing below her. She prayed it was Harri and not a fish or other lake creature tangled in a broken line.

With her new super eyesight, a shadow of a figure twisted and turned, fighting something she couldn't make out. It floated another twenty-five feet down from Aisha's position. No, not floating. It was drifting toward the bot-tom. As she watched, its struggles faded.

Aisha aimed for the shadow. Flying through water wasn't much different than flying through air. Despite her new powers though, she still needed to breathe. Her lungs ached, reminding her of that little fact.

She reached the shadow, grabbed its arms, and launched them both towards the surface. The taste of air was incredibly sweet when she breached the water. She wrapped her arms under those of her law partner and flew the short distance to where Eddie waited on the dock.

Aisha laid Harri gently on the scarred wood. Water sloshed inside her helmet. Eddie knelt on Harri's other side. Together, Aisha and Eddie unlatched the helmet from the rest of the suit. Harri jerked and coughed up a bunch of lake water.

"Get her on her side," Eddie ordered.

Aisha was pissed at him, too, but she needed Harri alive in order to yell at her about her stupidity. Together, they gently rolled Harri onto her left shoulder.

Harri coughed up a lot more water. But she was breathing. That was all Aisha cared about.

She laid down on the dock beside her friend, sucking in as much air as she could.

"You okay," Eddie asked as he banged on Harri's back.

"No," both women said at the same time.

"And stop pounding on me," Harri snapped.

Aisha rose up on her elbows and glared at her partner. "What the hell were you thinking!"

"We need to question him," Harri bit out. "It's the only way we'll get Rey back."

Aisha cocked her head. "And you planned to do that by pretending to be a super?"

Harri's mouth opened and closed before she turned away.

"I have to agree with Aisha on this one," Eddie said.

"Shut up, Lewis." Aisha sat upright. "You were acting just as stupid as she was."

His eyes narrowed. "Hey! I didn't go up against a super by myself."

"And where's your backup, Special Agent?" She waved a hand at the silent and empty dock.

He turned away from her, too.

Aisha climbed to her feet. "That's the real reason your marriage fell apart. You two are too much alike." She scanned the surface of the dark water. "Where is he?"

"I don't know," Harri said in between coughs. "I literally shot my last gas pellet up his nose, and he dropped like the proverbial sack of flour. I tried to get back to the dock before I totally lost power."

Aisha looked down at her partner. "You dropped an unconscious man into Lake Del Oro?"

"I don't have super strength like some people," Harri snapped back.

"That's manslaughter at best." Eddie stared at his ex, disbelief all over his craggy features.

Good. Aisha folded her arms over her chest. At least, she wasn't the only one who thought Harri had lost her marbles.

Eddie looked up at Aisha. "How deep was she?"

She shrugged. "I didn't take a depth monitor with me."

"Dammit, Aisha!" Anger flicked across his features. "She could develop decompression sickness if she was too deep!"

"The bends would serve her right for this stupid-ass stunt," she grumbled. He was right though, and she sighed. "I'm not sure. Maybe fifty, sixty feet down."

"Shit," Eddie muttered. "You both will probably be okay, but we'd better not take any chances. Get her in the backseat. Tim has a decompression chamber we can use."

"I'm fine," Aisha growled.

"Do you really want to take a chance with the baby?" he said calmly. Too calmly.

She glared down at Harri. "Did you tell him?"

"No." Harri rolled her eyes. "He guessed, and you just confirmed it."

"I deducted," Eddie said. He grabbed the discarded helmet and rose to his feet. "It's what detectives do. And we need to get out of here, ladies, before the local rent-a-cops find out the Ghost Owl is my ex-wife." He marched to the driver's side of his SUV and climbed in the seat.

Aisha crouched to pick up Harri.

"No! I can do it myself." Harri swatted at Aisha.

She swung her partner unceremoniously over her shoulder and strode to Eddie's vehicle. "Quit acting like a baby, or so help me, I'll spank you."

"You wouldn't!"

Aisha heaved Harri in the backseat. A quick glance confirmed Eddie had engaged the childproof locks before she slammed the back door shut. She climbed into the front passenger seat.

"You two are paying for the upholstery cleaning. You both smell like lake." Eddie turned his SUV around and headed for the vehicle exit for the docks.

"How'd you get back here anyway?" Aisha asked.

"It's amazing what an FBI badge will get you." He winked at her before he looked in his rearview mirror. "Harri, there's a blanket in the cargo compartment. Cover up before we hit the guard post."

"For the love of—this smells like dog! You know I'm allergic!"

Aisha snickered. "Serves you right for tonight's dumbass stunt."

Harri sneezed all the drive home.

Chapter 26

⟡

After a round in Tim's decompression chamber, a couple of allergy pills, and a shower, Harri almost felt normal again.

Until she was summoned to the firm conference room by a very somber Arthur.

When she arrived, Eddie's lecture didn't match the one Patty launched into once she was sure everyone was okay.

"Look, Harri, I get your mommy issues when it comes to Rey. I'd do anything for Grace."

Tucked in her infant carrier, the baby burbled in response.

"But you endangered Rey and Aisha's lives by going after this imposter by yourself." Patty flung her arms toward the ceiling. "And don't get me started about their baby. What if Aisha died from an air embolism?"

"Don't forget outing Tim's secret identity," Eddie offered.

"You're not helping," Harri said under her breath.

"He's right!" Patty slammed her palm on the table surface. "After all your bitching about the damage both heroes and villains do to the city and how the taxpayers are screwed with the repair costs, you decide to go vigilante, too? You said you wanted Tim out, but you jumped in with both feet!"

She turned toward Arthur and Miguel. "And you two decide it's a good idea to help her? And drag poor little Francisco in to your scheme? What the fuck were you thinking?"

Her voice rose in pitch at the end of her rant, and Grace responded with a wail of her own.

"Now look what you've done!" Patty scooped the baby into her arms and crooned, "I'm so sorry, sweetie. Mommy didn't mean to upset you."

Eddie leaned forward, his elbows on the table. "Did your fake Captain Justice make any appearance, public or otherwise, after he went down in the lake?"

Arthur shook his head. "There's been nothing since he injured Tim last night. And no reappearance on radar or CCTV after Harri dropped him into the lake."

Whatever relief Harri got from her shower died under Arthur's words. "Tried to kill Tim, you mean." When everyone looked at her, she shook her head. "The fake admitted his intentions when I was trying to capture him. He thought I was Tim and was shocked to see the Ghost Owl."

"Anything from the RFID tag?" Aisha asked.

Arthur shook his head. "It was probably shorted in the battle."

"When Harri tased the imposter," Miguel added.

"So what do we do now?" Patty murmured. Her expression looked as bleak as Harri felt.

They were all right to blame her. Her eyes burned. She had to do everything her way, and damn the consequences. However, the worst damage had been to herself and her marriage. This time?

This time, someone she cared about like a son could be dead. And the man she'd fallen for lay in a hospital bed because she couldn't be honest with him.

"Are we sure the fake is dead?" Eddie said softly.

"I doubt it," Harri said at the same time Aisha said, "No."

She looked at Aisha who stared back.

"You go first," Harri said.

"According to Harri's comm reports during their . . . encounter, the gas had very little effect on our imposter." Aisha shook her head. "He may have simply been stunned by the pellet up the nose. Or she delayed him long enough to ruin whatever he had planned. According to a voicemail message I received from Sparx, there were several alarms across the city tonight. Enough to keep every Canyon Point superhero busy."

Alarm buzzed across Harri's nerves. "Nix was supposed to be watching Tim."

Aisha smiled. "Don't worry. She stayed with him the whole time. Apparently, Sourpuss called in their grandmother. I don't think the jewelry store robbers were expecting an octogenarian getting in their way."

"I thought the same thing about the fake being stunned," Harri said. "It's the only reason I can think of why he didn't come after me. Or he thought I was leading him into a trap when I tried to make it back to shore."

"Our imposter could have swam down the Rio Diaz where there aren't any cameras, and it wouldn't be hard for him to fly below radar if he retreated back to his lair," Arthur said. "Besides, supervillains always pop out of nowhere when you least expect them."

"You mean like Professor Venom popping out of my evergreen bushes?" Harri snapped.

"Harri, stop it." Patty's nasty expression countered her soft words.

"I'm sorry, Arthur."

"Wow, an actual apology," Aisha muttered.

Harri blew out a deep breath. Everyone in the conference room was going to hate her idea, but she'd really screwed up tonight. It was the only way to rectify things. She cleared her throat. Everyone except Grace looked at her.

"I'll call Trubble and make the trade."

"Trade what?" Aisha stared at her as if she'd lost her last marble.

Maybe she had.

"Whatever he wants for Rey."

Aisha's gaze dropped to the tabletop. "You don't even know if Rey's still alive."

"Harri, if you do this . . ." Eddie paused and shook his head. "Corvus will have a hold on you for the rest of your life."

"And what about the rest of us?" Arthur stared at her with a feverish intensity in his brown eyes. "What if what Trubble wants is the rest of us? Me. Grace. The rest of your clients. Are you going to throw Sparx and Cobblestone back into Corvus's grip?"

"Grace tested negative for being a super." Patty's lower lip trembled.

Arthur stood and laid a hand on her shoulder. "Testing negative at birth means nothing, and we both know it. I tested negative when I was born, and both of my parents were normal." He tapped his temple with his free hand. "My brain power didn't kick in until I hit puberty."

"I wouldn't do that," Harri protested. "I wouldn't turn you all over to Corvus."

"Yeah, well, I never though you'd go vigilante either." Aisha shoved her chair back from the table, jumped to her feet, and stalked out of the conference room.

Miguel wearily pushed to his feet as well. "Aisha is right. I helped you because I thought I wanted Rey back for her sake. But I was selfish. I think of him as one of my own, and I forgot about the other four boys' welfare in the process." He trudged out of the conference room, too.

"Tomorrow morning, you are going to spend the entire day with Tim." Patty trembled as she spoke. "And you are going to be supportive and reassuring while he recovers. Your lying by omission has nothing to do with attorney-client privilege. He's in that hospital bed because of you." She strode out of the room with Grace in her arms.

Arthur merely gave Harri a resigned look before he grabbed the infant carrier and followed Patty and the baby.

She'd messed up pretty bad if both Aisha and Patty were furious with her. But the guys? Dammit, they'd gone all in with her plan, then threw her to the wolves when things went bad. This is exactly why she didn't depend on anyone.

Everyone left her, even the man still sitting across the table from her.

Harri watched Eddie. "Aren't you going to say anything?"

"Sarah thinks I'm having an affair with you."

Harri blinked. "What?"

He pushed to his feet. "All the late night and weekend emergency calls about your supers? She thinks I'm lying about where I'm going and what I'm doing." He raked his fingers through his dark hair. "But tonight though . . . Aisha's right. Never in a million years would I have imagined you going vigilante. And Harri?"

He rounded the table and leaned over her. "If I catch you doing it again, I will arrest you." He sauntered out of the conference room.

Eddie's unspoken assurance he wouldn't wreck his marriage for her lay thick in the atmosphere. Harri couldn't blame him. He had everything he'd ever wanted.

If anything, Patty was right, too. She was ignoring the man who did care about her in her pursuit of her own interests.

She was so damn good at knowing the solution for everyone else's problems. How the hell did she solve her own?

Harri curled up on her couch in her loft with her second tumbler of scotch. When she had finally limped through the door, she knew wine just wouldn't cut it tonight.

Of course the instant she found a semi-comfortable position, someone knocked on the loft door.

"It's open!" Maybe she'd get lucky, and Rey's doppelgänger had come to kill her.

The door rolled open to reveal Aisha floating a couple of feet above the floor. "Well, that's a plea for suicide by supervillain if I ever heard one."

"I was trying to protect you and the baby." It was a lame excuse, and Harri knew it. But it was the only thing she had left to give.

"I know." Aisha closed the loft door. "It's the only reason I'm talking to you right now."

She zipped to the kitchen and fixed herself a glass of orange juice before she floated to the living area and lowered herself to a chair. Over the rim of her glass, she eyed Harri while she sipped her drink.

"Was there anything you left out earlier?" Harri gulped the second scotch. Its fiery path down her throat didn't begin to punish her for her sins.

"A lot, but I think you're right about one thing." Aisha's eyes met Harri's. "You need to call Trubble in the morning and try to cut a deal."

Harri blinked a few times. Maybe she'd already had too much alcohol. "But you said Rey was probably dead?"

"Corvus has been after Rey for the last fifteen years because they want to know what makes him tick. If they had taken Rey, why the hell would Trubble substitute someone with his exact powers?"

When Aisha was on a scent, she could be damn scary. With superpowers, she was absolutely terrifying.

Harri shook her head. "The imposter has to be faking Rey's powers somehow."

Aisha set aside her glass on the Ikea end table and leaned forward. "Corvus can't track Rey. Neither can Tim. Arthur was hoping to get some kind of reading from the imposter when we sent Sparx and Nix after the Ghost Owl last night." Her hand swiped through the air. "Nothing. You were up close and personal tonight. You know what Arthur picked up from your telemetry?"

Harri ran through Aisha's scenarios and realized what conclusion Aisha had already made. "Nothing?"

"Nada." Aisha sharply nodded. "I don't think Trubble's behind Rey's disappearance."

"But—" Harri started to sit upright, only to have her back remind her of her crash landing.

Aisha frowned. "Did you take some Vitamin I?"

Harri chuckled. Everyone had picked up Tim's nickname for ibuprofen. "As much as I safely could." Sobriety hit her hard despite the amount of scotch she'd drunk. "But Trubble's the only one who's been after Rey all this time."

"What if he's not?" Aisha cocked her head. "Who's really controlling those freaky parrot-lizard things that attacked us?"

Cold sweat broke out on Harri's forehead. "Have you been talking to Arthur?"

"About the parrot-lizard things?" Aisha's eyebrows drew together. "Just what I've said to you all after our encounter . . ."

"He threw out the idea earlier tonight that the imposter lured you to Westerville Park to kidnap you."

Aisha leaned back against the chair. Her frown deepened. "Why would they want me?"

"Leverage against Rey."

Aisha's shoulders sagged and an expression of relief swept across her face. "That would mean he's still alive."

"Still want me to call Trubble?"

Aisha nodded. "Let's find out—"

"—what he knows about other parties' interest in Rey." Harri swiped at the dampness on her forehead. "We'll find him, sweetie."

"Yes, we will." Aisha stood. "G'night, partner."

Harri chuckled, more out of relief that Aisha wasn't going to walk out on their firm for her screw-up tonight. "G'night."

———•———

Aisha stared out across the city skyline. It was the type of quiet only three in the morning could bring despite the glow of the bright lights.

She'd reviewed the telemetry from the city's radar system as well as the input from the Ghost Owl suit Harri had appropriated. Arthur was so good about labeling files clearly and correctly on the internal network. But for a genius, he was terrible about hiding his password.

The imposter had to be using Westerville Park as a base. And if not there, then the national forest on the other side of the state park.

Harri had the right idea. Her problem had been the execution. Going alone after the imposter was her big mistake.

It was a mistake Aisha wouldn't repeat. And for her, one of the regular Ghost Owl suits would do just fine.

CHAPTER 27

The next morning, Aisha sat in Harri's office while they discussed client matters when Patty knocked on the door.

Harri rolled her eyes. "Would you please call the temp agency, and get someone back here?"

Patty ignored her. "You need to see this." She crossed over to Harri's desk, snatched the remote and turned on the TV.

A vague image of two figures against the night sky appeared on the screen. The video had obviously been shot by an amateur, but the screen froze the instant the figures became clear.

Aisha groaned. There was no hiding from this one.

"This exclusive footage was given to us by a local viewer." Essie Morales's voice echoed from the speaker. "It shows Captain Justice battling the infamous Ghost Owl. Allegedly this fight happened over Lake Del Oro, south of the causeway, last night during the Cannons game. Action 12 News! has reached out to the representatives of Captain Justice, but they have not returned our calls."

Patty set down the remote and crossed her arms. "So far, I'm sticking with no comment, but you should know Nella Lopez said your exclusive contract and the pay rate is cancelled. She was pretty pissed."

As if on cue, the phone in the reception area rang. Patty's arms dropped to her sides before she strode from Harri's office.

"Shit!" Harri slammed her pen on her desk. It bounced once before it rolled off the edge and hit the carpet. "We can't afford to lose that money."

Aisha picked up the pen, stood, and set the pen back on Harri's desk. "We haven't. Yet. You make your call before you head for the hospital. I'll take care of this other crap."

"How can you be this calm about—" Harri waved a hand at the newscast still playing.

"Because this I know how to handle." She glanced at the screen and back.

"Who do you think engineered Captain Terrific's comeback after he over-dosed at that brothel in Nevada?"

Harri's shocked expression turned to guffaws. "You never told me that!"

"NDA." Aisha shrugged. "But now that we're partners, you should be warned if he decides to move his legal business to us."

She headed for her own office to start dealing with the fallout from the fake Captain Justice. Now, if only she believed the crap she'd just spouted to Harri.

———— •●• ————

After smoothing Nella's feathers along with a couple of Rey's sponsors, Aisha called Qiang at her day job office. "I've got your contracts back. They've agreed to everything."

"When would you like me to come over and sign them?"

"Actually, do you have any plans for lunch today?" There was a slight pause on the phone line after Aisha's question.

"While I really wish you were offering to buy me lunch, I have the strongest feeling you want another favor." Sarcasm dripped from Qiang's voice.

"I need your opinion about a professional matter." Aisha tapped her pencil against the legal pad sitting on her brand new used desk. Only a few scratches marred the cherry finish. "I'm . . . too close to the situation, and I can't trust my partner to be objective."

Blood roared in her ears as she waited for Qiang to answer. Nor could she fault the super if she said no. Aisha hated cleaning up other attorneys' messes. She could only imagine what the supers thought of each other.

"There's a food truck at the empty lot on 9th and MLK. I know how much you like Mexican. Meet me there at noon." The line abruptly died.

Aisha breathed a little sigh of relief. Qiang was willing to listen for the price of a few tacos. That was all she could ask.

———— •●• ————

Heat shimmered off the concrete while Aisha waited patiently by the truck. It sat on the remains of a parking lot. The building that had stood on the lot had been lost to a battle between Seismic Shift and Doctor Malevolent ten years before.

The property owner had foolishly let his private supervillain insurance lapse. Since the building had been one of the oldest in Canyon Pointe, the grants under the federal and state Supervillain Recovery Program hadn't been enough to rebuild under the current codes.

Last Aisha had heard, the owner had taken the payout and went to live on one of the Caribbean islands ruled by a cadre of supervillains. His blistering letter to the editor in the *Tribune* was published shortly after the owner left Canyon Pointe. He claimed he felt safer under criminals than the so-called law-abiding heroes. While rectification bills wound their torturous way through various legislatures to prevent villains becoming unjustly enriched with taxpayer money, Harri, as Canyon Pointe's city attorney, had declared war on the supervillains' assets.

Actually, it was a wonder someone, besides Arthur, hadn't taken potshots at Harri before this year.

When Qiang walked up exactly at noon, the accountant by day wore a bright red sheath dress and huge sunglasses. Her blue-black hair was pulled back in a tight ponytail. She looked like any other white collar woman working in Canyon Pointe.

"With all the bullcrap the other night, I didn't tell you I like the new color and cut." Qiang grinned, an expression Aisha rarely saw on the woman.

"Uh, thanks?" It wasn't too often a super threw Aisha off her game. But then Qiang was usually in her superhero togs and acting like a badass, not . . . a professional grabbing a quick lunch with a colleague before rushing back to the office.

Qiang moved to get in the rapidly forming line. "You brought the contracts for me to sign?"

"Yes." Aisha quickly followed the accountant. A lot of people were walking towards the truck. "This place must be popular."

"Best tacos in town." Qiang leaned closer. "Don't tell Marta I said that. We'll grab lunch and snag a bench in the park." She nodded toward the Allen George Memorial Park across the street and froze.

"What is it?" Aisha fought the need to look behind her.

Qiang smiled, but it was obviously forced. "Has Molly mentioned a tan Honda to you?"

"We already knew about the car when she brought it up." Ice crept up Aisha's spine, and she had to concentrate to keep her feet on the ground. She couldn't float into the air. Not in such a public place. Nor could she let on Molly had informed her through Serena since the student PA wasn't registered. "The person driving it has been watching us."

"He belongs to the flock." Qiang's subtle way of saying she knew he was with Corvus.

Static made the fine hairs on Aisha's face and arms stand on end. So she wasn't the only one nervous about their unwanted spectator. After being under Corvus's thumb for years, Qiang had every right to be upset.

They moved forward in the lunch line.

"Do you know his real name?" Aisha asked softly.

"D.B. called him Cade." Qiang shook her head slightly. "Can't tell you if it's his first or last name. I only saw him twice. I have no idea what his skill set is."

D.B., AKA Darryl Bloch, AKA Seismic Shift, the disgraced superhero who died mysteriously in police custody. The FBI had taken over the investigation from both a superhero and civil rights perspective. It would be damn difficult for non-super law enforcement to prove Shift's death wasn't natural causes. Was that the real reason Eddie had been so eager to help her and Harri lately? Bloch had been actively trying to kill Harri and frame poor Arthur for his attempts. When Harri had been arrested on false charges, Bloch sent in Black Death, who not only let Harri live, but he called Aisha at home and told her to grab Eddie and get their asses down to the jail before Bloch could do anything else.

After that little incident, Eddie had to suspect Black Death was behind Seismic Shift's demise. Had Tim let Harri's ex know about the recent stalking?

Not that Aisha really gave a damn about Shift. Some of his associates were responsible for trashing Aisha's precious BMW. And with the recent craziness, she and Harri hadn't been able to go car shopping as they'd planned.

The folks in front of her and Qiang finished their transaction and moved aside. At the counter, the women quickly placed their orders. Aisha was more than happy to pay. Qiang's confirmation of Black Death's name alone was worth a million taco lunches.

"Want me to short his car's electrical system?" Qiang whispered as they strode toward the crosswalk.

Aisha chuckled. "As tempting as that is, I don't want to tip our hand just yet. So far he's only approached and spoken to Harri. And he did it as a civilian the second time."

"He was suited up the first time? And she lived?" Qiang sounded incredulous.

"Do you know his code name?" Aisha asked.

The light changed and they started across the concrete. Despite the mid-nineties temps, she shivered as they both tried to nonchalantly passed the Honda. In her peripheral vision, Black Death's head turned to follow her and Qiang.

"No. All I know is he was in the extermination department."

Extermination. Wetworks. It didn't matter the euphemism. It still equaled murder.

Aisha wasn't about to point out Bloch had sent Qiang to kill Harri after Black Death supposedly failed. No, she needed Qiang in a good mood for the favor she was about to ask.

Maybe she should tell Qiang about Black Death. Not telling anyone at the Lechuza Building about the fake Rey had been a big mistake. Tim had paid the price for it.

"I'm going to tell you the same thing I told Molly. Stay away from Tan Honda Man no matter what his real name is." Aisha gulped in the hot air. "We have reason to believe he's Black Death."

Qiang faltered for a moment before she resumed their strolling pace. "No shit."

"I'm not joking." Aisha pointedly looked at the other woman.

"Okay. Does he have anything to do with the favor you want to ask?"

"No."

"Does this have anything to do with last night's multiple alarms?" Qiang said. She pointed to a bench under a pin oak. It would give them a little relief from the relentless summer sun.

"Yes and no." Aisha sat down and opened her bag. Grilled sweet onions accented the odors wafting from the waxed-paper-wrapped tacos. "Our fake Captain Justice apparently has a crew working for him. They were supposed to keep the rest of the heroes in Canyon Pointe busy while he did something else at Alpha Cola Stadium."

Qiang paused in mid-bite and stared at Aisha. "What was he planning?"

"We aren't sure." She took a bite of her fish taco. Qiang was right. The gals who ran the food truck could give Marta a run for her money. Aisha chewed and swallowed. "Jatz'om Kuh intercepted him over the lake before he reached the Stadium."

Qiang gave up on taking a bite, laid her soft chicken taco on its wrapper, and wiped her fingers with a napkin. "He's not available." She scowled at Aisha. "Come clean now, or we're done."

Aisha scanned the area around the picnic table. No one was close enough to hear them, and Black Death had stayed in his car, probably with the A/C running, the bastard.

"There's more than one person wearing the costume." She set aside her own taco and faced Qiang squarely. "Including me."

That obviously wasn't what the super was expecting. Her mouth worked silently a few times before she grabbed her diet soda and took a huge gulp from the bottle.

"H-how'd you lose him last night," she finally asked.

"It wasn't me who intercepted him." Aisha sighed. "The anesthetic gas didn't work. Neither did the tasers."

"How'd Winters get away from him?" Qiang asked.

"I didn't say who it was," Aisha pointed out.

"You didn't have to." Qiang laughed and shook her head. "Only Winters would be more idiotic than her boyfriend to take on the fake CJ by herself. Glad to know you're not that stupid. When are you going after him?"

"Tonight."

"Who else is going with you?"

"I was going to ask Molly," Aisha said.

Qiang nodded in what Aisha hoped was approval and reached for her taco. "I'll call her sister. Between the four of us—" She paused in mid-bite for the third time. "Do we know how Corvus is faking CJ's powers?"

"Therein lies the problem." Stomach acid swirled around the fish in Aisha's stomach. "He's not faking the powers, and we no longer think Corvus is behind this. Harri's working on confirming our suspicions."

The minute the words left Aisha's mouth, she knew why Black Death tailed her this afternoon. Trubble must think she was up to something, and Harri was a distraction. Aisha would bet her grandmother's cornbread stuffing recipe that Trubble had no clue about Black Death's extracurricular spying. Otherwise, why risk such a valuable asset being seen by his target?

"Okay, I give up." Qiang laid down her taco, rewrapped it, and slid it back in the brown paper bag. "I'll eat later." She pulled off her sunglasses and stared at Aisha. "What on earth makes you think Corvus isn't behind this? They're the closest thing to an archenemy Rey has."

Aisha filled Qiang in on her analysis of last night's telemetry, told of her encounter with the parrot-lizard things that had attacked her and Fake Rey in Westerville Park, and added Arthur's suspicion the parrot-lizards were really after her to get the real Rey to cooperate.

"Cooperate with what?" Qiang asked.

"We have no idea." Aisha shrugged and sipped her lemonade. "We know Rey's mom was on the run when she came here from Honduras, and she was murdered by something no one at the time could identify. Some kind of creatures attacked Rey two years ago, something that could actually cut through his skin. He barely escaped. He has no clue what his mom was running from. Right now, our best guess is whoever is behind this thinks Rey knows something or has something of Maria's."

"That makes more sense than anything I can come up with. So what's the plan?"

Aisha laid out her strategy.

"Sounds better than some of Winters' insane ideas." Qiang checked her watch. "I need to get back to work. You have those contracts?"

Aisha pulled the paperwork and a pen from her shoulder bag. Qiang signed on all the spots marked with sticky tabs. Aisha handed the super her own copy, and they both stood.

"What time do we want to meet?" Qiang asked.

Aisha cocked her head and regarded the super. "You sure you want to do this?"

"I don't mind doing favors for one of my kind." Qiang grinned as she slid her sunglasses back on.

"I'm not—" Aisha sputtered.

"Yeah, you are. Say nine p.m. on your roof?"

"Fine, but I'm not—"

"One of us, one of us," Qiang chanted as she headed for Ninth Street.

Aisha shook her head as she strode toward the public parking garage on MLK. The Honda was still parked on the street. She resisted the urge to wave at Black Death. Considering his obsession with Patty and Harri, he had to be following her under Trubble's orders.

Which went back to the chess game between Harri and Trubble. He didn't like losing, and not only had he lost control of Shift, Sparx and Cobblestone, he'd lost any opportunity to snag Rey quietly, thanks to Harri.

Which brought Aisha's thoughts full circle. Was she totally wrong about Corvus's involvement in Rey's disappearance?

The whole thing made her head ache. Or maybe it was the stuffiness in her car. The rental car's A/C couldn't keep up with a Canyon Pointe summer.

Between the heat and the traffic, part of her wished she could simply fly back to the office. If these powers turned out to be permanent once the baby was born, she'd need to make some serious decisions about her future. She just prayed Rey would be making those decisions with her.

———— •◆• ————

Harry sat on a bench under a pecan tree in Founder's Green. It seemed strangely empty in the summer afternoon heat. With the fire Seismic Shift had started gutting City Hall, fewer homeless and transients wandered the park or sought shelter under the random trees. The city staff were scattered across Canyon Pointe in temporary offices. The blue collar guys still clearing out the charred interiors were less likely to give a money hand-out than the pink collar ladies, though Harri noted a few of the workers brought extra sandwiches they shared willingly with the shabby people trying to survive.

One of the homeless men walked in her direction. Harri's muscles tightened as she recognized the shuffling gait.

Crazy Jim, AKA Valentine Delante. One of the Corvus operatives who didn't have powers.

The lack didn't make Delante any less dangerous. Two months ago, Tim had Rey look through the Corvus personnel files to identify the man after he tried to strangle Harri in this very park. If it hadn't been for Rey the day of the City Hall fire, she'd be one dead attorney in more ways than one.

She patted her purse. The hard shape of the Taser reassured her. Between that, the pepper spray canister on her keyring, and her secret weapon a few yards away, she had a fighting chance to get away if this turned out to be a set-up.

"Miz Winters." Delante nodded to her before he plopped on the bench beside her. His stench made her eyes water. He took his role a little too seriously. Maybe the pepper spray was a waste.

"Need a sandwich and some coffee, Jim?" she drawled. How many times had she fed this asshole, thinking he suffered from a bipolar disorder and was off his meds?

"I'm good." He grinned the same gap-toothed grin she remembered from her City Hall days. Now that she knew what to look for, she could see which teeth were blacked-out.

"This meeting was supposed to be with your boss, not you, Jim." No sense revealing she knew his legal identity.

"Well, he also said you weren't supposed to bring anyone with you." Delante glanced around the park before he focused on the elderly woman quietly reading on a nearby bench. "Though I was hoping you'd bring one of the hotties you represent."

Anger ground underneath Harri's skin at his sexist bullshit, but it wasn't worth getting into a fight with him. He'd probably been ordered to provoke her.

"You obviously didn't learn a damn thing when Captain Justice pounded you." Harri smiled at Delante. "Maybe I needed bigger guns to make the point."

A murderous glint shone in his eyes for a split second. Her comment had poked a hole in his ego, like she knew it would. Before he did anything stupid, his gaze shifted to something behind her, and he flinched.

She turned slowly to find a familiar man despite only meeting him in person once. This time, retired general Byron S. Trubble wore olive-colored cotton twill pants and a beige button-down short-sleeved shirt. Like their previous encounter, his smile didn't reflect in his eyes.

"The fact Ms. Winters brought Rue Liberty means she doesn't think either of us are that much of a threat, Jim." He stepped closer and waved a hand in a shooing motion. "Why don't you go harass some people for pocket change while the grown-ups talk?"

Fury flared on Delante's face, but he rose and shuffled off without saying another word.

Trubble took the vacated seat on the bench, his gaze drifting over the other people in the park or meandering along the sidewalks. "I thought we'd reached a modicum of trust, Harriet."

She didn't rise to the bait of her full name. "So did I, Byron."

"I expected you to bring your snake in the grass instead of a retired super. Where has she slithered off to this afternoon?"

A test since he used the awful nickname Aisha had acquired from some assholes in law school. Which meant a Corvus operative was following her on her lunchtime errand. Thank goodness, she was meeting with someone Trubble already knew.

"Meeting with a client."

His gaze finally locked on Harri, his black eyes unblinking. "And?"

She regarded him for a long moment. "I wasn't going to say a damn word when you had Black Death kill Seismic Shift, but you abducting the real Captain Justice is a whole 'nother matter."

Trubble's eyebrows crinkled, but otherwise, his expression didn't change. "You can't blame me for your boy losing control, Harriet."

"That asshole is not Rey, and we both know it." She shook her head. "You send in a spy and think we're not going to be able to tell the difference? You're slipping, Byron. I get that you're pissed about losing Sparx and Cobblestone, but you were the one who fucked up, trying to turn them into killers."

Trubble blinked a few times, but didn't say a damn word. The truth struck her in her gut. He had no clue about the switch. Aisha was right. Nausea filled Harri. How the hell could they find Rey if they didn't know who'd taken him?

She waved her right hand airily. "Your shapeshifter's good, but not perfect. And his efforts to trash Captain Justice's reputation are downright laughable."

"Even after his so-called battle with the Ghost Owl last night?"

"Fake news." She narrowed her eyes. "I'll give you until midnight to deliver Rey to our office at the Lechuza Building. Otherwise, everything we know about Corvus goes public." She stood and looked down at Trubble. "And before you do something stupid, like trying to blow up the Lechuza Building to prevent us from disseminating anything, the info's already been delivered to a third party."

Trubble snorted. "Calvin Johnson doesn't have the jurisdiction to do anything, and Edward Lewis doesn't have the power in the FBI he thinks he does."

Of course, he naturally assumed she and Aisha would call their ex-husbands. It never occurred to men like him that a woman might have other resources.

"Who said I'd give anything important to either of those yahoos? We divorced them for a reason." Harri mustered the most innocent expression she could manage before she headed for the café up the street.

As Harri passed the elderly woman on the nearby bench, she looked up from her book and winked.

Harri winked back and continued walking. She'd been a little surprised Aisha had volunteered Nix's grandmother to watch Harri's back during this meeting. But Rue Liberty had been more than willing once she heard who Harri had an appointment with. The retired superhero claimed the last two days had been better than bingo at the senior center.

It was also pretty obvious she knew who Trubble was and what Corvus did. It was equally obvious she didn't like them one bit. In fact, she insisted Harri call her once Harri got back to the hospital.

Harri turned the problem over in her mind as she walked. The pager system for superheroes was totally controlled by the NSB. Corvus was an unauthorized arm of the NSB. Rey had been summoned by someone with access to the pager system.

Except Trubble was the type of man to gloat over his successes. He was thoroughly confused by her accusation of abducting Rey.

Had their mythical mysterious third party infiltrated the NSB or Corvus? If so, they weren't so mythical after all.

Well, she'd cast her line with some decent bait, and she stirred the water a little with Trubble. It was a matter of waiting to see who actually bit the hook.

CHAPTER 28

Harri returned to Tim's hospital room before the orderly brought him back from radiology. The last thing he needed in his recovery was the stress of knowing who she had met while she'd been out to grab some lunch.

"Please tell me you snuck real food in here for me," Tim pleaded once both the orderly and his nurse left.

She shook her head and took his hand. "I'm not screwing you up any more than you already are."

He laughed, then immediately winced. "First, I don't think anyone can screw me up more than I already am." He squeezed her palm. "Second, don't make me laugh. It really hurts."

Tim's expression turned serious as he regarded her. "I half-expected you not to be here when I got back from my x-rays."

Harri groaned before she kicked the visitor's chair closer to the bed and sat. "I'm under orders from Princess Patty not to leave your side. If I didn't have to eat, and by the way, the crap they serve in the hospital cafeteria doesn't count as real food, I wouldn't have left."

"You're not afraid of anyone, especially your assistant." Tim squeezed her hand again. "Five feet of rage topped by two inches of woman, remember?"

Harri tried not to flinch at her ex's description of her. "Haven't you noticed how scary Patty's become now that Grace is here? Arthur's the only one taking her power-tripping in stride."

"I think Mr. Drallhickey has a thing for dominant women." Despite all the tubes and his pale complexion, Tim managed to lasciviously leer at her. "Which I totally understand."

"You're incorrigible, Canyon." Harri laughed despite herself. "I swear all of you men in our building have some weird fetish. I just haven't figured out Miguel's."

Tim's smile faded. "Did Rey come home?"

For a split second, she considered lying or changing the subject. But doing either thing would make her the biggest hypocrite on the face of the planet when it came to the subject of honesty.

"Didn't any of the supers tell you it wasn't Rey who attacked you the night before last?" she said.

"They didn't have to." Tim grimaced and shifted in his bed. "I figured out that little tidbit all on my own."

"How—"

"Sweetie, I've been sparring with Rey for the last two months." He chuckled and winced again. "This guy was making the same sloppy moves as Rey did in the beginning, relying too much on his speed and super strength. It's the only reason I survived as long as I did. I guess part of me hoped the real Rey might have escaped from Corvus by now."

Tim's freckles stood out on his pasty skin, and sweat drenched his hairline. This conversation was taking more out of him than Harri felt comfortable with.

"Tim, press the button for your meds," she said softly. "You need them." Lord help her, she never thought she'd be encouraging anyone to take opiates given her family history, but he was in obvious pain.

"No," he wheezed. "I want to be clear for this conversation. You knew that guy wasn't Rey, didn't you?"

She nodded.

"Why didn't you tell me?" He scowled at her. "Hell, why didn't you tell Aisha? She's your closest friend, not to mention she and Rey are living together."

Harri swallowed her discomfort. "She's the one who figured it out and told me."

When Tim shot her a suspicious look, she rolled her eyes. "Come on, she sleeps with the guy. You think she's not going to know the difference?"

Harri looked away for a moment. Those dark indigo eyes of Tim's were more dangerous than a polygraph machine.

"That still doesn't explain why you two didn't tell the rest of us," he murmured. "Corvus—"

She met his gaze once again. "That's the reason she and I went out two nights ago. We had a rough plan of getting him to expose himself—"

Tim grinned at the unintentional double entendre.

"As an imposter, you pervert." She laughed and shook her head. "The trick was how to tell the rest of you without tipping off the fake."

"You don't think I'm that good of an actor?" Tim's eyebrows rose.

"Arthur and Miguel's boys would be the real problem, not you." She shrugged. "As I said, we were trying to work details when the stuff at the children's health fair hit the fan."

"I'm assuming the ladies weren't able to find him after they called the ambulance for me."

"No. Thank goodness, the imposter didn't come back to the loft either."

"Corvus—"

She gave a little shake of her head. "There's a distinct possibility Corvus isn't behind this."

"What makes you think that? They've been after the real Rey since he was a little kid."

"Give me some credit," she said. "I've been a lawyer almost as long as you've been running around in your Underoos. I can dig up dirt with the best of them."

"So, who does the imposter work for?"

"We don't know yet."

"Where is he?"

"I, um, managed to lose him."

The EKG machine sped its rhythm. "What do you mean you managed to lose him?"

Harri sagged in her chair. Guilt pricked at her, but she needed to tell Tim the truth. It was her fault he was lying in that damn bed.

She couldn't face him though. "Um, there's something I need to tell you. I really screwed up. I accidentally destroyed our only method of finding this jerk."

"What do you mean?"

"I, uh . . . borrowed your exoskeleton and Ghost Owl suit."

Tim remained silent.

"I'm really sorry, and I'll pay for the damages," she added in a rush.

"You what?" The EKG hooked up to Tim's chest flashed erratically in her peripheral vision.

As hard as it was, she told him about Miguel and Francisco helping her finish the exoskeleton with the kid's rocket pack attached and her encounter with the man pretending to be Captain Justice, including how she fried the RFID tag in Rey's spare outfit with the Taser in Tim's suit.

"Like I said, I'm really sorry I damaged your suit in the process," she finished.

"What the hell were you thinking?"

Her head jerked up at his low, dangerous tone. Well, his face was no longer a pasty white. His skin was nearly as red as his hair.

"I was trying to apprehend an identity thief before he hurt someone else I care about." Out of everyone, she assumed Tim would understand why she'd gone after the imposter.

"You're damn lucky you didn't get yourself killed!" he roared. The EKG beeped in a hard, staccato rhythm.

"Tim," she said through gritted teeth. "You need to calm down before you give yourself a heart attack or restart the internal bleeding."

He totally ignored her. "I can't believe you did something so monumentally stupid!"

Harri jerked her hand from his. "Now you know how I feel every time you—"

"This isn't about me!"

"Hey!" The door to Tim's room swung open, and his nurse glared at them. "I will not have you two disrupting my ward." She shook a finger in Harri's direction. "Ms. Winters, you need to leave. You are upsetting my patient."

"No problem." Harri grabbed her bag and marched for the door. "Sorry for the scene."

"Harri, wait," Tim called from his hospital bed.

She whirled to face him. "I've heard enough, Mr. Canyon. I'll pay you back for the damaged equipment."

"Out," the nurse growled.

Harri stomped out the door and to the elevator. She knew what she'd done last night was stupid. If Aisha had pursued the imposter with that flimsy of a plan, Harri would be yelling along with Tim. But she . . .

She poked the down button and slumped against the wall as everything clicked in her brain. It wasn't fair to flinch at the same crap she would have been dishing out. She expected Tim to treat her differently because they were sleeping together. Then she'd made everything worse by letting her temper get the better of her.

Too bad Aisha was pregnant. This would be a perfect problem to solve over margaritas.

Harri sighed and fished her phone out of her pants pocket. She couldn't be selfish and leave the hospital in a huff over her hurt feelings. Someone still needed to watch over Tim in case the imposter pretending to be Captain Justice came back to the hospital to finish what he started. She pushed away from the wall and headed for the floor's waiting room. One of the chairs was positioned where she could keep an eye on the door to his room. She thumbed the controls and brought up the bestseller on her phone's book app she'd been meaning to read.

If Tim couldn't deal with her directly, fine. But she'd still stay and watch over him until Jeremy and Leonardo came to relieve her in four hours.

— •◆• —

"Well?" Aisha looked expectantly at Miguel.

They stood in front of the case holding a mannequin dressed in one of the Ghost Owl's older costumes. It was the only one any photographer had ever managed to snatch a decent picture of over the last twenty years. One of the toy manufacturers immediately reproduced a replica for mass consumption, under the theory the real Ghost Owl couldn't sue them without revealing himself.

They were right on that count.

What surprised everyone was its popularity. Most vigilantes were roundly derided by the civil authorities and the super community, but the Ghost Owl had eluded capture for two decades. Even her nephew Devon had been seduced by the legendary outlaw super, much to her sister LaShun's mortification. Devon was a pretty laid-back kid, but he demanded this version of the Ghost Owl costume for Halloween last year. It seemed only right to wear the known outfit if she were going to be the Ghost Owl for this one night.

Aisha smiled to herself. If only she could bring Devon down here to the official Owl's Nest, she would be the most awesome aunt ever. Too bad Tim was a client.

And here she was, planning to "borrow" her client's supersuit.

"All of you are loco, you know that?" Miguel shook his head.

"I don't need a brand-new suit." Aisha crossed her arms. "This is a one-time deal. Tim's only a couple of inches taller than me so it'll fit. I just need a disguise, and this outfit is publicly known. Besides, Harri nearly outed us all last night." She lifted and lowered one shoulder. "And the more people who see Jatz'om Kuh while Tim's in the hospital, the less likely anyone will connect the two."

"You may have superpowers, Aisha, but you are still carrying Rey's son." Miguel turned and cupped her cheek. "He will not consider his life worth losing you and his baby. Please think twice about this. You're the closest thing I have to a daughter."

His words made her eyes burn and water. She took his hand, gently pulled it from her face, and squeezed it before releasing him.

"You're not that much older than me," she protested, trying to ease the emotion swirling through her.

"Ah, so you believe he needs an even older woman." Miguel stroked his chin. "I believe Nix's grandmother is single."

Aisha snorted. "You and Rey put together couldn't keep up with Rue Liberty."

Miguel chuckled and gave her a rueful look. "I still wish you'd reconsider this crazy plan."

"Unlike Harri, I'm taking backup." Aisha smiled at him. "And I promise I'll be careful."

"We need to tell everyone, or else we'll have another brouhaha like last night."

The intercom buzzed. Miguel strode over to the wall and pressed the answer button. "Yes?"

Harri's voice filtered through the speaker. "Is Aisha still with you?"

"I'm here." Aisha strode towards the unit. "What's up?"

"I think you were right. You two want to come upstairs, and I'll give you the rundown of my talk in the park."

Aisha glanced at the clock on the wall. "Aren't you supposed to be at the hospital?"

"She told Tim about her stupid stunt," Patty spat over the intercom. "Now she can't understand why he might be upset. The nurse threw her out for causing a scene."

"Actually, she only tossed me from his room," Harri said dryly. "I stayed in the waiting area where I could see Tim's door until my relief arrived. Jeremy and Leo got to the hospital a little earlier than they thought. Several of their appointments for today canceled after news got out about last night's crime wave."

Miguel gave Aisha a pointed look.

She cleared her throat. "We need to cover a couple of other things on my end as well. We're on our way upstairs." She tapped the off button.

"Sure you don't want the armor?" Miguel's moustache twitched. "You may need it when you tell the ladies upstairs what you're planning for tonight."

CHAPTER 29

Contrary to Miguel's speculation, Arthur was the one who threw a fit when Aisha revealed tonight's quest.

"Honey, calm down." Patty laid a hand on his arm. "You're going to upset Grace."

However, the baby didn't make a peep. She continued sleeping in her infant carrier.

"Corvus is behind Rey's disappearance—" Arthur started.

"Stop right there." Aisha held up her hand. "Harri, what happened during your meeting with Trubble?"

Patty, Arthur and Miguel's head slowly swiveled to stare at Harri. It would have been funny if the situation wasn't so scary.

"Please tell us you didn't." Patty's lower lip quivered.

Harri leaned her elbows on the conference room table. "At first, Aisha and I suspected Corvus, too, but a lot of things didn't add up. And before any of you start lecturing me, I took backup."

"Thank goodness you took Eddie with you." Patty sagged in her chair.

"Better. I took Rue Liberty." Harri shook her head. "There's no love lost between her and Corvus. I think they're a little scared of her. Both Trubble and his backup behaved themselves."

"But what did Trubble say?" Aisha pressed.

"He tried to play things cool, but from his body language, I don't think he knew about the switch." Harri frowned. "But he didn't try to refute my accusations of kidnapping either."

"He knew you wouldn't believe him," Patty said.

"No." Aisha met Harri's gaze. Her partner had already come to the same conclusion. "He's got more problems in-house than Shift."

Harri nodded. "That's what Rue Liberty suspects as well. I gave Trubble until midnight to return Rey. Trubble will make a point of looking for Rey himself because otherwise, I'll release everything we have on Corvus. And after all the crap with Seismic Shift, Trubble now knows the Ghost Owl is helping us."

Aisha nodded. "My parties will arrive shortly before nine p.m."

"I'll call in the civilian authorities after you leave." Harri had the scary smile she wore before she ate somebody's lunch in court. "We should have him back tonight, one way or another."

"And if we don't?" Aisha asked, wishing she felt as confident in their success. It had to be said. She wasn't the only one who cared about him.

Miguel's calloused hand covered both of hers. "We will get him back. You will get him back. We have to have faith."

Except she wasn't sure how much she had right now. Not under the overwhelming fear that threatened to drown her.

— • —

For the first time since Aisha had become pregnant, nicotine cravings hit her hard while she waited for the other female supers to arrive. When she walked out to the Lechuza Building's garage to pace off the nervous energy, Harri followed her and perched on the half-wall that protected the pedestrian walkway from vehicle mishaps.

Something not so good had obviously happened between her and Tim at the hospital, but Aisha didn't ask. She simply couldn't deal with both hers and Harri's issues right now. Thankfully, they gossiped about innocuous issues, like whether or not Jeremy and Leonardo would ever get married.

Or they did until Harri said, "You don't have to go after Rey's doppelgänger tonight."

Aisha paused in midstride. "Why? Because you're afraid I'll be able to bust him when you screwed it up?"

"Hey!" Harri's eyes narrowed. "I got enough shit from Tim this afternoon, and that's after you and Patty dished it out last night. I admit I fucked up. Get over it!"

Aisha blew out a deep breath. Well, now she knew what had crawled up Harri's butt. "Who tattled on you?"

"I tattled on myself."

Well, that said just how much she was into Tim. Aisha couldn't remember a time when Harri had admitted any wrongdoing to Eddie.

"And you apologized?"

"More than once," Harri snapped. "And I said I'd pay for the damages."

Yep, she was definitely pining over Tim Canyon.

Aisha crossed to the half-wall and hopped up to sit beside Harri. "He'll get over it. The fake Rey may have stomped on his body on purpose, but you just accidentally stomped on his—"

"Ego?" Harri growled.

"Feelings," Aisha corrected. "He couldn't protect his family, and now he's scared shitless of losing you."

Harri stared at Aisha a long time before she muttered, "Oh, fuck." She buried her face in her hands. "I'm such an asshole."

"It's okay." Aisha nudged her partner's arm. "Everybody already knows."

A car honk drew their attention to the garage entrance.

Aisha shook her head and tried not to let her amusement show on her face. For once, Nix didn't arrive on her motorcycle. Instead, she arrived with her sister Sourpuss in a 1967 Wildcat convertible with the girls' grandmother behind the wheel. All three women were grinning when they climbed out of the vehicle.

Aisha and Harri jumped down from the retaining wall to greet them.

"What are you doing here?" Harri asked as she hugged Rue Liberty.

"It sounds like you might need some help watching the children while the girls are hunting tonight." The older woman smiled, showing strong white teeth for someone her age. "I may have fought in the Cold War, but it doesn't mean I've forgotten how to fight."

Harri's gaze flicked toward Aisha, her irritation plain.

"Hey!" Aisha held up both palms. "I didn't ask her to come over."

"You didn't have to, dear." Rue Liberty grabbed Aisha in an embrace that resembled an anaconda squeezing its prey but smelled of talcum powder and brandy. "When you're unsure of who's behind these recent shenanigans, it's best to take all the help you can get."

Once inside the building, the silver-haired superhero pulled Aisha aside while the rest headed toward the elevator. "Thank you for talking Molly out of that idiotic moniker she originally chose."

Aisha smiled. "We've all made decisions in our younger years that may not have been for the best."

Rue Liberty gave an unladylike snort. "More like she takes after her mother."

The super shook her head. "I swear I thought my daughter would outgrow her predilection for bad boys. At least by the time she turned forty."

Her words almost felt like a rebuke. Aisha's face grew hot.

Rue Liberty grabbed Aisha's hand and patted it. "I don't mean you and your Captain Justice, dear. He's a hero, and one of the good ones from what I hear." She shook her head again. "Monica had a thing for supervillains and vigilantes. Her father and I presumed it was just a phase, but she became pregnant . . ."

She patted Aisha's hand and released it. "Nevermind. I'm rehashing events I can't change." She headed for the elevator. "We've nearly ruled out Corvus's involvement in this fiasco. Are you absolutely sure Captain Justice doesn't have a twin brother who became evil?"

"We're not sure of anything at the moment, ma'am," Aisha said as she walked beside the older woman. "Other than the man currently wearing the costume is not the real Captain Justice."

— •◆• —

Aisha stood still while Miguel fastened the Ghost Owl tactical jacket. The material was one of Tim and Jeremy's creations, lighter and more durable than Kevlar. Not to mention surprising comfortable.

Between its composition and styling, Jeremy's twin degrees in chemistry and fashion made sense.

Arthur snapped his fingers in front of her nose. "Pay attention, Aisha!"

"I am. You've amped the baton to one hundred times the power of Harri's over-the-counter Taser."

The computer geek sniffed, and she half-expected him to poke at non-existent glasses on his overly large nose. "I'm glad one of you listens to me. If it weren't for Javier watching Grace, I wouldn't have gotten all this done this afternoon." He hesitated of a moment before he added, "May I ask for an advance on my salary so I can pay him?"

She grinned. "Harri and I already have it covered, so don't worry about it."

"You overpaid him," Miguel mumbled as he guided her right foot into its matching boot and buckled the straps.

"Are you joking?" Aisha looked down at him. "Have you priced out daycare in this city?"

He glanced up from his kneeling position. "Yes, I have."

"Then you know Javier is a bargain." She lifted her leg to step into the left boot. "And Francisco earned every penny we gave him for his help down here."

"All I can say is you'd better come back alive," said a feminine voice.

Aisha looked over her shoulder. Harri leaned against the doorframe with a scowl on her face.

"I can't run this law firm by myself," she added.

"I thought you were already looking for my maternity leave replacement." Aisha deliberately smirked at her partner.

"I can't replace your brain."

"Did Serena drop off the ultrasound?" Tim's invention would be a backup measure in case Fake Rey came back here to cause some mayhem. Aisha wished she had thought of the device sooner. It would have saved part of Tim's exoskeleton from ending up at the bottom of the lake.

"Yeah, she left it with Patty this afternoon while we were both out." Harri hesitated. "Sparx and the girls are waiting for you on the roof."

"She's early," Aisha commented. "Where's everyone else?"

"Major Foxstar tournament at Miguel's tonight." Harri chuckled. "The boys borrowed both my game unit and Arthur's. Sorry, guys."

"De nada." Miguel rose and grabbed the Ghost Owl helmet from his work bench. "There's worse things they could be doing."

"As long as they save some food for us," Arthur added. "Where's Patty and Grace?"

Miguel slipped the helmet over Aisha's head and connected it to the costume's electrical system. This wasn't as fancy as the exoskeleton Harri had borrowed, but Aisha had her own flight capabilities.

"At the party," Harri's muffled voice said. "Rue Liberty was cooing over the baby, and Patty was kicking Dom's ass on the game when Nix buzzed me Sparx had arrived."

"I thought we were getting the boys their own game system," Aisha said. The vocal modifier in the helmet made her sound just like Tim's creepy Ghost Owl voice.

Harri crossed her arms. "We were also supposed to be shopping for your new car. When have we had time to do either?"

"I'm the one driving a rental. What are you bitching about?" Aisha shot back.

"Stop." Arthur held up his hand. "Please just stop, Aisha. You sound like Samantha from *Sex and the City* trying to be Batman. My brain can't handle the contradiction."

"He's right, you know," Harri said with a smirk.

Aisha used both hands to flip off her partner.

"You've got the comm units for the other three ladies?" Arthur asked.

"Yes." She patted the right pouch of her utility belt.

He punched some keys on Tim's laptop before he looked up and nodded. "The comm units are synched, and the trackers in your belt pouch are all responding. If Sparx or Nix can't knock out our fake, all you have to do is attach one to his clothing or skin. Throw it at him. Don't get close enough to touch him if you can help it."

"Why?" She checked to make sure the flap was secured on the left pouch, which held the trackers. "Will they stick to me?"

"No." He closed the top of the laptop and set it on the work table. "I don't want you to get hurt."

"Don't plan on it." Despite the sass in her voice, anxiety crawled through her. If it were only her life, she wouldn't care. But with three other women and her unborn baby with her, she didn't have a choice.

If it came down to the idiot masquerading as Rey or everyone else's lives, she'd kill him.

* * *

As soon as Aisha was out of the room, Harri nodded to Arthur. He crossed to another desk and flipped on the security monitors. All of them showed various views of the Lechuza Building, including the three supers waiting for Aisha on the roof.

All except one monitor which showed the viewpoint of someone moving at superspeed.

"We're receiving her signal and recording," Arthur reported

"You're spying on her?" Miguel almost sounded relieved amid his offended tone.

Harri stepped closer to the monitor.

"Sparx will sense the body cam," Miguel said.

"She already knows." Harri leaned on the desk for a closer view. She really needed an appointment with an ophthalmologist when this mess was over.

"The rate you and Aisha lie to each other is highly disturbing," Miguel added.

"And here I thought you all were upset because we both failed to reveal we knew about the fake Rey," Harri drawled. She reached over Arthur and punched the button for the direct line to Eddie's cell phone.

Someone picked up on the other end, but there was a moment of hesitation before Eddie said, "Yes?"

"Here's the signal for my GPS." She rattled off the numbers on the screen with Aisha's hidden camera. The software would alter her voice. She would sound like the Ghost Owl to Eddie. "Follow my coordinates, but keep your distance until we secure the man pretending to be Captain Justice. We don't want any of your personnel to get injured."

"Wait a minute—" Eddie knew damn well it wasn't Tim talking. No sense giving him a chance to accidentally say someone's name.

"Sparx will contact you when we have him." Harri stabbed the button, ending the call.

And as she half-expected, her personal cell phone started ringing. She pulled it out of her pocket, thumbed the answer icon, and hit the speaker phone. "I thought you were worried about your wife thinking we saw too much of each other, Edward."

"Harri . . ." The low, growly sound coming out of her ex-husband usually preceded him punching something.

Or someone.

"Yes . . ." Two could play that game.

"Where are you?"

"On my way to Miguel's loft for food and a Foxstar tournament. You, Sara, and the rugrat wanna join us?"

"If Drallhicky thinks I'll cut him any slack—"

"Cut me any slack over what?" Arthur interjected.

"Please tell me Miguel or one of his boys aren't—"

"Say one more word, Special Agent, and I'll have my boss sue you for profiling," Miguel snapped.

"Where's Aisha?" The hamster in Eddie's brain finally caught up with last night's events.

"Having sex with her boyfriend." Harri had to work hard to keep from laughing at her ex. "Trust me, you do not want to hear that. You want to accuse my goddaughter of wrongdoing next?"

"I know you are up to something," Eddie hissed.

"Look, I spent a very long day with my own boyfriend." Harri made a point of emphasizing the last word. "You know, the one in the hospital. So, I'd really like to hang up and get some food unless you have a specific point to make."

"Eat fast. I'll be at the Lechuza Building in ten minutes to pick you up."

From the abrupt severing of the connection, she had the impression her ex wanted to slam a receiver.

"Shit," she muttered as she stuffed the phone back in her pocket.

"What do you want us to do, Harri?" Arthur stood like a soldier waiting for orders to jump into action. Maybe Tim wasn't that far off in his analysis of what the supervillain turned IT and childcare expert needed from the women in his life.

"I need a jammer." She considered her options for a moment. Last thing she wanted was to leave Arthur and Miguel defenseless if the imposter came back here. "Also, do you guys have anything that would emit hypersonics like the portable ultrasound scanner?"

Both men nodded.

Arthur handed her one of Tim's tiny jamming machines.

Miguel crossed the lab and pulled a small device from the shelves. "He uses this to break glass. It's not as powerful as the ultrasound, but if this *hiro de puta* gets within a few feet of you, it should do the job," he explained as he walked back to her.

"Thanks." Harri accepted the device from him. It was a fairly simple one-button gadget. No way she could screw this one up.

"I'm sorry for dumping guard duty on you two all the time, but Rue Liberty is upstairs." Harri yanked on her ponytail to make sure it was secure. "She can back you up in keeping Patty and the kids safe until Aisha and I get back."

Arthur nodded solemnly. "Don't worry We've got it covered."

"Thanks." She smiled. "You're a good man." She looked at Miguel. "You both are."

She strode out of the Owl's Nest with the two gizmos, exhaustion and pain from last night plucking at her muscles. If Eddie was going to arrest her for vigilantism instead of dragging her ass to the park, she couldn't stop him.

But she crossed her fingers that if she did spend the night in jail again, Black Death wouldn't make good on his original orders to kill her in her cell.

CHAPTER 30

Aisha tried to keep her game face on as she flew behind Sparx. Or she did until she remembered no one could see her behind the Ghost Owl visor. Then she grinned like a fool. Not even her fear for herself and the baby or her worry over Rey could block the exhilaration of flying above the city.

Nix huddled in Aisha's arms, her face tucked against Aisha's shoulder. The super's mask didn't block the wind on her cheeks and lips, and despite the hot day, air flow at this speed would have chilled all four of them to their bones without their hero togs.

Per their agreement on the roof before they left, all four women maintained radio silence. No sense giving someone below any indication of their presence. Everyone's supersuit was some combination of black, gray, or white, except Sourpuss's deep eggplant. People on the ground would be hard pressed to spot them against the moonless, partially cloudy night sky.

Sparx skimmed only a few yards above the rooftops with Sourpuss in tow on one of her magnetic disks. Instead of a direct route, Sparx flew well north of the causeway before she cut across the lake. Aisha followed, and per Sparx's previous instructions to avoid radar detection, she managed to keep a fairly even fifty feet above the waves.

Sparx slowed as they approached the smaller docks along the edge of the park, the ones used for pleasure craft. At this time of night, they were empty. The canoes for rent were neatly stacked on their racks, waiting for the morning's visitors.

As soon as they landed on the grass sloping up towards a set of picnic tables, Sourpuss said, "Holy crap! What is that stench?"

"All I smell is the lake," Nix said.

Sourpuss shifted to her feline form, which resembled an oversized tabby walking on her hind legs. Her tail lashed the air while she prowled the edge of the brush to the right of the docks. She sneezed several times before she shook her head. "These parrrot-lizards of yourrrsss, Owl, must be rrrolling all overrr the parrrk, marrrking theirrr terrritorrry frrrom the level of ssstench."

"Crap. There goes my plan for you to track them," Aisha murmured.

"If they were attracted to you and Captain Justice like you said, they'll show up eventually," Sparx commented.

Aisha pulled her baton from her belt. "Let's give them some bait then."

—— •◆• ——

Harri walked out of the parking garage when Eddie's government-issued SUV pulled to a stop in front of the Lechuza Building. The passenger door swung open. Inside, a scowling Eddie straightened.

"Get in."

"Why?"

"If you aren't the Ghost Owl tonight, then you know who is." Eddie's glower deepened. "Don't make me arrest you for obstruction, Harri."

She sighed and scanned the street. No one walked remotely close enough to them to hear what he said. Black Death wasn't parked anywhere on this side of the block either for once. She turned back to Eddie. There was no arguing with him when he was in FBI mode. She climbed into the passenger seat and slammed the door shut.

He floored the accelerator. The tires squealed before they caught the pavement, and the SUV shot down the street.

"Who called me tonight, Harri? I know damn well it wasn't the real Ghost Owl."

She stared out the windshield. It wasn't like Eddie to play coy either. Did his superiors suspect his links to Tim? Was his SUV under surveillance? She dug into her purse for paper and a pen and scribbled "BUGGED?" on the notepad.

At the next stoplight, she held it up for him to read. He grimaced and nodded.

She motioned for him to continue questioning her while she pulled Tim's jammer from the inside pocket of her bag where she stashed it.

"Dammit, Harri!" Eddie slammed his palm on the steering wheel for show. "Your license and my career are on the line. Who called me tonight?"

Ahead of them, halogens lit Ted Meadowfield's smarmy face on the side of the Action 12! headquarters. Their giant antenna would be a good excuse. She pressed the button on the scrambler. "Ten seconds to tell me what's going on."

"Boss got an anonymous tip I was covering for you and you are conspiring with the Ghost Owl. You?"

"Aisha took Sparx, Sourpuss, and Nix to catch the asshole pretending to be Captain Justice."

"Nix?"

"Used to be Screaming Orgasm," she muttered. "Off." She jabbed the button and stowed the device back in her bag. Now, she knew what they were up against.

Eddie smoothly shifted verbal gears as if he'd been arguing with her the whole time. "—don't seem to get how much trouble you are in."

"Yes, I do," she protested. "But I can't tell you who he is because I don't know!"

Other than the folks living in the Lechuza Building and her clients, the only person who could have called in a tip was Serena.

Unless . . .

Harri silently mouthed a few choice obscenities. Why the hell hadn't she taken Trubble's comment this afternoon about Eddie and Cal for the subtle threat it really was?

An idea fluttered through her head, a bad one, but hell, if the truce with Corvus was off anyway . . .

"Byron Trubble and his boys at Corvus know who the Ghost Owl really is."

Eddie glanced at her, confusion wrinkling his craggy features more than usual. She motioned for him to go with her line of conversation.

"I thought you had a deal with him, so he'd quit harassing your super clients."

"I have a feeling Trubble is behind both Captain Justice's abduction and the jerk who replaced him and is trying to trash CJ's reputation. Trubble's pissed CJ hired me instead of accepting Trubble's offer to become a black ops agent."

Eddie grinned. He understood the best lie was the truth. "Are you sure? Have you tried to contact General Asshole?"

"Talked to Byron this afternoon. I got the 'couldn't tell you if I did it' speech—"

"Which means he did," Eddie finished. "That still doesn't answer the Ghost Owl question." He guided his SUV onto the last exit before the freeway turned into the causeway. The road curved under the highway and merged with Shoreline Drive.

"I'm in the same boat you are. I get a tip from him once in a while to pass on to Captain Justice or Sparx, like when he let me know he'd rescued Miguel's son from Seismic Shift." Harri smirked as she recognized Eddie's destination. Reflective tape outlined the sheriff and police departments' boats on the law enforcement dock. Not so with the boats belonging to the FBI.

The three craft were thoroughbreds compared to the workhorses of the local departments. They were designed to pursue and apprehend supervillains when a superhero was unavailable. Eddie pulled to a halt next to the other FBI vehicles parked at the dock, and they both jumped out and headed for the boats.

"What the hell is she doing here, Lewis?" a tall man barked.

"Weren't you listening to the wire you insisted I wear?" Eddie said dryly. "By the way, Harri, this is my boss Howard Dreyfuss. Special Agent in Charge Dreyfuss, my ex-wife Harri Winters."

"Thank you for including me, Special Agent." Harri stuck out her hand. "As I told Eddie on the way here, one of my clients got a tip from the Ghost Owl earlier this evening that the man impersonating Captain Justice may be hiding in Westerville Park. Eddie confirmed the Ghost Owl gave the same tip to the FBI."

Dreyfuss blinked and shook her outstretched hand, apparently overwhelmed by her rapid patter.

She released his hand and glanced up at Eddie. "Got some Kevlar in extra-small."

"We'll get you situated." His lips twitched as he tried very hard not to smile. He turned to board the closest boat. Harri followed.

"Hold it right there!"

They both turned back toward Dreyfuss.

He jabbed his index finger in Harri's direction. "You aren't going anywhere. You're a civilian."

"With all due respect, Special Agent in Charge—" She smiled sweetly at him. "—I'm not a super, but I've held my own against professional assassins as well as superheroes like Sparx and Seismic Shift. And I'm one of the few people who can say she walked away from an encounter with the infamous Black Death. I'm more qualified than a lot of your agents." She whirled, brushed past Eddie, and climbed aboard the speedboat before Dreyfuss could say another word.

CHAPTER 31

Once on the deck of the FBI interceptor, another agent handed her a Kevlar tactical vest. He smirked as he asked if she needed help donning it, but his humor seemed to be aimed at Dreyfuss, not her.

"No, thanks." She yanked the bulky vest over her torso. At least, it seemed bulky after wearing Tim's exoskeleton.

"Eddie," another agent called out. "That signal you gave us has reached the eastern shore of the lake and stopped."

"Where?"

"The Westerville boat docks," she answered.

Eddie looked up at Harri, and she shrugged.

"They're probably giving Sourpuss a chance to pick up the imposter's scent," she said.

"I thought you said the Ghost Owl contacted one of your clients," Dreyfuss asked. He made a point of sitting as far away from Harri as he could manage in such tight confines. "You're not listed as Sourpuss's attorney of record."

"Nix is our client, and she's the one who called her sister in."

"Sourpuss's sister is Screaming Orgasm," the agent with the tracking tablet said.

"She's now Nix. She changed her codename on the recommendation of her attorney." Harri rolled her eyes. "Unfortunately, we made the announcement yesterday, and it got lost in the fake Captain Justice stupidity."

Eddie laughed while he finished untying the last rope. He jumped aboard, still chuckling. "Hit it, Quartermain."

The FBI agent at the throttle revved the engine, and the speedboat leapt across the waves.

The night remained quiet while Aisha led the three supers to the parking area overlooking the picnic tables and boat docks. Between her new super eyesight and the visor's night vision, everything stood out crystal clear.

Including the huge black eyes of a toad hidden in the grass.

"Anything, Sourpuss?"

The superhero bent and sniffed around the grass and concrete before she shook her head. "Nothing out of the orrrdinarrry. Humansss. Petsss. Wildlife. The ssstench of your parrot-lizarrrdsss is lessserrr herrre."

An idea struck Aisha. "What do I smell like to you?"

"A prrregnant human," Sourpuss said. "But you'rrre Jatz'om Kuh. I wasssn't going to crrriticize."

Both Sparx and Nix turned and stared at Aisha.

"Are you fucking insane?" Sparx blurted.

"That explains a lot." A mischievous grin lit Nix's face. "The pregnancy is messing with your powers. No wonder you've had trouble staying on the ground lately."

Sparx stalked towards Aisha. "You are going home right this minute." She jabbed her index finger in the direction of Canyon Pointe.

"My pregnancy is my personal—" Aisha started.

"Too late!" Sourpuss's growly voice turned into a full-throated roar. "Incoming!"

Her warning barely registered before something grabbed Aisha, and her assailant swept her up in the sky.

CHAPTER 32

"I'll kill you this time," someone shouted in Aisha's ear. Or close enough for her helmet's external microphone to pick up the words and add a few squeals of its own to her earbuds.

She twisted in his arms. Yep, the asshole pretending to be Rey. She reached up and tore off his cowl. The cloth fluttered away in their wake.

"It's over," she said. "We know you're not the real Captain Justice. Surrender and tell me where he is. The DA will cut you a deal for your cooperation."

Her receiver crackled to life, but it was Sparx's voice this time. "Cut loose, Owl, so I can have a clear shot at him."

Aisha glanced over her captor's shoulder. Sure enough, Sparx kept up with them.

All of Aisha's anger rose to the surface, but just hitting him wouldn't make him drop her. She cupped her gloved hands and slapped his ears.

The imposter howled in pain at the same moment he released her. In free-fall, she panicked for a moment and flailed in the air.

Lightning discharged above her. The visor darkened to compensate, but the shock was enough to bounce her out of her terror. A little concentration had her hovering few feet above the water.

Sparx was right. Aisha should be thinking about her baby. But Sparx was up there alone with that asshat. Aisha had more than enough of his shit, and he was their only link to getting Rey back, wherever he was.

With that determined thought, she shot up toward the battle.

— • —

The three FBI boats were about three quarters of the way across Lake Del Oro when the lightning strike blinded Harri. Before she could blink, a sharp clap of thunder blasted her. It was followed by a sonic boom. Between the spots in her vision, she saw everyone on the speedboat had clap their hands over their ears like she did. Everyone except poor Quartermain at the wheel. He winced and ducked his head, but he kept control of the boat.

"Anybody see anything?" Eddie shouted.

"Night vision goggles are recalibrating, sir," one of the other FBI agents called out. He looked a lot younger than Rey or Dom. A lot skinnier, too.

"The Ghost Owl tracker says he's about a thousand feet over the eastern lakeshore and climbing," the agent with the tablet said. "Two thousand, three—"

"What?" Dreyfuss yelled. "Since when can the Ghost Owl fly?" Everyone ignored him and scanned the sky.

"Got visual on him!" shouted the kid with the night goggles.

Harri looked upward but couldn't make out a damn thing in the dark.

"He's gonna slam into Captain Justice!" Another sonic boom followed the agent's play-by-play. "Holy crap! I think he just sent Captain Justice into orbit!"

"That's not Captain Justice," Eddie snapped.

"Sorry, sir." The kid sounded contrite. "Uh-oh. Static around Sparx—" He ripped off the night goggles.

Everyone on the boat ducked their heads as another bolt of lightning ignited practically on top of them, accompanied by a sharp crack of thunder.

A third sonic boom rattled Hari's brain despite her hands over her ears. She peered through squinted eyelids. A flash of white and dark rocketed toward the park. The tops of pines wavered and disappeared on the bluff. The sound of a multitude of logs cracking echoed over the water.

Quartermain slowed the engine. The two boats behind them followed suit. He looked over his shoulder.

"Hey, Lewis! You sure we want to get any closer to a super battle?"

"You want to be in this boat if one of them lands in the water too close to us?" Harri snapped. She was a decent enough swimmer to make it to shore, but losing the weapons if the speedboats were overturned or sank meant she and the FBI would be snacks for the monsters Aisha had seen in the park.

Eddie grinned at Quartermain. "You heard the lady."

"Wait a minute! I'm the agent in charge!" Dreyfuss protested.

Illuminated by the spotlights of the other two boats, all the agents looked at him with various degrees of worry, disgust, and amusement.

Dreyfuss's jaw worked for a moment before he said, "Cut the lights, and get us to the park docks, Quartermain."

Their pilot's whistle sounded like a freakin' freight train over the water. All three boats cut their lights. The kid, with his night vision goggles back in place, stepped up beside Quartermain, who opened up the throttle. As the boat eased forward at a fraction of its previous speed, the kid called out any obstacles like partially submerged logs and boulders. The other two pilots lined up and followed the course Quartermain and the kid set.

Eddie reached for his sidearm holstered beneath his shoulder. He drew the gun and handed it to Harri butt first. "Just in case."

"She's a civilian," Dreyfuss barked. "She shouldn't be carrying a weapon."

"She's a better shot than you," Eddie replied smoothly. He unzipped the duffle bag beneath his legs, pulled out a belt holster, and handed it to Harri.

Quartermain and the woman watching the dimmed laptop screen snickered.

"I taught her when we started dating because I didn't want some prick I arrested to come after her when I wasn't around," Eddie added as he handed Harri two extra magazines.

The two agents immediately stopped their not-so-silent laughter.

"What about you?" Harri automatically started checking everything, mainly by touch in the weak, scattered starlight. She didn't like the thought of carrying a gun again. But if Aisha was right, her monsters would be prowling the park, and Harri sure as hell didn't have any superpowers to protect herself.

"Mine's bigger." He reached back into the duffle bag at his feet and pulled out a grenade launcher.

"Seriously?" She stared at her ex in disbelief. "You think that will hurt him?"

"It fires gas grenades, and teargas will make even a super cry like a baby." His teeth gleamed in the dark shadow of his face. "I've also got anesthetic gas in the second set."

"Just don't hit one of my clients with any type of grenade," Harri muttered. She clipped the holster on the belt of her jeans. Her belts had become more than a fashion accessory since she'd started working out with Tim.

"So the Ghost Owl *is* your client," Dreyfuss crowed.

Harri's glare was wasted in the dark, but she made the face at him anyway. "The person wearing that costume is not my client. But frankly, he's on our side right now, and I'd like to keep it that way since our opponent has the same skill set as Captain Justice, who *is* my client."

She just prayed they got some answers out of the imposter before someone really did get killed in this fiasco.

— ·•· —

Aisha arrowed toward the furrow caused by the imposter's crash landing.

"Owl, hold up," Sparx murmured through the bud in Aisha's ear.

"He's down."

"Are we sure?" Sparx said. "I lost track of him in the falling trees."

Aisha opened her mouth, then changed her mind about arguing. Sparx knew more about the mechanics of superheroing than she did.

"I lost him, too," she finally admitted.

"Sourpuss? Nix? Either of you have eyes on him?"

Instead of an answer, an earsplitting shriek screamed over the comm. Thank goodness, Tim's little devices automatically compensated. Otherwise, they'd all be deaf from Nix's sonics.

"No," Sourpuss growled a moment later. "Owl's parrot-lizarrrds attacked the moment you went afterrr herrr."

"They're pretty adamant we don't go in the direction of their buddy pretending to be CJ," Nix added. Another shriek echoed over the comms.

"Where are you?" Aisha asked.

"The hiking trrrail passst the playgrrround," Sourpuss said.

Aisha blinked rapidly three times. The suit's system dialed Eddie's cellphone. One ring. Two rings. *God, please have your phone with you.*

"Lewis." His voice was muffled.

"Where are you?" she growled.

"The park's boat docks. You have the imposter in custody?"

"Not yet, but Sourpuss and Nix are in trouble. Parrot-lizards attacked them."

"Parrot-lizards?"

If Aisha hadn't already encountered them, she'd be incredulous, too. "You'll understand when you see them." She relayed the sisters' location. "Be careful. They're a bitch to take down." She blinked three times to end the call.

"Sourpuss, Nix, the FBI are at the docks and headed your way," Aisha said. "Sparx and I will do what we can to secure our fake superhero. Too bad we can't stick him in a bucket of water."

"Not funny," Sparx snapped.

"Actually, it kind of was."

Even Tim and Arthur, their resident geniuses, had to admit Harri's plan for containing Sparx two months ago was novel and scientifically on the ball.

"Just for that, you're buying me tacos for the rest of the year," Sparx said.

"Was already planning on it," Aisha responded with a smile even though the super couldn't see it. "How do we tackle the imposter?"

"Slowly and carefully." Sparx drifted toward the end of the giant furrow at a pace Aisha would have been comfortable jogging.

After checking she still had the titanium handcuffs she'd borrowed from Tim, she flew after Sparx. She crossed her toes the cuffs would be sufficient to hold the imposter. After watching the way Rey demolished her old condo when Corvus had sent Cobblestone to hurt her, she wondered if they would be enough.

— •◆• —

Harri jogged behind Eddie into the playground clearing. Nix and Sourpuss must have been forced to retreat. They stood on top of the jungle gym, making a stand against Aisha's parrot-lizards.

The second the three teams of FBI agents turned their flashlights on the monsters, the brightly plumaged critters scrambled for the underbrush. Harri shook her head. Aisha's description hadn't exaggerated their ugliness. Instead of wings, they had feathered forelegs with what looked like razor-sharp claws. Two shots at the retreating figures sent blue feathers into the air.

Sourpuss leapt down to the cedar chips cushioning the area beneath the playset while Nix swung down from the monkey bars. Adrenaline must still be coursing through them from their jerky motions as they reached the grass.

Harri jogged up to Nix and her sister. "You two okay?"

Sourpuss shivered and resumed her human form. "Cats and birds rarely mix." She waved at the bloody cuts showing through the rents in her costume. "But they don't seem to like Nix's sonics too much."

Dreyfuss joined them. "They've scattered through the woods. I doubt they'll bother us again." He patted the rifle under his arm.

"I wouldn't count on it." Harri shook her head. "The Ghost Owl said they hunted as a pack when he encountered them."

"Maybe he knows more than he's letting on." Dreyfuss sneered. "Hell, for all we know, he's controlling these things."

Nix moved as if she would hit him, but her sister stepped between Dreyfuss and Nix.

"Why?" Sourpuss asked quietly.

"Why what?" Dreyfuss said.

"What's the Ghost Owl's motive for luring us out here?" Sourpuss crossed her arms. "Or for setting those parrot-lizards on us?"

Harri bit her lower lip to keep from grinning. The girl was smart. Very smart. Asking all the right questions. She'd make a hell of an attorney.

"Yeah, boss," the agent who still had the signal tracker sidled up next to Harri. "According to witness statements, the Ghost Owl stopped the fake Captain Justice from killing that jogger a couple of nights ago. Not to mention, the amateur video from the party boat made it look like the fake was definitely trying to kill the Ghost Owl last night."

Harri shivered at the memory. The imposter would have succeeded in killing her if it hadn't been for Eddie and Aisha.

"The Ghost Owl contacted me because I know CJ's civilian friends and family," Nix added. "None of them knows where he is. And this freak?" She jabbed a thumb in the general direction of the imposter's crash landing. "He's definitely not CJ. Even I can tell the difference."

A red glow from the corner of her eye drew Harri's attention to her left. Eddie's buddy Quartermain stood near the edge of the woods, facing the trees. The red glow around him faded. He slowly turned around and raised the rifle to his shoulder.

Pointing the barrel towards their little group.

Horror mixed with bile in her throat. "Down!" She whirled and dived into Nix and the FBI agent as sound exploded inside her head.

CHAPTER 33

Shouts and the squawking of parrots penetrated the ringing in Harri's ears. Someone pushed her, and she flopped on her back in the grass.

"She's bleeding!" A feminine voice.

"Harri!" Definitely Eddie speaking. Except he shouldn't be here.

"Tim? Tim! Where's Tim? Is he okay?" She flailed at the hands trying to pin her to the grass. Her eyes refused to focus. Everything was dark. Too dark.

"Who's Tim?" A different woman's voice.

"Her boyfriend," Eddie muttered. He sounded angry. Why was he angry? He's the one who filed for the frickin' divorce.

"Is Tim out of surgery?" Wetness trickled down her temple and into her hair. Dammit, she was not a crier!

"Harri, listen to me," Eddie murmured in her ear. "Tim's fine. Remember? Sparx got him to the hospital."

She reached for her head. The liquid on her temple felt weird. Too sticky to be tears.

"Did you pour syrup on me?" she said.

"No, Harri."

Someone shone a flashlight in her face, and she squeezed her eyes shut. Someone poked her eyelid.

"That hurts!"

"Stop fighting us, Harri," Eddie said. "Nix, talk to her while I check her pupils."

"Ms. Winters, you're going to be okay," the first woman's voice murmured. She sounded terribly young. "Agent Lewis is checking your wound."

Nix?" Harri tested the word. Someone pried her left eyelid up and flashed a light before releasing her.

"Yes, Ms. Winters?"

"You're one of our clients." The same idiot with the flashlight wrenched up her right eyelid.

"Yes, Ms. Winters."

"What on God's green earth made you use Screaming Orgasm for your name? Were you trying to give your grandmother a stroke? She's a perfectly lovely woman, and you went out of your way to embarrass her."

"I'd say she's fine," Eddie said dryly.

Someone had been pointing a gun at Harri. "Quartermain!" She tried to sit up, but Nix and Eddie held her down.

"He's out cold and cuffed thanks to Nix and Sourpuss." Eddie dabbed at Harri's forehead with something very cold and very wet. "Everyone else is okay. The bullet grazed you though."

"Something had control of him," Harri murmured. "I saw a red glow."

"Yeah, so did Anson," Eddie said as he continued to clean her wound. "Those damn four-legged parrots charged us when Quartermain opened fire." He glanced around. "Sourpuss seems to have everything under control."

"Let me up," Harri demanded.

"Let me bandage you first!" Eddie finished cleaning her wound. "Otherwise, I'll cuff you and have Keel haul you back to the docks."

"Keelhaul." Harri snickered. "Have you turned pirate, Eddie?"

"Shut up and hold still, Harri," Eddie muttered.

"Sir?"

Harri looked up. The female FBI agent with the tablet stood over them, her attention locked on the screen.

"What, Anson?" Eddie squeezed a tube along Harri's forehead. Whatever came out cooled the burning streak that pounded in time to her heart.

"The Ghost Owl's signal is erratic." Anson shook her head. "It's dancing all over the place." A lightning strike and an immediate crack of thunder punctuated her words.

"I'd say our fake Captain Justice is still giving the Owl and Sparx fits," Harri said. "We need to get those gas grenades to them."

"Hold still," Eddie ordered again. "Let me finish!" He placed the gauze, then slapped on the tape a little harder than necessary.

"Ow! Hey! Watch it!"

This time, Nix let Harri sit up.

"You're a sadist," she muttered.

"You're really trying to fill those last two inches with rage," Eddie shot back. "Any dizziness?"

Harri climbed to her feet. "No." She wouldn't mention the headache or the nausea because he would follow through on his threat to cuff her and leave her behind. "What the hell happened to Quartermain?"

"We don't know." Eddie sounded worried. "Nix hit him with her powers. Two of the team are taking him back to the boats."

Harri sighed. "Well, that explains the ringing in my ears."

"Hey!" Nix protested. "You were on the ground and behind me when I cut loose."

"Not to mention the bullet grazing your skull didn't help," Eddie added.

"We need to get to Sparx and Ai—" She swallowed hard. Maybe the close call had rocked her brain more than she thought. "And-and the Ghost Owl."

Eddie was terribly still for an instant, but instead of calling her bluff, he turned to the other agents. "Let's move out."

— •●• —

Aisha darted to her left. The remnants of the pine tree trunk Fake Rey threw at her bounced before hitting another tree with a loud crash.

Sparx zipped behind him and hit him with a jolt of electricity. Little brush fires were dotted around the clearing his impact had created. If this battle had taken place later in the year, they'd be facing wildfires.

The imposter whirled to face Sparx, but she'd already shot straight up and out of the way. Her lightning strikes seemed to slow him, but the mega-volts of electricity weren't taking him down as they had hoped. They needed Nix.

Aisha hefted another tree trunk at his exposed back. The pine shattered like glass when it hit him and flew in all directions. She breathed a prayer of thanks for Tim's armor and headgear as shards bounced off the suit and pinged against the helmet. The last thing she wanted was to put her skin and bones to the test.

But for the first time, he staggered at their onslaught. Maybe they were wearing him down. Too bad she didn't have a refrigerator handy to beat him over his head, like Rey did to Cobblestone.

They needed to subdue him before someone really got hurt. Maybe she'd depended too much on using Nix's sonics after what Tim's modified ultrasound device had done to her and Rey back at their building.

As if in answer to Aisha's silent plea, she caught a glimpse of Sourpuss running in their direction. Nix couldn't be far behind her sister.

Aisha needed to keep his attention on her and away from the younger superheroes. She snagged a rock and launched it at Fake Rey. It shattered against the side of his face. And she needed to keep him on the ground where Nix could reach him.

Instead of throwing something back at Aisha, the imposter charged her. She dived to her right, but instead of landing on her side as she expected, she zipped along, flying three feet above the trees that had been knocked over. She oriented herself and concentrated on getting her boots back on the ground.

Fake Rey skidded in the debris and whirled, his intent to inflict bodily damage obvious in his enraged expression. His eyes widened as Sourpuss launched herself into the air. The super's extended claws aimed for his face.

His alarmed shout echoed against the trees still standing. He tried to toss Sourpuss off him, but her claws dug into Rey's extra uniform.

Light flashed, the concussion knocking Aisha over before the electronics of Tim's suit kicked in to dampen the sound. When the spots cleared, she looked up.

Sparx hovered over her. A red nimbus surrounded the superhero, but it was the sparking static that alarmed Aisha.

"Sparx, stand down!"

The superhero gestured. Out of sheer panic, Aisha launched herself straight up.

— • —

"What the hell!" The earth beneath Harri's feet shuddered with another sonic boom. Everyone with her halted. The FBI agents raised their weapons and scanned the trees still standing.

Her endurance was better since she started working out. The shame of representing superheroes along with the attempts on her life had motivated her. However, the debris from the imposter's crash meant Nix and the FBI team couldn't move any faster than she could.

Sourpuss had bounded ahead, and from the sounds, Sparx and Aisha were still going full tilt against the imposter. Sourpuss should have reached them by now to assist the other two women. Part of Harri had truly hoped he had been faking Rey's powers, but if he was holding his own against three other supers for this long, they were all in trouble.

"Come on," Nix urged. "We can't stop now."

"Except the sounds of their fight are getting closer," Eddie said.

Harri closed her eyes and concentrated. Despite the headache and the ringing in her ears, her ex was right.

A gust of wind blew past her face. Her eyes popped open as her ex-husband yanked her to the ground. Sparx flew towards them, but something was wrong. A faint red glow surrounded her, just like the glow around Quartermain before he opened fire on his own people.

"Nix!"

The superhero vaulted over a fallen pine and planted herself directly under Sparx's path. Static sparked and crackled along Sparx's body, but Nix didn't hesitate. She screamed.

Harri slapped her hands over her ears at the godawful sound. So did the FBI agents around her.

Sparx shuddered. The red glow faded. She lost control and tumbled through the air.

Another shadow blasted past them from behind and caught the falling superhero. The pair drifted to the ground.

Harri's breath caught in her throat. If she hadn't known Aisha was in the Ghost Owl costume, she'd be fangirling right now. And Aisha had all the right moves. No one would suspect an IP lawyer behind the visor.

"What the hell is going on here?" Dreyfuss shouted.

Harri ignored him and ran after Nix to Aisha. She still held up a woozy Sparx.

"Why'd you attack me?" Even through the helmet's voice modifier, Aisha's anger came through.

"I-I didn't have any control." Sparx sounded as wobbly as the rest of her.

Harri looked at Aisha. "The same thing happened to one of the FBI agents. A red glow appeared around him, and he opened fire on us."

"Are you okay?" Aisha asked.

Harri had the distinct impression her best friend was staring at her forehead. "A scratch from diving for cover." She didn't like outright lying to Aisha, but the woman needed to focus on the business at hand. "Nix's powers seem to disrupt the mind control. You two go. I'll take care of Sparx."

"You're under arrest for vigilantism, Ghost Owl!" Dreyfuss charged up to their little group.

Harri rolled her eyes and slid Sparx's left arm across her shoulders. "I've got her. Go do your job. I've got something that'll work almost as good as Nix."

Ignoring Dreyfuss, Aisha scooped Nix into her arms and shot straight up into the air before turning toward the way Sparx had come from.

Harry couldn't help a slight smile. Aisha definitely had a better handle on her powers than she did a week ago.

Dreyfuss rounded on Harri. "You advised him to leave. I'll have you arrested for conspiracy, Winters!"

"I think I'm going to be sick," Sparx muttered.

But before Harri could do a thing, vomit exploded from poor Sparx and coated the special agent in charge's chest. Dreyfuss gasped and sputtered.

Eddie appeared on Sparx's other side. Together, he and Harri walked the super to a fallen log and sat her down.

"Anson!"

At his shout, the female agent jogged over to them. "Yes, sir?"

"Keep an eye on Sparx," Eddie ordered. "We've got a mental manipulator in the middle of this crap. If she glows red again, grab the syringe of morphine from the med kit and stab her with it."

"Can't I have the morphine now?" Sparx said. She barely got the words out when she leaned over and threw up again.

Screeching came from the direction Aisha and Nix had flown. Harri and Eddie looked at each other.

"More of those damn mutant parrot things?"

"Yep," she answered.

"We can't leave Sparx and Anson here alone," he muttered.

"Yes, you can," Sparx called out. "Even if that asshat took me over again, I can barely stay upright."

Harri shrugged. "She's right, and Nix did knock out Quartermain. Leave another agent with them if you're worried about Anson coming at us from behind."

"You two are not in charge!" Dreyfuss was still dabbing at the puke that decorated the front of his Kevlar vest.

"I'll stay, Lewis." An agent that had been on one of the other boats stepped forward. His square jaw and rugged looks must look great on the FBI recruiting posters.

"Wait," Sparx said weakly. She slid her right forefinger and thumb beneath the stretchy material of her cowl covering her cheek and ear, and she produced one of Tim's communications earbuds. "Take this to coordinate with the other three, Harri. Last thing we need is your FBI friends shooting at a super accidentally, or one of them thinking you're supervillains in the woods."

"I should—" Dreyfuss reached for the earbud.

Sparx yanked her hand back. "I'm only giving this to someone I trust, and you're not it."

Her words hit Harri hard. The two of them were too much alike. Trust didn't come easy. But if Sparx considered Harri more trustworthy than the FBI agents, it said how far the two of them had come in the last couple of months.

"Let's get everyone home intact," Harri said.

Sparx held out the earbud. Harri took it and slipped it into her own right ear canal. No wonder Sparx was worried. Things really weren't going well against the fake Captain Justice.

Harri looked up at Eddie. "We need to hurry."

He nodded before he turned to the rest of his team. "The rest of you, let's move." He leaned over and whispered in Harri's left ear, "I hope you have a plan for the mental manipulator."

She patted the bag slung over her body. "I do. I just need you to get me close enough to use it."

CHAPTER 34

Aisha and Nix arrived in time for Fake Rey to launch Sourpuss into the air. "Drop me!"

Aisha dipped low enough so Nix didn't break any bones in the fall before she shot upward to catch Sourpuss.

"Trying to whittle down those nine lives?" Aisha asked.

Sourpuss chuckled, which sounded more like a cat trying to cough up a hairball. "Worried I wouldn't land on my feet, little birdie?"

Fake Rey rose into the air.

"More worried about who's with me when I fall," Aisha answered. Once again, she dipped, low enough for Sourpuss to leap to safety.

When Aisha regained some altitude, the imposter glared at her before he arrowed straight for her.

Harri pushed past the brush that clung to the hill she climbed and hit the ground. "Douse the lights," she hissed to the people behind her.

The tableau looked like something from historical photographs of bomb tests. The imposter had skipped along the tops of the three small hills she and the FBI agents had crossed to land in this depression. Trees were flattened in a semicircle. His landing had been hard enough to bounce boulders and rocks to the surface.

And the situation was just as bad as it had sounded over the comm. More of the parrot-lizards had poured into the cleared area. They attacked Sourpuss and Nix, keeping the two superheroes on the defensive and unable to help Aisha.

Meanwhile, Aisha and the imposter traded blows in the air above the clearing. Any time Aisha came close to the ground, the parrot-lizards would leap, trying to get a grip, pull her down so the rest of the flock could ravage her.

"Boss?" The kid with the night goggles from their boat nudged Harri in her left ribs. His chin jutted towards the opposite side of the clearing. "Got someone in the woods to our left."

Probably the kid acknowledging her as the leader was meant as an insult to Dreyfuss, but he sounded so damn sincere. On the other hand, none of the other agents, including Eddie, showed any signs of humor.

She narrowed her eyes, but she couldn't make out anything in the shadows. Hell, the only way she could keep track of the supers was Captain Justice's uniform, Nix's white-blond hair, and the occasional reflection of ambient light from Canyon Pointe off of Aisha's visor. "You sure it's not one of the monsters?"

"Heat signature's closer to human." He shrugged. "Most likely a super. Did your peeps call anyone else in?"

Harri shook her head. "No."

Eddie crept up next to her right. "Our mental manipulator?"

"Probably." She wished she and Aisha had been wrong about an unknown third party being behind their recent troubles. This would have been so much easier if Corvus had been behind all this crap. Now, they were dealing with a possible super whose abilities had only been hinted at.

"I could unload the gas grenades, and we sort out the mess once everyone's unconscious or crying," Eddie said.

"And we can arrest them all," Dreyfuss snarled from Eddie's right.

"We're still not sure they'll work on the guy pretending to be Captain Justice," she murmured. In fact, she was pretty sure the anesthetic ones wouldn't, but she couldn't tell the truth in front of Eddie's superior without both of them ending up in jail cells. "If we take out the supers on our side, but not the unknown super and those damn parrot-lizards, we'll be—"

One of Nix's sonic blasts hit the side of the hill below their position, blowing top soil and debris into the air. Harri and the FBI's little army ducked and covered their noses.

"—sitting ducks," she finished when the dust settled and they could all breathe again.

"We need to take out the person in the woods before he realizes we're here," Eddie murmured. "Otherwise, he will set us on each other again."

"Can we use one of the teargas grenades on him?" Harri said. "Flush him out?"

Eddie stuck his right index finger in his mouth, yanked it out with a sucking sound, and held it up in the air. "Wind's out of the southwest. About four-five miles per hour. The teargas will blow right into the clearing."

Harri tapped her right ear, the one with Sparx's comm. "Then we flush him out."

Eddie nodded.

"I thought those supers were your clients."

She could hear the sneer in Dreyfuss's words. Her fist curled into a ball, but before she could deck the asshole, Eddie wrapped his large hand around hers.

"Now's not the time," he whispered in her ear.

He was right. Tim would have said the same damn thing if he were here. That knowledge made her relax her fingers.

Instead, she said, "Owl, ladies, we've got a second hostile in the southwest corner of the clearing—"

"For the love of—" Aisha said. "I'll distract him. Hit him with the damn teargas already!"

Harri couldn't help grinning. Of course her partner had been listening to Harri's conversation with the FBI. "Owl says do it."

—— ·◆· ——

Aisha cried out as the jerk pretending to be Rey hit her with a particularly nasty left cross she couldn't dodge in time. As long as no video conferences, court hearings, or mediations were scheduled for the next week, she wouldn't have to worry about any adverse publicity over the bruising on her face.

Assuming she survived this fight.

But the person Harri and the FBI spotted? Someone controlling the guy impersonating Rey, plus plastic surgery and some kind of illegal genetic enhancement to give him powers? Yeah, that would explain a lot.

She concentrated and dropped like a rock. With Nix and Sourpuss dealing with the parrot creatures, Aisha hadn't dared throwing anything at the fake, afraid she'd miss him or he'd knock it aside, both of which could result in killing the sisters. But now . . .

Now, it was time to stop fighting defensively.

Her actions drew the parrot-lizards toward her. She hefted a tree trunk and swung it like a two-handed hammer. Her swipe took out a bunch of the monsters. The others scrambled out of the way. On her second twirl, she released the trunk at the imposter. He zoomed out of the way, but the remnants of the pine landed a bit north of the position of the second possible hostile Harri reported.

Muffled thumps came from the hill at the south end of the clearing.

"Gas away," Harri reported in Aisha's ear.

"Harri, have your boys give me a couple of those gas grenades." Nix's voice crackled through the comm. "Two right in front of me."

"Got your back, sis," Sourpuss said.

Unfortunately, Aisha's respite wasn't long. Fake Rey bodyslammed her into a still standing tree.

Well, through the standing tree.

He may be stronger, but she was faster. She channeled her fury into arching her flight path up. The idiot stared at the broken trunk as if he couldn't believe what he'd done. And the rest of the tree tottered in his direction. She shot forward, adding her momentum to gravity's pull on the pine. The resulting powerdrive buried him in the tough, root-filled soil.

Something tickled her instincts. The imposter wasn't acting like any of the supervillains she'd seen in action, whether live or on video. Sure he hadn't held back any of his punches.

Except it didn't explain why he hadn't touched her abdominal area. His hits and kicks had been aimed at every other part of her body. Now, why the hell would he care about hurting her baby?

— • ● • —

Gunfire erupted as the couple of FBI agents with rifles and night scopes picked off the parrot-lizards that weren't caught between the four gas grenades Eddie had launched in the middle of the clearing.

With Tim's sonic device in hand, Harri scrambled down the side of the hill that still had some vegetative cover, dragging the kid with the night vision goggles with her. The trees gave them some protection from Nix's sonic scream. The superhero used her powers to create a wall. The vibrating air kept the teargas around their unknown participant and from blowing into Nix and

Sourpuss. Nix's efforts drove their unknown supervillain out of the noxious cloud and toward Harri and the kid.

Centered in the beam of their flashlights, the old man skidded to a stop, shock on his weathered features. A red glow emanated from a stone amulet hanging from a leather thong around the old man's wrinkled neck.

An amulet that looked awfully similar to the one Rey's mother had given him.

The old man's expression shifted from surprise to craftiness. He pointed to the FBI kid and mumbled something that was neither English or Spanish.

The kid stumbled. The same red glow that had covered Quartermain when he shot Harri flouresced around the young agent. He reached for his sidearm.

The stone. It had to be the old man's source of power. Just like Rey's kept him hidden from the monsters.

Harri raced forward and crashed into the old man. They tumbled to the ground. She pressed the button of Tim's sonic device, and the old man cried out.

Something hard cracked the back of Harri's head. The sonic emitter dropped from her nerveless fingers, and the old man pushed her off him.

She rolled over to see the barrel of a gun aimed at her head. The FBI kid started to squeeze the trigger.

"No." The old man pressed a hand on the kid's arm.

The agent lowered his sidearm. There was nothing in his slack expression to indicate he understood what was happening.

Harri tried to get up, but she couldn't make anything work quite right. Maybe the kid had finished the brain damage started by Quartermain.

"I have a better use for her." The old man pulled a knife from beneath his denim jacket. Its blade gleamed bloody from the glow of the stone.

She moaned and kept her eyes slitted. If he got close enough, maybe she could use him as a shield. Surely, he wouldn't command the kid to shoot him in order to take her out. All she needed to do was get that damn amulet off him.

Right, Harri. Why don't you wish for a ride on a space rocket, too, while you're at it?

"I need her heart."

Adrenaline jolted through her at his threat. It was all she could do to keep her breathing even.

The old man knelt beside her, the blade aimed up as he started slicing her polo shirt. She grabbed his hand holding the knife with both of hers and shoved upward with everything left in her.

He grabbed her hands with his left and barely stopped her from slashing open his throat, but she'd achieved her objective. The knife was inside the leather thong hanging from his neck. She joined his effort to push the knife out and away from him.

The blade sliced through the leather, and the stone dropped to Harri's bare abdomen. She heaved and the old man toppled. She snatched the stone, rolled to her feet and staggered toward the clearing. If her guess was right, the damn parrot-lizards wouldn't touch her.

If she wasn't . . . well, death was better than some jerk using her for a sacrifice.

The old man yelled something in his strange language. Something Harri was pretty sure wasn't complimentary. But the expected bullet in the back never came.

She touched her ear. The comm unit was still there. "Aisha! Get the stone off the fake! That's how he's being controlled!"

CHAPTER 35

Before Aisha could dig the bastard out from under the huge pine tree, Fake Rey burst from beneath it in an explosion of wood shards. Beyond him, Nix finally had to release her wall of sound in order to breathe. Tear gas drifted into the clearing, no longer impeded by Nix's barrier.

Aisha winced at Harri's shouting through the receiver, but her partner's words made sense. She should have yanked the damn amulet off of the imposter the first night she noticed it. Despite Aisha's watering eyes, or maybe because of them, she focused her attention on the amulet's outline, barely visible beneath his costume's design and rose into the air.

He gasped and coughed as the main wall of teargas rolled over him. She wouldn't have a better chance.

Aisha sucked in a deep breath of air, prayed the helmet's filtering system worked as well as Miguel claimed, and darted for the fake Captain Justice. He grabbed her arm at her feint. She pivoted and wrapped her legs around his waist. She dipped the glove of her left hand beneath the torn neckline where she'd ripped off his cowl. Her fingers found the thong.

"What the hell are you doing?" Confusion and anger twisted his face. Tears ran down his cheeks.

"Freeing you," she said as she clasped the amulet. She yanked. The leather snapped.

And they both tumbled to the ground.

⸺ ◆ ⸺

Harri ran into the clearing. Dead or vomiting parrot-lizards covered the ground. Nix was bent over, out of the way of the cloud of tear gas. Her chest heaved, trying it replace the oxygen after such a long sonic scream. Sourpuss kept the remaining parrot-lizards away from her sister. The FBI couldn't shoot anymore for fear of hitting the superheroes.

As one, the parrot-lizards stopped their attack and their vomiting. They looked at Harri with an intensity that reminded her of Quartermain before he opened fire.

Crashing in the brush behind Harri drew her attention. The old man stumbled into the clearing, the knife still in his hand.

The parrot-lizards looked at him, then Harri again. They reminded her of the German Shepherds in CPPD's K-9 unit waiting for the signal from their officer. She couldn't stop her vicious smile.

"Get 'em, boys," she said.

The surviving parrot-lizards squawked unanimously and charged toward the old man. Terror filled his face. He whirled and raced into the woods, the flock after him in their odd reptilian stride.

Sourpuss straightened from her crouch. "You do realize you set loose a pack of monsters on public land, don't you?"

Harri ignored the superhero's sarcastic question and stared across the clearing. The teargas had dissipated to reveal Aisha cradling Rey's lookalike in her lap.

"You folks okay down there?" Eddie called from the top of the hill.

"Cuts, bruises, and a definite concussion," Harri called back. She touched the back of her head. She had another lump to match the one on her forehead, but nothing wet or sticky to indicate blood. Her ponytail had taken the brunt when the kid had pistol-whipped her.

"You might want to send someone into the woods to collect your agent with the night vision goggles," she added. "Our mentalist put the whammy on him, like he did Quartermain."

She shoved the stone into the front pocket of her jeans and trudged toward Aisha. Behind her, Eddie's deep voice issued orders, only for Dreyfuss to stridently countermand them before giving the exact same order. Was Dreyfuss Corvus's inside man at the FBI, bent on making Eddie's life miserable out of spite for being married to Harri at one point in their lives? Or was Dreyfuss just that much of an insecure idiot?

It wasn't her problem. She and Eddie were over. Yep, she traded one set of husband problems for another set of boyfriend problems that were even weirder. And that was assuming she and Tim were still an item after their fight at the hospital.

Fake Rey was obviously out cold. Aisha had been smart and already cuffed him.

"Hey, you did good." She reached out and laid her hand on Aisha's shoulder. "Way better than I did."

Aisha tapped the side of her helmet to turn off the comm system and cracked open her visor. Harri pulled out the one in her ear and shoved it in the back pocket of her jeans.

"Do we turn him over to the FBI?" Aisha whispered. She opened her right hand, showing the amulet she'd removed from him. "If he was being controlled, he's innocent. And if he knows where Rey is—"

"There's also the fact that whoever he is, he's an unregistered super with Rey's powerset." Harri crossed her arms. Despite all the crap the bastard had put them through, she felt a little sorry for him. "Corvus will ensure he never makes it to a federal court for his arraignment hearing."

"What do we do th-then?" Aisha's voice caught.

"I don't—"

Light exploded around them. Light so bright and white Aisha slid her visor back in place and Harri had to raise her hands to block it.

"Thank you. Thank you so much for finding my son," a feminine voice said.

CHAPTER 36

Aisha still squinted, even though her visor had automatically darkened to its lowest setting.

A woman stood in the center of the light. Or the light came from her. Aisha couldn't tell which.

The woman appeared to be about Harri's height, but her dress and jewelry were something out of Dad's research books on Central America. Not to mention, she floated a couple of feet from the ground.

Aisha carefully laid Rey's duplicate on the ground and stood. "Who is he? Who are you?"

"He is my son, Hunahpu. I am Xquic."

This was NOT happening. The name were all too familiar from the book Dad had written on Mayan mythology. If this whole situation weren't insane from the beginning, Aisha would have laughed in the woman's face. Except this woman, whatever she wanted to call herself, believed she was a Mayan deity.

What if she was?

"He has a twin brother, doesn't he?" Or Hunahpu did according to the story of Xquic. *Please say no. Please say no.*

"Oh, my god," Harri muttered. "An evil twin? Seriously?"

"Shut up, dumbass," Aisha hissed.

"Yes." Hope glimmered in Xquic's face. She clasped her hands together. "Have you seen him?"

"He, uh . . ." How exactly did you tell an ancient Mayan goddess you were living out of wedlock with one of her sons? Aisha swallowed hard. "Xbalanque's a friend. We know him as Rey, the name your nurse gave him to blend with mortals. He has been missing several days. Hunahpu—" She pointed at the unconscious man. "—replaced Rey. Someone was controlling Hunahpu, attempting to fool us." She held up the amulet. "He was wearing this."

Xquic reached for the odd jade piece. The heat from her body penetrated

Aisha's glove. Her touch wasn't uncomfortable, but it was a clear indication she wasn't a normal human.

Xquic frowned as she examined the stone. "There is a matching stone." Her white hot gaze settled on Harri. "You have it."

"Yes, ma'am." Harri dug another amulet out of her jeans pocket. "I took this off an old man in the woods." She pointed at the other side of the clearing where several of the parrot-lizard corpses still decorated the ground. "He was using it to control those creatures, too. When I managed to get a hold of his amulet, the creatures obeyed me. I told them to go after the old man to keep them from killing my friends."

Xquic took the second amulet from Harri's outstretched hand. She held it up and examined it. "You took this from the sorcerer and set his death parrots on him?"

"I get a little pissy when someone tries to cut out my heart."

Xquic smiled. "You are a brave woman."

"Wait a minute," Aisha interjected. "If you're Xquic, why don't you know where Rey, I mean, Xbalanque is?"

The goddess sighed. "When I sent my sons and their nurses away shortly after their birth, I gave them protective magics to hide them from their uncles who wished my children dead."

"The amulets you gave your sons and their nurses hide them from you as well, don't they?" Aisha said.

"Yes." Xquic bowed her head. "It had to be that way. I knew someday they would learn of their abilities. When they could protect themselves, then it would be safe to see them again." She raised her head, and crystal tears traced paths down her translucent skin. "I never dreamed their uncles would find them before I did."

"Uncles?" Harri frowned. "Was the old man who was controlling your son and the parrot thingies one of the uncles?"

"No, he was merely one of their servants." Xquic crushed the two stones between her palms. Gray-green dust drifted to the ground. "You gave him the fate he deserves."

She floated down to their unconscious imposter and picked him up as easily as Patty would Grace before she headed toward the center of the white light.

"Wait!" Aisha cried out. "What about Rey? I mean Xbalanque?"

Xquic looked over her shoulder. "I don't know. I fear the worst. I hope for the best. All I can do is save the son in my arms."

The light, the goddess, and the imposter simply disappeared.

Aisha dropped to her knees. She didn't believe in magic, but she couldn't deny what had just happened either. Had Rey been sacrificed so his uncle's agent could control Rey's brother? A scream of fear and frustration clawed at her throat, but she couldn't release it. Not here. Not now.

Harri crouched beside her. "Girl, you need to pull it together and get the hell out of here. Eddie's boss wants to arrest the Ghost Owl in the worst possible way."

Aisha pushed past the numbness threatening to engulf her. Harri was right. They couldn't endanger Tim's secret identity by Aisha's arrest for vigilantism.

She pushed herself to her feet. The FBI agents were headed their way. She released her tenuous grip to the earth and zoomed into the sky.

CHAPTER 37

Harri winced at the sonic boom that echoed over the lake. At least, Aisha waited until she was clear of the park before she cut loose. Harri pulled the comm out of her back pocket and slipped it in her ear. If she were arrested, she wanted a copy of everything said, and knowing Arthur, he was recording everything.

"Why the hell did you let the Ghost Owl go?" Dreyfuss shouted. He stomped through the debris toward Harri. Eddie and a couple of other agents followed him. "He's under arrest! And where the hell did Captain Justice go? He needs to be held accountable—"

"Captain Justice is dead," she stated flatly. Even if Rey wasn't, and she prayed that Trubble delivered him to their front door in a couple of minutes, his superhero persona was definitely a goner. All that work for nothing.

The ramifications to their law practice didn't even begin to cover what Aisha was facing if Corvus didn't produce Rey.

"Where's the body?" Dreyfuss threw his hands in the air.

"His mother took it," Harri replied. Damn, she felt tired. Aisha was so much better at the PR stuff than she was.

"Harri, start from where you and Keel ran into the woods to intercept the mentalist," Eddie said gently. His right hand wrapped around her left bicep, tugged her to a fallen log, and patted it with his free hand.

Her legs had turned rubbery in those few steps. Grateful for the seat, she lowered herself to the smooth bark. She laid out what happened in the woods to her and Keel, the kid with the night vision goggles. When it came to Aisha, Harri had to alter the story a little.

"The Ghost Owl could see a similar thong on Captain Justice after she ripped off his cowl and a small lump beneath his costume. She calculated our mentalist was using a similar amulet to control Captain Justice and ripped it off him. That's when he collapsed and died."

"Where are these amulets?" Dreyfuss demanded.

"The woman claiming to be Captain Justice's mother destroyed them." Harri shrugged. "She said they were too dangerous to exist."

"Sparx didn't have one of these amulets on her," Dreyfuss pointed out. "Yet, the mentalist controlled her."

"Neither did Quartermain or Keel," Harri said. "Nix's sonic power easily disrupted the mentalist's hold on Sparx and Quartermain. His control of Keel didn't slip until I grabbed the stone from him and ran.

"Wait a minute," Dreyfuss snapped. "You referred to the Ghost Owl as a her. What are you trying to pull here, Winters?"

"The real Ghost Owl is dead, too." Harri didn't have to fake the emotion that made her voice tremble. "The video of his and Captain Justice's battle a couple of nights ago? According to the woman in the Ghost Owl costume, Captain Justice drowned the original Jatz'om Kuh in Lake Del Oro that night."

"Who is she?" Dreyfuss demanded.

"I don't know." Harri shook her head. "She raised the visor enough I could see her lower face. Her natural voice was definitely female. But I didn't recognize her." Thank goodness, she still had one of Tim's comm units. Nix and Sourpuss could hear every word Harri said, too. Hopefully they'd back up her story.

"You still haven't answered why you didn't stop her!" Dreyfuss was going to give himself a stroke at this rate.

His stupid questions were making her even more weary. "Special Agent Dreyfuss, I am not a super. How do you expect me to stop someone who was tossing around fifty-foot pines like they were toothpicks?"

"Captain Justice was your client." There was a little too much glee in Dreyfuss's voice. "If a woman with his abilities was wearing a Ghost Owl costume, that means you know more about the Ghost Owl than you're admitting. I can have you and your records subpoenaed."

"Sir, think about it," Eddie calmly said. "Our unknown super may have the same power set as Captain Justice, but she was wearing the Ghost Owl's only publicly known costume. At least, the only publicly known one until that video from a couple of nights ago. It's not that hard to get a voice modulator. They sell them as children's toys these days. Do you really think a subpoena on Ms. Winters will pass muster?"

One of the FBI agents ran up to their little group, thankfully interrupting

Dreyfuss's tirade. "We followed the trail, sir. It went cold about a mile north-west of here."

"In the middle of the woods?" Dreyfuss didn't bother to hide his incredulity.

"Yes, sir." The agent shook his head. "It's like both the man and the monsters simply vanished at that point."

Harri glanced at Eddie and followed his line of sight. There were fewer corpses of the parrot-lizards then there had been, and the ones that remained looked a little funny. As she watched, she realized why.

Their plumage turned gray before the carcass disintegrated into a pile of dust. The slight breeze scattered the little that remained across the clearing.

"Call in a truck. We can have the lab analyze these damn bird monsters and find out which supervillain created—" Dreyfuss turned around and waved toward the piles of dust.

Eddie was definitely trying to hide his smile at his supervisor's dumbfounded expression at the loss of the parrot-lizard corpses. Harri didn't bother to suppress her chuckle.

Dreyfuss's shock turned to rage. He stomped around in a tight circle, swearing a blue streak, for a good minute. Finally, he stopped. "So, we have nothing to show for tonight's work. No suspects. No evidence. Nothing but dust."

Harri's humor died. Rey. She and Aisha had promised the kid the sun and the moon. All they'd done was paint a giant bullseye on him. Putting him in the spotlight had drawn the very attention his foster mother Maria had feared.

They'd bet their law firm and their professional reputations on a man who may not be human, and who might even be dead. Harri swallowed the lump in the back of her throat. By the time all the dust settled from the past two weeks, nothing may be all she and Aisha had left, too.

— ◆ —

Aisha floated above the city, reluctant to release the faint peace the view afforded. But she couldn't avoid reality anymore. As she approached the Canyon Block, she spotted someone pacing the sidewalk in front of the Lechuza Building.

Byron S. Trubble, general, retired. And he was alone.

She stayed in the shadows until she landed on the overhang above the main entrance. A quick search in the appropriate pouch produced a smoke pellet. As he walked away from her, she leapt and landed lightly behind him.

When he pivoted and saw her, he jumped. His hand dipped towards what was no doubt a weapon hidden on him. A curl of satisfaction at surprising him lifted a little of the night's emotional turmoil. The man wore a suit in this summer heat, but she didn't think that was the only reason why his forehead gleamed with perspiration.

"You didn't deliver, Trubble," she said.

"Winters or Franklin couldn't even bother to meet me?" he said in a dry tone. He carefully and slowly relaxed the hand that had been reaching for his weapon. "And they sent you?"

"We both tried to recruit the Garcia kid." Aisha shrugged. A little truth made the best lie work. "The ladies beat us out, but I'm not the one taking his rejection personally."

"Except you didn't have your own people undermining you," Trubble said bitterly. "I've got some things for Winters in my pocket."

At Aisha's nod, he slowly, carefully reached into his jacket pocket and produced a medium-size manila envelope. "Winters was supposed to meet me here tonight."

"You had your pet at the FBI drag Winters out into the middle of Westerville Park this evening." Aisha forced a chuckle. "Did you really think that will stop her from outing you?"

"Then I want to talk to her partner."

"No, you can't talk to her partner. None of us trust you after what you've done to supers. You have to deal with me."

"Fine. Tell Winters I'm . . . asking for a twelve-hour truce." Trubble's jaw muscles twitched. This request had to be killing him. "Have her review the file. We have a mutual enemy." He held out the envelope.

Aisha laughed outright. "You're really using 'the enemy of my enemy is my friend' bullshit?"

"Yes." No mockery, no condescension came from Trubble. He was deadly serious. "I'll meet her at the same bench at noon. No tricks from me."

"That's no different than a scorpion saying he won't sting."

Trubble let out a long-suffering sigh. "It's the best I can offer."

"I'll let her know your terms when she returns," Aisha said, and she took the envelope from his outstretched hand. "On one condition."

Trubble stiffened. "Which is?"

"Black Death needs to stop following her and her people."

"Black Death is nothing more than the supers' boogeyman," Trubble retorted.

"So am I."

The wait seemed to stretch for an eternity before Trubble's posture eased a fraction. "I only had him follow Franklin today because I had to assume Winters wanting to meet with me was a distraction for whatever her partner was up to." His feral grin was back. "None of you can blame me for being suspicious."

"I don't mean just this afternoon," Aisha said.

His awful smile faded. "What are you talking about?"

"Sounds like you need to have a little talk with your boy, but remember this one thing—" She stepped closer to Trubble. More satisfaction flowed through her when he retreated a step. "If Black Death touches anyone in this building, I will kill him. And then I'll come after you."

Aisha threw down the pellet hidden in her right hand at the sidewalk. Smoke rose in a white cloud tinged with orange from the streetlight. She flew only as far as the overhang where she crouched to see what Trubble would do next.

Coughing, he stepped out of the smoke cloud. He looked around, and to his credit, he even looked up. Most people forget to do that, she recalled Tim once saying. Yet, if Trubble spotted her, he didn't give a sign.

Instead he pulled out a phone and texted someone. A minute later, an all-too-familiar black SUV pulled up in front of the building. Trubble climbed in, and the vehicle sped off.

— •◆• —

The second Eddie dropped Harri in front of her building, she ran inside. She paused long enough to double-check she had reset the security system before she raced to the elevator.

She'd nearly had a heart attack when Patty had reported through the comm

Trubble had arrived at the Lechuza Building without Rey. Even worse, Aisha had met with Trubble as the Ghost Owl.

Sparx had managed to fly Nix and Sourpuss back to the Lechuza Building from Westerville Park. All three supers offered to stay until Harri arrived, as had Rue Liberty, but Patty sent them home with the promise she'd call if they were needed.

Despite Harri's pleas over the comm, Aisha hadn't answered during the long boat ride back to the Canyon Pointe docks and the even longer ride in Eddie's SUV. Nor did she pick up her phone, though Patty had assured Harri Aisha was in her loft and Arthur was with her.

The elevator doors opened, and Harri ran to Aisha's loft. She rolled the door open. Arthur sat at the little steel and glass kitchen table with his laptop and a bunch of papers on the surface. He looked up with a weary smile.

"Glad you made it home okay," he said. "We all were beginning to worry."

"I'm fine. Where is she?"

"She went to take a shower." Arthur jabbed his thumb in the direction of the bedroom. "But before you go back there, you need to see these." He tapped the papers on the table. "They were in the envelope Trubble brought for you. And yes, I did scan everything for bugs."

Harri tentatively crossed to the table. Instinct said her night was about to get a whole lot worse.

And the first photograph proved it.

She had seen crime scene photos when Eddie had been promoted to homicide detective years ago. But these . . .

"Did Aisha see them?"

"Yeah." Arthur refused to look at her. "We weren't sure how soon you'd be back, and she didn't trust Trubble enough to wait for you."

It had been a rough week, and the man had been nothing but a trooper through it all. Everyone was right. She had been too hard on him over the last couple of months.

"Arthur, I'm not mad at you or Aisha." Harri dropped wearily in the chair. "I would have done the same thing in your position. Thank you for going above and beyond what we pay for."

When he said nothing, she flipped through the rest of the photos. The first dozen were taken at a lab. If the massacre had been staged, it was done by an expert. The blood spatter patterns met Eddie's explanation from when they'd been married. Red splotches were everywhere, including the ceiling.

The last eight photos looked like standard corporate ID photos. No one smiled in them. Not even the last guy, an elderly man.

The same man who had been in the woods, controlling the parrot-lizards and Rey's brother, if the strange woman who appeared out of thin air was telling the truth.

"H-Have you identified these people?" she choked out.

Arthur looked up at her and nodded. "They are all Corvus personnel. Research division."

Harri held up the photo of the old man. "This one in particular."

Arthur turned his laptop so Harri could see the screen. The picture on the website was of a much younger version of the man from the woods. She recalled enough Spanish to piece together his story, and that story made her fear for Rey's life.

"You're back." Aisha walked out of her bedroom in a bathrobe, drying her short hair with a towel. From her bloodshot eyes, she'd taken the shower so Arthur wouldn't see or hear her cry. "Dreyfuss give you a lot of shit?"

"Enough." Harri shrugged. "I had to tell him both Captain Justice and the Ghost Owl are dead. Eddie made a case that the woman in Owl's costume was a cousin of CJ's from another country sent to stop him, and that Dreyfuss might not want to start an international incident."

"Dreyfuss is one of Trubble's moles." Aisha crossed to the refrigerator as she talked. "Arthur confirmed it."

Harri chuckled. "Eddie and I kind of figured when Dreyfuss forced Eddie to wear a wire to entrap me."

Aisha held up a bottle of water, and Harri nodded. Aisha brought three bottles back to the table and passed two to Harri and Arthur before she sat down.

"Trubble wants to meet with you tomorrow at noon at the same bench as before in Founder's Green," Aisha said before she sipped her own water. "Take someone with you."

"Why not you?" Harri asked. "You're stronger than anyone else besides Cobblestone or Captain Mojave."

"That's exactly why I can't go," Aisha said softly. Her hard-eyed stare scared

Harri. "I don't trust myself not to kill him. And he can't find out I'm carrying Rey's son. We'll never get a moment's peace if he does."

Harri glanced at the stack of photos. The idea of Aisha or her baby ending up as Corvus's lab rats churned her stomach. Her partner was right though. If Trubble knew, he wouldn't stop.

"How do you plan to hide it?" Harri asked. "In a month or two, you're going to have a baby bump on that flat stomach of yours."

"I'll talk with Jeremy." She shrugged. "I'm sure I can challenge his fashion sense. Take Rue Liberty with you again."

"All right." Harri pushed back from the table and stood. "I'll give her a call in the morning. If you need me—"

Aisha faked a yawn. "I just need to sleep. Too much exertion tonight for the mom-to-be."

Arthur collected the photos, envelope, and his laptop. He didn't say a word as he followed Harri out of the loft. Instead of stopping at the elevator, he walked with her to her door.

When she rested a hand on the door handle, she said, "You didn't have to walk me home. Aisha and I are on the same damn floor."

Arthur ignored her statement. "You know what Trubble is trying to insinuate with those photographs. You can't possibly believe him."

The same thought had already run through her mind. And the same worry was probably why Aisha had been crying in the shower.

"You didn't see those parrot monsters Aisha ran into a few nights ago." Harri shook her head. "They were waiting for us at Westerville Park. Sourpuss and Nix had problems. The girls got some pretty good cuts from those things, and those were near misses. If they are what killed Rey's foster mom and attacked him a couple of years ago, Trubble may not be insinuating anything. He may really be upset about losing his personnel and a super he's been after for years. If those idiots did abduct Rey and took off his protective amulet, the monsters would have come. Just like they did before."

Arthur stared down the hallway a moment before his somber brown gaze returned to her. "No offense, Harri, but I hope you're wrong."

"So do I, Arthur." Her eyes stung. "So do I."

CHAPTER 38

When Aisha finally slept, nightmares plagued her. If she weren't so damn tired from the battle in Westerville Park, she wouldn't have gotten any sleep at all. When her alarm rang, she stumbled through her morning routine out of sheer habit.

Despite her restless slumber, she made it downstairs to the office at five after eight, Patty greeted her with a big hug before their assistant pressed a large mug of peppermint mocha into her hands.

"Thanks, but I need decaf—"

"It is," Patty answered.

"Would you please call the service and get a temp back here?" Aisha said. "You're supposed to be on maternity leave."

"I will after Harri's meeting this afternoon."

"Promise?"

"Promise."

Aisha sipped her mocha on the short walk to her office door. Patty was probably just saying she would call the temp agency to mollify both Aisha and Harri, but Javier couldn't keep watching Grace while both Patty and Arthur were working. Not with school starting in a couple of months.

The intercom buzzed before Aisha even sat at her desk. She punched the button. "Yes?"

"Essie Morales is on line one," Patty said. The investigative reporter turned news anchor at Action 12 News!

And so it begins.

"Put her through." Aisha dropped in her chair as the phone rang. Wishing she had stayed in bed, she picked up the receiver. "Aisha Franklin."

"Tell me it isn't true." Essie sounded on the verge of tears.

"You need to be more specific, Essie."

"Dammit, Franklin. Don't fuck with me. My contact at the FBI said both Captain Justice and the Ghost Owl are dead." There was an odd sound, suspiciously like a sob.

"I can confirm Captain Justice is dead." Aisha cleared her throat. "Jatz'om Kuh, the Ghost Owl, allegedly drowned in Lake Del Oro a couple of nights ago. Did your source say whether they found the body yet?"

"He, uh, he said his information was based on a formal statement your partner gave."

"Harri was only relaying information to the FBI that a third party gave her," Aisha said firmly.

"So, it's true that an unknown female super is acting under the Ghost Owl alias?" Essie asked.

Aisha forced a laugh. "I didn't witness the events at Westerville Park last night. If that's what the FBI and Harri said what happened, I can't add anything."

Essie was silent for a long moment, which was totally unlike the reporter. "Tell, um, tell Captain Justice's family I'm sorry for their loss. He was truly one of the good guys."

Aisha's eyes burned at Essie's heartfelt sentiment. "Thank you. I will."

"Can I set up an in-studio interview with Sparx and Screaming, ur, I mean, Nix for the evening news about last night's events?"

Aisha released the breath she didn't realize she'd been holding. This she could handle. Essie had at least skimmed the press release.

"Let me contact them," Aisha said. "I'm not sure the ladies will be up to it though. It's always hard losing a colleague, but in this case—"

"It would be good to have eyewitness accounts," Essie said. "There's a lot of rumors flying right now. I don't want his last legacy to be that of a villain, and I don't think you do either."

Aisha resisted the urge to sigh. Between the lines, Essie was warning her that her co-anchor Ted was planning to publicly lambast Captain Justice.

"I . . . understand." Aisha hesitated for a moment before she added, "I'll call you by three to let you know one way or another."

Essie sniffed. The reporter was losing her battle to remain professional. "Th-thanks." The line abruptly died.

Aisha's vision blurred in response. The truth hurt too much. Rey wasn't coming home.

No, she couldn't lose it now. Once the work day was over, then she could hide in bed and cry. She blew her nose, sipped her mocha, and hit the power button on her computer.

As she waited for the boot-up, there was a knock on her door. Harri stuck her head around the doorjamb. "Got a minute?"

"Don't start on me about being five minutes late," Aisha snapped.

"Whoa!" Harri held up both palms. "Simmer down there. I was just checking to see how you were doing. Patty said Essie called."

"I—" Aisha stared at a bare spot on the wall. She'd been meaning to put up some of her Sara Golish prints. The past two months had been so insane. And she couldn't think about Rey. "I don't know right now. I'm concentrating on not bouncing off the ceiling."

"That's . . . a start. Just to let you know, I'm heading over to the hospital before I meet with Trubble." Harri played with her ponytail, a sure sign she was upset.

"You're afraid it's over between you and Tim," Aisha stated. She didn't have the patience to let Harri come to the conclusion herself. Not today.

"Sorry," Harri murmured. "That's kind of selfish of me with everything going on right now."

"No, it's not. It's—" The intercom buzzed. Aisha shook her head as she hit the button. When it rained, it poured, as Grandma Franklin used to say.

"Aisha, it's Mr. Boswell from the calendar people," Patty said. "He needs to talk to you about the Captain Justice calendar."

"Do you want me to handle him?" Harri asked softly.

Aisha shook her head. "Essie actually gave me an idea of how to spin this. Go take care of your stuff. You've called Rue Liberty?"

"Next on my list."

"What line, Patty?" Aisha made shooing motions.

"Line two."

"I want a report as soon as you're done with Trubble." Aisha picked up the receiver and stabbed the appropriate button. "Good morning, Mr. Boswell."

— • —

As Harri pulled the office door closed behind her, Aisha extolled to Boswell how they could turn Rey's calendar into a memorial collector's edition.

Harri shook her head. How Aisha could keep her shit together on a morning like this was incredible.

Patty looked up from her computer monitor. "How is she doing?"

"She's conning the company into selling next year's Captain Justice calendar as a commemorative thing for charity instead of pulping them."

Patty blinked. "I guess that's good. Better than all that paper going to the landfill."

"Did Tim give you Serena's number?"

Patty nodded.

"Have her drop by and check on Aisha while I'm out, please." Harri glanced at her partner's closed office door. Aisha buried herself in work after her emergency surgery for her ectopic pregnancy. And she did the same thing when her marriage fell apart. If Rey never came home—

"Arthur and I are worried about her, too," Patty said softly. "He told me about the photos Trubble gave Aisha."

"If anyone else calls about Captain Justice, confirm he is dead, any memorial service is pending, and we'll release details once they are confirmed."

"You've given up hope?" Patty's lower lip quivered.

"Not on Rey, but Captain Justice is over." Harri swallowed hard. "He has to be for Aisha and the baby's sake."

She turned and stalked back to her own office to collect her keys and bag. If she didn't, she'd join Patty in her crying jag.

— • —

Harri turned off the radio the instant her Honda started. She couldn't deal with any more talking. If Essie knew about last night's incident at Westerville Park, it meant word was spreading among the other media. And none of them would get the story right.

None of them could.

The bunting in windows and doorways of shops and homes caught her attention first as she took the back streets to the hospital. Fourth of July decorations had been taken down a couple of days ago. No, the streamers and ribbons were only red and white.

Then came the signs. RIP. Luv U CJ. And many others in both English and Spanish extolling their sadness and appreciation.

More signs on store fronts proclaimed they were out of Captain Justice merchandise. Billboards at churches announced memorial services for the hero in the evening, although Harri saw impromptu gatherings in front of a couple of places.

People donned t-shirts. And homemade costumes. More than a few men wore black ribbons or bandanas around their biceps.

And the sentiment continued when she crossed River Street. By the time she reached the hospital's parking garage, tears trickled down her face and snot clogged her nose. After she pulled into a slot, it took her a couple of minutes to gather herself and blow her nose.

When she reached Tim's floor, Cobblestone sat in the waiting area. A pretty redhead in scrubs perched on the couch beside him and held his hand. She must be the pediatric nurse Cobblestone had a crush on.

"Miz Winters." His skin made a grinding sound when he rose. "It's true? About Captain Justice?"

Harri couldn't help smiling. "I think that's the first time you've ever used his registered name."

The huge superhero shrugged. "My mama taught me not to speak ill of the dead."

Harri's smile faded. "I'm sorry, but yes, he's gone."

"What about the asshole behind his death?"

"With any luck, he was eaten by the bird monsters he created," Harri said sourly.

"I'm Claire." The redhead held out her hand. "Cobblestone has spoken a lot about you."

"Nice to meet you, Claire." Harri shook the nurse's hand. "He's spoken quite fondly of you as well."

"When's the next time you need me to watch Mister Canyon?" The superhero jabbed his huge left thumb in the direction of Tim's room.

"I think we're good now that the threat's been neutralized."

"You sure about that, Miz Winters?" Cobblestone cocked his head as he regarded her. "If you don't have the body of the bad guy in hand, it usually means he'll come back to bite you in the ass."

"He might," Harri admitted. "But it won't be today."

"If you need me, you know how to reach me." The superhero saluted her before he and Claire headed down the opposing hall way.

Poor guy probably didn't dare to take the elevator.

Harri headed down to Tim's room. She knocked lightly on the door before she pushed it open enough to peer inside.

Fewer wires and tubes came out from under his hospital gown, and his skin no longer blended into the white sheets. Even more surprising was his wry smile.

"I wondered if you'd come back," he said.

"Yeah, I wondered if I would, too." She stepped into the room and closed the door.

"I do have a bone to pick with you about Captain Justice—" He held up the one hand not encumber with an IV and made quote marks with his index and middle fingers. "—killing me."

"Tim Canyon or Jatz'om Kuh?"

"The guy you claim runs around in his underwear." He scratched the auburn and gray stubble on his chin.

"Sorry about that." Harri took a couple of steps toward the bed. "We had to come up with something on the fly between some amateur footage and Eddie's FBI supervisor breathing down his neck about me."

"You as in Harri Winters, or you as in the Ghost Owl?"

"Yes," she said.

"I'm actually impressed you kept my name out of the news."

"Other things took precedence than a random jogger who was mugged."

"So I saw on this morning's news. I was jogging, huh?" Tim chuckled. "That's an incredible feat on these knees. But it is weird not to be a headline as me." He gestured toward the guest chair. "Sit down and tell me what's really going on." When she hesitated, he said, "I'm not going to bite."

Harri crossed to the chair and gingerly sat. Quickly and quietly, she poured out everything that had happened since the night of Tim's surgery. For once, he didn't interrupt.

"I'm meeting with Trubble at noon." Harri sagged in her seat. "And yes, I have super backup going with me."

"Do you really think Rey is dead?" he asked quietly.

"I don't want to, but I know nothing would keep him away from Aisha and their baby," she said.

When they both fell silent, Harri realized she and Tim were holding hands.

CHAPTER 39

Harri sat on the bench in the park. The unrelenting sunshine left damp spots beneath her arms despite her super-strength antiperspirant. How the guys gutting City Hall could survive this heat in flannel shirts over their t-shirts, heavy jeans, and gloves was beyond her. But the work was proceeding, and it wasn't her problem anymore as city attorney to find the money to fix the destruction wrought by supers.

"Did he give you my package?"

She looked over her shoulder and shielded her eyes. Byron S. Trubble stood behind her. Sunbeams created a halo about his white hair, but he sure as hell didn't look godlike. No, he looked like someone who'd lost his prized Mercedes on a bad bet at the country club golf course.

Or maybe Dreyfess's news of a new, female Ghost Owl had his underwear in a twist.

"Yes," Harri said. "Are the eight people part of the team who were killed at the lab?"

Trubble circled the bench and sat beside her though he didn't meet her gaze. "Yes, but we're still trying to piece all the bodies together."

"Did any of the blood types or DNA match Hector Gonzalez-Estes?"

"Who?"

"You knew him better as Martin Villanova, your lab chief." A feral grin lifted the corners of Harri's mouth. "Of course, the public knew him better as Professor Paranoia."

Trubble's jaw muscle twisted.

Oh, god, he was really that stupid.

Harri scowled. "He was a supervillain aiding one of the factions during the Honduran civil war twenty years ago, and you willingly hired him? What the fuck is wrong with you, Trubble?"

"He had skills—"

"He made the Nazis and their Final Solution look like a fucking Sunday school picnic!"

"Keep your voice down, Winters," he hissed.

She glanced around them. Rue Liberty watched them, her book forgotten. Harri gave a slight shake of her head. The retired superheroine relaxed a fraction.

"Besides, he's dead. Those pictures were taken two weeks ago."

"You sure he's dead?"

Trubble stared at her.

"He was alive and well and controlling the Captain Justice duplicate in Westerville Park last night."

For the first time, Trubble seemed surprised. "A clone?"

Harri crossed her arms. "You tell me. Is that what Professor Paranoia was doing at your lab?"

"It wasn't his original project."

"So it was the mind control shit," Harri snarled.

"After the Seismic Shift incident, I needed a way to ensure loyalty," Trubble snapped.

"Has it occurred to you that Professor Paranoia might have his own plans of what to do with your supers?"

"So it would seem." Trubble looked at her long and hard, as if he were weighing something. Finally, he exhaled. "We found strange DNA inside the facility."

"Let me guess." Harri let the sarcasm drip from her voice. "Did it look like a mix of parrot and lizard DNA?"

Trubble's expression shifted to an appraising look. "Some of it."

"And the rest?" Harri prompted.

"Whatever your boy was, he wasn't human."

Her heart threatened to choke her. "You found R-Rey's body?"

"If I did, would you exchange it for the duplicate's?"

"You already know we don't have the duplicate's corpse."

"You could get it back from the super who took it." The sly look returned to his face.

"No, I can't," she whispered.

"A pity." Trubble shrugged. "Frankly, I wouldn't want Miss Franklin to see the pile of bits that used to be her boyfriend either."

"Our deal—" Harri started.

"Was for me to return Rey Garcia alive. I can't because I never had him. Nor did I authorize his abduction." His expression turned to the same cold reptilian one he had the first time they met. "You can blame me all you want, but we were both fooled."

"We knew we had an imposter on our hands." Harri shook her head. "However, we didn't invite a snake into our bed, and then were surprised when he bit us."

Trubble's lips pressed into a hard line, and his jaw muscle twitched again. Harri was sure he was going to leave.

Instead, he said, "You release any information about me or Corvus, and I'll make sure Franklin never sees hers and Garcia's kid once it's born."

Harri gritted her teeth. Corvus agents were going through the Lechuza Building's trash. It was the only way they could know about Aisha's pregnancy.

"Someday you are going to screw up, Trubble."

"I haven't survived this many years without playing the long game, Winters."

This time, he did stand and stroll away like he didn't have a care in the world.

———•———

Out of the chaos after Rey's death, Aisha never expected another superhero to defect from her old law firm. She gestured for the Reinhold sisters to take a seat on the couch before she closed her office door and grabbed her trusty legal pad and a pen. It wasn't until Kerry Reinhold, AKA Sourpuss, took off her sunglasses did Aisha realize why Kerry had always worn them indoors at Dewey & Cheatham. Her irises were vertical like her namesake.

Aisha perched on the edge of the matching plush chair. "What made you decide to change firms, Kerry?"

"Because it is so totally awesome the Ghost Owl is my attorney," Molly squealed. "I told her that's why you're so clued in about superhero branding!"

"Last week was a one-time deal," Aisha admonished. "It is not happening again."

"Why not?" Kerry asked with a frown. "You were great at it. We worked well as a team."

"The man pretending to be Captain Justice needed to be dealt with," Aisha said. "It's over."

"But—"

Molly jabbed her elbow into her sister's ribs. "Shut it. CJ was her boyfriend."

Kerry winced. "Ooohhh! I'm sorry." She hesitated before she added, "Are you sure the package Byron Trubble left here wasn't doctored?"

Alarm bells rang in Aisha's head. "How did you know—"

"Harri told Grandma," Molly said. "Some of us don't have any manners." She glared at her sister. "Or respect for other people's private phone conversations."

The light-head feeling rose to the surface, but Aisha shoved it aside. She needed to work. Work made everything better.

She smiled her professional smile at Kerry. "Let's focus on the real purpose of this visit. Have you served your thirty-day notice to Dewey & Cheatham?"

"Yes, ma'am." Kerry pulled a folder from her tote and hand a page to Aisha. It was a copy dated two weeks ago.

Before Rey disappeared.

Aisha blinked a few times to clear the threatening tears.

"I gave them notice after Stuart Cheatham grabbed my ass," Kerry continued without missing a beat. "I'd been trying to get them to take Molly as a client, but they kept saying no. Cheatham said if he and I made a private arrangement, he could get the partners to change their minds. As much as I wanted to rip his throat out, I know hitting 'em in the wallet is more effective. I'm done with them."

Aisha raised an eyebrow. Stuart pulled those stunts with the staff all the time, but she'd never heard of him pulling this crap with a client. Maybe he was getting bolder since she'd left Dewey & Cheatham.

"Did you tell your grandmother?" she asked.

"Hell, no!" Kerry exclaimed. "She would have disintegrated him! I want to punish him, not kill him."

"That makes only one of us," Molly grumbled under her breath.

"Did he harass you, too?" Aisha asked.

Molly nodded but wouldn't meet Aisha's gaze.

Time to have a private chat with Rue Liberty whether Sourpuss wanted her to or not. Or maybe the Ghost Owl could have a little chat with the bastard. Yeah, that might be the better approach.

"Neither of you have to deal with him ever again." Aisha smiled, a real one this time. "What exactly are you expecting from Winters & Franklin?"

"Well . . ." Kerry pulled another sheaf of paper from her folder. "All of my endorsement contracts, except one, are up for renewal this year. I'm hoping you could negotiate better deals and expand into some new areas . . ."

CHAPTER 40

Six weeks later . . .

Rey grabbed the clean towel from the top of the pile and pressed it to his side. Wrapping the roll of duct tape he'd found around his torso hurt like hell. But if the bleeding didn't stop, there was no way he could sew up his wounds.

Not with the normal stainless steel suture kits his captors had in their cabinet. The needles wouldn't penetrate his skin.

He tried to ignore the bodies, or pieces of them, scattered around the lab, both human and monster. The people who'd abducted him hadn't believed him when he warned them not to remove his amulet. But then, he hadn't believed them when they said they were from the NSB either.

They'd paid for their mistake. The monsters made sure of that.

Despite their intentions, he would have tried to save them, but the anesthetic gas they pumped into the glass cage where he'd been placed kept him barely conscious. It wasn't until the surviving monsters broke into the cage that he could breathe clean air and fight the damn things.

Rey shuffled over to the table where his carved jade amulet lay. His captors had tested the leather thong until it was destroyed, but the stone itself was intact. He picked it up, and its familiar warmth was comforting.

He needed something to hang the jade from. And clothes. He needed some clothes.

"Freeze, asshole." A woman's voice behind him.

Rey winced at his rookie mistake at not securing the door. Tim had taught him better than that.

"Put your hands up," the woman commanded.

"Don't shoot." Better to comply until he could make a plan. He raised his hands as high as he could.

"Higher!" Her voice was shaky.

"I can't. Aren't you Corvus?"

"What if I am?"

That answered one question. She obviously wasn't, but an innocent civilian wouldn't have stumbled across this massacre. *Dios*, it hurt to breathe with his hands raised. "I'm not Corvus either. We both need to get out of here before more of these creatures arrive or Corvus reinforcements show up. I'm going to turn around very slowly." Not that he really had a choice. "Don't fire your gun. The bullets may ricochet off me and injure you."

He slowly pivoted to face a very beautiful woman. Silky dark hair framed her delicate features and large purple irises. But he recognized the hard look in her wide eyes. He saw it too often from others who'd grown up on the street like he had.

She waved her gun toward the wounds along his right ribs. "If you're an invulnerable super, how'd you get hurt?"

"These creatures." He waved at the furry, feathery, and scaly parts on the floor. "I've never run into something that could hurt me except these things."

"Do you know what they are?"

"No, but something like them killed my mother when I was seven."

The woman cocked her head. "Do you know where you are?"

"Some Corvus facility. They've been after me most of my life, too."

"Oh, kid." She lowered her gun and holstered it. "You're in such deep shit."

"Why are you here?" Rey frowned. Was he wrong about her? She could be Corvus, someone they planted to get information about Tim out of him. But at the expense of so many lives?

Innocent lives hadn't mattered to the head of Corvus when Seismic Shift had gone rogue. General Trubble could have stopped the carnage long before he actually raised a finger.

Heck, he hadn't raised a finger. Harri had.

"They brainwashed Captain Justice to kill my ex-boyfriend. He was a nice guy. I'd hoped down the road we'd get back together. Now, I'll settle for revenge." She brushed past Rey. "We need to find you some clothes."

"Wait? What?" He turned to follow her, but his wounds reminded him that sudden movements weren't a good idea.

She looked over her shoulder. "Was he a friend of yours?"

"Your boyfriend?"

"No, Captain Justice." She pulled out some scrubs, checked the size, and tossed them aside.

"Um, it's complicated." He shuffled over to her. "Who's your ex-boyfriend?"

"The Ghost Owl."

Tim? Spots flashed in front of Rey's eyes. What had his doppelgänger done?

And if the imposter had harmed Aisha or the baby, he'd rip the bastard apart with his bare hands.

Will Rey make it home? Will Corvus try to take his and Aisha's baby? And what is Black Death really up to? Find out in *Hero De Novo*! Turn the page for a sneak peek!

HERO DE NOVO

©2019, Suzan Harden

Rey Garcia stared at the woman with the gun, her words ringing through his head. *They brainwashed Captain Justice to kill my ex-boyfriend. The Ghost Owl.*

No. Tim couldn't be dead. And how could I have killed him if I was a prisoner in this Corvus lab?

Despite the sick feeling in his stomach at the strange woman's words, Rey tried to laugh, but pain shot through his side. The monster's claws had cut deep enough to see bone, but he was pretty sure they hadn't puncture his lungs. He wouldn't have been able to draw a proper breath for his weak chuckle if they had.

"C'mon. The Ghost Owl is a Canyon Pointe urban myth," Rey said. "How could Captain Justice kill a children's tale?" Despite the drugged haze the morning he was abducted, he definitely remembered the man who looked just like him. *Dios*, if his doppelgänger had killed Tim, how could he live with himself? Bile rose in the back of Rey's throat. And if the imposter had infiltrated his real life, that meant Aisha and their baby were in danger as well.

The woman gave him a suspicious look.

"I grew up on the east side of the Pointe." He shrugged. "Everyone knows the story. Jatz'om Kuh, the Ghost Owl, is nothing more than the Robin Hood tale for this century."

"No, he exists. Here." The woman poked around the shelves of the lab some more. She pulled out a set of scrubs and shoved them at Rey. "These will work until we get to the mainland."

"The mainland?" He accepted the wad of blue-green clothes. "What mainland? There aren't any islands in Lake Del Oro."

She paused and stared at him. "You really have no idea of where you are, do you?"

He shook his head.

"We'll discuss it once we're out of here." She continued rummaging through equipment and supplies.

"No. We need to discuss it now." He was fairly certain he heard the rhythm of the sea, but it could be the Gulf of Mexico or the Pacific Ocean for all he knew. A shiver ran through him. What if Corvus had taken him from the U.S.? How would he ever get back across the border? Harri Winters, one of his attorneys, had pulled a lot strings to make it look like he was born there, even though Mama had said more than once she had carried him to the U.S. from Honduras.

The woman sighed and shook her head. "We're on an abandoned oil rig off the coast of Java."

"What?" His heart sank. He had no ID with him. "You mean as in the capital island of Indonesia Java?"

"Why are you stalling? You said you were worried about Corvus agents coming back here." She stopped shuffling through the last supply cabinet. Again, the suspicious look from the woman.

"I am, but for all I know, you could be one of them," he said.

"How'd Corvus get you here?"

"I'm not sure."

When she raised her gun and pointed it at him again, he tried to look non-threatening. He couldn't risk injuring his only potential ally.

"The last thing I clearly remember is getting a text about an emergency and to come into work early." He shook his head. "I got dressed and was flying—" He swallowed hard at his slip. "Down the freeway." He hated lying to anyone, but as both Aisha and Harri repeatedly pointed out, total honesty could be a detriment in the superhero business.

Her eyes narrowed. "Are you registered?"

Dios, she was sharp. But given her admitted rage at Captain Justice, telling her he was the real thing wasn't smart.

"My attorney was working on it before Corvus abducted me." Which was true if he stretched the definition of truth. He sighed. "I'm not even sure how long I've been here, much less if it was really Corvus." The head of the top secret organization had taken a personal interest in Rey years ago. He couldn't imagine General Trubble not coming in to gloat over Rey's capture. But as far as Rey knew, Trubble had never come here.

The stranger lowered her weapon again.

Rey ran his tongue over his dry lips. "What happened to the Ghost Owl in this epic battle between him and Captain Justice? If the real guy is as good as the myth—"

"Because the Ghost Owl wasn't a super." The woman slid into an undamaged chair and popped a flashdrive into a port on the last functioning computer work station. "He had enough tricks up his sleeves to fool a lot of people, but in the end, he was a mortal man."

"So are you going after Captain Justice?"

"Not exactly." The woman sagged in her seat. "According to the rumor mill, an unknown female super claiming to be the Ghost Owl killed him."

"A woman? But you said . . ."

The stranger looked at him and rolled her eyes. "I know, right? So insecure she couldn't create she own super persona? What a pussy!" She turned back to the monitor.

"But you just said the Ghost Owl was your ex-boyfriend, and you don't know who she is?"

"I'm guessing she's a family member." The woman's fingers danced across the keyboard. "An illegitimate daughter or something."

"If Captain Justice is dead, there's no one to exact your vengeance on," Rey said.

"I'm going find this woman, and then I'm going after Corvus, like I should have done years ago."

"What's your issue with Corvus?"

"Besides the possibility they were the ones who were mind-controlling Captain Justice?" She whirled on the chair to face him. Anger sparked in her eyes. "Those assholes used the Supervillainy Act of 1947 to take my daughters from me."

Acknowledgements

While I've been reading comic books for nearly fifty years, the movies are what brought my husband, my son, and millions of others into superhero fandom. As I write this, we're two weeks and two days from the premiere of *Captain Marvel*. Four days ago, *Black Panther* lost the Best Picture Oscar, but the concept of a superhero movie even getting the nod was unthinkable a couple of years ago. Two months ago, *Aquaman* swept through the holiday box office like the proverbially tidal wave. In the meantime, *Wonder Woman 1984* is penciled on my calendar for next year.

Genius Kid will be the first one to tell you I'm reliving my childhood. And it's totally AWESOME!

My own entry into the world of superheroes wouldn't be possible without the following people . . .

Jaye Manus of QA Productions, who tolerates my foibles and obsessions,

Elaina Lee of For the Muse Design, who takes my vague ideas and turn them into art,

Joseph Bradshire, a fellow comics fan and superhero writer, who has patiently listened to me natter about this project for years (you should check out his Miss Marathon series!),

And most of all, my Darling Husband and Genius Kid for accepting that spaghetti, tacos, and cereal are the only food groups while Mommy is trying to edit three books at the same time.

About the Author

Suzan Harden is a recovering attorney who writes fiction to regain her sanity. She currently lives in the Great Lakes region with a husband who believes writing is a practical career option and a kid who thinks she's too enamored with superheroes.